NOVELS BY DAVID DARLING

The Noah Hunter Series
The Tipping Point
Grave Choices
Course of Action
Hunter's Gambit (forthcoming)
The Silent Takedown (2026)

Novella
Grim Measures

Standalone
Serve in the Shadows: Recruitment
The Egyptian Enigma

Science Fiction/Fantasy
Edge of Time
Edge of Eternity
Edge of Infinity (forthcoming)

The Sorcerer's Circle (2025)

YA Fantasy
Guards of Twilight (early 2025)

"In Egypt, the past is but the beginning of a beginning.
What lies beneath the sands may change the world."
    —*Ancient proverb*

THE EGYPTIAN ENIGMA

When a mysterious black ankh appears and fades away at the scene of a gang member's death, Ryan Petey's reality begins to unravel. As the symbol reappears with each new fatality he witnesses, Ryan becomes desperate for answers. His quest leads him to Dr. Crystal Kowalska, an Egyptian curator at a Toronto museum.

But Ryan's troubles are only beginning. Unknowingly, he reveals an ancient technique known as stone singing, effortlessly moving a massive granite slab with a single touch. This demonstration sets off a chain of events that thrusts Ryan and Crystal into a dangerous game of cat and mouse. Powerful adversaries, determined to unlock the secrets Ryan holds, will stop at nothing—including kidnapping and murder.

Long-lost abilities and mysterious symbols are only the beginning. Ryan and Crystal must outwit their opponents, recover ancient records, and safeguard a priceless treasure that could change the world. Meanwhile, a long-dead god has other plans.

David Darling Books

Cover Design by Norm Jolin
First Edition: November 2024

CHAPTER 1

Fight or flight is an acute stress response. The two choices are built into a lifeform's genetic makeup to ensure the species' survival. When cornered, the most timid creature will attack should escape be impossible. But there is a third option.

Ryan Petey crouched behind a blue dumpster in a Toronto alley, his heart pounding against his ribcage like a trapped animal. Morning light failed to pierce the shadows, leaving him enveloped in a cloak of darkness. The sound of glass crunching beneath his knees and the sting of fresh cuts on his palms were insignificant compared to the terror gripping his mind. Thirteen feet away, voices clashed like a brewing storm.

Ryan's view through a wooden skid was enough to verify the danger mere steps away, and his hands trembled. Options were few, and he remained still, hoping the danger would pass.

The group leader, a short Vietnamese man with a gray hoodie, wore a gaudy gold necklace. His fingers glinted with either brass knuckles or multiple rings. "Ya should know better, G-Way," his deep voice mocked. "You stumbled into *our* house."

The Vietnamese man addressed two black men dressed in tracksuits who weren't worried. Attitude rolled off them in nearly palpable waves.

"Do ya think we're alone, biotch?"

Had they found him? *Oh, shit!*

The Vietnamese man reached inside his hoodie and paused as a smaller man ran up and whispered in his ear. Five large men had spread out across the narrow lane on the sidewalk. Anticipation stretched like the moment after the lightning strike and before the thunder.

Ryan's gaze darted back and forth between the opposing groups as his dry tongue rasped across the roof of his mouth. In an explosion of energy, the tension was released.

Darting hands grabbed pistols stored in waistbands of track pants or inside sweatshirts. Weapons were fired as the shooters ducked and ran backward. Two rounds thunked into the dumpster and another off the wall above his hiding place. With each shot, brass casings fell like rain on an asphalt pond.

Too afraid to scream, Ryan curled into a ball, forehead pressed against the glass. *Oh my God!* He lost count after eight bullets ricocheted off the pavement and sides of buildings. The screams and curses rose in a chorus, making his teeth grind as he waited to die.

A final pistol shot was followed by everyone running. Pounding footsteps replaced gunfire, and Ryan was left alone with the sounds of the city in the distance.

The first minute of waiting felt like an hour.

The second was an eternity.

Gasping, he raised his head to look through the wooden skid slats, expecting a dozen bodies in a sea of red, but there was only one. The young Vietnamese teenager in jeans and a gray hoodie who gave the warning knelt in a growing pool of blood—Ryan revised his age—maybe twelve. The kid's arms hung limp, chin resting against his chest. It looked like he was praying.

"Are you all right?" Ryan tentatively stood and took a step to the side. Glass crushed underfoot. They were the only two in the alley. A glance at his surroundings showed graffiti-covered walls and piles of garbage in the corners but no windows or cameras. *Why did I take a shortcut through the alley?*

"You are chosen, Ryan." The bubbling whisper was faint but made the hair on Ryan's arms stand on end.

"Did you say something? Pardon?" Ryan's jaw dropped, not believing his ears. "How do you know my name?"

He's dying.

"Hello?" There was no answer. Ryan fumbled for a cell phone in his front pocket. "Hold on. I'll call an ambulance."

His fingers shook as he punched in the security code, dialing 911.

"Police, fire, or ambulance?" The woman's voice was calm and brooked no nonsense.

Ryan winced at the growing pool of blood. "Uh … ambulance. Someone's been shot."

"Location? Is the person still alive?" As the woman typed, a flurry of keyboard strikes sounded like hail on a window pane.

"East of Jane Finch Mall. In the alleyway between the towers. And … huh …"

Ryan couldn't answer while staring at the ground. It wasn't the repeated *sir, sir* over the phone but the kid's shadow growing across the pavement that made him hesitate.

The morning sun was still low in the sky and not visible inside the dim north-to-south alley, but the shadow still grew.

"Sir? Are you still there?"

"What the—"

Thirty feet across the alley, a black glowing three-foot symbol pulsed against the far wall. The shape was a letter T with an oval on the top, giving a vague impression of a cross. Each pulse was slower than the last until it faded away.

With a gurgle, the Vietnamese kid toppled forward in a heap.

The symbol disappeared, along with the eerie black light.

"Police and an ambulance have been dispatched. Can you hear me, sir? Help is on the way."

"The kid is dead." Ryan didn't have to check. He should have been freaking out, but a blanket of warmth calmed his mind turning the moment surreal—dream-like—a nightmare.

"Sir, remain on the line and—" He placed the cell phone on the ground and walked around the body to the far wall.

Every square inch of the hundred-foot alley was covered in various designs, tags, or artwork. Ryan ran a hand over the brick, leaving a faint blood smear against the spray paint.

Nothing.

Whatever made the symbol was gone. *Maybe I imagined it? Did a stressful situation break my mind?* When a siren approached, Ryan was jarred from his thoughts. A Toronto police cruiser drove into the alley with blue and red strobe lights, turning the area into a rave.

Help had arrived, but too late.

CHAPTER 2

Ryan sat on the ambulance's bumper, wincing as an older paramedic picked glass out of his palm with tweezers and then used a clear fluid squeezed out of a bottle to wash the cuts. "You'll be fine. Keep them clean and covered. Use Polysporin or something like it. You're lucky to be alive after that shoot-out. Stay here until you're allowed to leave."

"Thanks."

In the alley, a cluster of people stood around the body, taking pictures and securing evidence. Yellow placards with numbers littered the ground as an officer photographed everything.

One police officer, nearly six-foot-five, questioned him repeatedly as others arrived. *Was Ryan a part of a gang? Why were you here? Did you know the person who was shot? Do you want a lawyer?* Ryan was hustled out of the alley as yellow barricade tape was tied around a bus stop sign, then knotted on the driver's mirror of the police vehicle. The ambulance had reversed on the sidewalk, and the tall officer told him to stay put. The paramedic's partner, a slim young man, wrote on a clipboard near the body.

A woman in a suit jacket and jeans glanced over her shoulder at Ryan and spoke a few more words to the tall officer before heading toward him. She was slightly taller than him and between forty and fifty years old. Her quick strides made her jacket flap open, and the gold badge on her belt next to a holstered gun caught his eye.

"Mr. Petey, I'm Detective McCallan from the guns and gangs task force. Before we begin, are you okay? Injured?"

Ryan showed his palms. "A couple of scratches. I'm good."

"Just a few confirmation questions. Date of birth?"

"November second, two thousand." Ryan tried not to watch a crowd gathering behind the yellow tape and kept eye contact with the detective.

"Place of employment?"

Ryan shook his head. "I'm a freelance graphic designer working odd jobs and getting by."

"Married?"

He shook his head again. "No."

"Start at the beginning. Take your time." She pulled a notepad and pen from a pocket, flipped to a new page, and gestured for him to start.

"Okay." He swallowed and took a deep breath. "I was heading to the Ministry of Transportation at the mall to get the manual. I don't have my license yet. I keep meaning to take the test but haven't gotten—"

"Focus on the incident, please," McCallan interrupted.

"Sorry." Ryan ran a hand through his hair. "I was going to the mall and took a shortcut through the alley. I had too many energy drinks this morning and wouldn't have reached the bathroom. So, I went behind the dumpster to take a leak, and a bunch of guys appeared at the end of the alley." He gestured behind the office where they had stood and continued. "I don't have much money, just a cell phone, but I didn't want to get mugged. I know the area isn't the best, and"—at a look from the detective, he got back on track—"but they didn't see me, and I ducked down as two guys came in from the other end."

The detective took notes as Ryan continued to describe the confrontation.

Then she stopped him. "One man called another G-Way?"

Ryan winced. "I think so, but not one-hundred-percent positive."

McCallan flipped pages, and Ryan took a moment to look around. A man lifted the yellow barricade tape and pushed a stretcher underneath. By this time, a dozen police officers were on the scene, and one kept the growing crowd back. Everyone was likely hoping to get a glimpse of the body or find out what happened. A female reporter wearing a red dress and a CTV on a white placard on a microphone raised her hand, waving an officer over.

Through the gap in the crowd, Ryan locked eyes with a bystander, and his heart froze.

It was the Vietnamese man from the alley.

Ryan's eyes widened as the Vietnamese's eyes narrowed. The sweatshirt was gone. He wore a white T-shirt and a Blue Jays baseball cap, but the gold necklace was unmistakable. A finger rose to his lips in the *hush* gesture.

"Mr. Petey?"

Ryan blinked and shook his head when he realized the detective was asking questions. "Sorry, I missed it. What was that?"

Her brow furrowed. "Can you describe any of the men in the alley?"

Ryan's mouth remained open while he paused. *Holy crap! What should I do?* He hated rapid-fire decisions and preferred to explore options to find the best course of action. While he couldn't describe all the men well, there was little doubt *they* knew what he looked like. Self-preservation chose for him.

"No. I stayed in a ball crouched behind the dumpster and didn't move. I would have been seen."

Ryan tried to remember a video he had watched once on lying. Don't look away. Keep eye contact? Don't look up? He didn't know what to do, so he kept eye contact for a moment, then stared at his hands.

She wrote a bit more, then asked for his phone number and gave him a business card. *Detective Trish McCallan, Toronto Police Services*. "My work phone number is on the front, but I wrote my cell number on the back. If you remember anything further, give me a call."

"I will."

Ryan casually scanned the faces behind the yellow tape but couldn't see the Vietnamese man. He didn't know what was worse: not knowing where he was or seeing him.

"One more thing, Mr. Petey."

"Yes?" Ryan's heart rate spiked at the tone in her voice, and he swallowed the sudden lump in his throat.

Her eyebrows rose. "I think it's safe to do up your zipper now."

Cheeks burning, he spun around to make the correction. The tall officer returned Ryan's identification and cell phone a few seconds later. Keeping his head down, Ryan disappeared into the crowd.

CHAPTER 3

Ryan barely made it through the front door at home and into the bathroom before his breakfast splashed into the toilet bowl. During the walk, he kept looking over his shoulder, expecting to be followed while visions of a dead kid danced before his eyes. The paramedic had called him lucky, and Ryan felt anything but that as he flushed. He dug around under the sink and found ointment and Band-Aids. Only one cut in the middle of his right palm needed attention, and the rest were minor. The bandage the paramedic used was already falling away, and he switched it to a fresh one.

Ryan lived with his divorced mother in an older bungalow in the North York district of Toronto, and he hadn't seen his father since he was eight. Ryan had his father's build and his mother's features and complexion.

Fair skin, a thin nose, and a near lack of facial hair made many revise his age lower.

He needed a distraction, or he would be hugging the toilet all day. After college, the basement had been converted into his office and bedroom. A six-foot table held three monitors and acted as his workstation next to a double bed, and a light brown couch sat against the opposite wall. The only door in the room led to the laundry and storage. For the last two years, he has been designing company logos and letterheads and has recently expanded into website design from the basement. Ryan had trouble concentrating after checking his email and sending a quote for a webpage. A sketchbook and pen were always within reach, and as he tried to block out what happened, Ryan drew the symbol he'd seen when the kid died. Over and over, he sketched the cross and loop in pencil, then applied detail with the black pen.

Did I imagine it? Temporary insanity? Did the kid really say my name?

A new thought made him wince. He had to let his mother know. She was a receptionist at a dental clinic downtown and worried excessively. Ryan would tell her tonight and sit through her lecture. *"Everything comes with a lesson if you are careful enough to learn from an experience."* One of her favorite sayings, and it drove him crazy at times.

Out of the corner of his eye, a shadow had passed across the window above the bed. Ryan's head snapped around at the movement, and nausea made his mouth water.

In North York, which is not the best neighborhood, security bars were installed on the lower windows, and beefed-up locks were on all the doors. The only weapon at hand was an old, dented aluminum baseball bat—a remnant of a failed attempt at sports.

Ryan swore to go down fighting or at least to hold an intruder off long enough for the cops to arrive. He gripped the bat tight with damp palms as he went upstairs, ensuring each window was locked. From behind the curtains, he studied the street. All clear. The only thing out of place was the shed in the backyard.

The shed door was opened five inches.

Ryan threw the two deadbolts and dropped the security bar from the kitchen exit. Outside, he took two steps toward the shed and called out, "If you're in there, you're going to get a beat down. Show yourself."

He held the bat cocked over his right shoulder, ready for a home run, but nothing happened. Two steps closer, Ryan froze when something moved.

The black and orange cat stepped outside. Yellow eyes bored into him with disdain.

"Jesus Christ."

Clutched in the cat's mouth was a twitching field mouse trying to escape.

In a flash, the cat darted under the wooden fence and disappeared. After a nervous laugh, Ryan lowered the bat and returned to the house. His cell phone rang after locking the back door.

Out of breath, he answered. "Hello?"

"Hi, honey. There's been an accident, and I need you to pick me up in an hour or so." His mother sounded upset and short of breath.

"What's wrong? Where are you?"

"I'm okay. It's just a case of two left feet. I fell at work and sprained my left wrist."

A woman in the background yelled, "It could be broken."

His mother sighed. "Don't listen to Heather. She's a pain."

Ryan once met Heather, a petite woman with curly brown hair and large round glasses who worked as an office records clerk. "Where are you?"

"Heather drove my car, and it's parked in the east lot at Humber River Hospital."

"Okay, I'm on my way. I'll call once I'm there." Ryan did the math and figured it would be ninety minutes with two bus transfers. Damn, he needed his full license, not just a learner's permit. A car would be great as well.

"Thank you. Love you, sweetie."

"Love you, too."

The morning's close call was momentarily forgotten as he put on a clean T-shirt and darted out the door. Two steps later, Ryan felt he was being watched and stopped. The cat from the shed sat near the tree on his lawn. It was easily the largest house cat he had ever seen. It calmly tore the head off the mouse, and golden eyes followed the young man as he ran to the bus stop.

CHAPTER 4

Ryan had traveled on the T.T.C. (Toronto Transit Commission) busses for most of his life, and no matter the time of day or how busy they were, an unspoken set of rules was followed. Students usually crowded the rear with their backpacks, headphones, and cellphones. Older adults, mothers with strollers or kids, and single riders sat near the front. The middle was usually designated No Man's Land, where he spent most of his time. When the students became too plentiful, they would fill the bus from the back to front, shuffling like zombies in the aisle. While he wasn't claustrophobic, Ryan preferred the window seat directly across from the rear exit for no other reason than the blast of fresh air you would occasionally receive when someone left. The stench of too many people gathered in a tight spot would make him ill. Sitting elsewhere on the bus made him anxious.

Normally, Ryan would join the others staring at his phone as he scrolled through social media or played games. But he stared out the windows today without seeing the urban scenery. The gunshots echoed in his mind, making his heart race, and he struggled to gain control of his breathing. The stifling air and unwashed bodies weren't helping.

He pressed the next stop button. Once outside, the bus left with an obnoxious plume of diesel heading south on Jane Street. Ryan ran a hand through his hair and walked around the corner to Sheppard Avenue West to catch the Humber River Route. When the next bus arrived, he sent a text. *Will be there in ten minutes.*

His phone chirped as Ryan stepped off the bus and crossed the parking lot to the emergency entrance. *Going in for X-rays, I'll be a bit longer xo.*

A line of cars snaked through the lot like a fast-food restaurant dropping off or picking up patients. The last thing he wanted to do was wait inside. Ryan sat on a bench and watched the traffic or the occasional patient shuffle into a waiting vehicle.

When a two-door Honda Civic pulled into the drop-off, a feeling of dread made the hair on the back of his neck stand on end. The car was white with gold rims and a ground effects body kit and spoiler, making it resemble a race car. The windows were dark enough that you couldn't see the driver or passengers, and Ryan felt subtle bass from the stereo system in the metal bench.

The driver got out, and another man crawled out of the rear passenger seat. Both wore gray track pants, matching hoodies, and bright white running shoes. The hoods were pulled forward, covering their face, but Ryan had seen the outfits previously. The black men that the Asian gang confronted were all dressed similarly.

Oh shit! They knew I saw everything.

The front passenger door opened, and the two men reached inside and helped a third out.

Ryan gripped the edge of the bench, and the metal slats dug into his palms as fresh cuts oozed blood. He was ready to dash through the emergency room doors at the first sign of danger.

The third man was dressed the same and hunched over with his hood down, clutching his stomach. Ryan rose an inch as the adrenaline surge overrode his mental process. *Run! Flee!* The two men carried the third to the bench beside Ryan before darting back to the Honda and driving away.

Confused, Ryan settled down as he gained control of his rapid breathing. The figure slumped on the bench as his hand removed the hood. The black man was around thirty years old with short hair on top and shaved at the sides. He was clean-shaven, except for a small patch of hair under his chin. His eyes remained closed, and his moans carried to Ryan's ears.

"Do you want me to get a …" Ryan's question faded as he stared at the wall behind the bench. Next to the *no-smoking* sign, the black symbol appeared. It was the same as the previous one in the alley, nearly three feet tall. Ryan's eyes flicked back and forth between the mark and the man.

"You're going to die." As with most of his life, his mouth had engaged without the benefit of his brain.

The man's right eye opened and eventually focused on Ryan. A short bark of laughter made the man wince. "Looks that way. Sit with me. I don't want to die alone."

Ryan stood and pointed to the hospital doors. The instinct to run was still coursing through his body. "I can get help, and they can save you."

The man groaned, and two hands clutched his stomach. "It's too late. I already can't feel my legs. Don't worry, man. Just sit for a few minutes."

The first step was the hardest, and the second was easier. Shaking, Ryan found himself beside the dying man on the bench. "I'm Ryan."

"Collin. Sorry if I don't shake your hand."

"That's okay." Ryan looked over his left shoulder at the symbol. It was within arm's reach, and its strange warmth felt good on his skin. A projection couldn't be felt. Ryan filed that away for later. "I saw you earlier today. I'm sorry you got shot."

Collin's eyes opened wide, and despite the pain, he looked surprised. "How do you know, man?"

Ryan swallowed the lump in his throat. "I was behind the dumpster. I had to take a leak, so I hid when the other guys showed up."

Collin started breathing heavily, and his chest rose and fell rapidly. "Good call. Thanks for sitting with me."

"I can still get you some help." Ryan felt compelled to mention it.

Collin shook his head, and they sat silently for a minute. Collin asked, "Do you have a family?"

"My mother." The symbol was pulsating like a heartbeat: *Lub dub, lub dub*.

"Good… listen to her… and always do your best. Stay away from the wrong crowd ... it never works out in the end. Tell my mom I love her for me. Will… you… do that?" Collin was gasping for breath with each word.

The symbol began to fade from the wall, and Ryan knew what it meant even if he didn't understand it. He whispered, "It's time. Goodbye, Collin. I'll let your mom know."

"Thanks, Ryan." With those last words, Collin stilled, and the muscles in his face relaxed. The grimace disappeared. His hands fell to the sides, showing a large dark red stain soaking into the sweatshirt. Ryan smelled something he didn't care to admit was the faint, unpleasant odor of shit.

Ryan took several deep breaths and then screamed, "Help!"

He darted inside the hospital like the devil was chasing him.

CHAPTER 5

Ryan found a security guard in the waiting room and beckoned him outside to help. At the bench, the guard shouted into his two-way radio. A flurry of activity revolved around a doctor and two nurses when they arrived. The guard moved Ryan backward to give them room to work.

Collin was lowered to the ground, and a nurse began chest compressions. Ryan couldn't look away and knew it was too late. The symbol didn't reappear. *What's happening? I should be losing my mind.* However, Collin *really* died and was stretched out on the sidewalk as the nurse attempted to revive him. The waking dream continued with a tap on his shoulder.

"Well, look who it is. How are you doing, Mr. Petey?"

When he spun about, Detective McCallan took a step back, and the look in her eye made him want to run—a predator ready to pounce on its prey.

"What are you doing here?" Ryan's mouth spoke before he could think. Again.

"My job. I usually follow up with all the hospitals in the area after a murder. I think it's time we talked, Ryan." Unblinking, she stared into his eyes, studying him like a bug under a microscope.

"I'm just here picking up my mom." Her intensity made him shuffle back, but he bumped into the security guard.

"I've been doing this job for twenty-six years. Do you know what I've learned? Coincidences are rare, if not impossible." She nodded toward Collin as he was being placed on a stretcher. "What happened?"

Warning bells were going off in Ryan's head, loud enough that he almost missed what she was saying. Keep it simple. You did nothing wrong. Relax. "I was waiting for my mom, and two guys dropped him off. When he died, I ran inside and got help. That's it."

"Why didn't you get help *before* he died?" She tilted her head slightly.

Ryan swallowed. He was on treacherous ice and had to watch his footing. "He wanted to talk for a minute and didn't want help. I *did* ask him! He refused."

Collin was wheeled into the hospital, and the security guard watched the exchange from the doorway.

Nothing was left behind except a wet, dark stain on the sidewalk.

"What did you talk about?" the detective pulled out her notebook and pen from an inside pocket. "Exactly."

"I asked if he needed help, and he said to sit for a minute. He didn't want to die alone. Collin asked about my family and told me to listen to my mother. He wanted his mother to know that he loved her. When he stopped moving, I got help."

"His name was Collin?" The pen scratched on the notepad.

"Yes."

Ryan glanced at the wall where the symbol had vanished. As before, no marks were on the bricks. The high roof had no means of hiding anything that would project on the wall either. Despite the elaborate circumstances, there was a nagging doubt that he was being set up for a practical joke, and it was hard to shake that feeling. When he spotted the cameras above the emergency entrance and corners of the building, Ryan didn't know if he should be afraid or relieved. Surely, any recordings would back up his story.

"Have you ever met Collin previously, Ryan?" McCallan's dark eyes bored into his.

Shit. Don't lie. She will know. "I've never met him but may have seen him earlier today. I can't say for certain."

Her eyes widened slightly. "Was Collin in the alley near Jane and Finch? Was he involved in the gang shoot-out?"

"I think so."

Detective McCallan frowned and flipped back through her notes. "This morning, when I asked you if you can describe any of the men in the alley, you said, and I quote, 'No. I stayed in a ball crouched behind the dumpster and didn't move. I would have been seen.' Are you saying you'd like to revise your previous statement, Mr. Petey?"

Her frigid tone could have chilled a polar bear. A panic rose in Ryan's chest, and heat flushed his cheeks. "I couldn't describe the men, but that was the outfit from the guys in the alley. They were more or less dressed the same. I couldn't see his face, though."

McCallan asked a series of rapid-fire questions about the alley, the confrontation, and the clothing of anyone he could or may have seen. Then she asked about the men who had dropped off Collin and the vehicle. She also wanted to know what he had done between leaving the alley and taking the bus to the hospital.

After fifteen minutes of answering questions, Ryan felt like he had run a marathon. Sweat dripped from his brow, and the T-shirt clung to his back.

"Falsifying a statement is contrary to the criminal code of Canada and can result in a fine and up to six months imprisonment. These are some serious charges,

Ryan. Is there anything else you'd like to add or change?"

There was only one thing Ryan had left out. The symbol. He would be locked up and given a psychological evaluation if he mentioned the mysterious sign that vanished when a person died. They'd throw away the key.

His throat was dry, and he could have drank a bottle of water. "Nothing. That's everything."

"I'm going to check the security footage, and if there are any discrepancies, you and I will be having another conversation at the precinct. Understood?"

"Yes, ma'am."

The detective gave him a strange look, then went through the emergency doors. As if that was the signal, his cell phone chimed with an incoming text.

I'm done. Where are you?

With everything that's happened, Ryan hoped his mom was okay—after being grilled by the detective, telling his mother about his day would be a piece of cake.

He was wrong.

It was worse.

CHAPTER 6

Despite her five-foot-three frame, Julie Petey had never been one to be pushed around, and when her temper flared, men twice her size backed away. She slammed the detective's business card on the kitchen table. "You should have told me earlier!"

She still wore her blue scrubs with her left arm in a black sling to keep it elevated until the swelling receded. Her wrist had ballooned too much for a cast, and she wore a brace held with Velcro straps. A small bone in her wrist had broken, but for now, there wasn't much anyone could do. She would go to the fracture clinic in a few days for a plaster cast.

"I was going to, but things were happening too quickly, and I had to go to the hospital and pick you up." Ryan had grudgingly told her what happened on the way home. She was overprotective and took things personally—protective mama bear. While he was twenty-two years old and considered an adult, he felt like a kid around his mother. Especially now.

Like a switch had been flicked, Julie sat across from Ryan at the table with concern in her eyes. "How are you feeling? Let's talk about it."

He tried not to groan at the Dr. Phil approach. "I'm good, Mom. Seriously."

"You've seen two people die today and were nearly killed! There's no way you are good."

Ryan thought it over and privately agreed that his mom was right. He should have been an emotional mess, but everything seemed fine now that it was over and he was home. Well, not one-hundred percent fine. There was the small matter of his sanity and seeing strange glowing black symbols. Besides that, he was fairly normal.

"For now, I'm okay. But if that changes later, maybe we could talk about it?" Ryan reached out to squeeze his mother's hand.

Her eyes narrowed. She agreed with the same look when Ryan was up to something. "Deal." She gestured to the sling and injured wrist. "I need you to help out more around the house until I'm better. That should take your mind off things."

"No problem." Ryan smiled. "Now, what happened to you? How did you fall?"

Julie leaned back in the chair, ran a hand through her shoulder-length brown hair, and shrugged. "I was getting the mail outside from the lockbox when a huge cat ran by chasing a squirrel. Scared the hell out of me, and I tripped."

Cat? I saw a huge cat today as well. Weird.

Ryan got an ice pack from the freezer and wrapped it in a towel. "If you need anything, I'll be in the basement."

"I'll be watching TV. I'm here if you want to talk." Julie kissed his forehead before going to change.

Downstairs, Ryan sat at his computer. A quick search showed the shooting in the alley, but Collin dying at the hospital didn't make the news. However, he got a customer response on designing a website for a mobile dog groomer in Richmond Hill. While he had never been there, the city was a thirty-minute drive north, and he knew enough about it and the business to start the project. Eagerly, Ryan threw himself into the project—a welcome distraction. After a series of back-and-forth emails, he secured the domain name.

"Are you hungry?" Julie had changed into shorts and a Rolling Stones concert T-shirt from the nineties, her unofficial loungewear. She came up beside Ryan and looked over his shoulder. "Busy?"

"Setting up a new client's website." A series of clicks saved the work. "Hopefully, they'll ask me to manage it as well. Easy money."

"Looks good." She moved his sketchbook to the side and tapped the top page. "Are you doing an Egyptian theme?"

"Huh?" Ryan turned to see the drawing of the symbol under scrutiny. "What do you mean?"

"It's an ankh. I can't remember what it means, though. Something about eternal life." Julie shrugged. "Your old mom still knows a thing or two, ya know?"

"Oh, that. It's nothing. Just doodling." The fact that there was a name to the symbol piqued his interest. "How about pizza?"

"Sounds good."

When Julie went upstairs to order, Ryan read everything he could find on the ankh and searched hundreds of pictures. There was zero doubt in his mind that it was the symbol. What confused him was that the sign was supposed to represent the key of life in ancient Egypt, not death. A Google search of people randomly seeing the character didn't help, but it was worth trying. The ankh, pronounced *aangk*, was over five thousand years old and most likely the source of inspiration for the Christian cross.

Julie wasn't religious, except when swearing, and Ryan had grown up similarly. While they did celebrate Christmas, they were more about Santa and family than any spiritual background. Ryan remembered asking about God when he was younger. *You can make up your own mind when you're an adult. It isn't up to me to push my ideas on you.* He was open to the concept of a god, but believing in something on just faith seemed foolish. Show me proof, and then I'll believe.

If Christianity was based around Jesus, which was only two thousand years old, give or take, and most sections of the Bible were created in A.D. 400, but the ankh was possibly three thousand years older than the Bible. Ryan wasn't sure if that lent more credibility to Egyptian beliefs, but three thousand years was a long time for a culture to believe in something. Things changed when the Romans called their belief system paganism and killed those who didn't convert to Christianity.

Further research seemed fruitless. There were articles arguing both or three different sides of any topic on religion. Ryan wasn't interested in such discussions but wanted actual facts. He found the earliest recorded use of the ankh as a symbol was in 2700 B.C. As with everything else, archeologists were mainly guessing at the signs used. They were *educated* theories nonetheless, but in the end, they didn't know for sure.

"Pizza!" Julie called from upstairs.

"Okay, I'll be right there."

Ryan checked to see if the new client wanted any further changes to the layout design. He paused when the ads appeared along the screen's right side. He had searched the ankh enough that the sponsored advertisements were targeted specifically to his recent history. An article on the R.O.M. (Royal Ontario Museum) in Toronto had an Egyptian mummy exhibit; click *here* for tickets. The cursor hovered over the ad, and he hesitated. When Julie called for him again, Ryan powered down the computer. The day seemed unreal, and putting it behind him may be the best bet.

CHAPTER 7

Nightmares of being chased by shadows startled Ryan from a deep sleep several times throughout the night, and before the sun rose, he sat on the edge of the bed holding his head. After a quick trip to the kitchen, he returned to the basement with a cold pizza slice and an energy drink. He didn't like coffee but enjoyed the benefits of caffeine in the morning. Today had nothing to do with loving the drink. He needed it to function. Last weekend, he had friends over for an all-night Call of Duty session, and he had a dozen cans left over.

"I may need them all to get through the day." Ryan groaned.

Out of necessity, he had been getting up early for the last year to get work for his growing business. Ideally, Ryan preferred going to bed in the middle of the night and waking up around noon. At one point in the morning, Julie called down the stairs that she was going to work and left. She could still do her job as a receptionist with her wrist in a brace and sling. She joked that Heather could get the mail from now on.

After sending the final information to the dog groomer for her website, Ryan looked at the hours of operation for the Royal Ontario Museum. A quick search on the T.T.C. website showed it would take sixty minutes to travel on the bus and then the subway. However, he could be there with an Uber when the doors opened at ten o'clock. Before he could change his mind, he called for the ride and got ready.

Dressed in another black T-shirt and jeans from the day before, Ryan grabbed his phone and waited at the front door when a four-door black Toyota Prius pulled up to the sidewalk.

After climbing in the back seat, Ryan confirmed he was the client. The driver was an older man with an English accent. Tufts of white hair stuck out randomly, and he wore a collared blue shirt with a black tie. "Please buckle your seat belt."

The Uber turned east on Finch Avenue. The tablet mounted to the dashboard tracked their location on the map in real time. The estimated time of arrival would be thirty-three minutes. "Going to the R.O.M. for school?"

Ryan shook his head. "Just some research."

Despite being twenty-two, he was mistaken for a high school student on so many occasions that it was commonplace. He looked forward to being able to grow a beard so he wouldn't be asked for identification everywhere he went. His friends knew the doorman would ask for his ID every time.

The driver wasn't up for chatting, and that suited Ryan fine. He stared out the window as other vehicles buzzed around them like hummingbirds on a feeder. The Uber driver wasn't one for going over the speed limit and enjoyed every moment of agony it caused others around him. At times, the traffic and others driving only a few feet away from his bumper were why Ryan postponed getting his license. If there were enough room for a car to squeeze in front, they would do it, and that frayed his nerves.

Shortly, they turned south on Allen Road, and Ryan tried not to groan as he followed their progress on the map. The drive ahead had just switched from green to orange, then red. That meant the traffic had increased and would take longer. At least Uber wasn't like a cab company where he would pay per kilometer, just a flat rate.

After they passed Sheppard Avenue, the traffic had increased, and the driver tapped the screen. "Sorry, there's an accident ahead and not many choices. We'll 'ave to ride it out."

"No problem." Ryan shrugged. He didn't have any real plans, including going to the museum. The northbound traffic was sporadic, and the southbound was crawling. Fifteen minutes later, the distant flashing lights of a police car and fire truck were visible near the Highway 401 overpass. An ambulance flew past the line of cars with sirens and lights going south.

"That doesn't look good." They moved just enough to see part of the twisted wreckage behind the firetruck.

Ryan privately agreed, but his attention wasn't on the first responders but on the overpass. Above the accident was the 401, a major twelve-lane highway. A narrow guard rail had separated westbound traffic on the cloverleaf, but a section was missing. A car had gone through the fence to plummet fifty feet onto Allen Road. Police were keeping the traffic on the main highway away from the opening, and more officers worked below to keep the area clear to allow the paramedics and firefighters to work.

A sinking feeling made Ryan groan when the ankh symbol appeared on the overpass immediately above the accident.

"It will be okay, lad. God willing." The driver reassured him.

Ryan didn't have the heart to mention that what upset him wasn't the accident but an ancient symbol that only he could see. The ankh didn't seem to represent the key of life but death. *Was it causing deaths? Could it be prevented?*

Questions ran through his mind as they passed the firetruck and what used to be a car. The twisted pieces of blue metal had been pried apart to get the driver out and sat like a demolished pop can on the road. A huge ring of various fluids was controlled by something that resembled kitty litter. A crew of firemen and police officers stood around a person on a backboard. As they crept forward under the direction of an officer, Ryan kept one eye on the ankh. The glowing back symbol flared once before fading away.

"Oh, Jesus. That isn't good."

A kneeling paramedic pulled a light blue sheet over the body as they drove by. The look of sorrow from the EMT made Ryan's breath catch in his throat, and he slumped low in the seat to avoid watching.

Whatever had happened yesterday wasn't over yet. Either Ryan's mind had gone off the deep end, or something was occurring he didn't understand. As they accelerated, leaving the horrible accident behind, Ryan had the urge to call his mother and tell her everything. However, he left the phone in his pocket and ignored the voice in his head. Now wasn't the time or place. Hopefully, he could discover some answers at the museum. If not, he would be in a straight jacket and shipped off to the funny farm fairly soon.

Only one question kept running through his mind.

Why me?

CHAPTER 8

The remainder of the journey was silent, and Ryan kept his eyes on the screen, marking their progress. When they arrived, he thanked the driver, promising him a five-star rating. The entrance to the Royal Ontario Museum was an abstract design with towering flat angles made of brass and glass that carried the eye. Ryan was vaguely reminded of the Sydney Opera House in Australia with the conceptual design. Not that he had been there, but he studied architecture in his graphics design class at college.

Ryan thought the museum would have been empty this early on a Friday morning, but he was wrong. Throngs of school children followed their guides or teachers carrying flags of varying colors, and he trailed them into the lobby. After navigating the roped-off line, he bought a ticket and went inside. In the first gallery, a massive dinosaur skeleton occupied most of the space, and various entrances to different exhibits led from the main room. To the side, Ryan found an information placard. The African-Egyptian exhibit was on level three.

Ignoring the various displays, he took the stairs to enter a new world. All the lighting and displays made it feel like he was in Egypt, with the tan and varying shades of brown on the floors and walls. A wall section was sloped outward and turned into a replica of a section of the Great Pyramid. Several dozen displays in Plexiglas contained pottery, a sarcophagus, and a skeleton draped in a linen blanket. The exhibit wasn't too busy, but a class of nine-year-olds followed a guide.

Ryan didn't know where to start and ended up following the tour. They stopped at a display showing examples of hieroglyphics on a gray tablet. Many of the kids had cell phones and took pictures of everything. He scanned the tablet, but the ankh symbol wasn't there.

"Follow me inside and take a seat." The woman led the children into a theater classroom at the end of the gallery hall. Ryan stood in the doorway, and a woman dressed in a white lab coat stood behind a podium, smiled, and waved him inside.

Ryan took a seat in the third row near the door. As soon as he sat, the presentation began.

"Good morning. I'm Doctor Kowalska, an archaeologist and one of the curators for the Egyptian exhibit." The speaker reminded Ryan of a younger Scarlett Johansson with large round glasses and shoulder-length brown hair in her late thirties with a pointed chin and prominent cheekbones. "Today, we will go over the history of the pyramids and the Sphinx."

Behind the podium, the white wall turned into a projection screen. A bird's eye view of the three pyramids made his jaw drop. The details were amazing; it looked like the theater had become a flight simulator.

Dr. Kowalska continued, "The largest pyramid was built in 2560 B.C.E. by Kuhfu, the second king of Egypt's fourth dynasty, over a period of twenty-seven years and is considered one of the natural wonders of the world."

The scenic view changed and came to rest at the pyramid's base. "The base is a square with each side measuring seven-hundred and fifty-six feet, and over two point three million blocks of limestone and granite were used." The camera angle shifted, and large stones filled the screen from each corner of the room. "The average stone was two-and-a-half tons, and the largest is over eighty tons. Scientists have various theories on how each stone was moved. Does anyone here have any ideas on how it was done? Remember, they didn't have our modern technology."

A young girl in the front row called out, "Aliens?"

Her classmates laughed as a boy in the back shouted, "UFOs?"

"Stone singers."

"Time travelers!"

When the students calmed down, Doctor Kowalska paused the movie and, to his surprise, she turned to Ryan. "Excuse me, did you say stone singers? Can you elaborate?"

He sat upright in the plastic chairs and looked around. *Oh my God, she's talking to me.* His mouth had started without the benefit of his brain … again.

Ryan cleared his throat. A brief image of a man singing with two palms pressed against red granite blocks the size of a car came to mind while another moved it around. "Uhh. It's how they moved the big stones. Without the singers, none of that would have been possible."

Dr. Kowalska seemed at a loss for words. "And how do you know this, sir?"

Everyone in the theater was staring, and Ryan wanted to be anywhere else but here. His cheeks were burning red, and he mumbled. "Something I must have seen on YouTube. The singers softened and lightened the great stones. Sorry, I interrupted."

She stared at him for a brief moment, then shrugged. "Sonics are one of the methods we're researching, but nothing is definitive. Yet." With a quick smile to the rest of the class, the movie resumed. She talked about the precision of the buildings and how they were perfectly aligned with magnetic north.

"The predynastic Egyptians shaped the granite using various copper chisels, stone hammers, and dolerite to pound the rude material off the rough limestone and granite." The video shifted to a man bouncing a rock the size of a bowling ball off a granite boulder, pounding it into shape.

Ryan chuckled. "I don't th—" with an effort, he shut his mouth with an audible click. *What's wrong with me? They are going to kick me out!*

Dr. Kowalska gave him another glance but didn't stop discussing the tools and possible methods to shape the stone and statues. While she spoke about the Sphinx's age, Ryan shook his head. *She's off by fifteen thousand years.* Somehow, he managed to keep his mouth shut. *I've watched too many videos online. I'm suffering from psychological trauma, and Mom will have me committed.*

She ended the lecture by discussing the undiscovered tombs and preserving the treasures for future generations, then asked, "Does anyone have any questions?"

A dozen kids put their hands in the air, and Ryan chose that moment to slip out of the theater. He had embarrassed himself enough. While interesting, he had learned nothing about the ankh. "Focus," he mumbled to himself.

As another class tour began at the gallery's far end, Ryan was at a display monitor, pressing the buttons to advance the screen. Hieroglyphics and their various meanings scrolled by, and he found a carved ankh with the definition "symbol of life." He hasn't been able to find more information on the character haunting him since yesterday.

Frustrated, he was about to bring his fist down on the button when a shadow appeared behind his left shoulder.

"Hi there, sorry to bother you." Dr. Kowalska smiled.

Ryan's cheeks flamed red once again. "Ughh … sorry about disturbing your class."

She was the same height as Ryan, five-foot-five inches, with pale blue eyes, and his flush deepened for another reason. "That's perfectly fine. You had a great idea for the sonics. Not many know about that possibility. There are marks in the solid granite where the stone was *scooped* out of the bedrock, and the possibility of sonics is gaining popularity."

This time, Ryan knew what she was talking about; he had watched the thirty-minute video online last night. He cleared his throat and ignored the scent of vanilla. "Not sure where I got the stone singers idea. Must have been something I've read."

She chuckled. "That's okay. You wouldn't believe the answers I get daily from the young kids. I noticed you were going to say something when I was talking about the dolerite shaping stones."

Ryan tried not to groan. He wasn't getting off that easy. "They're too heavy for that kind of repetitive work."

She touched his shoulder and winked. "Come with me."

Ryan was led through the exhibits to a side room where three granite slabs, half the size of his kitchen refrigerator, rested on a carpet of white sand. "This is the interactive exhibit where you can try the dolerite stones on the granite."

A dozen black rocks with white veins running through the surface rested in the sand. She stood at the nearest red granite slab. "The stones are not heavy, maybe a pound and a half. Go ahead and try it."

Ryan stood in the sand and picked up the rock. There were grinding marks where hundreds of tourists had pounded it against the solid stone, and a light coating of dust rested on the surface. The dolerite wasn't as heavy as he thought, but he shook his head. "It would have taken thousands of years to shape any stone with these. You mentioned the Great Pyramid was completed in twenty-seven years." Ryan closed his eyes and ran the numbers. He was always good at math and didn't need to be precise.

"You said there were over two million stones in the Great Pyramid?" When she nodded, he continued, "If it was built in twenty-seven years, that's over two hundred stones *per day* they would have to move from the quarry and shape. It can't be done with these."

He hefted the dolerite with one hand. "I think they were movers. If you place a few of them under the stones, they were easier to push, like marbles under a cookie sheet."

Ryan looked around for something to use as a demonstration and rested one hand on the granite slab. The memory tugged at his conscience, and he closed his eyes. Ryan recalled the nameless tune the stone singers hummed. Unbidden, the deep vibration came from his chest and slowly gained volume like a tuning fork plugged into an amplifier. When Ryan opened his mouth, the guttural bass note didn't carry far, but Dr. Kowalska drew in a sharp breath as the air in the small gallery became charged, and the hair on his arms stood on end.

Fifteen hundred pounds of solid granite tipped to the side as Ryan slid the dolerite rock underneath. He shook off the stone singer's dream and took a step back. Ryan dusted his hands together and slowly realized what had happened.

Dr. Kowalska gasped. "Holy fuckin' Christ on a stick!"

CHAPTER 9

Crystal Kowalska stood at the rear of the crowded security office as her boss, Dr. Ashraf Dali, worked with the chief security officer. The primary curator was in his late seventies with a short white beard and hair. The small round glasses constantly slid down his nose to perch on the end, driving her crazy. The security guard was in his mid-twenties and seemed competent with the equipment. The array of monitors was impressive, covering the entire wall in the office and detailing every second within the museum.

"Right there." Dali pointed to the black four-door car that stopped outside the main doors. A young man wearing jeans and a black T-shirt exited the backseat and stared at the building entrance as the vehicle drove away.

"Unable to get a detailed image of the plates." Fingers danced on a keyboard.

The scene shifted inside the lobby as the man lined up and bought a ticket.

"Timestamp, ten-forty-five a.m." The guard wrote a note before allowing the footage to continue.

Crystal leaned forward and understood the reason for the accuracy. The man had paid for his ticket by tapping a credit card.

Over the years, she asked thousands of adults, students, and small children how the ancient Egyptians moved the stones, and today was the first time *stone singers* came up. He had seemed so sure of his answer that her interest was piqued. Aliens and time travelers came up so often that they were common, along with lost Atlantian technology. What had shocked her was the demonstration. That granite slab was *solid*, and it would take five strong men to move it a few inches, but he had done it with one hand. *One hand!* The man had seemed as stunned as she was, then bolted before she could say anything.

She had closed the interactive exhibit and canceled the next class before running through the museum. When she burst into the offices, she was still in shock, and her mind sought a logical answer, but nothing made sense. Dr. Dali was on a phone call, and she practically dragged him down the hall to the Egyptian gallery. Dressed in his usual brown suit and tie, he had grudgingly followed. They had tried to move the granite block, thinking it had been replaced with a prop, but their efforts were in vain.

Maybe it was the look on her face or the dolerite-shaped stone *underneath* the granite. Dr. Dali caught her excitement, and a few minutes later, he knocked on the security office glass door.

"We lose sight of him here when he enters lecture hall 3-2b."

There were no security cameras inside the classroom. Crystal had taught with the R.O.M. for six years and knew the building well.

"Here we go." Dali sat on the edge of the chair and pushed his glasses back up.

Crystal watched herself approach the young man and lead him into the interactive exhibit. The camera angle switched under the guard's fingers, and she asked, "Is there audio?"

"No, sorry. Just video."

She heard Dali swear under his breath. She would have loved a copy of the guttural humming the man had performed as well.

The video feed flickered and jumped after the man laid a hand against the granite. The young man ran out of the hall when the image became clear. The stone rested at an angle.

"Uhh?"

"Hold on. There's another position." The guard made a series of clicks with the mouse, and the scene shifted. The camera was in the corner ceiling behind the stones. Crystal watched as she encouraged the man to try the stone against the granite. He talked briefly, then placed his hand on the large rock. The camera flickered once, and then the recording ended.

"That's not possible." The security guard pulled up the main menu and shook his head. "It's listed as a corrupted file, and that camera is now offline."

Dr. Dali leaned back in the chair and pressed his fingertips together. "I need a copy of everything. Can you get me the financial transaction details as well?"

The guard shook his head. "You'll need the CEO to order the chief financial officer to release the information. That has nothing to do with security."

"That won't be a problem. Thanks for your help." Dr. Dali received a thumb drive with all the video footage. "Dr. Kawolska, join me in the office, please."

She followed briskly up the stairs to the third-floor offices. Dr. Dali had his own office at the end of the hall, and Crystal had to share one with Tammy, but they worked opposite shifts, so space was never an issue.

Crystal sat in the visitor's chair as Dr. Dali sat behind his desk, and he pulled out a notepad and pen. "What do you know of this man? Have you seen him before? Impressions?"

"I'd never seen him before, and at one point, I thought he seemed rather smart. The problem with the number of stones in the pyramid versus the alleged years to build it, he figured that out in his head."

At university, that problem was refined. With two-point-three million stones in the pyramid, the final math showed that each stone had five minutes to be quarried, transported to the building, and shaped. Her archeology professor had mentioned that the timeline was either flat-out wrong or there was another method used that they had yet to discover. The number of limestone and granite blocks was accurate and couldn't be disputed. Many in the community knew of that mathematical problem and chose not to address it.

"Did you smell alcohol or believe he was using an illicit substance? Do you think he used a mechanical device to help tip the stone?"

Crystal shook her head. "He seemed sober, and you saw him. He carried nothing. I wouldn't have believed it if I weren't there."

Dr. Dali smiled. "That's where I'm at right now. Sorry for all the questions. I'm just trying to understand what happened. If that block hadn't been moved, I would also have had trouble believing the story. Can you describe the singing?"

She would never forget that moment for the rest of her life. "It wasn't singing as much as it was humming, then he vocalized the same deep pitch. I was somewhat reminded of an Australian didgeridoo, but a note that was more felt than heard."

"I'll keep the interactive exhibit closed while I run a few tests and forward everything to some colleagues." Dali took off his glasses and raised his eyebrows. "However, if you run into this young man again, physically sit on him and call me. I'd love to have half an hour with him or hire him. Trust me. There would be no lack of funding, and he could name his price."

Crystal knew firsthand how much was spent on digs, and several donors had bottomless pockets. "I'll handcuff myself to him if I have to."

"If you could take pictures of the stone from all angles and forward them to me. I'll make a few phone calls and see if that video can be cleaned up."

The adrenaline high hadn't left her body yet, and Crystal sprung from the chair. "I'll get right on it. Oh my God. I can't even imagine what this could mean."

"Talk to you soon and Dr. Kawolska." Dr. Dali cleared his throat. "As a precaution, don't mention this to anyone."

"Yes, sir."

Ashraf closed the door to the office and ensured the lock was engaged. He sat behind the desk and inserted the thumb drive into the computer. He flicked through the various captured videos and stopped when the kid placed his palm on the granite. From the elevated camera above the arched entryway, the image showed static interference, but you could still see the moment when the stone was tipped. After that, the recording was garbage. The security guard had added the footage of the young man fleeing the building. Once outside, he turned east and then was out of range.

Crystal's pictures arrived on his phone, and he forwarded them to his email.

"Okay, kid. Time to find out who you are."

Ashraf wrote an email to his long-time colleague at the archeology faculty in Cairo, Egypt. Despite the seven-hour time difference, Mahmoud should still be at work. If not, he would call him at home and risk waking him up. He wouldn't mind at all. With his resources and connections, no stone will be left unturned.

CHAPTER 10

"Psychedelic mushrooms and cocaine? That's the only answer." Ryan mumbled, thrust his hands in his pockets, and continued walking south on Yonge Street. He had run a city block until the pedestrian traffic forced him to slow down. He occasionally looked over his shoulder to see if he was being followed, but it was getting close to lunchtime, and the downtown traffic was picking up.

Ryan's friends must have spiked the energy drinks, and someone slipped mushrooms on his pizza. He should be tripping right now, but mostly, he was confused.

"Arghh! What's wrong with me?" A woman gave him the side-eye and pulled her children away from his path.

The image of a dark-skinned man in long white linen robes laying two hands on the stone seemed like the memory of a dream. He *must* have seen it somewhere, maybe on the computer or television, but Ryan couldn't recall. As the white fog coated his brain, he remembered the stone singer's exact pitch and tone. When the moment had passed, he stood in disbelief. Coupled with seeing the strange symbols and the deaths, running away from the problem seemed the best bet.

Ryan didn't consider himself a fighter, and avoiding conflict was better for his nerves and health. However, there had been times when there wasn't any choice. In grade seven, he had been picked on by a group of kids for weeks. One day, they had been waiting for him outside of school. The biggest kid threw the first punch, and Ryan snapped. While never having been in a physical fight before, he had watched the hockey game the previous weekend. Colton Orr, from the Toronto Maple Leafs, never backed down from anything. Colton's left fist would wrap in his opponent's jersey while his right fist fired like a jackhammer. The pummeling wouldn't stop until two referees interrupted the fight. The big kid, Larry, tried to run away, but Ryan wrapped his hand in the shirt. Other kids kicked and punched his back, but he never let up on Larry's face. Through tears and swelling eyes, Ryan grabbed the next kid, and his right fist blurred repeatedly. The others ran away, and he had never been bothered again in public or high school. He thanked number twenty-eight for the lesson.

Ryan felt he was in the same situation today. Events over which he had no control were thrown at him, but there was one difference. There was no one to fight. He never got to ask the woman at the museum about the ankh and if there were any special meanings or stories.

Lost in thought, he found himself standing outside the Eaton's Center. The indoor shopping mall had four floors and hundreds of stores, and the place would be packed during lunch on a Friday. An idea began to form, and Ryan followed the crowd inside. After taking the escalator to the lower floor, he sat at the edge of the food court.

Each vendor had a lineup of twenty people or more, and the Tim Horton's outlet had two lines of fifty. The food court was nearly shoulder-to-shoulder people as they stuffed their faces. Ryan wasn't watching the people as much as the walls, signs, and ceiling above the crowds.

He had thought of a way to fight back, even if he lived in a delusion.

Prevent the symbol from claiming a life.

Ryan wasn't trapped in a corner yet, but he didn't want to play the weird game any longer. The advantage would be his if he could force the unknown player's hand.

Fifteen minutes passed with no results. The Eaton's Center should have had the largest concentration of people in the area, but nothing was happening except that the grumble in his stomach was becoming painful.

For two hours, he walked the mall before giving up. Ryan managed to eat a burger and fries once the crowd thinned out at the food court before finding himself outside on Yonge Street again. While the lunch hour was over, the city of Toronto never slowed, and clusters of people hustled along the sidewalks, darting into various stores. After he left the air-conditioned mall, sweat made his T-shirt cling to his back within moments as the sun made an appearance through the skyscrapers.

With no sense of planning, Ryan headed south and turned right on Queen Street. Immediately, the foot traffic eased, but he kept scanning the shops and alleyways. He crossed University Avenue heading west, passing old City Hall and the Sheridan Center. The towering office buildings were left behind as the city transitioned into the never-ending storefronts with apartments above.

Ryan had given up on the endeavor and was going to go home when his jaw dropped.

Across the street was Steve's Music store, and to his back, a building was covered in scaffolding and walled off due to construction. Queen Street was a four-lane road with street car tracks along the middle lanes. A three-foot ankh lay on the road in the far lane, directly in front of the music store, but no one was on the sidewalk or in the immediate area.

"What the hell?" Ryan darted across the street and dragged a foot across the sign with the toe of his shoe. While he couldn't touch it, it was very real. Heart racing, he moved to the sidewalk.

Two high-school students left the music store carrying guitar cases, and Ryan moved out of their way. When he was little, he wanted to play guitar, and the urge never faded. A flash of light made him wince when he looked through the glass window at the instruments.

Across the street, a white car pulled away from the side of the road and performed a U-turn. The afternoon sun reflecting off the windscreen was blinding.

A westbound red T.T.C. streetcar couldn't stop in time and T-boned the Chevy. An explosion of twisted metal and glass made Ryan jump, then cringe as the car was pushed twenty feet. The streetcar squealed to a halt as the horn sounded from the Chevy. Fluids poured out of the engine, and steam rose under the hood.

Ryan had vowed to fight back. Before he knew what was happening, he darted toward the passenger door of the wrecked vehicle. The airbags had deployed, and the locking mechanism automatically disengaged, but the car had taken a beating. It was bent and crushed from the impact.

He banged the passenger window with a fist and screamed, "Are you okay? Can you hear me?"

Ryan couldn't access the driver's side of the car. The nose of the streetcar rested where the center console would have been. Frantic, he tried the rear door, and it squealed open.

"Hello?" Ryan crawled in the back seat but couldn't go far, and there was no point.

The construction worker who had jumped behind the wheel was a bloody mess. His face and torso were crisscrossed with deep cuts, and the angle his head rested wasn't natural. The door squished the body, and he lay half in the passenger seat. Blood trickled from the man's mouth as his eyes remained fixed on a distant sight—unblinking.

Not ready to give up, Ryan tapped the man's shoulder. "Sir? Can you hear me?"

Ryan could barely hear himself over the vehicle's horn. The man's head lolled to the side.

"Is he okay?" The T.T.C. driver stood by the door.

"No." Ryan winced and shook his head. He found himself gasping for breath. "Not good at all."

The driver quickly looked inside the car, then took two steps and vomited. Ryan didn't blame him. People were already gathering on the sidewalk, and vehicles had stopped in both directions. A wailing scream of despair rose inside like a tidal wave, threatening to swamp his sanity. Before he ended up pulling his hair out, Ryan ran from the horrific scene like a gazelle being chased by a lion.

CHAPTER 11

Constable Mike Peebles, from 52 Division, was the first to arrive on the scene, and he quickly called for an ambulance, fire, and backup while keeping civilians away from the accident. Mike has been with the Toronto Police Services for fourteen years and was known for being the strong, silent type. At six-foot-five and wearing the vest and gear, he appeared larger than life. The short beard added to his bulk, but his wife thought it made him look like a teddy bear. However, one look from him could diffuse most situations without violence or being physical—which was fine for him.

While the streetcar was full of passengers, no one, including the operator, was injured. The driver of the Chevy Malibu was dead, and he had no way of extracting him from the car. This was not his first accident scene or death on the job. Just yesterday, he worked in another division due to a staffing shortage, and the victim was a twelve-year-old boy. He was also a qualified S.O.C.O. (scene of crime officer) and had to take pictures and fingerprints of the aftermath of the gang conflict. After his shift last night, his wife and children received extra hugs. Throughout his career, there had been many such moments, sometimes daily.

Fire Station 332 was a few streets over and arrived within four minutes, and Constable Peebles shut down the road in both directions. When his patrol sergeant arrived, he was ordered to gather witness statements and help with scene management.

The streetcar driver swore everything happened too fast, and he couldn't react in time. A quick survey of the pedestrians wasn't successful. They had arrived after the accident. A few passengers from the streetcar confirmed the driver's story.

The T.T.C. inspectors arrived, and the hard drive was unlocked from the interior. The video cameras showed the driver turning without looking, signaling, or warning. There would be no charges against the streetcar driver. Mike spotted a security camera above the door to Steve's Music, and while he didn't have to duck to go inside, it was close. The staff was helpful, and they went over the external footage.

"Can you go back another three minutes?" he asked the manager.

"Not a problem."

Mike leaned over the counter, his face a foot from the small monitor, when his eyebrows rose. "I'm going to need a copy of the footage. Hopefully, that won't be an issue?"

"No, sir."

A few minutes later, Peebles stood outside digging through his wallet until he found the business card from yesterday. Detective McCallan will want to know what one of her witnesses was doing on Queen Street West. He would as well.

▲ ▲ ▲

Trish McCallan sat at her desk and rewound the footage for the tenth time. Ryan Petey runs south across Queen Street and pauses in the second lane. His toe marks the spot, and then he steps on the sidewalk. Thirty-three seconds later, the streetcar smashes into the white car. The body ends up where Petey's toe had tapped the road.

Exactly.

"That's three deaths tied to Ryan Petey within a twenty-six-hour span. Is that enough to justify surveillance? I could bring him in for further questioning." She paused the video and turned to her boss, Inspector Carl Davidson. "What do you think?"

Davidson read her reports on the shooting and the "coincidental meeting of the subject" at the hospital, but the video evidence was the final nail in the coffin. "I'll make sure the warrants are approved for advanced surveillance." After a glance at his watch, he grunted. "It's a Friday night, but I'll make things happen quickly. I'll get things ready and let you know when we implement them. Good luck."

Trish nodded. "Thank you, sir. I'll make the calls. I have no idea how Petey pulled off that last trick on Queen Street, but we'll find out."

By the morning, there wouldn't be many secrets Ryan Petey had that she wouldn't know. With a few keystrokes, McCallan reclassified the 415 Queen Street West accident to a homicide.

CHAPTER 12

Ryan reached an alley near Spadina Avenue before the burger and fries decorated the pavement. Sirens from the accident echoed down the street as tears and snot rolled down his face. "What the fuck is going on with me?"

Shooting up digital bodies in Call of Duty was one thing, but seeing three dead people in two days was three too many, as far as he was concerned. Or was that four? Confused, he wiped his hands on his jeans. Ryan noticed a dark brown streak.

"Jesus Christ!" His right hand had blood on the palm from the accident. He scrubbed up as best he could with his T-shirt while trying not to hyperventilate. After pacing back and forth in the alley, Ryan calmed enough to think rationally again.

Using his phone, he ordered an Uber to the corner of Spadina and Queen Street West, not caring about burning through any money he had made on the last job. He wanted to get home at any cost. *Needed* to be home. Ryan also discovered a series of text messages from his mom that he had missed. She's going to kill me.

I'm alive. Talk to you tonight. Hopefully, the quick reply will calm her down.

His ride showed up, and forty minutes later, Ryan unlocked the front door of his home. His mom would be done work in a few hours, and he had to clean up. Clothes went into the wash, and he climbed into the hottest shower he could stand to scrub himself thoroughly.

The mental fog had lifted enough that he just felt numb. Ryan moved like an automaton going through the motions of life. After dressing in his pajamas, he heated the last slice of pizza and sat in front of the television without eating or seeing anything.

"I need help and answers," he mumbled. Looking for answers is what started today's nightmare, and he ended up with only more questions. Ignoring the food, Ryan went downstairs to search the internet, and twenty seconds later, he was scrolling through a thirty-eight-year-old woman's profile on social media.

Dr. Crystal Kowalska graduated with a master's degree in archeology from the University of British Columbia and a B.A. in anthropology from the

University of South Dakota. Her profile picture showed a young woman wearing a pith helmet and holding a trowel and brush. In the background, a pyramid rose against a clear blue sky. Ryan also found the usual pictures of food, selfies taken with friends, and memes.

He logged into his profile and sent Dr. Kowalska a message:

Sorry, I wrecked your display at the museum. I wanted to ask you a few questions on a different subject. I need some help. – Ryan.

Before he could change his mind, he pressed send.

"Hope there's no such thing as museum police." Fatigue made Ryan's eyes heavy, and he couldn't stop yawning. "Come on, nightmares. Let's see what you got."

Turning out the lights, he crawled into bed and was sleeping within seconds.

CHAPTER 13

2560 B.C. Giza Plateau

The day's scorching heat plummeted as the silky smooth sky of pinks and purples announced the night's calm. As if marking the fiery orb's former location, a brilliant star appeared a finger's width above the horizon, twinkling like a polished jewel against a black cloth. A symphony of crickets sang to each other as bats feasted upon mosquitos and moths in the enveloping darkness. A beige rat scurried from a pile of rocks with a twitching scorpion in its jaws. Immune to the repeated stings, the furry rodent feasted at the water's edge.

An hour later, when a glowing constellation appeared in the northern sky, a robed man stood with his back to a granite outcropping while unrolling a banner.

To the untrained eye, the papyrus was covered in random ink lines and showed signs of wear—thirty-six holes of varying sizes perforated the material, but a trained eye knew differently. While in his fourth decade, he had the physical attributes of a man half his age. Corded muscles that shifted beneath the cloth were more suited to physical labor than a scholar. Dressed in tightly wrapped white robes and sandals, he stood two inches above five feet, and his tanned skin gleamed in the starlight.

The sheet was carefully aligned with the bottom edge against the horizon, and when the constellation could be seen through the holes, a nervous excitement made the man's pulse race. Grinning, he counted seven lines to the left, and a yellow-white star flickered through the page. A calloused finger counted the crossing dashed lines—three.

After rolling the scroll tight, the man slipped it into a deep pocket and picked up his pack and a reed cage. Inside, a goose with a tan plumage and brown-colored mask about the eyes appeared uniform gray in the low light and seemed unperturbed at the traveling accommodations.

The leather sandals made gravel crunch underfoot, but soon, the silent sands of the desert cushioned each step as he strode northwest, leaving the oasis behind. Dry and cracked lips murmured prayers learned, not only to appease his soul but to measure the pace. The path led over dunes a hundred feet high and across open expanses where the sand barely covered the limestone shelf beneath. The glimmering yellow-white star guided his steps, and at the end of the third repetition of praying, it was nearly lost as one jewel among many when his journey ended.

Unsurprised to find a dune at his feet, the man placed the pack and cage to the side before digging. The day's heat was held in the ground but soon gave way to the cooler temperatures as the hole deepened. Throughout the night, he toiled in silence with only brief breaks to sip tepid water from a container, and as the faint blush of dawn arrived in the east, the capstone was revealed.

The polished red and black flecked granite slab was eighteen inches wide, twenty long, and three inches thick, and the man was surprised to find no carvings or writing blemishing the smooth surface. Further digging showed the stone to be sitting on a limestone shelf.

The legends are real! He quickly added, *not that I had any doubt, my God.*

The man gathered his pack and cage, pausing to watch the sunrise. The longest day of the year had begun. Heat waves already rippled above the sands, making the sun shimmer and dance on the horizon. The afternoon winds would erase any trace he had left on the journey, including the hole. Turning from the light, he sought the darkness.

The capstone shifted to the side with minimal effort, and he slipped into the cool tunnel beneath. The shaft was five feet tall and wider than his shoulders, with plenty of room to walk nearly upright. He removed an oil lantern from the pack and used a metal striker to light the wick. The goose honked and shifted within the confines of the reed cage, and its dark eyes watched the man struggle to replace the stone. With a huff of effort and grinding of sand, the sixty-pound weight slid into position. Any vestiges of light from the outside world were extinguished.

The tunnel sloped downward through the bedrock and, after one hundred paces, performed a ninety-degree right-turn into a chamber. The ceiling was constructed of massive curved granite blocks that met twelve feet above the man's head. Each stone was an example of perfection and design; a grain of sand would not fit between the gaps. Contrary to the exquisite work above, the floor was rough-hewn limestone and dust-covered. However, the man's attention was drawn to the end of the long room where an eight-foot statue appeared to be emerging from the wall behind a table.

"My, Lord."

He dropped to both knees and pressed his forehead into the rugged floor.

The jackal's head and body were solid stone, and brilliant green eyes glimmered in the lamplight. A muscular arm held a balanced scale in the left hand and a staff in the right, and around each wrist, golden bracers were decorated with symbols. The god of the afterlife looked ready to enter battle or pass judgment.

"I have come bearing bad tidings, my Lord." The man remained on the floor but raised his head. "I am the last from the great temple. The rest have been slain in the name of your usurper."

The high priest prompted his harrowing escape and subsequent journey. His mentor's last-minute instructions and knowledge have led Aken to the secret temple of Anubis with the raiments of the order—such relics can *never* be lost.

Aken stood and brought the caged goose to the stone table. The solid granite slab was precisely six feet long and three feet wide, with the right side being three inches taller than the left, giving the surface a definite slope. A copper knife made quick work of the cage door, and the bird was placed on the table.

"Please accept this humble offering as a token of—" Aken's head snapped around when a distant grinding echoed down the tunnel.

The capstone was being moved.

I have been followed!

The blade flashed twice to either side of the goose's neck as the hurried sacrificial offering was completed. Knowing her life was ending, the goose's wings gyrated as if taking flight, and feathers landed in the growing pool of blood. Aken threw the bird aside and opened his pack, removing a ring and necklace. His hands shook as sweat beaded across his brow.

"Guide me, my Lord," he pleaded.

The hushed tones of men talking replaced the echo, and they were barely heard over the dying bird but were unmistakable.

My eyes see all.

Eyes? The glint from the lantern made the emerald crystals sparkle, and Aken had the answer. Two thumbs pressed inward, and a muffled click allowed the table to slide a foot back, revealing a small cavity underneath. The relics fit inside, and the table slid back into position with ease.

The goose found a corner to die as multiple footsteps approached.

Join me.

"Yes, my god."

Anubis was the lord of the dead, and the command only meant one thing.

Aken sat on the table and didn't hesitate. The copper blade slashed deep across his left wrist, nearly to the bone. The steps were mere feet from the chamber as the razor-sharp knife slid across the side of his neck through his carotid artery. As the last priest of an archaic order lay flat, blood arced in a sheet across the wall and floor with each beat of his heart. Three men stormed into the chamber, shouting victory and clutching knives, but their cheers were short-lived as the earth shifted and thunder rolled from above.

A granite wedge weighing two tons fell from the ceiling at the entrance, trapping everyone inside. Aken's lifeblood ebbed across the table as the dim light of the oil lantern faded, but the grin on his face grew as the Osiris priests panicked.

In the absolute darkness, the eyes of the jackal watched the folly of men, and a brief glint of light betrayed the god's anger. The setback would cost hundreds of years, if not millennia, but the ancient conductor of souls was nothing if not patient.

CHAPTER 14

Ryan swung his legs off the bed and kicked the covering to the side. His mom must have tucked him in; the blanket was from the couch upstairs. Every detail of the dream seemed vivid, and his limbs still shook with adrenaline. The soft dusty feathers of the goose to the cold knife parting the flesh on his wrist like butter were more a memory than a dream. He ran a thumb over his left wrist, expecting to feel bone, and was surprised to find it whole.

Bleary eyes widened when he saw the time. He had slept six hours! Ryan never liked sleeping during the day and would only do so if he was sick. He would have slept throughout the night if his stomach wasn't growling like a hungry bear.

"I think I'm okay."

Once he turned the light on and stretched, Ryan felt rather normal. While the sight of the dead was disturbing, it was now in the past. Whatever mental anguish he had suffered had been washed away and had become manageable, and despite it being ten o'clock at night, a new day had begun.

He was going upstairs to get something to eat when the flashing light on his phone caught his eye. Dr. Kowalska had written back!

Ryan, I'd love to meet up, and I will, of course, answer any questions that I can. As you can guess, I have a few of my own! – Crystal

After researching her background, Ryan felt confident she could help or point him in the right direction. His stomach growled again, and he wrote back.

I'm starving. Do you want to go out for a drink so we can talk?

As soon as he sent the message, his heart started racing. It looked like he was asking her out on a date. "Oh my, God."

Ryan was about to unsend the text when she replied. *Yes! Where and when?*

One of his favorite places was around the corner and a fifteen-minute walk, The Harp and Clover. The pub served amazing chicken tacos with over two dozen beers on tap. He wrote the location, and she agreed to meet in thirty minutes. While clearly not a date, Ryan threw his usual black T-shirt aside and chose a blue and white collared dress shirt with clean jeans.

After grabbing his phone and wallet, he scrawled a quick note for his mom and left it on the kitchen table before slipping out the front door. He didn't want to wake her up. After a few steps, he paused and looked back at the darkened home. He pulled out his phone and punched the security code to arm the system. Enough had happened to him lately, and it was better to be safe than sorry.

Dr. Ashraf Dali smiled at his good fortune. Crystal had trusted him with valuable information, and moral decisions were quickly pondered and discarded. He sat at his desk in his condo, shuffling through a stack of paperwork and signing forms. The building was on Front Street, and the penthouse had a view of the C.N. Tower and the Harbourfront from his balcony and Lake Ontario. Tonight, the tower was lit with blue and yellow lights, and the smell of the water and a cool breeze came through the window.

Ashraf had reached out to an old colleague, and after a flurry of discussions with Mahmoud through email, they ended up talking on the phone for nearly an hour. The possibilities were staggering and would rewrite Egyptian history and possibly the stone walls of Peru,

Easter Island, and Stonehenge. Ashraf had watched videos on a man who lived in Florida City, Florida. In the early 1900s, Ed Leeskalnin had single-handedly built a coral castle entirely of limestone on his property. The average weight of *each* stone was fourteen tons. Some of the rocks carved were over twenty-five feet tall, and the heaviest weighed thirty tons. Ed never used modern equipment, and when asked how he performed such miracles, he stated he had 'discovered the secrets of the pyramids.' For several decades, the eight-foot-tall revolving gate was on a perfect pivot point that could be rotated with just one finger. The gate weighed nine tons and was shaped by *one* diminutive man. Truly astounding! Mahmoud thought the secrets had been discovered again by a Canadian man, and so did one of his acquaintances. Mahmoud's friend believed in the discovery so much that he forwarded Ashraf a retainer fee, with promises of more just to keep him updated on any further findings or the man's whereabouts.

Tap.

Five hours ago, he printed off his bank statement and shook his head at the seven-figure balance. In the last forty-five years, Ashraf has been pursuing knowledge around the globe, treasuring each kernel of information gained or teaching others about the wonders of discovery. All for a fraction of that sum. Archeology had some of the most poorly paid professionals anywhere in the world. At seventy-one years old, he never thought the day had come, but with a slanted pen stroke, he signed his resignation letter. He would scan the document and send it to the appropriate people in the morning.

"Come on, let's see how much the last bit was worth to you." His index finger tapped the F5 key, refreshing the laptop screen.

Crystal had called, literally bubbling over that she had made contact with the man from the museum; his name was Ryan Petey. She would meet him at an Irish Pub in North York, Toronto. Ashraf told her to be cautious but to get as much information from Ryan as she could, then bring him to the museum so he could test the man's abilities—reminding her that money was no object.

Tap.

Ashraf had no intentions of ever seeing his colleague again, as pleasant as she was, but to disappear on a morning flight, returning to Cairo, Egypt, after a month-long layover in Morocco.

Tap.

It was time to pass the gauntlet to another so they could rewrite history and explore new knowledge.

Tap.

Sweet Mother of Mary!

The amount in his account had quadrupled. His phone vibrated with an incoming text:

Your assistance is no longer needed. We have it from here.

His shaking fingers pulled the battery out of the Android phone and removed the sim card. While he had done nothing illegal, just sharing information, it was time to make his exit.

"Good luck, Dr. Kowalska."

Ashraf looked around at the condo he'd been renting for five years and shrugged. He wouldn't miss it in the slightest. "Now, where are my suitcases?"

CHAPTER 15

Ryan ordered a Wheaten Kings, an Ontario craft beer while waiting. The pub was mainly polished brass and oak with knickknacks on the walls: old instruments, Guinness posters, and shelves holding pottery, mugs, and books. The shine on the bar was from the sleeves of countless patrons, and the lowered lighting was heartwarming. On the far side, a man cleared tables from the stage before setting up a microphone and amplifier. From the guitar cases on the floor, live entertainment would happen soon. Until then, music was piped in from hidden speakers in the ceiling. The pub was half full of patrons, and more were arriving by the minute. The place would be packed on a Friday night, and he was glad to get a booth for privacy.

Ryan flipped through the menu while keeping one eye on the door, trying not to be nervous.

Answers. Ryan needed answers and, hopefully, a way to return things to normal. Egyptian symbols, dead people, and moving heavy rocks like they were balsa wood weren't ordinary, and those abilities could disappear at any time if he had the choice.

When she walked through the door, it took a moment to realize it was Dr. Kowalska. She wore black leggings, a tank top, and a short denim jacket. With her hair in a ponytail, she looked closer to his age than forty. She clutched a small green purse inside the entrance, scanning the pub. He noticed her glasses were missing— wearing contacts? Swallowing the lump in his throat, Ryan stood and waved her over.

"Thanks for coming." He gestured to the restaurant. "Hope this is okay."

"Are you kidding me? I wouldn't miss this for anything!"

She sat across from him in the booth, and the waitress brought his order, placing the pint glass onto a coaster. Dr. Kowalska ordered a Guinness and Ryan chicken tacos.

"Okay, where do we start?" Now that he had the opportunity, he didn't know where to begin.

"First, you can call me Crystal." Her grin set him at ease. "Tell me about yourself."

Ryan nodded. "I grew up in Milton, just west of Toronto. My family moved here when I turned six, and two years later, my parents divorced, and my mom kept the house. After high school, I studied graphic design at George Brown College for two years. Now, I'm working out of my mom's basement designing websites, logos, or any work I can find."

Crystal seemed genuinely interested in what he was saying. Absolutely nothing in common with a date he had last month. *Not that this was a date!* Ryan felt his ears burning, and he took a sip of beer.

"I grew up in Vancouver, British Columbia, and digging up fossils has always interested me since I was a young girl." Her beer arrived, and she placed it to the side before continuing. "I went to the University of British Columbia for my doctorate in archeology and an understudy for my bachelor's in South Dakota for anthropology. I spent two years in Pakistan and four years in Cairo before taking the curator position with the exhibit. To be honest, I needed the money."

Crystal made crawling into tombs or mountain caves sound exciting. His food arrived, and she gestured for him to eat while she continued. She spoke of her findings and mentioned frustration with the Egyptian government on their tight grip on excavation permits to new technology and the use of LiDAR, which can find buried walls, forts, or structures, even through the rain forest canopy.

Ryan pushed his empty plate away, knowing there was no good way to mention the last two days. He cleared his throat before beginning. "Before I start, I want you to know that I'm not crazy and to keep an open mind."

"If I thought you were, I wouldn't be here." Her quirky grin was reassuring.

Ryan spun his coaster and decided that if you remove a Band-Aid, it's best to do it with one quick yank instead of a slow, prolonged effort. "Yesterday, I hid behind a dumpster as two gangs had a shoot-out. A kid was shot, and I saw this symbol on the wall."

He dipped his finger in the beer and drew the ankh on the tabletop.

Unable to meet her eyes, he added, "When the kid died, the symbol disappeared."

Once he had started, the rest of the story poured out like a broken damn. Ryan talked about Collin dying at the hospital and the accident. "Each time, this symbol was there. When they died, it disappeared."

Ryan kept his head down, staring at his drink, waiting for the laughter. Instead, her hand reached across the table to hold his. "Are you okay? Oh my God. I can't imagine what that would have been like. I'd be a complete mess." Crystal squeezed his hand once before pulling away. "As far as anyone knows, the ankh symbolized the key of life or the Nile. The sun god, Ra, was usually depicted holding an ankh in his right hand,

and Anubis had one affixed to his staff, representing eternal life. But to be honest, I've never heard of an ankh foreshadowing someone's death. Sorry."

Ryan was lost in her sympathetic eyes and slowly nodded. He expected as much and was about to mention his dream when the music turned off. The pop of a guitar being plugged into an amp came from the speakers. He glanced at the banner behind the player, *East Coast Experience with Bill Quigley*, but ended up locking gazes with a man sitting at the end of the bar. The dark-skinned man's eyes widened briefly before snapping down to look at his phone.

Mental alarm bells rang, and a kernel of fear settled in his stomach.

"Can you talk about what happened at the museum?" Crystal laid both arms on the table and leaned forward.

Ryan scanned the crowd, and one man at a table of four briefly looked his way before returning to the conversation. The kernel grew a little larger.

"Evening, folks. I'm Bill Quigley, and let's get this party started!" The guitar player lifted a pint in the air. "Sociable!"

"Ryan?"

Cops? Gang members? The men at the table had the same haircut, short on top and nearly shaved to the skin on the sides and back. It's the same style as the man at the bar. Not gang members. Not a chance. Am I being paranoid?

"I think I'm being watched." The feeling of unease grew. "I need to ask a favor."

"Depends …" When her left eyebrow arched, he blushed.

The performer strummed the opening notes of a Tragically Hip song, and the patrons cheered.

Ryan leaned closer to be heard over the music. "Nothing like that. I'm going to the bathroom. Can you see if anyone watches me?"

Crystal nodded, and he couldn't read the look on her face, but he didn't waste time. Keeping his chin lowered, he walked to the end of the seating area, then down the long hall to the bathrooms.

Ryan didn't need her confirmation. Their gaze felt like daggers into his back, and his skin crawled.

CHAPTER 16

Bobcaygeon's last notes were lost to the pub's roar as Ryan slid into the booth. A look of worry flickered across Crystal's features. She nodded without saying anything. Ryan lifted his arm to call the waitress over and asked for the bill. He tapped his credit card on the reader, leaving a tip.

Once she left, Crystal asked, "What will you do?"

A strange calm washed through his body like a wave. *This* was the real world. He had done nothing wrong despite the bodies and wasn't worried. Ryan smiled. "I need to make sure. Just stay here."

Her mouth opened as if she was going to say something else, but then she changed her mind. "Okay."

As the musician began another song, Ryan bolted for the exit. While he wasn't running, he wasn't taking his time. Side-stepping a group of college students and an older couple that had just arrived, Ryan crashed through the double doors. Once outside, he ran along the length of the building. Heart pounding, he skidded to a halt at the last window on the corner overlooking the dining room. Not only was the table of four men rushing to get outside, but also the black man at the bar and a woman.

"Fuck!"

Instead of sprinting through the parking lot, Ryan hugged the wall and raced around the rear of the building. When he came to the emergency exit, he removed the drink coaster wedged between the lock and frame. Without being spotted, he slipped back into the pub. The initial calm had disappeared. The adrenaline made his muscles twitch and his heart rate spike. The men's washroom was the first door on his left. He went inside and locked himself in a stall. He may not know what was happening, but he had watched the Jason Bourne movies enough that he powered down his cell phone, and nearly five minutes passed before he regained control of his breathing. Ready, he returned to the dining room and slid into the booth.

Crystal's look of shock made him chuckle. He grabbed his beer. "Follow me."

He led her to the rear dining area, where a few couples ate in a snug room. Most importantly, there were no windows, and they couldn't be seen unless someone walked inside.

Crystal gasped, "How?"

Ryan shuffled into the corner seat, and she sat across from him. "Someone left the emergency exit open."

Her jaw dropped, then she laughed. Dimples appeared, and her eyes sparkled as she took a healthy sip of her drink. "What now?"

Ryan hadn't thought that far ahead yet. "Not sure. Probably call an Uber and go home."

"You're being watched." Crystal shook her head, and an errant strand of hair fell across her face. She tucked it behind an ear before touching his hand. "I have another idea."

Any suggestions were good ones. "Well?"

"I get my car, drive around back, and pick you up. No one's watching me."

His mouth nearly got away from him again, yet he still blushed at the near comment. Crystal was easily the best-looking woman in the pub. That's one of the reasons he had to confirm they were watching him and not her. He wouldn't have blamed the men at all.

"Sounds good, but I need to ask a favor." Ryan waited until she nodded. "Can I use your phone to call my mom? I turned mine off, and she doesn't know what's happening. I don't want her to worry."

"Of course!" Crystal opened her purse and unlocked the phone with a circular pattern. He called his mom and wasn't surprised it went to voicemail. It was nearly eleven o'clock at night, and she didn't know Crystal's number.

"Mom, I met a friend for a late drink, and everything's okay. My phone isn't working. I'll call when I can. Don't worry. Love you." Ryan disconnected and slid the phone back. "Thanks."

"No problem. Now, I think I've been very patient … please tell me how you moved the stone. Please!" She clutched the pint glass and leaned across the table.

Ryan knew this moment was coming, and he took a deep breath. "You may not like the answer, but it's the truth. I don't know." A look of pain flickered across her features, and he felt the need to elaborate. "I don't know where I heard or got the name stone singers from, but I could hear their song in my head, like an old memory."

"But you could do it again. Right?"

While the moment was hazy, he recalled the thrumming from his chest and answering vibration in the granite. For a brief moment, the stone slab was an extension of his hand, and there was zero effort in tipping it. He could have flung it onto its side if he wanted. He could have shaped the hard stone like putty if he had the right tools. Where did that idea come from? *I'm losing it.*

"I could try."

"Good, because I'm going to hold you to that." Crystal finished her drink and stood. "Give me two minutes, and I'll meet you at the back door."

Ryan counted down, left his beer on the table, and casually walked down the hall to the bathrooms. Outside, an older blue Kia Sorento sat waiting. He crawled into the backseat and lay flat.

"I didn't see anyone. Here we go!"

Feeling like a spy, Ryan kept low while an archeologist navigated the parking lot, helping him escape. Escaping *what* exactly, he wasn't sure. However, when six people follow you to a restaurant to keep an eye on you, it generally isn't for a good reason.

How did they know I would be there, and why were they watching me? Ryan didn't realize he was going to the pub until he had messaged Crystal. *Oh, shit.* As he stared at her profile, Ryan wondered if she was in on it or if someone had cloned his phone. *Was my house bugged?*

The car accelerated, and they were driving too fast to jump out safely. Either way, it was too late. He was trapped.

CHAPTER 17

"I think you're safe." Crystal had been driving for fifteen minutes, occasionally making random turns and backtracking. "What's next?"

Ryan sat up and looked out the windows. He wasn't sure, but he thought they were near Eglinton Avenue West. There had been many red lights where he could have jumped out and made a break for it, but a nagging doubt kept pestering him. Crystal was innocent. He had a feeling after looking into her eyes; it wasn't much. Ryan was fairly sure he wasn't thinking with another body part. Mostly.

"I have to go home sometime."

She cleared her throat. "Whoever's watching you would know where you live and could be waiting. I'd invite you back to my apartment, but it's pretty small.

But we have a staff lounge at the museum, and I'd like you to meet my boss, Dr. Dali, in the morning."

"Umm," Ryan ran a hand through his hair and shook his head. "I'm not sure about that. I was hoping to keep a low profile."

"Dr. Dali has worked on hundreds of digs and is an authority on many archaic subjects. If anyone can figure out what the ankh means, he would be the one."

Ryan thought it over and grudgingly agreed. Options were few, and he didn't want to bring trouble home.

"We have one stop to make, and we'll be there in twenty minutes." Crystal performed a series of turns and headed east on Bloor Street. Ryan glanced at the dashboard and realized it would be midnight in twenty minutes—the witching hour.

There was never-ending construction, though the traffic was lighter than normal. When Crystal ran into a store, Ryan moved to the front seat. He pulled out his cell phone and debated turning it on to see if his mother was okay and not worrying about him. He was going to help out around the house with her wrist—possibly broken— but that wasn't possible at the moment.

The remainder of the drive wasn't too bad, and Crystal turned south on Queen's Park, then the next right into the shipping/receiving area for the Royal Ontario Museum. She parked between a security vehicle and a green dumpster.

"I won't have to move until the morning." A green parking pass was left on the dashboard before walking to the building's security doors on the east side. Ryan kept looking over his shoulder. Being out in the open was putting him on edge.

Crystal pressed the button on the stainless-steel panel and held the drink tray and brown paper bag to the overhead camera. With a click, the door unlocked.

The hallway ended at another security door with a window on the left. An older man in a navy blue security outfit grinned through the Plexiglas. He wore frameless glasses, short white hair, and an impressive mustache twirled into points. "Nothing better to do on a Friday night, Dr. Kowalska?"

Crystal chuckled. "Work never stops, Tim. Signing in a visitor."

The security guard glanced at Ryan and winked. "Come on through."

The second door opened, and Tim stepped out of the office and sat behind a desk. An array of monitors decorated the rear wall. The guard pulled out a thick binder and spun it around so Crystal could sign him in.

"This is for you and Luke. I guess he's on patrol?" Crystal slid the Starbucks drinks and bag across the desk.

"Thank you, ma'am." Tim had a quick peek in the bag and smiled. "He's training a new guard and making the rounds."

Crystal finished filling out the paperwork, and the guard handed a yellow visitor pass to Ryan. "Make sure you always wear this while in the building and hand it in when you leave."

"Thank you." Ryan clipped the pass on the breast pocket of the dress shirt as Crystal pulled out her security identification. She slipped the blue lanyard over her neck, tapped it against the reader, and opened the next door.

"Make sure you share with Luke!"

As Ryan followed her down another hallway, the sound of Tim chuckling faded when the door closed behind them. Walking through the museum at night was a surreal experience, and he expected to be yelled at for trespassing. The most disturbing thing was the echo of their footsteps in the foyer and the low lighting. Random spotlights enabled them to walk through the building safely, and Ryan noticed the large dinosaur with the long neck in the second gallery was lit from underneath with an LED light string that changed colors.

"It's a little eerie, but you get used to it and relax. Nothing in the museum will come to life." Crystal grinned at his discomfort. "That I know of."

She led him under the dinosaur skeleton to a spiral staircase with an eighty-foot totem pole in the middle. As they ascended, Ryan studied the various carvings, but the horned owl's deeply carved eyes gave him the creeps, and he focused on his steps.

The third floor was designed so people would go through the exhibits in a circular pattern. Leaving the totem staircase behind, Crystal led him through a set of stone pillars. "This is the Byzantium area, and then we go to Rome."

The display cases had silverwork, vases, and decorative weapons on display, along with pieces of jewelry. Ryan thought he had seen an ankh several times, but they were elaborately detailed crosses from the sixth century.

She pointed to her right. "That way is the Egyptian exhibits, which you know, and the ancient Greek displays to the left. Tammy handles that side of the wing, and I have the other."

Instead of going farther, she held her badge against a reader opposite the emergency staircase. Motion lights turned on as they entered a long hallway, and when she passed the first door on her right, Crystal tapped it with her knuckles. "This is the office I share with Tammy, and the next is Dr. Dali's." At the end of the hall, she pointed to two blue doors. "The first is the washroom, and the second is the staff lounge."

Against the far wall was a kitchenette with a sink, toaster, coffee maker, and microwave. A smaller apartment-sized refrigerator took up one corner, and an open shelf of mugs, paper plates, and cutlery in the other. A round yellow table with black plastic chairs was against one wall, and two brown leather couches filled the opposite corner. A narrow window by the table was covered with bent plastic horizontal blinds.

"It's not much, but it's safe."

"Thank you." Ryan sat on the couch inside the door, holding back a yawn. He didn't sleep well last night, and the day's events were catching up quickly. He was coming off the adrenalin high like an addict and about to crash.

"There are muffins and donuts in the fridge that should be good still, and bottles of water if you want." Crystal stood in the doorway and gestured down the hall with her thumb. "I'm just going to my office for a bit. If you need anything, let me know."

"Sounds good. Thank you. Hopefully, everything will sort itself out in the morning." Ryan covered his mouth with the back of a hand as he yawned.

"Rest up. I'm sure you've had a long day." Crystal turned off the light and closed the door. Ryan leaned back, and the cushions were soft and welcoming.

"A little nap wouldn't hurt."

An hour later, he didn't stir as Crystal laid down to sleep on the other couch. Their soft snores competed against the clock ticking on the wall until Ryan's eyes snapped open at three o'clock in the morning.

CHAPTER 18

Danger approaches. Awake.

Heart pounding, Ryan swung his legs to the side and sat upright, confused. It took a moment to realize he wasn't in his bedroom but on a couch at the museum. A faint light from the window showed Crystal sleeping on the other couch. Who had spoken? Was it a dream? Was it paranoia when everyone was out to get you? Maybe he *was* being set up. Once that line of thought began, he couldn't shake it. In the end, Ryan was too trusting of a pretty face. A pretty face with gorgeous eyes. Ughh! *What was I thinking?*

Quietly, he opened the lounge door and slipped into the hallway. Ryan's running shoes squeaked on the tiles before pausing in front of Crystal's office. The door was open a few inches, and the light from the monitor flickered inside. Pushing open the door revealed two desks against each wall with packed bookshelves above each. The far desk barely had room for two monitors, and the near desk had a single monitor with an active screensaver. Next to the keyboard sat Crystal's purse and cell phone charging on a stand.

After a quick look over his shoulder, Ryan sat in the chair. He didn't bother with the computer. No doubt, a password would be required. Recalling the pattern Crystal used to unlock her phone, he was in, and seconds later, scrolling through her text messages.

The only current communications were to an A. Dali: *Let me know when you check your email.* The most recent text was just after midnight: *I'll see you in the morning. I hope to crack a millennia-old mystery with you!* Dr. Dali hadn't messaged back. Tentatively, Ryan checked her email, and the bottom dropped out of his stomach. His name and the place where they had met had been sent to her boss. Crystal *was* in on it.

"Fuck this shit. I'm outta here."

He placed the phone on the charger. He left the staff area in the hallway and turned right toward the totem pole staircase. The last time he had left the museum, he was running in panic, but now he fought to control a wave of rising anger. *What a bitch! I trusted her.*

When he came to the staircase, his steps slowed. A janitor's cart had tipped onto its side, and rolls of paper towels, bottles of cleaning fluid, and garbage had spilled across the polished wood floor. Three steps down the staircase, a dark-skinned man dressed in dark blue overalls lay on his back. A stream of blood had oozed down the steps like a sluggish river, pooling on the first landing. The hole in the man's forehead resembled a third eye, and the stain on his chest was the size of a dinner plate. Back-peddling, Ryan spun in circles while gasping for breath.

"What the hell?" Thoughts of a robbery were quickly dismissed. What did Detective McCallan say the other day? True coincidences are rare.

An echo sounded deep within the third-floor exhibits. Had it happened during the day, he wouldn't have heard it over the crowds, but at night, it was like a distant chirp of a cricket. When Crystal held her security pass against the card reader, Ryan had listened to that same noise earlier.

He wasn't alone.

Fighting with fists was one thing, but being shot was another. With a final glance at the body, Ryan tried walking along the edges of his shoes so they wouldn't squeak. A pair of golden armor knights guarded the next gallery's entrance. The lighting was minimal, with plenty of shadows in which to hide. He only had to wait until the police showed up. Tim would have made the call or pressed a button by now.

Another beep followed the thud of a door closing. To his right, a long, rusted sword rested on a wooden rack inside a display case. Ryan stepped over the velvet-roped barrier and quickly lowered to his knees. The only light in the arched ceiling cast a shadow on the far side of the case. *I should have worn my black T-shirt!* Ryan would have thought the museum would be completely silent at night, but the whirl of exhaust fans from the HVAC system didn't stop. Some displays had their own lighting and were individually climate-controlled, contributing to the background disturbance.

A flashlight beam flickered against the walls in the hallway from the Egyptian exhibit near the staff lounge. Ryan held his breath for a moment. When they turned the corner, he would be seen. Rising to a crouch, he slipped off his running shoes. He tucked them close to the display case and darted through the exhibit. Mannequins dressed in archaic clothing, displays of odd-shaped furniture, and animal pelts passed in a blur. The layout reminded Ryan of an Ikea with no straight lines from one area to another.

"Ryan Petey. Come out now. We just want to talk." A deep voice yelled from the darkness.

Ya, sure, they just want to talk. Tell that to the janitor, asshole. He wasn't waiting around and went into the next gallery. The displays were built into the walls, and many busts were on pedestals in the middle of the floor. The Asian gallery was wide open, and there were no hiding places. *Shitshitshit!*

The low rumbling of men talking came from behind. They were getting closer. Ryan stood behind a floor display of a three-foot-tall vase and spotted two flashlights sweeping the area. Unable to control his fear, he bolted. A cry of victory was followed almost immediately by shoes pounding the floor. Ryan hunched over, expecting a bullet as he ran.

The hallway on the right was dark, and when he came to an end, Ryan tried not to scream in frustration. He had come full circle and was back in the Egyptian gallery. *Where the hell are the police?*

Keeping to the left wall, he was about to hide under a bench when he spotted an emergency exit ahead. *Yes!* Struggling to breathe, Ryan was about to move when another flashlight beam bounced around the end of the Egyptian gallery.

He was trapped.

CHAPTER 19

Behind the sarcophagus display case was the interactive exhibit with granite blocks and dolerite stones. A black velvet rope stretched across the entrance before a *closed/fermé* sign on a brass stand. Inside, the lights were off. Ryan didn't have long, only a few seconds, and he didn't waste it. Keeping low, he snuck around the display and slid under the velvet rope.

While the lights were off in the exhibit, dim light came in from the hall. Nothing had changed since he'd been here last. Three granite slabs rested in white sand, and the dolerite stones were scattered like dark Easter eggs. The stone was still tipped with the rock underneath. He crouched behind the third granite slab and tried to control his rapid breathing. The vein in his forehead pulsed with each beat of his heart and threatened to burst.

A bead of sweat trickled down his back, and he forced himself not to move quickly. Ryan felt around and discovered the sand was only six inches deep. His fingers also brushed against four dolerite-shaping stones, the smallest being the size of a football and the others a few inches larger.

"Did you see him?"

"Found his shoes. They were still warm," a deep baritone responded.

"Thought I saw him running this way." the voice called out with an English accent.

Three men. I don't stand a chance.

The flashlights flickered all around, but the granite slab kept him hidden.

The Englishman ordered, "Get in there and look. We don't have much time."

Ryan heard the scrape of the sign being dragged on the tiles and the ends of the velvet ropes clanking against the poles.

"Ryan? Are you there?" Crystal called out down the hall.

One of the men whispered, "Check that out. No witnesses."

No witnesses? Maybe she wasn't with them. I need time to figure things out!

Use your abilities.

Huh? The voice wasn't one of the men in the hall, but he could hear it just as clearly. The same voice warned him of danger and woke him up. It's a hell of a time for my subconscious to turn crazy. When Crystal cried out, and the sounds of a struggle carried, Ryan had made a decision.

"Leave her alone!" He stood behind the stone slab.

Two flashlights shone on his face, blinding him.

"Step on out with your hands up. You're coming with us," the man on the left growled.

Ryan shuffled back a step in the sand, and his heel bumped into the shaping stone.

Abilities?

The flashlights separated, and suddenly, the overhead lights came on, blinding everyone temporarily.

Stone singer.

The dream memory reasserted itself, and he knew what to do. The granite slab was too large to use, but the dolerite shaping stones would work. As Ryan reached down, a deep rumble came from his chest, making the hair on his neck stand on end. With one hand, he picked up the largest dolerite. The three-pound stone was feather-light.

"Don't move!" The man who hit the light switch was the jock with short hair and shaved on the sides and back. He wore a brown T-shirt and jeans. He held a yellowed-bodied gun aimed at Ryan's head. The other man was older with glasses and a brimless cap and had a silenced pistol in one hand, also pointed at him. Both men looked mean, muscular, and hard as if chiseled from stone.

"Enough fucking around. Hands up. Let's go." The man with the gun pocketed the flashlight and used two hands to aim.

Ryan took half a step back and opened his mouth, and the note made the granite slab resonate.

Brown T-shirt Man swore. "We don't have time for this." When he glanced at his companion, all hell broke loose.

Ryan grunted and threw the three-pound stone like a baseball—sidearm.

The dolerite hit the Englishman under the right clavicle, and the sound of pulverized bones echoed throughout the gallery with a sickening crunch. The man's feet left the ground as he was hurled backward, and the stone ricocheted off his shoulder into a display. The Plexiglas shattered, and the rock hit the sarcophagus with a boom that was heard throughout the museum's third floor. When the man spun in mid-air and slumped to the ground, he was already dead. The pistol skidded away into the shadows.

"You fuck!" Brown T-shirt Man pulled the trigger, and a sound like a firecracker popped. Two electrode darts hit Ryan, one in the side of his neck and the other in the chest, but instead of 50,000 volts traveling through the thin wires, nothing happened.

Ryan ignored the stings to his flesh and grasped another dolerite. The sub-vocal note changed slightly, but it didn't matter to him. The lighter stone traveled thirty feet as if shot from a cannon; his aim was better this time. The man's head was flattened between the rock and the wall. The body stood briefly, connected by lengths of flesh and sinew, as if the torso didn't know the head was missing. The man's left arm rose to shoulder height, dropping the Taser before his knees gave way. The headless body twitched on the tiles twice before remaining still. The dolerite rested sixteen inches inside a solid concrete wall.

"If you fucking move one inch without me telling you to move, she dies." The black man he had spotted at the bar held a pistol to the side of Crystal's head while another hand clamped over her mouth. They stood at the edge of the doorway outside the interactive exhibit. Her screams were muffled, and the wide-eyed panic in her eyes cleared up any misgivings Ryan had. Crystal was afraid for her life; no one could fake that look of horror. He allowed the internal rumbling to fade.

"Step towards me and keep your hands in the air!" The man had a look of panic in his eyes, and before he could accidentally shoot anyone, Ryan complied.

"That's good. No farther. Now turn on your fucking phone. One *strange* move, she dies, and you're next. Move now."

Confused and frightened, Ryan removed his phone from the front pocket of his jeans and powered it on. For the next thirty seconds, he struggled to gain control of his breathing while reassuring Crystal everything was going to be okay with his eyes. He got a dozen notifications when the phone finally connected to the network.

"Check your text messages." The man hunched lower, throwing Crystal off balance as he used her for cover.

Ryan wasn't surprised to find a message from his mother, but his heart froze when he opened the texts. The last picture made him cry out and drop to his knees. "No!"

The man spoke. "If you don't cooperate, your mother will die."

His mother was tied to the kitchen chair with blood dripping over her right eye and cheek from a cut on her forehead. A handgun was being held to the side of her head.

"Do you understand, Mr. Petey? For your mother's sake, I hope you do."

He pushed Crystal away, and she collapsed beside the older dead man. Her whimpers sounded like a dying puppy. "Both of you, get up. We have travel plans."

CHAPTER 20

The Toronto Police Intelligence Services obtained the copy of the electronic warrant for surveillance by seven o'clock Friday night, and Sergeant Annie Wickman went to work. She had access to Ryan Petey's bank records within the hour and was waiting on a separate e-warrant to gain real-time access to Ryan's cell phone. The investigating officer had to show probable cause and had different hoops to jump through. Most importantly, plainclothes officers were authorized to begin surveillance operations. The standard procedure of two at night and one during the day was implemented. Annie glanced at the time and sent a team to Ryan's home address and another to monitor his activity. The four officers were already briefed and waiting for the green light to proceed. She scheduled the relief teams for six a.m. After copying the subject's bank records, she forwarded the paperwork to the officer-in-charge, Detective McCallan.

Sergeant Wickman had been with the Toronto police for thirty-one years and looked forward to her retirement. She had worked in intelligence services for the last eighteen years and knew where to go digging. The bank account only had a few hundred dollars, and the VISA account showed minimal activity: the occasional Uber, meal, and a trip to the ROM earlier today. The Ministry of Transportation didn't have a driver's license on record, and no vehicles were registered in Ryan's name.

With last year's agreement with the police services board and the Toronto Transit Commission, law enforcement now had access to a person's electronic fingerprint. Annie could follow a subject in real-time by using the Presto card as they tapped on the streetcar, subway, bus, or train. The second batch of information regarding Ryan's recent commuting was sent to the OIC. While she worked on another case, sometimes juggling three or four at a time, the subject's credit card recorded a purchase, enabling an alert.

"And just like that, we have you."

Annie sent the team watching Petey's home to the restaurant. They were only a few minutes away but could not locate him. Shortly thereafter, like clockwork, the cell phone monitoring was approved, and Annie began the hunt with the tenacity of a terrier on the trail. Currently, the subject's cell phone was offline, but she was patient. Annie then matched the subject's GPS data through the cell phone provider.

Patience paid off when, at 03:22 hours, the subject's phone registered on the network in downtown Toronto. While the technology couldn't accurately pinpoint within feet, the tower at Queen's Park recorded the link-up.

"Why's that familiar?" Annie drummed her knuckles on the desktop while studying the map. After a snap of her fingers, she cross-referenced the financial statements. Twenty-three dollars was charged to the VISA account for a ticket to the R.O.M., which is *very* close to Queen's Park. She took her niece and nephew to the museum last summer and showed them the seat of Ontario's government afterward. It was less than a ten-minute walk between the locations.

"Gotcha."

Pleased, Annie began going through the subject's call history, and after checking the text messages, her jaw dropped. A quick cross-check confirmed the validity of the material.

Without any hesitation, Annie ran to the superintendent's office.

The silence was deafening as Ryan closed his eyes and focused on breathing. The worry for his mother was such that he felt ill and came dangerously close to vomiting.

I have to save my mom. Focus!

Ryan realized the man with the gun had been yelling at him. When he opened his eyes, Crystal gave him furtive glances, but if she was trying to convey something, Ryan had no idea.

"Pity session is over." The gunman kept a ten-foot distance and gestured with his pistol. "Help her up. Time to leave."

"She's done nothing. Let her go." Ryan helped her stand. Her hands shook, and her breaths were short and rapid. "It'll be okay. They don't want you, just me."

The man gave a short bark of laughter. "Not a chance. I think she'll keep you in line. Move."

"Can I get my shoes?" Ryan was stalling, but a planned rescue had yet to materialize.

"Not my problem."

After the Egyptian exhibit, they turned left down the hall, past Crystal's office, to the totem pole staircase. When Crystal saw the body on the stairs, she crushed Ryan's hand and gasped.

"Yup. Dead people all over the place here. Watch your step. Keep going." The man's voice was cold and void of any emotion. He could have been talking about the weather or announcing the next stop on a train ride. It's just a regular occurrence—no big deal.

When they got to the main floor, Ryan headed for the front door, but the man was having none of it. "Left turn. We're going out the side, past the security office. Enough fucking around. Move."

At the end of the hall, Ryan tried the door. "It's locked."

The gunman threw a security pass at Crystal's feet. "Use that."

The picture on the card was Tim's, and before the door opened, Ryan braced himself. The security guard was tied to the chair with his throat sliced ear to ear. His uniform, chair, and floor were sheeted in blood. A knife was driven through the back of his hand, pinning it to the desktop. Someone else was lying on the floor, and he could only see a pair of black boots and the dark pants of a security guard. Tim's partner, Luke, wouldn't be getting up again.

Crystal buried her face in Ryan's chest. "Oh my, God."

"Outside."

Three-thirty a.m. was the rare moment after the late-night crowd went to sleep, and before the early risers were awake, a stillness descended across the urban jungle. Night birds called out, raccoons raided garbage cans, and the cool breeze blew north off the lake.

"Time for a ride. Move." A white Toyota 4Runner was parked in front of the dumpster, blocking Crystal's car.

Ryan heard the vehicle first and glanced north on Queen's Park as a warmth spread through his chest. It was hope. He couldn't identify the make of the black four-door car, but he noticed a spotlight next to the driver's side window—an unmarked police car.

"Don't shoot me!" Ryan pushed Crystal to the side and held both hands in the air, palms out.

"What the fuck are you doing? Get in the—"

The red and blue lights came on, and the vehicle stopped. Ryan whispered to Crystal, "Get on the ground, lay flat!"

Ryan dropped at the same time as Crystal, spreading his hands out.

"Toronto police. What's going on? Place your hands where I can see them!"

Ryan's head turned right to see a grinning archeologist's face, and when he turned left, a uniformed police officer stood with his pistol drawn, leaning across the car's roof. He looked like he could bend steel bars for fun.

Ryan shouted, "He has a gun! He's killed everyone inside!"

The black man shuffled back and swore. "This isn't over, Petey. You're a fuckin' dead man."

"Let me see your hands!" the officer shouted.

The man didn't comply and bolted between the parked cars. He jumped the fence as if the hounds of Hell were on his heels.

The officer spoke into his radio, then asked, "Are you guys okay?"

Ryan got to one knee and nodded. "We're good. He's got a gun and has killed everyone inside."

"Stay right there. An ambulance is on its way." He jumped back behind the wheel. The spotlight pivoted and turned on, aiming at the side of the building. The tires squealed as the pursuit began.

Ryan helped Crystal to her feet. "Are you okay?"

The streetlights were enough to reveal a blotchy face with red and swollen eyes. "Not really, I guess. What's happening?"

"I'm not too sure, but they have my mom. I have to go." Ryan moved to the SUV.

"We have to wait for the police."

The passenger door was unlocked, and the keys were in the ignition, ready for a fast getaway. "Yes. You should wait for the police, but I have to go." Ryan pulled out his cell phone and showed Crystal the picture.

"Holy shit."

"Ya, that's why."

Ryan ran around to the driver's side and jumped in. He had to adjust the seat forward before turning the ignition. Before he could drop it in gear, the passenger door opened, and Crystal jumped in. "I'm not staying here alone."

He didn't have time to argue. Every second counted.

"Buckle up, and I'd like to apologize."

"What for?"

Ryan stepped on the gas, and they rocketed out of the parking lot and north on Queen's Park. "I don't have my license and very little practice."

Tires clipped the curb as he turned right on Bloor Street.

"After what we just went through, the last thing I'm worried about is an accident." Contrary to her statement, Crystal calmly clicked the seatbelt home.

I'm on my way, Mom. Hold on.

CHAPTER 21

Detective Trish McCallan was used to receiving calls at all hours of the day and night and was dressed and at work within twenty minutes. She had received a copy of the text messages sent to Ryan Petey's phone as part of the surveillance package, and a puzzle piece fell into place. He was being coerced into performing murders. Nothing else made sense. Units had been dispatched to the R.O.M. and were pursuing a subject. She didn't have details yet but knew firsthand how the officers would herd the fleeing subject, restricting his movements and eventual capture.

What did you do now, Ryan?

Julie Petey was being held hostage, and as soon as Trish sat at her desk, she contacted the unit watching the home in North York. They had checked in at 03:45

hours, reporting no activity, and the house had remained dark since arrival. She was tempted to ask for a door knock to verify a wellness check, but she hesitated after receiving the report from the intelligence officer. A witness had said, *"Everyone inside was dead, and the fleeing subject had killed them."* That was enough to kick the Toronto Police Services like an anthill and get everyone involved.

Trish signed out her Glock 19 and raced to her cruiser. Reports were one thing, but boots on the ground were another.

▲ ▲ ▲

Ryan wasn't used to the larger vehicle or driving in general, and after fifteen minutes of weaving in the lane and nearly rear-ending a pickup truck at a red light on Yonge Street, he parked beside the curb so that Crystal could take over.

They drove in silence for ten minutes as Ryan kept looking over his shoulder. Remembering the moment he checked Crystal's phone, he had to ask. "I've told no one where we were going or what happened. How did they know where we would be?"

She glanced at him and then kept her eyes on the road. "I only told my boss, Dr. Dali. I've known him for years; he wouldn't tell anyone else. I was trying to help you find answers and learn more about what you did."

Ryan thought it over and didn't respond right away, except to give directions. After driving west on Bloor, they turned north on Allen Road. He asked, "How well do you know him? I don't know your boss, and he's the only one who knew what was happening."

Crystal shook her head. "Apparently, not as well as I thought. I swear I didn't tell anyone else."

When she met his eyes, Ryan nodded. Despite having slept, he was traumatized and near the end of his rope. Help, any help, was essential. Without it, he wouldn't know what to do.

"Thanks for being with me then. It's appreciated."

"Now that we have time, why don't you tell me about stone singing and how those men died?"

He rubbed a hand across his face and nodded. "When I was in your class, the answer popped into my head. I hadn't even heard the words together before." He was going to mention the voice in his head but decided to hold that close. Things were strange enough as it was without Crystal detouring to have him committed. "I ended up placing my hand against the granite, and I knew what to do. It was like humming that turned into a single note when I sang—same thing with the small stones. I just knew what to do. When I picked them up, they weighed nothing."

"My boss tried to watch what you did on the security monitors. They are throughout the museum. But whatever you did shorted out the cameras, and nothing was recorded."

Ryan groaned. "So there could be footage of me killing two men by throwing stones?"

"Maybe." Crystal slowed and took the 407 off-ramp, heading south after the cloverleaf. "But I think when you were singing, it did something to the electronics. They glitched."

He could still feel the stings where the darts had embedded in his flesh. Was he singing then? The Taser didn't work; if it had, he'd be bundled up and taken—too many questions and not enough answers that didn't test his sanity.

"Take the next left. We're almost there." Ryan didn't know what to expect or what he could do. At most, he promised to call the cops so his mom had a chance. That was all that mattered.

They drove past the Jane Finch Mall and the towers where he first saw the ankh symbol. It seemed like weeks ago, but it hadn't even been two days. Traffic was nonexistent, and they made good time. It was nearly four a.m.

"What do you want to do?" Crystal slowed in the residential neighborhood.

"Park down the street. I have to see what's going on." Ryan pointed behind a Dodge Caravan. "Right here." Crystal turned off the engine, and they sat for a moment. "That's my house on the inside corner. Do you want to stay here?"

"Not a chance." She opened the car door before he could say anything and stepped outside. Sighing, Ryan followed suit.

One home behind him had a light on above the front door, but the remainder were dark, including his. Before Ryan could cross the road, Crystal whispered, "Ryan! Come here."

She pointed at the minivan when he joined her. The driver's window had been shattered. It wasn't the damage that startled Crystal, but the man slumped forward on the steering wheel. Mindful of the broken glass in his shoeless feet, Ryan shuffled closer.

"Holy shit." The bullet hole in the side of the man's head would have killed him instantly. Then he noticed the passenger and ran around to the other side. The door was unlocked, and the woman had slumped low, nearly on the floor. She was dressed in a blue collared dress shirt and clutched a pistol in her right hand. Ryan was sure she never got to fire it with the two bullet holes in her chest. Matching holes punched through the windshield. A camera with a telephoto lens and a hand-held radio was on the console between the bodies. From the passenger door, Ryan spotted a silver and blue badge on the man's belt.

"I think they're cops."

"Jesus Christ." Crystal looked like she was ready to run.

Ryan glanced at the dark windows of his home and down at the body. "Sorry, ma'am. I need this more than you."

His shaking fingers removed the pistol from her death grip. Her hand was still warm and flexible. Ryan's limited knowledge of weapons was gained from countless hours of action movies and video games. He left his finger outside the trigger guard, ensuring the muzzle pointed away from his body and Crystal. "I'm going in."

Ryan didn't wait to see if she followed. Keeping the pistol down the side of his leg, he ran along the sidewalk and paused at his front step. When he approached, the security light didn't turn on, and he found the door had been kicked open. The jam was splintered, and pieces of wood littered the ground.

He used the muzzle to open the door and listened.

There were enough lights on the electronics and the streetlight to show that the living room was empty. Ryan crept inside and poked his head into the kitchen. The light above the stove revealed a complete mess. The table had been pushed against the counter, and three chairs had been tipped over. The fourth chair was against the wall, and dark smears were on the tiled floor directly underneath.

Ryan darted down the hallway and confirmed his suspicions. The house was empty. When he returned, Crystal stood in the doorway, and he shook his head. "My mom's not here."

He placed the gun on the kitchen table and fixed the chairs. When Ryan's cell phone rang, Crystal jumped, and he came close to wetting his jeans. The display read *unknown caller*.

After a deep breath, Ryan accepted the call. "H-hello?"

CHAPTER 22

"Glad to finally talk in person, so to speak. Ryan Petey, I assume?" The man's voice was rich, and he spoke with an accent Ryan couldn't identify. Spanish?

"Yes. Who is this?" Ryan placed the call on speakerphone. He sat at the kitchen table, and Crystal joined him. He was waiting for the hammer to fall.

"That's not important, but what *is* important is that you listen to me. Can you do that, Ryan?" He swallowed the lump in his throat, and Crystal placed her hand on his and gave it a gentle squeeze.

"Yes. Go ahead."

"Glad you are so attentive. Your mother, Julie, a fine woman, is with me right now. If you take her place, she goes free. It's that simple."

Rage and worry made him grind his teeth. "What did you do to her? Is she okay?"

The man chuckled without any hint of humor. "She's a little banged up, but if she survives … well, that's up to you, Ryan."

He got up to pace the kitchen, unable to sit still. "What do you want?"

"To the point. I like that. You had an opportunity to meet me at Buttonville Airport, but that window has closed. It is quarter past four in the morning. You have one hour to meet me at Oshawa Airport, at the side door of the main terminal, if you can call it that. Things get worse for your dear mother if you're not here on time. She will lose a finger for every minute you're late. Once those are gone, other parts will go missing. Am I making myself clear, Mr. Petey?"

Ryan paused to get his breath. "If I show up, you let my mom go free?"

"That's the deal. You have sixty minutes. The clock is ticking."

Adrenaline made his legs twitch, and he wanted to run out the door. "Wait!"

The man sounded amused. "Go on?"

"How do I know my mom's alive?" Ryan's blood froze at the thought.

There was no immediate response, and he thought they had been disconnected until Julie's crying came over the speaker. "Ryan? Is that you?"

"Mom! Are you okay?" His heart nearly shattered at her voice.

"What's going on? Are you—"

The call disconnected.

Ryan wiped the tears from his cheeks and looked at Crystal. "I'm going."

"Don't you think the police should be involved by now?" She stood and rested a hand on his shoulder.

Ryan shook his head. "It's me they want, not my mother. I'm leaving shortly. You should stay here."

He didn't wait for her answer. The clock was ticking.

Ryan ran downstairs to find the basement had been destroyed. Dresser drawers were upside down on the floor, and clothes were everywhere. His computer had been opened, and the hard drive was missing. None of that mattered.

Ryan dug through the pile on the floor, finding a pair of clean socks and a black T-shirt. The closet produced an old pair of running shoes that he slid onto his feet. The toilet flushed upstairs as Ryan took a final look around. Impulsively, he opened the nightstand, picked up an old folding knife, and slipped it into a pocket beside his wallet.

"Phone, wallet, and knife. I'm ready." Regardless of the situation, his stomach reminded him that he needed food, and he flew up the stairs to the kitchen and opened the fridge. His eyes watered upon seeing two roast beef sandwiches in Ziploc bags on the top shelf. A note was written on a napkin: *here's your dinner when you're hungry. Love Mom xo*

"I'll be there soon. Everything will be okay," Ryan whispered.

He threw the sandwiches in a plastic bag along with four energy drinks. Ryan's hand hovered above the pistol and decided against it. He was going to make an exchange, not a gunfight.

"I'm leaving in one minute and—" he turned to find Crystal in the kitchen doorway.

"Hope your mother wouldn't mind." She had changed into an old navy Blue Jays T-shirt from his mom's closet. Crystal tied the bottom of the shirt into a knot and stood with one hand on her hip.

Ryan fought the urge to let out a wolf whistle but said, "No. It looks good on you."

Idiot! Focus. Now isn't the time.

"I've thought about it, and before you say anything, I'm coming with you."

"Fine."

Her eyebrows rose in surprise. "Fine?"

"There's no time to argue." Ryan held the front door open for her and set the lock. He stepped outside and asked, "Are you ready? You can—"

Crystal screamed.

"If you fucking move, I'll blow your head off." A woman's voice growled behind him as the barrel of a gun pressed into the base of his skull. "And you can shut the fuck up any time now, lady."

CHAPTER 23

"Ryan Petey, you are under arrest for murder. You have the right to seek counsel. If you can not afford a lawyer, one will be appointed to you. Turn around, place your hands on your head, and spread your legs." Detective McCallan slammed him against the house, kicked the inside of each foot until he was in position, took his plastic bag, and set it to the side.

"No! There is no time. I have to go!" Ryan pleaded.

The gun shifted to the middle of his back while he was being patted down. "Do you have anything in your pockets that will injure me?"

"You have to listen!" Crystal pleaded while Ryan's face was pressed against the brick wall.

"Stand back and don't interfere, or I'll arrest you for interfering in the performance of my duties."

Crystal shuffled away, helpless to act. "If we don't leave *now*, his mother will be killed."

A hand felt the front of his jeans. "Empty your pockets. The police will deal with any kidnapping or hostage cases."

The feeling of helplessness disappeared, and the kernel of anger turned into an inferno. Ryan spun in place so quickly that he caught the detective by surprise, and her gun was now pointed in a safe direction: the front door. He grasped her forearm from underneath while singing a warbled note from the bass registers. The tone made the glass panes in the screen door vibrate like an earthquake, and the bottom sheet cracked with a sharp retort.

"Do *not* resist arrest! You …" McCallan trailed off as she looked up at Ryan. Not that he was four inches taller, but she had sunk into the sandstone slab like quicksand. She tried to move and nearly fell. The stone had solidified over her feet, covering her ankles.

The front landing and walkway had been updated several years ago, and the landscaper recommended the natural stone for which Ryan was now grateful. He took a step back. "Sorry, Detective, but we really have to be going. There's no time to explain."

The detective's gun swung up as she aimed at his chest. "You're under arrest and not going anywhere."

"I'm unarmed. You won't be shooting me." Ryan turned and walked away. His back twitched between the shoulder blades as he waited for the impact, but it didn't arrive. A Ford Interceptor blocked the end of the driveway, and when he passed it, Ryan broke into a jog toward the white SUV. Crystal kept pace as they ignored McCallan's yelling and constant stream of obscenities.

"That was amazing. Holy shit!" Crystal turned the engine over when Ryan jumped into the passenger seat, right knee bouncing like an engine's piston.

Ryan's fingers flickered over his cell phone and pulled up the map function. The estimated time of arrival at the Oshawa Airport was forty-five minutes. They would make it, but there wasn't any time for side trips. He pushed *start* on the directions, and Crystal performed a three-point-turn, heading back to the Allen Road ramp to the 407 express toll highway east.

"Not sure if I could do that again, but glad it worked." Ryan was pressed into the seat as Crystal accelerated.

▲ ▲ ▲

Trish stared without comprehending. What Ryan Petey had done was simply the greatest magic trick she'd ever seen. She tapped the stone with the butt of her Glock and looked for wires or *something* but came up short.

Her radio was in the car, but she called dispatch directly with her cell phone.

"Suspect is Ryan Petey, age twenty-two, five-foot-five inches, male, Caucasian. Last seen wearing a black T-shirt, jeans, and dark running shoes. Accompanied by a female, brunette, Caucasian, approximately thirty-five years old. Fleeing arrest in a 2022 white four-door Toyota 4Runner. Last seen heading west on Dundee Drive. Wanted for multiple homicides."

She had tried to make out the tag but was too far away. Trish struggled but to no avail. She was trapped. There wasn't a chance her colleagues would ever forget this moment.

"Dispatch, officer needs assistance." She gave the address and added, "You'd better bring a sledgehammer."

Giving up, she awkwardly sat to wait.

After a few minutes, her skin began to crawl. She'd been in the game long enough to know when someone was watching her. Trish half-twisted around to spot a fluffy white cat curled up on the hood of her cruiser, watching.

"Fuckin' cat." She'd always been a dog person. Unless that cat happened to be carrying a jackhammer, it could go to hell. However, it wasn't the cat she focused on, but the vehicle parked down the street. She could barely distinguish a figure slumped behind the wheel and two spiderweb cracks in the windshield.

Detective McCallan's next call was to Sergeant Wickman in intelligence services.

CHAPTER 24

"Whoever owns this will be getting the bill for the toll road." Ryan chuckled when they passed under the network of cameras for the 407 ETR.

"Hope they charge them double." Crystal winked and merged onto the eastbound lane from the on-ramp.

Ryan dug into the plastic bag and handed over a sandwich. He popped the tops on the energy drinks, placing them in the center console cup holders. "I don't know about you, but I need this."

He took the time to explore the SUV and opened the glove box. Ryan was disappointed in finding the rental agreement and vehicle manual. He was expecting a gun—too much television. The rear seats were empty, and as far as he could tell, so was the back area.

"There's time. Why don't you close your eyes? I'll wake you before we get there." Crystal turned on the radio for some background music.

Ryan shook his head. "I don't think there's a chance I could sleep." To prove his point, he cracked another can.

"Those things are supposed to be bad for you." Crystal smiled, finished her drink, and threw the empty can over her shoulder into the back seat. "Not my car."

Ryan laughed and opened another for her.

He tried to focus on what may happen for the rest of the drive. There was little doubt someone knew of his new abilities, but he didn't understand them himself. Stone singing *just* happened. He would need a while to experiment, but there was no time. What baffled him was a very simple question. *How?* How did he learn the songs? There was also the problem of slipping sanity, but he chose not to dwell on the subject.

After thirty minutes, Crystal left the toll highway and drove south on Thickson Road. They were in the township of Whitby. "We'll be there in fifteen minutes."

Ryan sat upright. He didn't intend to fall asleep and must have been meditating. Looking out the window, he saw nothing but trees and farmland, and the eastern sky was getting brighter. The sun would be up within the hour.

"Thanks for driving." He rubbed the sleep from his eyes. It was almost game time.

"Ryan, I've been thinking." She turned left on Taunton Road into a town of small plazas, stores, and residential neighborhoods. "After we get to the airport, I'm going home. I don't want to get caught up in what may happen. No offense."

"I don't blame you. I'd have bailed a long time ago, except now, I have no choice." He saw the sign, *Oshawa Airport, 2kms ahead.* The city of Oshawa looked a lot like Whitby, with more stores and never-ending subdivisions. "I don't know how to thank you, but it's probably my fault you're involved."

"You've solved a mystery that has puzzled everyone for thousands of years. I hope we get to study what you do properly."

Ryan took a deep breath and understood what she was saying. *Only if you weren't going off to die.* "I'll do my best."

All too soon, she turned right at a medical center, past a military building with a wheeled tank parked out front, and then the next driveway led to the airport. The main terminal was on the right, with smaller buildings on the left. Crystal drove through the parking lot and service gate. She parked fifty feet away and turned off the engine.

The lights were off in the large building, except under the covered entrance. Three figures stood next to the double doors. The headlights briefly illuminated them, and Ryan saw his mother being held by a tall man in a leather coat. A dark-skinned, bald man dressed in a blue suit and white shirt raised his hand as if Ryan could miss them.

A woman appeared at the driver's window and tapped the glass with a gun. "Come join the party, sweetheart."

Ryan recognized the woman from the bar—short black hair, slim, and wearing a green jacket. Crystal whimpered but opened the door. Ryan started walking without them. As he approached the group, his mother cried out and tried to rush forward but was held back by the tall man.

"Mom!"

She let out a heart-wrenching sob. "Leave Ryan! Get out of here."

He ran forward, and his mother broke free when he was within a few feet. Her hug threatened to break his ribs, but he didn't mind. "It's okay, Mom. I'm here."

"Well, isn't this a nice reunion?" The man was six feet tall with a rough goatee and mustache, possibly sixty years old. Round glasses completed the dirtbag image. "I think it's time to—"

A cell phone interrupted him, and he pulled it out of his inner jacket pocket.

He listened for a few seconds, and his eyebrows rose. "Really? Thanks, Vincent."

The man put the phone away and turned to his companions. "Change of plans. The police followed Mr.

Petey. Someone apparently doesn't know how to turn off his phone."

The woman swore and held out her hand. Numbly, Ryan handed it over.

"I'll lose them and meet up with you later." She sprinted for the 4Runner and drove with the engine roaring across the parking lot.

Ryan pried his mother's arms away and turned to the man in the suit. "I'm here, now. Let my mother go."

The man winked. "A deal's, a deal. Ma'am, you're free to go. The two of you can board the jet." He gestured over his shoulder to the Gulfstream waiting on the runway. The engines started as the interior lights turned on.

"You don't need Crystal. You have me. Let them both go." Ryan stepped in front of his mother, and the man in the leather coat reached into his jacket. He looked ready to draw a gun.

"Ah, Mr. Petey. Our deal was for you to arrive on time, and I was to let one person go free. *You* decide who can leave and who can come with us. You have ten seconds."

Ryan's heart broke, but he didn't hesitate. "My mom goes free. Sorry, Crystal."

"Oh my, God." His mother clutched at his hand. "I'll stay with my son. Send the girl away."

"Mom goes free—the perfect ending for her. You two, get on the jet. Now. We could have company any minute. Sorry for the trouble, Miss Petey." The man in the suit stepped back and gestured for Ryan and Crystal to board.

"Goodbye, Mom. I love you."

"Ryan, no!" Julie dropped to her knees and wrapped her arms around his legs. The man in the leather jacket peeled her off and held her to the side. Ryan stepped toward the Gulfstream but stopped when his heart jumped.

On the ground in front of his mother was a black ankh. *Not a fucking chance!*

Ryan swallowed and turned to the man in the suit, crossing his arms across his chest. "Let her go. Now. If she's harmed in any way, I won't cooperate. You'll get nothing."

Suit Man turned to the Leather Jacket Man. "Let her go. Ma'am, I suggest you run as fast as you can."

When his hands let go, Julie stood with tears rolling down her face.

"Mom. Trust me. I need you to run away. Go call the police and get help."

"Yes, Julie. Call the police. We're leaving. Now." The man in the suit nodded to his companion, and the leather jacket man grabbed Crystal's arm, guiding her to the waiting jet.

"Mom! Run!" Ryan yelled while pointing across the parking lot. The message finally got through. Julie ran, and for the first time, the ankh disappeared without a death.

"Everyone get on board. I hope you enjoy the accommodation." The man in the suit had an Italian accent, the same as his grade ten math teacher—not Spanish.

With a lingering look at the rising sun, Ryan climbed the steps behind Crystal and boarded the jet. When he saw what waited inside, the man in the leather jacket drew his gun and encouraged him forward.

CHAPTER 25

The steel cage was six feet long, three feet tall, and three feet wide. The bars were flattened steel, an inch thick. The front seats had been removed, and the cage was secured to the floor against the bulkhead.

"We didn't anticipate you having company, Ryan. But after looking at your companion, I'm sure you won't mind. Get inside. Both of you."

Before he could move, the man in the leather coat spoke. "Before that happens, I need to confirm, sir."

Ryan was pushed face down on the cage and frisked for the second time today. The wallet, knife, belt, and shoelaces were removed. "Get inside."

Crystal was given the same treatment. Her shoelaces were added to the pile before she was ushered inside. She had no pockets in the leggings, but that didn't stop him from checking. There wasn't enough room to sit fully, so Ryan sat hunched over, with his knees into his chest, and once inside, Crystal numbly mirrored his position with their toes touching. The cage door swung closed. Instead of a key, a code was entered on a panel secured to the opposite bulkhead. A brief low hum came from the board as the doors were magnetically sealed.

"Snug as a bug. Perfect. However, I find your situation depressing." A black cloth was draped over the cage, turning the interior into twilight. "Ah, much better. No noise, or I'll resort to medical methods to keep you quiet. That's a good boy."

The stairs were lifted and locked in place; a few hushed words were spoken before his captors sat. Seconds later, Ryan felt the jet lurch and then taxi on the runway. Crystal laid her forehead on her knees and wrapped her arms around her lower leg, pulling them in tight. Her hair fell forward, and he couldn't see her face.

Ryan whispered, "I'm sorry, but I had to choose my mom."

Crystal didn't answer, keeping her head down, but her body shook with silent sobs.

The engine's roar increased, and Ryan was steadily pressed back into the cage wall. Crystal reached out to steady herself as the floor tilted. The transition to flight was smooth, and as they banked, the landing gear was retracted. The jet steadily climbed, and the floor eventually leveled out once they reached cruising altitude. Ryan worked his jaw back and forth until his ears popped.

The blanket didn't fully cover the prison cell, and Ryan peeked through the end gap. The leather and chrome interior of the jet was accented with dark wood—reeking of opulence. Leather Jacket Man, Ryan didn't have a better name besides asshole, sat facing the front allowing him to be studied. He wore khaki pants, loafers with black socks, a tan dress shirt, and a dark brown leather jacket. His six-foot-two-inch frame was packed with muscle, and he had a barrel chest with arms the size of Ryan's legs. Dark brown hair was short and brushed to the side, with hints of gray at the temples, placing him in his mid-forties. He was clean-shaven and had a bulbous nose and a cleft chin that Ryan would love to smash with a hammer.

Suit Man was out of sight toward the jet's rear, and Ryan turned his attention to his prison. There was barely enough room to slip a fingertip through the flat bars, so he gave up. The floor was the same as the rest of the interior, a burgundy all-weather carpet with gold flecks. Large bolts secured the cage to the floor.

When Ryan finished exploring, he looked into Crystal's red-rimmed eyes. She whispered, "This is because I fucked up and trusted my boss. It's my fault this is happening."

Ryan shuffled forward and held her hands. "You are not responsible for someone else's actions."

She nodded as fresh tears rolled down her cheeks. "Maybe they're taking us to the Bahamas."

Ryan grinned. "I could use a vacation after the last few days."

She squeezed his hands. "I can't sit like this for much longer. If we lay down together, there should be enough room."

After some contortions, Ryan laid down on his side with his back against the rear wall. Crystal spooned in front, using his arm as a pillow. He didn't know where to place his right arm and gave up. He held her tight, burying his nose in her hair.

Oh God, no. Not now.

He shifted awkwardly, but there was no room to separate. He tried thinking of hockey or counting sheep, but nothing worked. Crystal was shaking, and he felt she was crying, but when she turned her head, a grin made her eyes sparkle. "I thought you were searched for dangerous weapons?"

"I'm sorry. I just—"

"It's okay. Glad some things are still normal." She chuckled.

Crystal snuggled closer, and eventually, her breathing deepened. Once his ears stopped burning, Ryan closed his eyes and allowed the hum of the craft to lull him to sleep. He would take any chance at escape, even if only temporarily.

An hour later, Ryan's arm was dead, and they shuffled into another position with him laying flat and Crystal resting her head on his chest, curled up to his side. When her knee shifted over his leg, he couldn't fall back asleep but lay staring at the cage ceiling, two feet away from his nose. *Too bad I wasn't a metal singer. I could bend the bars to get out of here.* Was there such a thing? Last week, he would have laughed at such an idea, but today?

Ryan lost track of time as he dozed intermittently but was wide awake when the jet dropped in altitude. He couldn't tell how much time had passed, but his best guess was between four and five hours. A glimpse through the blanket showed Leather Jacket Man sleeping with the seat reclined. The wind noise changed, and Crystal and their captor woke when the landing gear deployed.

The blanket was ripped off the cage, and Suit Man grinned. "I knew there was lots of room in there. Hope I didn't disturb anything."

Ryan and Crystal separated to either end of the cage under his amused eye.

"We'll be refueling, and if you behave, there will be an opportunity to use the bathroom and have something to eat. I'd warn you to go easy on the fluids, though. The next leg of our journey will be a long one. How does that sound?"

Ryan nodded, but Suit Man had already returned to his seat.

When the Gulfstream's tires touched down, Crystal leaned forward, and her hands pulled his head in close as if they were going to kiss. Instead, her head turned at the last second, and she whispered in his ear, "I have an idea."

CHAPTER 26

The landing was smooth, and the Gulfstream taxied for a few minutes before coming to a halt. The engines powered down, and the pilot, a young man in a white shirt and black tie, turned the handle, allowing the stairs to deploy. Ryan didn't have much of an angle to view the outside, but he could tell it was cloudy and raining. Fresh air blew inside the jet, and it had never smelled so good. The pilot removed a dark blazer with stripes on the cuffs from a cupboard and went outside. Suit Man produced an umbrella and walked down the steps.

Leather Jacket Man pulled out a black-bodied pistol and entered the code on the panel. The cage door clicked, then swung open. He pointed to Crystal. "You. Out."

After five hours of being in an awkward position, she stumbled but gained her feet. The door swung shut, and he locked it again.

"Rear of the plane. You can use the bathroom."

"Thank you." Crystal tried to be pleasant—points for her.

The cabin was nearly fifty feet long from his brief glimpse of the interior. Toward the rear, two plush couches faced each other, and there were single seats before and after a group of four chairs facing each other with a table in the middle. The polished mahogany door at the rear must have led to the restroom.

"Leave the door open. No funny business."

Ryan winced at the callous attitude and wished he could call the ankh symbol to hang over his head.

Shortly, they came back, and it was Ryan's turn. He had the same problem as Crystal. After lying on the floor for so long, the circulation took a few seconds to resume proper flow in his legs.

The bathroom could have been in a billionaire's home. Polished stone countertops and an enclosed stand-up shower were opposite the toilet and bidet. Towels were rolled to perfection and stacked in a pyramid next to a vase of white orchids. Ryan tried not to stare at the landline telephone mounted to the wall next to the counter. He doubted there would be time to make a call with the door held open with Leather Jacket Man's foot. It was awkward having someone watch while you do your business would have been an understatement, but he had to go and didn't know when the next opportunity would arise. After flushing, Ryan ignored the man's gesture and washed his hands.

"Fuck that. Let's go."

"Almost done. Geesh." The hand towel was incredibly soft, and as a gesture of rebellion, he tossed it in the sink when finished. Fuck them. Someone else can pick that up.

Once locked back up, Ryan settled down to wait with Crystal. As she had predicted, it didn't take long for Leather Jacket Man to step outside—he was a smoker.

"Okay. Try it now!" she whispered, leaning close.

Ryan closed his eyes and hummed a deep note. He held it for as long as possible, but nothing happened. "Maybe I need stone to help it work? Sorry, not too sure."

"Keep trying. We may not have much longer."

He wasn't sure, but stone of any type was the key to making the singing work. How far away did the stone have to be? There was some in the bathroom, and the jet rested on asphalt. That was mainly stone … right?

Ryan called out to his subconscious, grasping at straws with growing frustration.

Help me!

To his utter surprise and dismay, there was an answer.

Faith begets the gods. Without trust, there is nothing.

Oh my …

Ryan had either jumped off the deep end, hit his head, and didn't know he had sustained brain damage, or someone was communicating with him. Was that so strange after he moved a granite slab with one hand or sunk that detective into solid stone? With no other options, he did something he hadn't done since he was a little boy at his grandmother's home.

Pray.

Ryan closed his eyes, and his lips tried to keep up with his thoughts but failed. The voice had mentioned faith, and he was beside himself for answers.

Please help me get out of this situation and ensure that Crystal isn't harmed or killed. I promise to be a faithful servant, and if you have a church, I'll start attending. I am not the strongest or fastest man, but I will do my best as long as I can do your will. Guide me.

It is done.

A door opened in his mind, and like a river bursting a damn, a rush of experiences flooded his being. Experiences that, suddenly, were now part of his memory. He recalled sitting down with his father, learning the tones and inflections that were part of his heritage. Knowledge his father had learned from *his* father and had been passed down for thousands of years.

He recalled the differences between each stone and knew how to identify flaws deep within crystalline structures.

The current of information, at first, was too much to bear. It was like trying to contain lightning in a jar without getting burned. Ryan's hands held his head together, fearful it may explode.

Stone singing varied with experts specializing in different aspects of the craft. Ryan suddenly *knew* how to transport a monolithic carving with only seven people. He *knew* where to dig to find the best sand for polishing granite to a mirror finish and a hundred other ancient tricks of the trade.

But most importantly, and with absolute certainty, Ryan Petey *knew* how to sing. When his eyes opened, he was momentarily confused. Gone were the hot sands and sounds of chisels shaping earth's treasures, and he stared at a metal cage.

The soft hand on his arm brought him back, and he nodded. Without hesitation, Ryan called to the stone in the deep earth. The notes were nearly inaudible but had the desired effect. The lights on the security panel for the cage blinked off for just a moment as the current was interrupted, but that was enough for Crystal to open the gate.

"I knew you could do it!" she whispered. "I'll go make the call. Hold him off as long as you can, and I'll lock the door."

Ryan shook his head. They had to leave before Suit Man or the pilot came back. His fighting skills wouldn't slow Leather Jacket Man enough to be worth it.

"When I nod, I want you to scream. Not loud, just enough to be heard outside. Okay?"

There was strength in stone, and a lifetime of shaping and singing had given him an appreciation for precision work. You can't be a stone singer without learning how to hold a mallet and chisel. They were the first implements placed into the hands of any worker. Ryan recalled the advice of a father he had never met. *The hand must be prompt to execute the design. Do not hesitate. Glory to the builder.*

He slowly unclipped the bracket on the red fire extinguisher beside the door, not to make any noise, and held the twenty-two-inch cylinder comfortably before nodding to Crystal. Even though he expected the scream, Ryan was still startled. She could have stared in a B-movie from the eighties.

A muffled curse carried through the open door, and when Leather Jacket Man reached the top step, Ryan was ready. The fire extinguisher slid through his hands like a pool cue and smote him with a hollow thunk on the forehead. Leather Jacket Man fell straight back and down the steps unconscious. *Timber, you fuck.*

"Holy shit!" Crystal gasped.

Ryan placed the extinguisher on the floor and held out his hand. "Let's go."

That was the moment something shifted within his thoughts. There's no way I could imagine a lifetime of shaping stone and escaping from the cage on my own. Ryan wasn't crazy and talking to himself. There was always an issue of believing in a god without proof and going on just faith. But now there was real evidence. He was now a believer.

Thank you, my Lord.

CHAPTER 27

The moment of realization and confidence vanished when he stood on the top step and scanned the airport. The terminal was to his ten o'clock, and an orange steel-roofed building to his two o'clock. The rain poured off the roofs in sheets, turning the tarmac into a puddle-strewn landscape. A white truck with an orange fuel container was parked beside the port wing, and a man in a hi-vis yellow rain suit connected the lines to the jet's tank.

The sign above a set of double doors on the terminal's right side would have been visible across the runway. *Welcome to Gander, Newfoundland.* He helped Crystal step around Leather Jacket Man and ignored the man's forehead. The crescent cut was deep, and the flap of skin hung loose. Head wounds usually bled fiercely, and this was no exception. While upside down on the steps, blood soaked through his hair, coupled with the rain, the stairs resembled a pink waterfall. Ryan didn't feel sorry in the slightest.

Hand in hand, they hurried toward the glass doors marked Gate 36. Ryan kept his head on a swivel, looking for Suit Man, but he couldn't see him. Walking without laces in his shoes was a new experience, and he turned it into a shuffle-glide. One hand held up his jeans. There was no time to grab his belt. Two people dashing through the rain—nothing to see here, folks.

"Over there." Crystal pointed to the oranged-roofed building. The first sign was Canada Customs, and the second was RCMP, beside double doors.

"They'll probably arrest me first." Ryan wasn't sure how well he would be received by law enforcement in Canada.

"I'd rather be in jail and alive than back on that plane."

Ryan nodded, and water trickled down his back. "Good point."

The lobby was styled with a generic government blue paint. On the wall straight ahead was a dedication mural to the city of Gander for their efforts on 9/11 with a Canadian and provincial flag. To the right were the doors for customs, and to the left were the police.

Before going inside, Ryan pressed his face against the glass, but he couldn't tell if Suit Man was inside. He flung open the door.

"Hello? We need help!" The small foyer had a counter separating an office with two desks, filing cabinets, and a hallway to the rear. It was empty.

Crystal called out, "Hello? Anyone there?"

"I'll be there in a second."

Ryan's nerves were frayed. He turned the deadbolt on the office door as a police officer emerged from the hallway holding a mug of coffee. The RCMP was dressed in a blue uniform and ballistic vest.

"We need help!" Ryan pleaded.

"We've been kidnapped!" Crystal cried.

The officer set his coffee on the desk and frowned. "Pardon? Are you guys serious?"

Ryan pointed toward the jet. "We were forced to get on board in Oshawa and kept in a cage. We just escaped and ran in here. You have to help us!"

The officer leaned forward with two hands on the counter. The nametag read P. Garnier. He was in his mid-thirties with a short beard and piercing eyes that studied Crystal and Ryan.

"Who kidnapped you?" He seemed to be slowly coming around to the idea that they weren't lying.

Crystal gestured to the approximate size while describing their captors. "Older man, bald with a goatee,

Italian accent, wore a suit. The other man is taller with short dark hair in a leather jacket."

The officer's eyes flickered back and forth before coming to a decision. He pulled a radio off his belt. "Gaston, return to base 10-18."

Over the speaker, a woman responded. "10-4."

"Come on through. I need details." He lifted the end of the counter, allowing them to enter the offices. "Are either of you injured?"

"No."

"We're okay."

"Tell me what happened, and where is the man who took you right now?" Garnier pulled a notepad and pen from his vest pocket and gestured to the two plastic chairs across from his desk. They didn't have time for this, and Ryan felt like pulling his hair out but still sat as directed. The only saving grace was Leather Jacket Man bleeding out on the steps. That left Suit Man, and two cops could deal with him. Ryan's next thought was to let his mom know he was okay.

Crystal shrugged. "He left the jet ten minutes ago and could be in the terminal."

Garnier's partner arrived from the hallway with one hand on her holstered pistol. The older woman with streaks of gray in her short hair reminded Ryan of Detective McCallan—tough as nails and didn't put up with any bullshit. "What's going on?"

"These two …" Garnier paused, "names?"
Crystal went first, then Ryan. "Say they were kidnapped and forced onto a jet."

Crystal had reached a breaking point. "There's no question of *if* we were."

Officer Gaston asked, "Which jet?"

"The closest one outside that just refueled." Ryan couldn't believe the officers' calmness and lack of action. His heart wasn't going to make it, and he began hyperventilating.

The hard exterior on Officer Gaston's face cracked slightly, and a bit of humanity escaped. "It's okay, sir. Everything is fine."

"You stay here, and I'm going to check out the registry of the jet and call the tower to ground the flight." Garnier grabbed a rain jacket from the back of the chair and slipped it on. "Officer Gaston will get more information from you both."

"One other thing." Ryan cleared his throat. "I knocked out the guy with the leather jacket so we could escape. He's probably on the stairs. And both of them were armed. I don't know about the pilot."

Garnier's eyebrows rose. "Anything else?" When Ryan and Crystal said no, he left through the hallway, and Officer Gaston took his place behind the desk.

"Everything's going to be okay now." Ryan tried to reassure Crystal—or himself—and she squeezed his hand. Then he realized that they had been holding hands since leaving the jet.

After a few minutes of pecking away at the keyboard with two fingers, Gaston asked, "Can you spell your name for me, please, along with your home address, date of birth, and phone number?"

Crystal went first, then Ryan.

The keyboard clicking paused, and Officer Gaston looked up at Ryan. "November twenty-second, two-thousand twenty-two?"

Warning bells were ringing. "Yes."

"Are you aware there is a Canadian-wide warrant for you?" Officer Gaston abruptly stood, not waiting for an answer. "You're under arrest."

"Fuck." Crystal whispered.

Arrested again, Ryan mentally added. He stood, raised his hands, and slowly turned around. The alternative was worse.

CHAPTER 28

The holding cell was eight feet long and five feet wide, with a bench running the length. Unfortunately, the barred metal door was locked with an iron key on Officer Gaston's belt. Crystal was also detained while law enforcement determined if she was a victim or an accomplice and placed in the same cell.

Three white walls were cinderblocks, and the fourth was steel bars. A single overhead light was recessed in the ceiling eight feet above their heads. Over the years, people had carved their initials into the wood or witty sayings: *Back again '94. Die pigs! This Airbnb sucks.*

"Out of the frying pan into the fire?" Crystal sat cross-legged with her back to the wall.

Officer Gaston read them their rights and frisked them in record time. They were escorted to the cell within three minutes as she called for her partner to return to the office. Crystal had asked for a lawyer, and the answer was *in due time*.

"Like you said, better here than in the cage." Ryan picked at the wood with a nail. "They'll let you go free, but I'll probably be transported back to Toronto. You know, throwing stones and killing people and escaping arrest. Minor stuff."

"That was self-defense, and we had to leave to save your mother. I'm sure everything will be just fine once we can explain."

Crystal picked at a growing hole in the knee of her leggings, and Ryan took a moment to pray for guidance. Being religious *suddenly* was difficult, but he was learning to adapt. *Ummm ... God? I don't know how to pray to you properly, so I hope this is fine. Thank you for the memories of the stone singing and helping me out of the cage. But I'm back in another prison, and if you could help, that'd be great.*

Ryan opened his eyes and looked around, but nothing had changed. There was no answer, nor was anyone talking in his thoughts. Maybe one miracle per day was the limit.

When gunfire rang out, Ryan and Crystal were on their feet instantly. A single door separated the hallway and the offices, and the noise was unmistakable.

"They're here," Crystal whispered.

Ryan stuck his head as far as he could against the bars, trying to see down the hall, but it was useless. Another single retort echoed in the building.

Crystal spun him so they were almost nose to nose. "You can get us out of here." She turned him again to face the wall. "You can do it."

Maybe the miracle for today hadn't expired.

Yet.

Ryan placed his fingertips against the cinderblocks above the bench, and the seeking song rumbled forth. The notes were to find quarries or minerals in a deposit or learn the composition of an unknown stone. Young eyes recalled his father licking a finger and tasting different rocks as a way to tell them apart before he knew the song. Strange how he could remember singing and the knowledge imparted by a man long since turned to dust, but he couldn't recall the language or the small details like clothing, food, or a mother. Interesting.

Ryan frowned. "The wall is mainly made with limestone, but there is a large portion of sand and other minerals. Stones can be moved alone, but this wall is nearly whole, only separated by mortar and another layer of blocks outside."

Crystal rested her hand on his shoulder and spoke, but he had already tuned her out. He focused on a single block, not the one he touched, but on the building's exterior. If Ryan pushed, he wouldn't be able to move it with the interlaced support. It would be like trying to lift the structure.

His voice dropped an octave, more of a nasal vibration, and the sand contained within the mortar vibrated in response. Outside the building, gray dust fell around the sixteen-inch blocks as if from an hourglass. Ryan hunched his shoulders, changed the song's pitch to a warble, then pushed.

At first, nothing happened, and his face turned red with effort.

When another bullet was fired in the building, Ryan screamed. Two cinder blocks shattered into pieces smaller than a golf ball and were thrust outside like scattershot.

"Hurry! They're coming!" Crystal knelt on the bench and kept watch.

Each block was eight inches deep and tall and sixteen inches wide. There wasn't a chance either of them would fit through the opening. But the hard work was already completed, and soon, another block landed on the grass intact.

"You go first."

She fit through on an angle, and then Crystal emerged on the lawn covered in stone dust without any problems. While Ryan wasn't built like a football player, he had a situation she didn't have—wider shoulders.

"Pull!" He managed to get one arm through with his head but was stuck.

Crystal planted one foot on the wall and began tugging.

"Well, isn't this an awkward position?" Suit Man stood outside the cell and chuckled.

"Harder! Almost there." Crystal nearly pulled his arm out of the socket.

"Great effort! I must congratulate you both on your escape. Well done, but you're too late."

Leather Jacket Man came up behind Crystal.

No! Grunts of effort turned to a primal howl of rage, and his vision turned black around the edges. His left fist blurred in an arc, smashing through the cinderblock like it was made of papier mâché. Shards of stone exploded outward, peppering Crystal and Leather Jacket Man's exposed skin with a dozen small cuts. With a forward roll, Ryan landed on the grass.

"Get your fucking hands off her!"

Leather Jacket Man looked like he had just walked off a movie set. The crescent skin flap on his forehead hung like a morbid eyepatch as blood slicked his cheeks and chin. Already, one side of his face was grotesquely swollen, turning fabulous shades of red. A new knife wound started on his cheek, through his left jawline, and narrowly missed the carotid artery. One of the officers had put up a fight. Despite the horrific visage, he remained calm. One hand rose to shoulder height, pointing through the new prison cell window.

"I love your enthusiasm, Mr. Petey. If I could have your attention for just a moment, that would be splendid. We have a few decisions to make." Suit Man held an injured Officer Gaston by the hair. Her hands were cuffed behind her back, and she was bleeding from the nose and a bullet wound in the leg. Gaston was dazed and didn't put up a struggle.

"If you come with us, this fine young lady will live to see another day. What choices are you going to make, Ryan?"

Panicking, he looked at Crystal. "What do we do?"

A shot rang out, and the police officer collapsed as blood and gray matter were sprayed over the interior wall. "Just a little slow on the decision. Let's try again, shall we?"

Ryan felt like he would be sick as Suit Man stepped over the body and quickly returned with a similarly bound Officer Garnier. The pistol was held against his right temple.

"How about it, Ryan? Will you willingly come with us on our magnificent journey?"

"Will you let Crystal go free?" he pleaded.

Suit Man grinned. "Not a chance. You're a package deal. Five, four, three …"

Ryan's shoulders slumped. "Yes."

"Good choice." Suit Man nodded to his companion.

A needle pierced the side of his neck, and Ryan ground his teeth, wincing at the sudden paralyzing pain. He tried to raise a hand, but his arm didn't respond. Crystal fell unconscious at his side. Ryan blinked, then once more, but couldn't open his eyelids. He didn't recall falling, but suddenly, the cool, wet grass was on his face. His heart rate slowed, and before he lost consciousness, a single gunshot made his ears ring.

Despair followed him into the darkness.

CHAPTER 29

2560 B.C. Western Giza Plateau

"Three, two, one. Heave!" Tehran-mun strained until a blood vessel burst in his left eye, and his sandals slipped on the sandy slope. Skin rubbed off his shoulders in thin rolls as blood slicked the granite slab. Black spots danced in his vision, and he nearly collapsed from the efforts. His companions, Akhethetep and Neferu, worked to either side in vain. Even if they had two dozen men, the granite slab wouldn't shift. You may as well attempt to move the sun.

The low flame oil lamp flickered, and the three men prayed for it to last, for without the feeble light, the darkness would be absolute. Tehran-mun had coaxed an extra hour by squeezing the wick to the end, ignoring the smell of burned flesh to make it happen. The three men had worked as fast as they could, exploring every seam and inch of the hidden altar chamber. Desperation washed away the fatigue and fear. Like a tomb, their fate was sealed.

"Rest. We'll try again later if we can."

Neferu was young and did not want to give up. "I'll check the body and table."

Tehran-mun nodded his approval, and the acolyte cradled the light in the palm of his hands while descending the slope, turning right into the chamber.

Akhethetep patted his brother on the shoulder. "At least we have each other."

He nodded, but the gesture wasn't seen in the darkness. "We still have a ritual to perform. Our God's wishes cannot be ignored, no matter the personal cost."

"The cost is high, my brother. Although, our reward may be great."

Tehran-mun, ignoring the aches and pains, shuffled forward. Fingertips brushed against the smooth wall as he followed Neferu to the altar chamber.

The young man was on his hands and knees, pressing every square inch of stone where the floor met the wall. The solid-stone carving of Anubis remained untouched by mutual consent. While the Jackal wasn't *their* God, few could doubt the power wielded by such a being, and it is best not to incur his wrath. No doubt judgment was already passed on the priests of Osiris, and their mortality hung in the balance.

"Brethren, we have to complete our divine task. The fate of the gods may hinge on our success or failure. I will begin, and when completed, the strength of our sacrifice will seal the ritual permanently. The last Temple of Anubis will be no more. May Osiris guide our hands and lay his blessing on the tuqus al'iinha'."

The termination ritual.

Akhethetep and Neferu faced him and bowed. "So mote it be."

The flight feather of the goose was perfect for the task. A sure sign fate was on their side. The copper knife trimmed the end, and Tehran-mun dipped the quill into the priest's neck. The hollow shaft of the feather acted as a wick, and fresh blood was drawn.

The smooth walls of the temple were a blank canvas, and Tehran-mun worked frantically. There would be no chance of finishing the work when the light was gone. He darted back and forth from the body to the wall while his companions prayed. Their low voices were reassuring and helped calm his troubled spirit. Knowing your life was about to end was disturbing, even to the most devout.

When the quill dropped from numb fingers, Tehran-mun nodded. "It is done. We shall seal the termination ritual thrice."

Each man dipped his fingers in the priest's blood and coated their hands in the cloying, sticky fluid. With reverence, palms were pressed against the granite, leaving their mark for the ages. The ritual was permanent and not reversible.

The flame flickered and dropped to half its height.

"It is time to join Osiris in the heavens above. I am proud of you both and the work we have accomplished. May your spirit be a guiding path for generations of our people to follow."

Tehran-mun knelt before the altar, and his brethren joined him in order of rank with Neferu on the end. "I join you, my Lord. May I be worthy of your embrace."

The copper knife easily parted the linen robes and buried in his torso below the heart. With a final gasp, the blade slid upward, sealing his demise. A shaking, bloody hand freed the knife and dropped it on the floor.

Akhethetep was next, and he wiped the handle on his sleeve before following suit. He did not go silently like his older brother, but his screams filled the altar chamber as the knife was buried deep before being removed and dropped in front of Neferu.

Tehran-mun had gone numb, and the cool sensation of the stone against his flesh had disappeared as his lifeblood spilled forth. The flame on the lamp was nearly gone as his brother twitched in a death spasm.

Neferu murmured a few words and crumpled in a heap. The ring of the blade against the stone was music to his ears, and he ceased any efforts to resist death's cold embrace.

I'm coming, my Lord. My final work is completed, and I hope you find me worthy.

When the last vestige of light disappeared, so did Tehran-mun's final breath.

▲ ▲ ▲

After thirty minutes, Neferu opened his eyes, but there was no point. He could not see in the blackness. The last year had been hectic for the fifteen-year-old as he was accepted into the order with an initiation ritual that still gave him nightmares. Sworn to secrecy on the penalty of death, he had complied with every demand, following Tehran-mun about the land. Temples were destroyed, and the order of Anubis was no more. When the three of them left the army's main body at midnight to follow the priest, he thought the journey would be easy, and they would return by dawn. But fate decided otherwise.

However, the final order was too much for the young man to bear. He couldn't follow through with the ritual and faked his death. His brethren had died not knowing otherwise, and the deception weighed heavily.

A thought had been pestering him since they were trapped. No one built such a structure without having an alternate exit plan. There was an area he wished to explore, but the beliefs of his older companions held him back—the statue of a dead god. They would rather die than make any attempt, but he had no such reservations.

Sandals slid through an incredible amount of blood before his fingers touched the altar table and the priest's body. The only sounds were his ragged breathing and linen robe hissing against his skin and stone. Neferu carefully made his way around the other side and, without any misgivings, explored the stone carving of Anubis.

The play of muscles in the arms and chest was so detailed that he wouldn't be surprised if the god moved. The necklace and bracers were the results of perfection at the hands of a master mason. His father was a stonemason, and prior to joining the order, Neferu had learned a few things, like the difference between painted limestone and granite. The statue was the former, and the walls, the latter. The god was not carved in place but added once the chamber was completed.

On tiptoes, thin fingers probed and prodded the muzzled snout and protruding ears, coming up short. When a blood-smeared thumb pressed against the left eye socket, the emerald sunk an inch inside the skull, and the statue swung open silently on hidden hinges.

Off balance, Neferu stumbled backward and slipped. He fell hard against the blood-covered wall, smearing a handprint with his shoulder.

"Yes!" Such bruises were inconsequential as the young man caught the briefest glimpse of light at the end of a tunnel. The tuqus al'iinha' was incomplete, but surely two sacrifices were enough to seal the ancient god's fate? Neferu pushed those thoughts aside as he climbed to the surface.

A jumble of rocks blocked the exit, and he quickly went to work. Fresh air and daylight were all the motivation needed. Neferu didn't notice when his heel pressed a flagstone into the ground. The statue of Anubis resumed its place, and sand filtered down from hidden reservoirs, filling the escape tunnel in a slow, methodical fashion.

Neferu stood on the surface like he was born again, treasuring the heat of the sun and the fact that he still breathed. He could bathe at the oasis and wait another day until he returned to the army and other priests of the order. There is plenty of time to develop an acceptable but altered tale. Only those who could say otherwise were dead or a disposed god.

History is written by the victors.

CHAPTER 30

Floating on a sea of thoughts, Ryan swam without direction. One second, he showed an apprentice how to sing or make paper-thin vases out of granite; the next, he sat in a college classroom learning about fonts and kerning. At one point, he was climbing dunes in running shoes and strolling in leather hand-sewn sandals on sidewalks. Images blurred as his mind absorbed the information of an ancient time and learned to cope.

Ryan's psyche needed not only forced rest but also his body.

A thirst stirred him from the depths, and he reached for the bottle of water on the nightstand, but his hand felt nothing but air. When his eyes opened a crack, the clock was missing from his dresser, and his bedroom had been replaced.

"Ah, I'm sure you'll have a fine scar to show to the women in no time, Francis." A man in a dark blue suit was suturing an injured man's forehead while wearing latex gloves. The needle pierced the flesh, and a dark thread tugged at the skin before it was held in place. The knot was tied and then cut with scissors.

Confused, Ryan turned his head to the side. A woman was stretched out on the leather couch with a saline bag suspended from the low ceiling. An IV was inserted into the back of her wrist and held with medical tape. When an earthquake shook the room, her arm fell to hang off the couch.

"There we are. You have certainly earned your bonus. Now, let's see—"

The patient gestured with a chin toward Ryan, and the man turned around with a shocked expression. "Well, that's new."

Suit Man placed the needle and thread on a silver tray, balanced on the man's lap, and hurried to Ryan's side. "I think a slight adjustment will fix things."

When he looked down, round glasses slid to the end of his nose. He moved the red plastic piece on Ryan's IV until the drip rate increased. "That's why I get paid the big bucks. Expertise. Night night, rabbit."

Realization dawned. It wasn't an earthquake.

It was turbulence. Ryan struggled against the medication upon realizing he was in the jet, but he didn't stand a chance. He was sent into a slumber beyond the depths of dreams, but this time was different. Ryan Petey wasn't alone.

Lavender had always comforted Ryan, reminding him of when he was a small child with his grandmother. Her subtle perfume brought back a sense of love, baking, and a hug that would sweep him off his feet. A single tear trickled down his face, and he wiped it away. An eye cracked open, expecting to see the inside of a Gulfstream jet. However, the room was even more disturbing, but for different reasons.

The wallpaper had a repeating paisley pattern that drew the eye into boredom. An antique mahogany wash-stand held a white ceramic bowl next to a matching pitcher. Folded towels hung on a nearby rack next to a wardrobe. In the right corner, a beveled mirror showed a reflection of a shirtless young, wide-eyed man. Ryan ran a hand through his hair and wiped the sleep from his eyes. On the bedside table, a glass-bodied lamp was dim but gave enough light not to disturb his rest. The door was closed, and a thick terrycloth housecoat hung on the back. To his right, thick red and gold curtains blocked any outside light. The faint scent of lavender came from an extinguished pillar candle on the nightstand.

Waking in this room set him on edge. Someone wanted Ryan to feel comfortable, but not too comfortable. He discovered a monitoring bracelet secured to his left ankle, and his clothing was gone. He threw the duvet to the side and slipped on the beige robe before opening the curtains.

The elevated view revealed a backyard where gardening was completed to a standard not found in Ontario. Geometric topiary bushes lined a cobbled pathway leading to an outdoor dining area with stone benches next to statues and flower gardens with various colors. There wasn't one weed marring the manicured emerald grass to either side of the path. The walkway continued to an iron-wrought gate leading to a trellis heavy with a growing green vine and large white and purple flowers.

An ornate iron gate led to lush meadows lined with trees and stone fences that carpeted the rolling landscape. The skies were overcast, and a recent rainfall had covered everything in a sheen. Drops of water made a majestic willow tree sparkle as a light breeze made it sway back and forth.

Movement from a nearby field caught his attention as two dozen dairy cows were herded. A man in a dark brown jacket and cap waved a stick, and a black and white border collie raced to the cow's heels then the stick pointed in the opposite direction, and the dog darted to the other side. The method was effective; once, through a gap in the stone fence, a gate was closed. The man and dog walked along the treeline until they disappeared.

"What the hell is going on?"

Ignoring the extra weight on his left leg, Ryan paced the room momentarily before trying the door. To his surprise, it was unlocked. "If they wanted to kill me, they would have done so by now."

The wide planked floor creaked as he walked to the top of the stairs. Wall sconces provided enough light. Gripping the banister, Ryan descended. Each step sounded like a gunshot as the wood groaned under his weight.

The home was musty, maybe because of the rain, but more likely due to age. He couldn't say for certain but guessed it was built well over a hundred years ago, maybe two hundred. The wiring for the lights appeared to be an afterthought with added conduit, controlled by a round panel with two buttons, instead of the lightswitches he had at home. The first room at the bottom of the stairs was a library with a dozen bookshelves covering two walls and a couch and an overstuffed chair on the other. An area rug, white with pale red flowers, gave the room a cozy feeling.

A door swung open at the end of the hall, and an older woman came to a halt when she saw him. She was a little taller than Ryan and had short, curly gray hair, a pointed chin, and sharp cheekbones. She wore dark pants and a yellow top under a frilly white apron. She held a folded bundle of clothes in one hand.

"Glad to see you're awake, young man."

Ryan blinked, and it took a moment to realize what she had said. Her English accent was thick, and the words blurred together.

"Where am I? What's going on? Where is Crystal?"

"You're at the duke's residence. No idea, and never heard of her." She thrust the clothing into his hands. "All washed."

Ryan stood as if poleaxed. An eyebrow rose, and she didn't let go of his clothing.

Oh, shit. "Uh, thank you, ma'am."

"That's better. Go change, and I'll make you some breakfast." A thumb jerked over her shoulder at the swinging door. "Through there on the right. If ya get lost, follow your nose."

At a loss for words, Ryan retraced his steps upstairs. He just realized who had most likely undressed him. When he hit the top landing, she called out, "If you're to make your bed, I wouldn't be upset in the slightest."

Ryan had just finished dressing and tucked the duvet under the pillows when a shotgun blast echoed across the field. It was close.

Before he could get to the window, a second shot was fired.

CHAPTER 31

Ryan rushed down the stairs and through the swinging door into a grand foyer to find a chandelier hanging above a polished marble floor and a circular stained-glass window centered on the front door. To the side was a coat rack filled with hats and a full umbrella stand. He was initially tempted to try the lock and escape, but the lack of clothing and information made him reassess. The scent of fresh coffee and bacon hit him, and he pushed another swinging door into a kitchen larger than his basement. Floor-to-ceiling cupboards filled one wall, and an island the size of a pickup truck matched the wrap-around counters. Everything was white, including the tiled flooring. Glass chairs and a table were in front of a bay window showing the garden. A bouquet of wildflowers was the only splash of color on the table. The door at the rear led to a mud room, then outside.

"What was gunfire?" Ryan's heart was still beating double-time.

The woman cracked an egg into a cast iron frying pan and chuckled. "You got that right. I'm fairly sure that means I'll have more work soon. Take a seat."

As soon as he sat, the woman produced a mug of coffee and placed it before him. "There's cream and sugar on the counter if that's how you like it."

"Thank you."

Ryan preferred an energy drink but felt the caffeine boost would be welcome. "I'm Ryan."

She used a spatula to slide the food onto a plate. She grabbed a knife and fork from a drawer and placed everything beside the coffee. "Gemma. Pleased to meet you. The duke will be here soon. Eat up and get some meat on your bones, lad."

The more she talked, the more he made sense of her accent. A triangular piece of soda bread and a fried tomato complimented four eggs, bacon, sausage, and hashbrowns. Ryan couldn't remember the last time he ate or how long it had been, but his mouth watered, and his stomach let him know it was time. Without preamble, he dug into the huge meal.

Gemma was washing the pan when the rear door opened.

The man from the field stepped into the kitchen with a shotgun over one forearm and two dead birds in the other. He wore a long brown coat and a brimless cap. Wisps of white hair stuck out to the side, and while he was slim, six feet tall, remnants of jowls jiggled below the jawline. The slight hunch to his shoulders was due to age, possibly in his late seventies.

Gemma gestured, using the towel as a whip. "Get those out of here right now, or there'll be hell to pay!"

"Jesus ..." he grumbled before returning to the mudroom. The calf-high boots were removed before coming back in. The two black and tan grouse were tossed on the island countertop, and the shotgun was placed near the door.

The man noticed Ryan but accepted a tea mug before sitting across from him at the table. "How are you doing, son?"

He held back a dozen questions after a quick glance at the gun. "Good." Gemma raised an eyebrow again as she took his empty plate, and Ryan hastily added, "Sir. And thank you for breakfast." She gave him a quick wink before placing his dishes in the sink and disappearing through the swinging door. His accent was similar to Gemma's but not as thick.

"Let's get the obvious done first." He removed the cap, placing it on the table. He was bald, with thin wisps of hair circling his head like a crown. He took a sip of tea before beginning. "I'm Clive Ackerly, the second—Duke of Wilsford, a title in name mostly. You're in England, and I'm in the procurement and assessment business. You seem to have a unique talent and, not surprisingly, a very popular conversation piece within certain circles."

Ryan sipped at the coffee and nearly spat it out with that information. "You are the one who hired those people to bring me here? Where's Crystal?"

"Yes. That's my job. I was contracted to bring you here to see what you can do, lad. As to your lady friend, she's safe."

Ryan's first impression was of a dotting grandfather, but that was quickly replaced by an old English coot with a screw loose and a total disregard for humanity. "People died! Why would you do that?"

"Unfortunately, yes." He had another sip of tea, not seeming bothered at all. "I asked for minimal collateral damage, but shit happens. As to why? You seem to be reasonably smart. I'm sure you can figure it out."

Ryan pushed the coffee mug away. He didn't want anything Clive offered.

"You're done. Good." He collected both mugs and placed them in the sink. "Grab your shoes and meet me at the front door. We'll be leaving in a few minutes. Don't wear them inside if you value your hide."

He went through a side door, leaving Ryan wondering if he had entered the Twilight Zone.

Procurement and assessment? Who hired the duke, and what would they do with him? *What the fuck is going on?*

Ryan found his shoes in the mudroom, lined up neatly on a rubber mat. He also found a box of shotgun shells, No. 4 birdshot, on the bench seat below a cabinet. The shotgun was still in the kitchen, and he was alone. The temptation to load the gun and shoot his way to freedom was strong. Too strong. But who would he shoot? Gemma? The housekeeper or wife didn't seem involved and treated him fairly. Duke Ackley? If he had to, but he didn't seem to be a threat. He could probably physically overpower him if required. Ryan sighed. He had never used a shotgun or knew how to load and fire it. If he survived, he would make the time to learn.

"Hurry up, lad," Ackley called out. "The car's waiting."

Outside the front door was a black Mercedes limousine underneath a covered drive-through carport. A middle-aged man in a dark suit, tie, and white gloves held the rear door open. The duke gestured for Ryan to get in first, and he followed. The driver closed the door and headed around the vehicle to get behind the wheel. Ryan moved to the far side, facing forward. The interior smelled of leather, and the cushioned seats were incredibly comfortable. Another two seats faced the rear with a bar cart in the middle. The divider was up, and the driver pressed an overhead button. His voice came through a hidden speaker.

"Are you ready, sir?"

Ackley adjusted his coat and settled in. "Go ahead, Paul. Ready."

He couldn't hear the engine when they proceeded down the circular driveway. It was just a slight vibration. On the left was a fountain, and tall hedges lined the property on the right. A security gate rolled to the side as they approached, and once on the road, Paul accelerated.

"Crap …" Ryan gripped the armrest, white-knuckled, as a small car drove by on the other side of the road. It was then he realized the driver sat on the right side of the limousine, not the left.

"Relax. We'll be there soon."

Ryan tried to focus on the countryside instead of the oncoming traffic. Farmland and small cottages were common and wholesome, but he missed Toronto and worried about his mother. He should have looked for a phone to call home.

They made a few turns on the narrow country roads and eventually slowed. A man in a yellow vest and security uniform stood beside a barrier crossing their path. The sign behind his shoulder read *Temporarily Closed, will open soon.*

The duke lowered his window at the touch of a button, and the guard bent over.

"Everything's ready, sir. We'll reopen when you're done."

He pulled a white envelope from his jacket and passed it to the guard. "A little beer money for you and your men. It's appreciated."

The envelope disappeared, and he stepped back. Two similarly dressed guards moved the barrier as the window closed.

Ryan didn't have to ask where they were. He had seen the pictures his entire life. After passing an empty parking lot for busses to drop off tourists on the left, Ryan winced. It felt like someone had driven a spike in his brain. It's worse than any hangover or headache.

The pain in his head worsened as the limo navigated the gravel road. His eyes watered while his hands held his head together. "*Holy fuck*, that hurts. Stop the car!"

When the limousine stopped, Ryan fumbled with the door and couldn't open it.

"Paul." Duke Ackley pressed a button. "Unlock the doors. You'd best hurry."

Once the vehicle's transmission was in park, the driver jumped out and opened the door in time for Ryan to collapse outside on his hands and knees. Vomit shot out like water from a firehose. Paul danced backward to avoid the splash as his breakfast came up. When nothing was left, Ackley handed him a small white towel and a bottle of water from the bar.

"When you're ready, we'll go on up. I think we can walk from here, Paul."

"Very good, sir."

The driver helped Ryan to his feet. The pain in his skull made him dizzy, but he focused enough to rinse his mouth. Luckily, nothing had landed on his clothes.

"You're not the first to throw up at Stonehenge, but usually, it's from the drugs or alcohol."

Ryan stared at the monolithic stones at the top of the hill and had no doubt that was the reason for the shooting pain in his head. "Something's wrong or broken. I can't tell." He handed the bottle and towel back. "I'm too far away. I have to get closer."

Paul lifted the yellow rope barrier lining the road. Without waiting to see if Ackley followed, Ryan marched across the lawn. At seven hundred feet, the monument was impressive, and with each step, it grew more so. But Ryan walked not just in the present but in the past. He knew how the lintel stones were lifted onto the uprights and had done such work countless times over the decades. They would only be thirty tons, maybe more, and not difficult.

Without realizing what he was doing, Ryan hummed the seeking song when he was within fifty feet. Soon after his mouth opened and the resonant vibrations escaped, a chill ran down his back. For the first time in either of his lives, something answered the call.

CHAPTER 32

Ryan stumbled, and a firm hand steadied him by the elbow. He made a mental note to reassess the older man's physical capabilities. "Easy, lad. I got ya."

"Why am I here, sir?" He swallowed the lump in his throat and turned to the duke.

White bushy eyebrows lowered. "Rumors and bad videos are not facts, and I will not base any assumptions without firsthand knowledge."

An energy pulse made him cry out, and Ryan's knees buckled. He was lowered gently to the ground. The piercing pain had returned, and this close to the stones, it was amplified tenfold. Ignoring the duke, he crawled through the grass until he was within arm's reach of a fallen upright. White lichen spotted the thirteen-foot stone, and he found a bare spot to press his hand and listen.

Ryan wasn't ready when another surge hit, and his muscles spasmed.

Ackley gasped. "What did you do, lad?"

One eye cracked open, and he groaned. His hand sunk an inch into the stone as if it were clay, forming a perfect imprint of four fingers and a thumb.

"I know what's wrong." Ryan ignored the offer for help and struggled to his feet, stumbling to the center of the henge. A distant memory was the only guide for the situation, but he would make it work. A builder had insisted on using a specific granite quarry for the great project, but a section of the deposit was flawed. When Ryan and his brethren had sung to the stone in an era long ago, the discord made them ill. The flaw had warped their notes, and the sensitive singers cried out in pain. After a lengthy collaboration, a new song emerged that would temporarily strengthen the crystalline structure so the stone could be removed from the earth without being destroyed. Many believed the flaws would be reasserted afterward, but the builder didn't care and had them proceed. Once the granite was in place, the other blocks would secure the damaged stone.

Stonehenge had been altered and destroyed slowly over thousands of years. Farmers had taken stones to use as foundations for barns. Souvenirs of past rulers to time and weather had changed the pattern. Despite the pain in his skull, Ryan grinned. He knew what the landmark was built for and could help. Temporarily, at least. The structure would need to be rebuilt, and another location would need to be adjusted, but it could be done.

Ignoring his discomfort, Ryan sang not the deep vibrational song of seeking but the high-pitched notes of healing and binding. His thoughts sank into the ground and the structure of the great stones. Flaws and internal cracks should have been fixed as the damage occurred, but singers were in short supply or nonexistent. Waves of despair nearly made him weep. Such a magnificent project was almost destroyed, and once it was gone, all of Great Britain would feel the effects. The fact that Stonehenge still operated as intended was a miracle.

The two vertical stones, with another across the top, were trilithons in their original location, but the third must have been moved or adjusted later. The bluestones, weighing two to five tons each, quarried from the Carn Menyn Ridge in the Preseli Hills of southwest Wales, were for a specific reason—they sang. They were more akin to a bell than a rock and acted like resonating amplifiers ready to increase the volume of an instrument. Ryan changed the pitch after soothing several flaws in the great stones and fixing an internal crack. He called out to the bluestones, and all forty-two answered. *No, wait! Forty-three.* One was partially buried. There should have been more circling the henge, and they'd have to be replaced. The bluestones of Stonehenge were not a decoration or aiding in charting celestial events but acted as loudspeakers.

At first, nothing happened. The decay of the henge slowed his work, but the bluestones redirected the song *back* to Ryan and the great stones, creating a feedback loop. The response lifted his being, and he wept, but this time not in pain, but pure joy. His throat burned while harmonizing with the feedback, and the henge dissipated the force. Before finishing, Ryan changed the song, like a conductor redirecting the energy, back into the healing song. Massive trilithons acted as a tuning fork, vibrating the anchor stone buried a hundred feet underground.

The ground shook in response enough that Duke Ackley whispered, "I could feel that."

Ryan nodded. "The henge is repaired, but it may not last long. This *really* needs to be fixed."

"Fixed?" Although the older man was his captor and held all the strings, he looked wary at the young Canadian.

"We have to go there." Ryan didn't look but pointed due north. "There is another—henge? Structure?—that feeds this location and is out of tune. Trust me. You'll want that adjusted."

Ackley frowned and shook his head. "I have enough information. We will be returning to the estate."

Ryan matched his expression with feet shoulder-width apart and crossed his arms. "This is too important. I have to insist."

The old man barked laughter. "You are not in any position to argue. Come, we're leaving."

Now that Stonehenge had been fixed, even slightly, those attuned could feel the energy. People sensitive to the world will feel a charge in the air and a heightened sense of awareness. Some things were easier in this location than elsewhere, and Ryan acted without thinking. Easier? Too easy. The ancient skill of moving pebbles was considered a crowning achievement of any stone singer upon reaching the peak of the profession and life. Usually, such abilities were draining and rarely done. Ryan stood in the center of the henge, where the impossible could happen at this moment.

His hand snapped out to the side, palm flat and fingers extended. A rock exploded through the turf, spraying dirt in a twelve-foot radius before flying into his grip. The two-pound stone was similar in size to the dolerite at the museum. If he threw this stone hard enough, Ryan could knock over a twenty-five-ton trilithon. And knew all too well the effects on a person. He tried not to think of the difference between moving a pebble the size of a thumbnail and what he now held. Brethren, who turned to dust thousands of years ago, wouldn't believe it either.

"You have no idea what will happen to this part of the world. We *will* be going."

Ackley turned white as a sheet, no small feat for an Englishman, and his eyes flicked from the stone in his hand to studying Ryan's eyes. He licked his lips and took a step back.

"Explain."

Ryan gestured with the stone as if it weighed nothing and was an extension of his arm. "Stonehenge isn't to map the stars. It's a speaker or a pressure-release valve. A place for energy to be dispersed. Nearby, another place redirects the energy here. I don't know how to explain it properly, but I'll try."

Noticing the duke wasn't paying attention to him, just the potential projectile, he dropped it on the ground. "Sound waves and energy are different sides of the same coin. Underneath the United Kingdom, large tectonic plates are shifting; if the sound generated by the rock doesn't have an outlet, it will build. Does this place get earthquakes?"

Ackley may have been apprehensive, but he wasn't slow. Understanding dawned. "Yes. All the time."

Ryan's hand circled his head. "If this is gone, they will be worse. A *lot* worse. Nearby, a series of stones will most likely need to be aligned. It shouldn't take long."

"Avebury."

Uhh? "Pardon, sir?" He needed something. It is best to be polite.

"There is another circular henge nearby called Avebury. It's only twenty-five miles or so north of here."

Ryan nodded. That made sense. He could feel the call while standing in the middle of the henge. Was repairing the henge the reason he had the memories of a dead man?

He followed the duke across the lawn, and with each step downhill, the energy dissipated. Stonehenge could have been rebuilt within a week if he had two other singers longer if they had to quarry new stones. Such monolithic structures were on each continent worldwide and weren't for show. They had a purpose. Maybe Ryan had found his.

Duke Ackley shook his head and gestured behind him. "Glad you were not here four days ago. It would have been a disaster."

Curious, Ryan asked, "Why's that, sir?"

"It was the festival for the summer solstice. Thousands were celebrating the longest day of the year."

Paul held the door, and they sat inside the limousine. Ryan's eyes grew wide as the dates sunk in. Four days ago, he was in an alleyway near Jane and Finch. That's when the ankh first appeared.

CHAPTER 33

For the first time since the building was constructed, the Royal Ontario Museum was closed for two days as an army of forensic investigators descended on the premises. Detective McCallan, despite her interest in the case, wasn't even allowed inside until late afternoon on the second day. All four levels and the basement were considered a crime scene and treated accordingly. Latex gloves were issued upon arrival, and protective boots were to slide over their shoes.

She shook her head, recalling the body count. Two security guards died in their office, with another on the fourth floor. A janitor was found on the third floor, shot twice, but the other maintenance workers on the second floor had no idea anything was happening—most worked with headphones on, listening to music. It was the two men next to the sarcophagus that was confusing. They had the murder weapons, but there wasn't any trace of the mechanism to launch the stones.

Trish McCallan was escorted to the third floor via the elevator. The main staircase was closed from the second to third levels by forensics. After seeing the damage to the exhibits and wall and the amount of blood on the floor, she knew the museum wouldn't be opening on Monday either.

"What do you think?" Inspector Percy from the homicide section of specialized criminal investigations led her to the hands-on exhibit. Two men in full-body suits were chiseling at the wall to remove the stone, and McCallan pulled out her flashlight. The sand was out of bounds pending casting of the shoe impressions, but she examined the area from a distance. Except for some activity around the tipped granite slab, the remainder was smooth as a beach, with no marks or impressions marring the surface.

She stood before the exhibit, using her arm as a sight line, and pointed her fingers to the wall and where the man died in the other room. "Whatever was used to kill the men was right here or behind this tipped rock. But no marks on the ground or sand suggest how it happened. Slingshot? How far can a strong man throw one of those stones?"

Percy, while older, retained the barrel chest and arms from working out at the gym. "I've thought about that. Did you know there's a chart for those stats? An average person can throw a two-and-a-half pound stone thirty-seven feet, right-handed." He pointed to the wall where they had nearly succeeded in freeing the dolerite-shaping stone. "The force needed to throw that into the wall far exceeded anything capable of a human. A machine had to have been used, or a mechanical device."

She still had red marks on her ankles where the firemen had used a jackhammer to free her from the front step. McCallan had *sunk* into the solid stone. The possible answers on how the rock got within the wall were no doubt related to what happened to her. The one thing in common? Ryan Petey. Dr. Crystal Kowalska had signed him into the building as a visitor, and the log was now considered evidence.

"Got it. Stand back."

The stone was removed from the wall using a six-foot prybar and caught before it hit the ground. Gloved hands turned the projectile over, and the taller technician whispered, "Oh, shit. Inspector? You'll want to see this."

McCallan joined Percy as the stone was rotated. Sunk an inch into the solid material was an outline of a human hand. With gloves on, she placed her right hand in the impression. The imprint was slightly larger than her own, but not by much.

Sir Arthur Conan Doyle said it best, "*When you have eliminated the impossible, whatever remains, however improbable, must be the truth.*"

She turned to Inspector Percy. "I think we need to talk, sir."

Thirty-five hundred miles and a five-hour time zone difference away, the exact moment detective McCallan placed her hand in the dolerite, Ryan Petey, stepped out of a minivan along with two burly workmen. Dressed in black and carrying shovels, they approached Avebury. While not as well known as Stonehenge, the sight was of a grander scale. At the stroke of midnight, they went to work. Neither of the workmen mentioned the task's impossibility or what was happening. They were paid quite handsomely for their efforts and continued silence.

Unlike Stonehenge, Avebury was not guarded or patrolled, and visitors were allowed to lay their hands on the monolithic stones. Not *only* did Ryan lay his hands on the stones, but they were shifted and aligned properly with his expertise and direction. One difficult stone, weighing eighteen tons, had to be rotated in position while another was moved eight feet to the west. Again, nothing was said except for the occasional grunt or direction the young Canadian gave.

Curiously, there were no late-night visitors or strolling locals. Ryan didn't have time to wonder if the duke had a hand in that oddity. There was work to do.

Twenty-four minutes after six in the morning, sunrise revealed three exhausted, dirt-covered men with scratches and cuts on various body parts. Ryan stood beside the largest sarsen stone at the northeast corner of the henge, weighing twenty tons. As sunlight bathed the top of the rock, he pressed two palms against the behemoth and sang. The note was carried to the remainder of the circle. The vibrations and resonance soon escalated beyond the range of the human ear before being directed south.

Twenty-five miles away, a fresh-faced guard working for the EH staff directed a special access or inner circle group for a tour at dawn. Twelve customers paid forty-seven pounds each for the privilege of standing within, but not touching, the ancient stone circle to witness the sunrise.

When a couple holding hands with a small boy passed out, he rushed to their side, then things worsened. A couple from Queensland was next, followed by a group of four from Arizona. Spinning about in a panic, he found the remainder lying on the plush grass, asleep or dead. He didn't know.

The young guard removed his earbuds connected to his phone, and his eyes rolled back in his head, not in pain but ecstasy. Overloaded by stimulus, his brain temporarily shut down, and he fell face-first across a woman's legs from Dublin.

The government released a press release citing that those underground gases had been freed and that everything was fine with no danger to future visitors. However, the inner circle dawn and dusk visits were canceled until further notice.

CHAPTER 34

Ryan lay in bed staring at the ceiling, reviewing what happened yesterday and throughout the night. He had operated with the same instinct a parent had when saving a child or consoling a loved one after a tragedy. Compassion and empathy were driving forces, coupled with the fact that he may be the only person in the world capable of making the necessary adjustments; there was no choice. He had no idea how much longer Stonehenge would function, but he had extended the expiry date, hopefully significantly. The only worry? It may not have been Ryan Petey in charge, but a man long since dead. He had been so deeply immersed in the past that he had lost the importance of the present. While his actions didn't deviate from or alter his current circumstances, the sense of accomplishment shed new light on matters and put a spring in his step.

After making his bed, he opened the curtains to find the sun was setting. He had slept all day. "I haven't done that in a long time."

Ryan had returned to the estate by seven o'clock, showered, and then collapsed. Duke Ackley had simply nodded and went outside to talk with his partners in crime. He had never learned the names of the two men, nor had he asked.

Yesterday's clothing was missing upon awakening, but this time he found replacements. Folded neatly on top of the bureau were new socks, underwear, and other essentials. He held the jeans up to his waist and figured they would fit. Instead of a T-shirt, he found a light gray collared dress shirt. Ryan couldn't find any price tags, but the quality was better than anything he owned.

On his way downstairs, he checked the other room, hoping to find a phone. The first door led to another similar bedroom, and the next was a sewing room. Bolts of cloth leaned against the wall behind a sewing machine and a fitting mannequin. The other two doors were locked. Maybe the library. Once downstairs, he quickly looked, but it turned up empty. A growling stomach found him in front of the refrigerator as Duke Ackley walked through the swinging door.

"Well rested?" Ackley wore a blue pin-striped suit and black tie. He looked ready to go out, minus the shoes, of course.

"Yes, sir." Giving up, he closed the door.

"Good. Sit at the table a moment."

He produced an oddly shaped silver key and handed it to Ryan. "You may as well take off the tracking device. It hasn't worked since your adventure yesterday."

Gratefully, Ryan unlocked and removed the monitor, leaving it on the table. He had forgotten about it … mostly.

"In the morning, you will be relocated. For your peace of mind, I have inquired into your ladyfriend, and she is in perfect health and not being treated poorly."

The sense of relief lifted a worry from his shoulders, but he still didn't know where she was or who was holding her. "Where am I going, sir?"

Ackley's eyebrows lowered with a quick head shake. "I'm not at liberty to reveal that answer. Suffice it to say, you will not be mistreated."

That left a lot that *could* happen to him and did nothing to quell his unease.

Gemma pushed the door open, placed two bags in the mudroom, and then turned to Ryan. "You're probably hungry. Hold on, lad, and I'll make something quick." She wore the same outfit as yesterday, but today's apron was pink with frills. "Those brown paper bags have a few more things for you."

"Thank you."

"No problem, dear. I'll be done in a few minutes. Go wash up."

Ackley stood. "I'll be back later, and we can talk if you like."

Not willing to say anything he'd regret, Ryan nodded. He was about to clean his hands when a siren blasted out of the speaker next to the swinging door, and a blue LED flashed, making him jump.

Duke Ackley held out a hand to Ryan. "Stay there."

Gemma stopped working, and her hands twisted the apron about in worry. A man he hadn't seen before rushed into the kitchen. He wore a black suit without a tie and a coiled earpiece. The tan-bodied pistol in his hand was held at the ready. "Sir, a group of men is breaching the gate. We have to get you to safety."

Ryan didn't even know there was security on the estate, let alone armed men.

Ackley asked, "How many? Can you handle them?"

The muffled sound of gunfire made Gemma burst into tears and cry out, "Oh my, God!"

A tall black man in the same style of suit rushed into the kitchen through the swinging door. A short-bodied SA80 rifle slung over his shoulder. "Sir, an unknown number of men have climbed the walls and are on the property. Time to go."

"One minute." Ackley stared at Ryan for a few seconds, then sighed. "Mr. Petey, things have changed."

Ryan was ushered into the mudroom. "Put on your shoes. Now."

The duke opened the cupboard, removing a mossy oak camouflaged hunting backpack. He placed it on the ground and stuffed the two paper bags inside. Gemma handed over some food wrapped in a towel and two water bottles, then darted away. They went into the pack as well.

"Put this on." Ackley removed his brown oiled jacket and hat from the pegs. Numbly, Ryan dressed in clothing too large for his frame.

"Go through the gate and follow the fence line north through the fields. You'll cross a road, then head east through the woods eight miles or so. You'll eventually come to a village where you'll contact Carrick. He'll help and get you to safety. I'll ensure he knows where your girl is being kept."

More shots were fired. They were close. Too close.

Ackley removed a flat wallet from his suit jacket and pulled out a sheaf of bills, thrusting them into the pack. "Things have changed, and someone can't wait for the auction."

"Sir, we have to go. *Now*. The gate is breached." The black man was on edge and brought the butt of the rifle into his shoulder.

Ackley ignored him and dug in the cabinet. Boxes of shotgun shells fell to the ground.

He removed a sheathed hunting knife and placed it into Ryan's hands. "Sometimes it's better not to be caught. Do you understand?"

Numbly, Ryan nodded.

"Go. I'm not apologizing for my actions, but this may balance the scales somewhat. Run and don't come back. Go change the world, lad."

The door closed in his face as the tall black man dragged the duke away.

Outside, the rifle shots echoed across the countryside for miles. Clutching the pack and knife to his chest, Ryan bolted for the garden gate. Seventy seconds had passed since the alarm sounded, and he didn't have time to process, only react. The latch was stiff, and his palm struck it several times before the gate squealed open.

The hail of gunfire had slowed, but a new sound made the hair on the back of his neck stand on end. A high-pitched buzz came over the estate's roof like an angry swarm of bees, and then a white light darted outside the second-floor windows with sharp, jerking movements.

A drone.

Ryan tucked the knife inside the pack and put his arms through the straps. Without looking back, he ran. Keeping the stone fence on his right, he was forced to slow. The sun had set, and he was having trouble seeing. There was partial cloud cover, and the moon wasn't up. A few stars peeked through the gaps, but not enough to illuminate. Yet.

Turning an ankle or breaking a leg wouldn't help things. Ryan was at the top of a cattle fence when the whirling rotors of the drone left the estate garden and shot out over the fields.

CHAPTER 35

The pack wasn't heavy, and he ran as fast as possible, putting aside the physical dangers. The distant crack of a rifle made him flinch and check over his shoulder. The drone zig-zagged across the main field and shouldn't have been able to find him, but the random flying stopped. Like a shot in the dark, the drone elevated to fifty feet before accelerating in his direction. Even if it was daylight and he could see the ground properly, he wouldn't have been able to outrun the quadcopter.

It circled his position, then rose to a hundred feet and hovered.

Ryan gained control of his breathing and wished for Ackley's shotgun. But maybe he had another weapon that was just as good. It didn't seem to matter which song he chose. They appeared to disrupt electronics. He decided on the seeking song and the low bass notes carried across the pasture. He sang for over a minute, but the drone was too far away.

At his back, the stone fence stretched for acres. Ryan picked up a field stone the size of a softball and hefted it in his right hand, and the deep bass notes of shaping vibrated the air. He was ready. However, throwing an object nearly straight above your head was almost impossible.

Ryan ran fifty feet to get a better angle, but the drone followed his movement.

"Quit wasting time. They know where you are!" Frustrated, he tossed the rock over his shoulder and ran north. After twelve feet, he stumbled on a tuft of grass and sprawled on his face. Any remnants of light from the setting sun were gone, and he had never experienced darkness like the countryside at night. In Toronto, there was *always* light from streetlamps, buildings, and cars that illuminated the entire city. Half a mile from the estate, enough stars were out to give a vague impression of objects without details. A thin sliver of a crescent glow on the eastern horizon was visible over the treeline. The waning moon was rising.

"It must have thermal imagery." He gave the machine a one-fingered salute and turned toward the stone fence. When he kicked a field stone, he turned north. While he couldn't see properly, if he sang the seeking song, he would know the location of the rocks like a blind man feeling the edge of the sidewalk with a cane or a submarine using sonar.

Singing while running was nearly impossible, so Ryan slowed the pace but made better time. After almost seven hours of work the night before, his throat was still raw, but there was no other choice. The seeking song rumbled, and the stone in the immediate area answered. The location was farmland at one point because the rock lining the fields was the same in the ground.

He tried to ignore the drone but found it impossible and was ready to give up, but the vibrations revealed a secret in the ground. A spring-fed meandering creek separated two fields in a low ditch and had been a watering hole for the cattle for a hundred years. The layers of mud and grass were gone, revealing a limestone shelf extending hundreds of feet in both directions. A flicker of hope made Ryan grin at the discovery.

The softer limestone is shaped with moving water, forming natural caves. Ryan recalled decades of experience with limestone; underground openings were common, and the chances increased with moving water. Instead of continuing north, he turned west along the creek bed, and the drone followed.

Ryan discovered a low, wide plank for the cattle to bridge the creek. Any caves in the lowland would be filled with water, but after he crossed to the north side, the ground steadily rose with the undulating landscape. He had also found the echo designating a buried cave.

No, two!

The limestone hillside was covered in a thin veil of earth. There were enough layers of stone that the pasture could have been turned into a quarry. But being elevated on the hillside revealed another problem.

Headlights were flying across the pasture in his direction.

There wasn't enough time to dig and hide in a cave until things blew over.

The crescent moon was a finger's width above the horizon, and the gentle white light allowed him to see. Nerves made him chuckle. "I've found the silver lining."

Backtracking, he headed east along the creek bed. The vehicle had covered half the distance to the estate and would be on him in a minute. Caution aside, he ran toward the stone fence separating the fields. Unless it was a tank, it couldn't cross the barrier.

Hundreds of years ago, the stone fence would have been four feet tall and made with field stones, but time had shifted the rocks into a jumbled mound. A deep vibration made the stones sing when he was within ten feet, and Ryan adjusted his course slightly. When his foot hit the first rock, he had already chosen where the next step would be. He darted up and across the barrier, surefooted as a mountain goat. Turning north, he tried to distance himself from the vehicle as much as possible, but it was nearly on him.

The drone lowered to fifty feet behind him, hovered briefly, then flew south.

It wasn't needed anymore. Headlights flickered across Ryan's body, and his shadow elongated across the field.

"Fuck!"

Ryan wasn't waiting to be caught but seriously thought about pulling out the hunting knife and putting up a feeble defense. He wasn't sure if he could take his own life. Not when he still had a chance.

The headlights stopped bouncing, and the sound of vehicle doors slamming carried across the field. He didn't waste time. The moon revealed enough of the landscape that he wouldn't run into a tree or rock, and he took advantage. Putting everything he had into the effort, Ryan ran north.

The sound of his breathing and pack slapping on his back covered any noise the pursuers made. After a few minutes, he had to take a quick look. Four flashlights were spread out across the field, running toward him. One light bobbed near the fenceline to prevent any escape to the west. Two hundred feet? Not much of a lead, and they were moving faster.

When Ryan came upon another fence stretching west-east with a ditch on the far side, he jumped. Pausing at the top of the wall, Ryan gulped air into his lungs with his hands on his knees. He could see the shadowy forms of the men, not just the flashlights. Between breaths,

Ryan also heard the trickle of water over rocks. A stream flowed downhill at the bottom of the ditch, and he didn't hesitate. The water was ankle-deep, then he scrambled up the incline, fingers digging into the soil for purchase.

The road was silver in the moonlight, and on the far side, the woods began.

Ryan ran across the road, then paused with a look back. He'd left wet shoe prints on the asphalt, pointing in his direction.

Flashlights bobbed across the field. They were close. He had less than two minutes.

Crying in frustration, he ran.

▲ ▲ ▲

Zhong Shi Chen jumped out of the Land Rover and gestured to the side, then forward with a knife hand. His men spread out, navigating the stone obstacle, but soon they were out of range of the headlights. The uneven ground slowed their movements. He turned on his tactical light, and the others followed suit to increase speed.

"ETA on the aerial view? Target was last seen moving north of my location, over." Chen keyed his microphone as he ran across the field.

"Two minutes, battery change complete. En route ASAP, over."

"Roger, out."

Now that the estate had been cleared, the remainder of the mission rested squarely on his shoulders. The target could not be harmed, and they were weapons-tight. Luckily, the thermal imagery from the drone picked up a signature fleeing the estate. Chen had argued for a halo drop with an approach from the north. A two-pronged assault would have had them on their way back to base, mission completed. There was enough room with the open pastures, yet it had been overruled. But who would listen to a sergeant with twenty years of experience? His head wouldn't be on the platter if they failed; that was all that mattered.

The subject had seen their approach, and Chen figured everything would be over within a few minutes, but the kid ran as if the devil were chasing him. Not to be outdone by his team, he gave a burst of energy but nearly wiped out in the mud. A quick look with the flashlight made him sick. It wasn't mud. It was cow shit.

When the target paused on top of a stone fence, Chen grinned. It would be over within minutes. His teammates also saw the young man and the race was on. He had promised a thousand euros to the man who brought the target down unharmed.

Vaulting over the stone fence, Chen slid down the ditch and jumped the creek. On the road, he called his men over. "This way."

They followed the prints across and down the ditch.

"Chen! Over here." Xia Shi Wu had climbed the far side and stood under an ash tree.

The flashlight showed a brown rimless hat lying under a branch. Chen peeled a glove down and felt inside with his wrist. "Still warm. It's him. Spread out."

They were fifty feet inside the woods when the drone flew overhead. The target didn't have a chance against T.I. "Talk to me. Where is he?"

"There's movement north of your position, but it could be wildlife." Huang stayed with the primary vehicle at the estate to use the drone remotely. "There's a smaller target moving rapidly to the west."

"That has to be him. Moving." Chen closed in with his left hand on the Taser and the right holding the flashlight. He could almost smell the Canadian. They were one minute behind. Tops. Ducking branches and dodging trees, he flew through the woods. "See you shortly, Ryan Petey."

CHAPTER 36

Dr. Crystal Kowalska crossed her arms, covering her bare chest while marching through the corridor. The cold tiles were slick, and she had to shuffle to keep her balance. Her guards would no doubt like it if Crystal fell. No men were present, but she still felt like she was sick and wanted to crawl into a hole and die.

She tried to pull Ryan through the brick wall one moment, and the next, she awoke on a lumpy mattress. The cell was four feet wide and eight feet long. Other than a mattress, there was a hole in the floor for a toilet. The cell door was unlocked twice daily, and a food tray was placed inside. The bowl of gruel was accompanied by a circular flatbread that Crystal used as a spoon. While the taste was bland, she consumed every morsel to quell the gnawing hunger.

Two days after being a captive, the door opened, but not to deliver a food tray. Four dark-skinned women in military uniforms pulled her upright and stripped her clothes.

"What are you doing?" Crystal pleaded. "Give me my pants!"

She tugged at the leggings, and the tall brunette slapped her. Dazed, she fell to the mattress with her cheek stinging. The cell door slammed shut, and the bolts slid into the steel frame. The lone lightbulb recessed into the ceiling, which has been on since she first awoke, and turned off. Naked, she curled into a ball on the mattress and cried. Eventually, she fell asleep but would wake up shivering every few hours, then every half hour.

Crystal had been keeping time by the regularity of the meals, but on the morning of the third day, the door didn't open. She knew enough to stay active and warm and tried a series of push-ups and stretches, but she didn't want to burn calories needlessly.

A day had passed since her last meal when the light turned on. Crystal closed her eyes and tried to cover her head. After being in the dark for so long, the light was painful. The cell door flung open, and her four guards had returned.

"Out." The tall brunette had eyes of steel, and not one ounce of emotion flickered over her hard features.

"What's going on? Where am I?"

Another guard slapped her on the back of the head and yelled, "Silence."

Weakened by the lack of food and sleep, Crystal couldn't put up a fight if she tried. She crossed her arms over her chest, not out of modesty as much as to keep from shivering while trying to learn as much as possible. The corridor was arched with conduit cables running the length. Every twenty feet, bare lightbulbs hung from the ceiling, connected by thick black wire. The guards wore a tan and dark green uniform without any insignia. Holstered pistols hung at their right hip along with a collapsable baton. A pouch with silver handcuffs was attached to the belt in the middle of their backs. When she tried to study the two guards behind her, a hand shoved the small of her back.

Her escort stopped at a green door and thrust her inside. "Shower."

The room hadn't been cleaned since she was in university. The subway tiles, once white, were now coated in a brown scum you couldn't remove with a pressure washer. Under the showerhead was a nameless gray bottle.

"I think I'm good. If I could have my clothes back that—"

Crystal was shoved hard enough that her head snapped back, and she skidded five feet on her stomach and hands.

"Shower." The brunette crossed her arms. "Now, or I'll do it for you."

She couldn't hold back the tears as she struggled to her feet. As predicted, there was no hot water. When she had finished, her lips were blue, and Crystal couldn't stop her teeth from shaking.

"Put this on."

Another guard threw a bundle of black clothing at her chest, and it took several moments to discover the material was a burka. While on digs in Pakistan, she had worn the pale blue garment for meetings and functions so as not to go against the local customs. However, a black burka was usually reserved for Arab countries. She had worked in Egypt too many times not to pick up on the traditions of the surrounding nations.

Only the eyes would be seen when worn properly, and the black material would cover all exposed skin. At times, a veil could also be worn, but it was missing.

Grateful for the warmth, Crystal slid it over her shaking, goosefleshed body.

"Keep your eyes down, no matter what. You will answer as briefly as possible if asked a question, leaving nothing out. Do not lie. We'll know. Don't volunteer anything or speak out of turn. One transgression and you will be shot dead. Understood?"

Crystal nodded and stared at the guard's black leather boots, reveling in the warmth. The tremors had nearly halted in her chest, but her hands still shook.

She was escorted to the end of the hallway and into an elevator. Crystal glanced up to see there were eight floors, and they were going to the top. With a whirl of gears, the steel doors closed. Her knees buckled as the elevator rose, and a hidden bell dinged at each level.

The difference from the basement to the eighth floor was nearly incomprehensible in her weakened state. Polished marble covered the floors and walls. The air conditioning was scented with flowers and carried a hint of freshly brewed coffee. The gold vase on the stone table held orchids and cost more than she had earned her entire life.

Her escorts remained in the elevator, and she was shoved out. Crystal didn't stumble this time; the small victory made her smile. No one could see her face as the burka acted like a mask. No one could tell if she was frightened, amused, bored, or yawning. Good. They can all go fuck a camel. She will take it as a win.

A male guard grabbed her right arm and gave her instructions while dragging her down a hall. She wasn't ready when they stopped before an intricate door of gold and diamonds, but no one seemed to care. The guard knocked gently and waited.

Crystal kept her eyes down.

When the door opened, he spoke. "I have brought the woman."

A man with a high-pitched Asian accent yelled, "About fucking time. Get her in here."

CHAPTER 37

Water rushed over Ryan's lower legs and knees, covering his hands to the wrist. A vehicle sped along the road and the sounds of men yelling carried for a quarter-mile in the countryside. Exhausted, his head hung low as he struggled to breathe slowly and steadily. Adrenaline-fed muscles shook, and a pounding headache made him wince.

Ryan didn't have the skills to evade the search, nor did he have a chance to survive a physical fight against four men. He had to switch tactics. The brown hat flew like a Frisbee toward the trees, then Ryan removed his shoes and ran down the shoulder of the road before crossing. He had jumped into the ditch as the men climbed the fence. Their voices carried, and Ryan crept away. If it *did* come down to a fight, he wanted to be near the stone fence, but finding the culvert was a surprise, and he couldn't pass it up.

The opening was thirty inches round and built of crumbling concrete. A large man wouldn't fit, and hopefully, it would be overlooked. Ryan hid his shoes and backpack under a bush, counting on the camouflage pattern to conceal them. Dropping to his hands and knees, he backed inside. Roots and pieces of stone protruded like tentacles or teeth of a mythical sea creature, and he was glad of the oil-skinned coat.

At first, the shallow water was refreshing and cooled him down, but he couldn't feel his legs or hands after an hour. The ache climbed up his limbs, and Ryan wouldn't last much longer. When something heavy crawled across the back of his neck, a hand swatted it. With a plop, it fell into the water before being carried away.

"Time to get the hell out of here." Ryan controlled a shudder that had nothing to do with the cold water and inched forward. Like a turtle, his head poked out of the culvert. He listened for ten minutes but couldn't hear anything over the trickling of the water. No one knew where he was, and he planned on keeping it that way. In this situation, he figured there was nothing wrong with laying low until the heat blew over. There weren't many choices, so during the last hour, he came up with a plan.

In the past, stone singer apprentices were given a myriad of tasks, from hauling refuse to sharpening tools. Later on, games were introduced that tested and pushed their abilities. One such pastime was the *linking* game. Working with stones the size of an apricot, they were balanced on each other while the singer hummed a nameless tune. The rocks were encouraged to adhere to each other as another stone was placed on top. Like connecting a series of magnets, towers or various shapes could be built. An older master, no longer capable of heavy work, usually supervised the apprentices and demonstrated the game. Ryan, or his past self, recalled a leather-faced man grinning as young men and women marveled at the inverted pyramid he had built. With a gentle push of a finger, the construct, made of small pebbles and stones, rotated like a top. When the master's song stopped, the rocks fell in a heap. It wasn't until he had been singing for decades that Ryan learned the trick. Like two pieces of steel spot welded, stones were tacked together. Miles of loose rock separated the fields, and the project he had in mind wouldn't take long. He hoped.

Ryan staggered out of the culvert, and his muscles screamed in protest. He grabbed his pack and shoes and crawled over a fallen section of jumbled blocks while humming. Ryan placed the first row four feet from the corner to outline the structure. The song changed with the second row, and he linked each piece to another, but he had to do it carefully. There was no point in creating a hiding place that resembled a cottage with perfect walls. Like building an igloo, the stone placement staggered inward, creating a dome. There was no lack of materials, and the project went quickly. Ryan could have built faster, but he paused to listen every few minutes. There was little doubt that someone was still searching and had not given up. Neither would he.

After fifteen minutes, Ryan threw his pack and shoes inside, rolling a large stone to seal him inside. While crude, it would pass scrutiny. The burrow was the same size as the cage on the Gulfstream jet, six feet long and three wide and tall. Before lying down, he did his best to move the stones underneath so they weren't digging into his back. But in the end, he didn't care as much. It was the first time he had slept on hard ground. Using the pack as a pillow, Ryan fell into a restless sleep.

He was safe, for now.

▲ ▲ ▲

Ryan's jeans were still damp when he awoke but were on the way to drying out. The stones reflected his body heat, staving off the chills, an added benefit of having a low-roofed shelter. Light didn't filter through the gaps, but Ryan figured it must have been close to sunrise when the drone returned. While muted, the distinct buzzing zipped overhead twice within fifteen minutes. Unsure that the machine could see a heat signature, Ryan had added an extra layer of stones. He had seen the movies and hoped his efforts were enough. Within fifty feet of the road, vehicles were loud, and car doors slammed, but no one came close to the hiding place.

Now was as good a time as any to pray to the god that spoke in mind, but nagging questions kept popping up. Was the voice *really* a god? If someone from the present went back two thousand years with a helicopter or a handgun, would the locals label the man as a divine being or a magician? This was where Ryan's memories conflicted with his present knowledge. The modern mind knew there had to be a scientific explanation for stone singing, and changing the molecular structure, even temporarily, with sonics was a mystery and impossible. How was it done? Ryan had no idea. And an uneducated person would believe he could perform magic or be a god. A slippery slope. How had Ryan been given the gift of memory and abilities? A god was as good an answer as anything. Putting aside the questions, he prayed.

Ryan poured out his heart and confided his deepest fears to the unknown deity, along with his desires and hopes. His mother was foremost in his mind, and to his surprise, Crystal. Like a raft adrift on the ocean, subject to the winds and currents, Ryan had been floating with circumstances out of his control. He was given the gifts and abilities, but *why*? What was the ultimate goal, and to which god did he pray?

Hours passed, and he sometimes cried or chuckled during his soulful confessions.

After everything he had gone through, he wasn't shocked but relieved when the response came. While hiding from his enemies and surrounded by stone, another door opened in his mind, and instructions were given. When the sun crested the horizon, a new day had dawned. The task was momentous, and Ryan didn't know where to start. One of his mother's jokes came to mind.

How do you eat an elephant?
One bite at a time.

CHAPTER 38

Sitting outside the shelter, Ryan searched the pack, finding the water bottles and food Gemma provided. A wedge of cheese, smoked sausage, and the heel of bread was wrapped in a hand towel. The money totaled three hundred and twenty pounds, but he wasn't sure how that was converted into Canadian dollars. Whatever the amount, it was better than nothing but short of what he could have used. He found new T-shirts, underclothes, and two collared dress shirts in the paper bags. He hoped Gemma survived so he could thank her for her kindness. In the pack's side pocket, he found a pair of hunting gloves, empty shotgun cartridge shells, and a few packages of earplugs left over from a prior hunt. Using the hunting knife, Ryan made a quick sandwich and drank sparingly.

The mid-morning sun burned through the clouds. He was about to unlink the stones forming the burrow when he changed his mind. Maybe a family of foxes will move inside. The thought comforted him as he jumped the fence and stepped over the creek. He had heard traffic on the road an hour earlier, but now it was empty. After crossing, he briefly looked for the hat, but it was gone.

Ryan had things to do, but none of them were in England, and the sooner he started, the quicker he would be completed. Ignoring the woods, he walked east on the shoulder of the road toward the village. The exercise soon warmed him, and he stuffed the coat in the pack before continuing. The occasional car would pass him on the road, and he couldn't shake the weird feeling of them driving on the opposite side.

Birds sang and flittered within the woods, and a light northern breeze felt good on his skin. Hiding in a stone cave served its purpose, but being outside made him feel alive. After unburdening his soul, Ryan felt lighter, with a bounce in his step—a new man.

Even when the Land Cruiser suddenly stopped and four Asian men dressed in T-shirts and khaki pants jumped out, his mood didn't change. One man pulled out a phone, looked at the screen, and then at Ryan before gesturing to his companions. "That's him. Get him in the car. Quickly."

"I need to go to town first, and then we can do whatever you have planned. Okay?"

The three men didn't bother listening. Before they could cross the road, Ryan pulled a pebble out of his jeans pocket and hummed. The stone hit the closest man in the chest with a flick of his finger. As the other two grabbed his arms, the first man dropped to his knees, ripping the T-shirt off. The pebble had sunk into his chest and disappeared. With a strangled cry, he toppled over, dead.

Along with his new purpose, Ryan could also recall more of his past memories. The child's game was never meant to harm anyone, upon punishment of death as a misuse of their abilities, but he had no other options. No builders were alive to pass judgment. A variation of the linking game, if you vibrated a pebble at a certain frequency and threw it, it would remain out of phase for a brief moment. Flicking pebbles at other stones made them stick as if they were linked, like a wild game of darts. A brush of a hand would make them fall. However, the flesh was softer than granite, and clothing even less so. As long as stones were lying about, Ryan would have ammunition. The entire planet was one big rock. A lesson he recalled too late.

"I have to go into town, but then I'll go with you. Deal?" Ryan ignored the two men holding him. They stared at their dead friend, and he couldn't blame them. He didn't pull a gun but hit him with a small stone the size of a thumbnail.

The man with the phone shook his head. "Get him in the car. Now."

Ryan guessed what would happen and hummed again while slamming the pebble in his left hand against the man holding him—in the upper leg.

The man held on briefly before screaming in pain, then fell to the ground, clutching his leg. Ryan wasn't trying to kill but incapacitate. "Are you ready to listen?"

The man with the phone was stunned and screamed, "What are you doing to my men?"

"I had to get your attention somehow, and I'm partial to not being stuck in a trunk or tied up in a cage." Ryan pointed west down the road. "I have an errand in town, and then I'll go with you. Willingly. Deal?"

The man looked tough and capable of picking Ryan up and running several miles, but he hesitated. Ryan's left hand was free, and he patted the pocket full of pebbles, making them rattle. The man flinched as his companion screamed again, then agreed.

The remaining two Asian men worked together to get the others in the vehicle. The body went into the back, and they tried getting the injured man in the seat, but he thrashed too much.

Feeling slightly guilty, Ryan shoved the two men aside and knelt beside the injured man. He didn't have access to the raw energy flowing out of Stonehenge, but he should be able to call the stone out. Humming under his breath, Ryan's hand passed over the entry wound, and when he turned it over, a bloody pebble fell to the ground.

"There, that should help him out. I'd apply pressure or something, but we have to get going." Ryan opened the front passenger door and climbed inside, trying not to show how much energy that cost. He placed the pack at his feet. Pressure was applied to the leg wound, and the man was carried to the back seat. Ryan was nearly out of his bag of tricks and wanted to be sick. His fingers intertwined, making him appear calm, but he did it so they wouldn't see the tremors or sweating palms. *Maintain appearances.*

He was in an unfamiliar country with no resources or passport, and there were little to no choices. His capture was bound to happen. It was just a matter of when. If his plan worked, no innocent bystanders would be killed or hurt. Ryan had no qualms or misgivings when *the bad guy* died. They chose that life, and as a result, they paid for their actions. He would try and throw up elsewhere.

"There's a village eight miles up the road." Ryan pointed west. The injured man and his companions were silent. The man with the phone drove. The woodlot continued on the north side of the road, and on the south, farmer's fields stretched as far as he could see. The landscape must have been incredibly hard to farm or clear. Stone fences in various states of repair bordered most fields and were rather picturesque.

To say the community was a village would have been an understatement. The built-up area consisted of an intersection of two main roads. The structures were older but well-maintained. One building wedged between a bar and possibly a post office was painted bright red with flower pots hanging to either side of the front door. Nearby was a bright yellow home with striped blue shutters. Across the street was another pub, and Ryan shook his head. The community couldn't have had more than fifty people, but there were two bars. A series of homes stretched west at the T junction, and more shops lined both sides of the road north.

"Just pull over here. I'll be back soon." The man was texting on his phone one-handed while driving, giving him side glances. Whoever he worked for would know of the capture while missing a few of the finer details, no doubt. The Land Cruiser parked across from the black and red tavern. Beer posters decorated a bay window, and to either side of the front door, three-foot iron pots held a variety of green plants and yellow flowers.

"Help your friend. I'll be back soon. Don't go anywhere. I don't have a car." Ryan picked up the backpack and slammed the SUV's door, leaving the stunned Asian men behind. After two steps, he wanted to cheer. He was an actor and didn't know the lines or what would happen. *I'm just playing my part and hoping it works.*

The red telephone box near the corner wasn't just for show. A young woman carrying a small dog had just left, closing the door before heading west. Having a god talk to him was one thing, but he needed to see if his mother was okay and let her know he was fine. But first, he had to find Carrick.

Ryan's hand reached for the door handle to the pub when he caught a glimpse of his reflection in the glass panel and gasped.

He would be dead within the hour.

CHAPTER 39

2560 B.C. Giza Plateau

Ptah-Du-Amun wiped the tears from his eyes, and sorrow broke his heart. Another temple had fallen, and not only had the priest been killed, but his family as well. The news struck like a dagger in his heart and was nearly his undoing. Tefibi had been his assistant for a decade and was not only a great man, but he was like a son.

After seventy-four years, the high priest was a bent, frail man, but his spirit blazed like a furnace in which many would bask in his warmth—even momentarily. As a man of faith, he represented the pinnacle of the order, but in later years, Ptah-Du-Amun preferred to become lost in his readings and to train his replacement. Death held no fear, for he knew the secrets others falsely claimed to possess. Fools.

The order of Osiris had gone too far in forming an army and imposing their will on the people. Instead of defending the land against the barbarians of the north, they systematically wiped out anything to do with Anubis. Pharaoh Djoser, the self-proclaimed high priest of the sun god, Ra, offered to remain neutral in the war. At the same time, the gods of darkness battled, Djoser stood in the light and couldn't care less. The pharaoh was busy and had petitioned the architects to design a temple in his name. The new location would be three or four days south of the Kher Neter plateau. He wanted to build as far away from the necropolis as possible but use the stone quarries nearby. The high priest shook his head. Ra did not speak to Pharaoh Djoser the way Anubis whispered in his ear—sacrilege for even voicing such an opinion, but the truth nonetheless.

Ptah-Du-Amun studied the temple complex and knew an era would end soon. The shelves containing the knowledge of the ancients would be burned, and all artifacts destroyed. But most of the material was copies, and the originals were hidden and preserved. Should the hall of records ever be destroyed, the gods would weep, and no one would escape their ire—in the physical world or beyond the veil.

If the last temple complex of Anubis were destroyed, the great carving of the jackal god would be next. The massive sculpture had been an affront to the Osiris priests for hundreds of years, but the builders wouldn't allow that to happen. Without the builders, the pharaoh's projects would never see the light of day, and the architect's planning would halt. Rumors of altering the jackal's face were whispered, but the lion's body would remain to appease the builders. Ptah-Du-Amun prayed that such speculations were wrong.

"Master!" Aken rushed into the temple's study, wide-eyed and sweating. The oil lamp shook in his hand, making the shadow leap. "The Osiris army is nearly here."

"How soon?" Ptah-Du-Amun brushed his robes and used the writing desk to stand. He reached out to grasp Aken's hand. He had proven a worthy student with a sharp mind and a devoutness that would be hard to surpass.

"Very soon." He placed the lamp on the table and laid both hands on Ptah-Du-Amun's shoulders. "There is time for you to leave. We can hide and get others to help. We can form our own army and take back the temple."

Ptah-Du-Amun shook his head. Raising a force was voted down decades ago by a gathering of priests, and he had honored their decision despite his misgivings. "Too late for myself, but *you*, on the other hand, have a chance. Come with me."

He led Aken into the dressing chamber where his robes and trappings of the high priest were on display.

He removed a sachel from a peg and then opened the display cabinet.

"No! You can't!" Aken held out a hand, but it was batted aside.

Ptah-Du-Amun removed the collar that had been passed down for thousands of years and confirmed him as the high priest of Anubis. Inscriptions were etched onto the precious stones, and the detail was such that the mind had trouble believing the images were not real. The feline on a polished diamond was no larger than the smallest nail on a man's hand. At the right angle, you could see each hair and the curvature of the ears. The eye of Horus, clutched in a falcon's talons, was engraved on a similarly sized emerald. The fist-sized ankh in the middle was made of a dark metal that could not be scratched, dented, or marred. One of the world's most priceless artifacts was tossed into the linen satchel like undergarments, ready to be laundered. Aken was speechless, but Ptah-Du-Amun wasn't finished yet.

The golden ring of Anubis was said to have been given to the original high priest of the order by the god himself. A prayer was inscribed on the inside band that no one could decipher. The direct words of the deity were said to predate language, or that of mankind, and any attempts at translation would be folly. Two ankhs rested to either side of a raised jackal head with emeralds for eyes. Silver and gold were mixed with an unknown alloy, and the ring never tarnished or needed cleaning.

Ptah-Du-Amun's fingers were too small, and he rarely wore them.

The ring was also tossed into the bag.

"Come. We are not done." Ptah-Du-Amun led Aken into his library and gestured to the top shelf. "Hand me the third scroll on the left, held with the leather band."

He was too old to climb the chair, but the young man could easily reach it. Ptah-Du-Amun had never opened the chart, but he had learned the secret at the feet of his predecessor. *I will see you soon, my friend.*

For the next ten minutes, he instructed Aken on how to read the chart and what the lines and dashes meant. Even if the scroll were to fall into the wrong hands, it would be useless without the prayer. Ptah-Du-Amun only had to repeat the chant a few times before Aken had it memorized.

"Where you go, place your trust in Anubis. For where he guides, your step will not falter." Ptah-Du-Amun embraced his brother and whispered, "Worry naught. For I will be with you as well."

Aken wiped the tears and slung the sachel over a shoulder as they walked to the temple entrance. "When should I leave?"

Ptah-Du-Amun pointed south toward the line of torches snaking across the desert. "It is time. Goodbye, Aken. May the great one watch over you."

The young man flew into the darkness, sandals flicking up sand in his wake.

"I once could run like the wind, my Lord." Ptah-Du-Amun turned to the north and bowed to the great sculpture. "Perchance, we shall race together all too soon."

Back in the dressing chambers, Ptah-Du-Amun dressed for a final time in the silver robes of the high priest. He made the final adjustments while gazing into a floor-to-ceiling mirror of polished metal. Satisfied and ready, he was about to step outside to greet the army when he stepped toward the reflection. Few things could surprise him at his age, but this was new, and he grinned. "Yes, my Lord."

He bowed to the mirror and recited while performing the prayer's first, second, and third movements. When Ptah-Du-Amun's palm touched the reflection, he spoke the words. The words were passed down in whispers for so long that they were lost in antiquity. Once completed, his mind shone with clarity, and strength flowed into his limbs. A lifetime of aches and pains was gone—a final gift before departing the land of the living.

"I am not worthy, my Lord."

The reply made him weep. Shoulders back and head held erect, Ptah-Du-Amun bowed a final time to the reflection and strode to the temple entrance. The torches were close, and it was time for a final prayer.

He would be dead within the hour.

245

CHAPTER 40

Ryan didn't blink as several seconds passed. The image of an older man with skin like aged leather and bright white hair disappeared from the reflection, but the intensity of the man's eyes lingered in his mind. In awe, Ryan placed his palm against the glass under the stylized Rose & Crown design, copying the man's last movement. Details were already fading, but the words and gestures the high priest imparted remained. This time, a god hadn't opened a door in his mind, but a man. Did the prayers allow the priest to send a message through time? It wasn't just a message. He had *lived* the last few moments of the high priest's life. He could smell the oil burning from the lamp and feel Aken's soft linen robe under his fingers. What other abilities Ptah-Du-Amun possessed, Ryan could only guess and wonder.

Grabbing the brass door handle brought him back to the present.

The tavern had booths lining the window side and seating in the middle. A bar ran the width of the building to the rear. An older, stout man stood behind the counter watching the news on a television mounted in the corner. A woman in a far booth worked on a laptop beside an empty plate and mug.

"Excuse me, but can I ask you a question?" Ryan spoke when the man turned. A bell hanging inside the front door announced his arrival.

"Ye just did."

"Pardon?"

The bartender winked. "You just asked a question, but if you have another, go ahead."

Seriously? "I'm looking for Carrick, and I was hoping you knew where I could find him."

The man wiped his hands on a white towel and shrugged. "Not too sure. Maybe if you asked down the—"

"Stanley! Don't be daft." The woman spun sideways in the booth, shaking a finger. She was his mother's age, in her late forties, with curly dark hair, black-framed glasses, and a black golf shirt with the Guinness logo on the breast pocket. "Answer the man."

"Sorry, Ruby." After a deep sigh, the bartender asked, "Who sent ya?"

Ryan wasn't sure how to answer but decided the truth wouldn't hurt. "Duke Ackley."

The woman whispered, "Holy shite."

"Have a seat, and I'll make the call." The bartender disappeared through a door into the back, not wasting time.

"Can I get you anything?" Ruby closed the laptop and collected her dishes.

From the center table, Ryan caught a glimpse of the red phone booth outside and nodded. He placed the backpack on an empty chair. "I could use some change for the phone. I'm unsure what I need or how much for a long-distance call."

"I think we can do one better than that." She placed the dirty dishes in a gray tub behind the bar and returned with a cordless phone. "Just dial zero-one-one, then the number you want to call."

"Thank you." Ryan's blood pressure spiked as he followed the instructions, dialing his mom's cell phone. Ruby disappeared into the backroom.

After the fourth ring, he thought it would go to voicemail when she picked up.

"Hello?" her voice had a strange echo with background static from the connection, but she had never sounded so good.

"Mom, it's me." Ryan's throat was already closing, and his eyes were watering.

"Oh my, God!"

He had to pull the phone away from his ear. To say his mother was happy would be an understatement.

"I don't have much time, but I had to let you know I'm okay. How are you doing?"

His mother was bawling, and a lone tear rolled down his cheek. "Where are you? What the *hell* is going on?"

"I can't explain right now, but I had to let you know I'm fine. Those people will not be bothering you anymore." Ryan didn't know for sure, but Suit Man's job was to bring him to England, not hound his family.

"The police are involved, and I had to get a lawyer. They want to know where you are and what's happening."

"If they ask, tell them I called, but you don't know anything more. I'm not sure when I'll be home, but everything will be cleared up when I do. Don't worry."

"Worry? Are you kidding me? I haven't slept in days thinking you're dead!" He knew that tone and winced.

"I know. I'm sorry. This is the first chance I had to call."

The bell chimed, and when the man walked inside, Ryan knew Carrick had arrived. The man's resemblance to the duke was without question. Tall, balding, with a ring of white hair above the ears, but this man had a bright white goatee and sideburns. He was smartly dressed in a blue shirt and black pants, and his cane thumped on the dark slate floor before sitting across from Ryan.

"Mom, I have to go. I'll call again soon if I can."

"No! Don't go. Where are you? I need to know what's going on!"

Hanging up on his mother was one of the hardest things he had ever done, and it tore at his heart. "I have to go, Mom. I love you. Talk to you soon."

"Ryan! I love you too, but—"

He placed the phone on the table and reached out across the table. "Ryan Petey. Sorry about that."

"Carrick Ackley, but from your expression, I'm guessing you already knew that." Instead of an English accent, the man spoke like an American. The man's grip was firm. Then he gestured toward the phone. "I hope everything is okay."

"No, but that's why I'm here."

"What has my little brother done now?" Carrick slid the cane between him and the table, interlaced his fingers on top, and leaned forward. "It must be serious because we haven't spoken in nearly twenty years, and he called me late last night."

How could you live so close to each other and not speak? As an only child, Ryan had no idea and didn't understand. "I'm not sure what I can say or should hold back, but he knows where a friend is being held and said he would let you know where."

Carrick leaned back, studying him. "Yes. He told me, but I want to know your involvement in all this."

Ryan didn't know who to trust, and despite being told to contact Carrick for information, he was hesitant to speak of what was happening. Hopefully, the duke's brother would be good with a partial story. "I was kidnapped from home and—"

"Canadian? Your accent gives it away." Carrick was sharp.

"Yes. I was brought here, and after the estate was attacked, the duke told me to run and mentioned you could help. That's why I'm here."

White, bushy eyebrows were raised, and a half-smile deepened the lines on his face into deep crevasses. "There are more holes in that story than a block of Swiss cheese. What do the men watching the building have to do with everything?"

Not only was Carrick sharp, but he apparently missed nothing. Much like his brother.

Ryan may be jumping from the frying pan into the fire, but options were limited. He had to help Crystal and go outside with the Asian men. Was she in the same place that they were going to take him? There were no guarantees, and it was time to roll the dice.

"It started last Thursday when I was on my way to the mall ..." Ryan didn't go into details, but he highlighted the last five days within a few minutes, then sat back to wait.

Carrick's face never changed. Ryan had seen slabs of granite with more expression. "Prove it."

A hand reached for the pocket of pebbles, but he didn't think tricks would convince Clive's brother. Ryan leaned down and placed the fingertips of one hand on the slate floor. He didn't call to the slate but to the stone cellar beneath the building and the limestone foundation. A few seconds passed while the deep resonate vibrations filtered through the different materials. When the building shook, a dozen liquor bottles rattled together on a shelf, and a wine glass fell from an overhead rack, shattering behind the bar. Carrick abruptly stood, and the chair tipped back. The cane rattled to the floor as dust fell from an overhead beam, spotting the table and two men like snowflakes. Ryan stopped singing and sat upright, waiting.

Ruby and Stanley rushed out of the back room, panicked, and Carrick whispered, "Okay, son. You'll have my help."

CHAPTER 41

Zhong Shi Chen sat in the Land Cruiser and glanced at his phone for the third time in five minutes. "We have to get going. How is your leg, Wu?"

"Painful. I still don't understand what happened."

Chen silently agreed. Nothing was making sense, but there was little choice. His team was committed. A short while ago, the old white man hobbled into the tavern, and Ryan Petey hadn't come out. Under the board and body, in the back, were pistols and rifles. The English overreacted to firearms in their country and were forced to keep a low profile.

Extraction was twenty minutes away at Martin's Flying Club, and they were under orders to proceed directly to the rendezvous. Chen was only missing one thing—the actual mission target, which he allowed to walk away. There would be hell to pay.

"I'm going in." He unbuckled the seatbelt but paused when the tavern's front door opened. A woman in a black shirt ran across the road carrying a white piece of paper. He tried to look away, but she ran around and knocked on his window.

"Here you go, dear."

The window was lowered an inch, and she shoved paper inside before returning to the tavern.

Thanks for the ride, but I had to leave. See you in Peru.

Zhong Shi Chen crumpled the note and threw it on the seat. "Peru? That makes no sense. Stay here."

He ripped open the tavern door and stormed inside.

The bartender asked, "What can I get for you?"

Chen ignored the man and checked the bathrooms and kitchen, but they were empty. The waitress sat in the booth smiling, and he wanted to shoot off her face.

"He went out the back door ten minutes ago. Sorry, sweetie. Would you like a menu? Will you be staying?"

Their laughter followed him outside as he sprinted to the vehicle. He took a picture of the note and sent it in. Chen ignored Wu's groans of pain and turned to the last member of the team, Mark Lim. "Did you see any cars leaving?"

"Nothing." Lim's hand was all bloody from keeping pressure on Wu's leg. Despite his training, Lim was the youngest on the team and had the least field experience, but he was holding up.

Chen's phone vibrated with an incoming message. "About time. We're leaving this fucking country. We'll be at the extraction point in thirty minutes. Petey isn't our problem anymore."

The Land Cruiser handled the winding roads as Chen followed protocol. The sim card was destroyed, pieces scattered along the countryside, followed by the phone. Escape and evasion training dictated that he ensured they weren't being followed, but with the tight time restrictions, he had to drive directly to the plane. Not that backtracking would have worked on the open roads. You could see for miles at a time, so when the white low-profile Ford police cruiser flew like a race car along the straight road a quarter mile behind, Chen had time. "Lin, ditch the guns out the window. Now!"

The young man struggled. "I can't get at them. Zhang is too heavy and blocking the hatch."

"Fuck!" Chen pounded the wheel. The phone was destroyed, and he couldn't call for backup or update command. He stepped on the gas, and the Land Cruiser shot forward.

"When we turn the corner ahead, I'm pulling over. Ditch Zhang and the weapons. We'll keep going, and hopefully, we'll just get a speeding ticket."

However, another cruiser was parked sideways across the lanes when the road turned north after the bend. They were trapped.

"We're fucked," Lim whispered.

Chen agreed. "No more English, and don't say anything to anyone unless it is through a translator and a lawyer. Understood?"

He pulled over as the Salisbury police officers used the roof to brace the H&K G36C carbine rifles. When the cruiser skidded to a halt on their bumper, blocking them, Chen turned off the engine and lifted his hands. He wasn't worried about the lengthy prison sentence. At home, he would have been killed instead of incarcerated. The crumpled piece of paper rolled off the passenger seat onto the floor mat, and Chen whispered, "Well played, asshole."

▲ ▲ ▲

Sergeant Annie Wickman replayed the audio recording for Inspector Percy. "The call was traced to southern England. We have the exact coordinates."

With the extended warrant, they had the full cooperation of the phone company and internet provider. While traumatized after her ordeal, Julie Petey was the only lead the Toronto police services had, and no resources were spared. The Durham Regional Police tactical helicopter was unable to track the suspect vehicle. Ryan Petey was believed to be in the north Oshawa or Peterborough area of Ontario until Julie's cell phone rang at 05:04 hours on Monday morning.

Percy had listened to the recording twice while reading from the transcribed notes. "Any chance Ryan is routing the call through a computer?"

Annie shook her head and tapped the screen. "Zero. Rural southern England. I found the location on Google Maps. I doubt they have internet."

Percy flicked the report with a finger. "This is enough for the chief to bring in the RCMP and CICIS so they can alert Interpol. Extradition procedures will bring him home if he remains in the area."

The Canadian Security Intelligence Services was the only agency in the country capable of alerting law enforcement overseas. Annie wished she could start the ball rolling without federal government oversight—time was wasted, and every minute counted. Detective McCallan had all the forensic evidence, from fingerprints and epithelial to video recording, that Ryan Petey was involved or responsible for eight deaths, maybe more.

"Anything I can do to speed things up?" Annie was ready to book a flight.

Percy chuckled. "Not right now. Maintain monitoring of the subject's mother. That will be the breakthrough. Your reports are detailed enough to, hopefully, expedite the big machine into action. Right now? Go home and rest. I have another project coming down the pipe and want you as lead. Good job, Sergeant."

Annie read the report again and listened to the audio before finding the answer. She knew how to speed up the process. At the twenty-two-second mark, the subject stated, "...*those people will not be bothering you anymore*." Ryan Petey could be on an international killing spree. Clearly, he was dangerous to the health and well-being of the United Kingdom. The updated report was filed and submitted for consideration, and the quote was highlighted. If that didn't light a fire under someone's ass, nothing would.

CHAPTER 42

"Get down, and if you say one thing we don't like, you're dead."

Crystal recognized the distinct sound of a slide being engaged on a pistol. Tears rolled down her cheeks before being absorbed into the material of the burka. She dropped hard enough to bruise her knees as her forehead flattened on the stone floor.

"Do you know where Ryan Petey is or where he could be?" The Asian man's accent was hard to understand.

"No."

The gun was pressed into the base of her skull, and she whimpered.

"Are you sure?"

"Yes!"

Another man spoke, and his voice was deep and smooth. "If you were to take an educated guess, where do you think Mr. Petey would run for safety."

Crystal hesitated, and the muzzle of the pistol pressed harder. "He would go home to Toronto. He worries about his mother!"

The pressure eased at the back of her head but didn't disappear. The same man asked, "And if he couldn't get home?"

"He would call."

The pressure disappeared, and footsteps walked away. Two men whispered to each other, and she strained to make anything out but failed.

"Miss Kowalska, with what you know about Mr. Petey's abilities, do you believe they are real?"

"One hundred percent real."

The Asian man yelled, "If you don't know where he is, you are useless!"

Crystal was about to speak, but no questions were asked. She was terrified, not stupid.

A full minute passed before the second man spoke. "What is your relationship with Ryan Petey?"

Shit. "He asked me questions at the museum a few days ago. I had never met him before and was only trying to find out how he could manipulate heavy stones. Nothing more."

The men whispered again, and the second man asked, "Where would someone go with his abilities? Your best guess."

"Cairo." The answer came to mind without much thought.

"Why?"

Crystal swallowed the lump in her throat. *I'm sorry, Ryan. I hope I'm wrong.* "He has the supposed abilities of the ancient Egyptians and can manipulate stone. Ryan believes that's how the monolithic rocks were moved and shaped."

The men spent a few minutes whispering before rough hands grasped her by the arms, nearly carrying her toward the elevator. Before the doors opened, the Asian's voice carried down the hall. "I can get men on the ground within the hour."

The other man added, "I'll handle the flight."

Once inside, she was turned around. As the doors closed, she glanced up through lowered eyes, then stifled a gasp.

▲ ▲ ▲

The older light green Fiat 500 was one of the smallest cars Ryan had seen, but while he was comfortable, Carrick's knees were a quarter-way up the steering wheel, even with the seat all the way back. Ruby handed over her keys, and moments after slipping out the back door, Carrick was on the phone with the police. The next call was to his brother.

The heated argument lasted twenty minutes as they drove on back country roads. "You wanted to help, and you're bloody well going to give it or shut the hell up."

The duke's raised voice came through the phone, but Ryan could not understand what he was saying. Carrick didn't seem perturbed and kept his eyes forward. While his brother ranted, the phone was lowered to his lap as they turned north and were quickly inside a small village. They parked in front of a bakery before the phone was picked up. "Are you done yet? Just make it happen, and text me the details."

The call was disconnected, and Ryan asked, "What's going on? Can you tell me where they're holding Crystal?"

"Dubai, in the UAE, but there are complications. I'm guessing you don't have a passport, and the authorities are after you."

"I have nothing, and I've never had a passport."

Carrick turned slightly in the bucket seat. "I don't have the resources Clive has, or had, at his disposal, but he wanted me to help you, and I've decided to do so."

Ryan didn't know where to begin and had a dozen questions. "What happened with you and your brother?"

"We worked together for many years fulfilling orders if you know what I mean, but I was nearly caught in New York. I couldn't do the job anymore, and I met a woman. I walked away, and he never forgave me." He gestured out the window. "I missed my country, so I moved back recently to where I grew up. I have a small home around the corner from the Rose & Crown."

Ryan had enough pieces to guess the answer, but he had to hear it. "What was your brother going to do with me?"

Carrick's fingers drummed on the steering wheel, and he took a deep breath before beginning. "If someone needed a piece of artwork or statue, we secured the item. Several people in the world could care less about certain legalities and would pay quite handsomely. We were selective on the clients and operated by word of mouth only, keeping a low profile. One job every few years soon turned into one every six months. However, Clive got a request from the black market auctioneer, and that's when I left."

"They just didn't sell artwork, did they?"

"No." Carrick had trouble meeting his eyes. "An incredible amount of money was being offered, and soon, my brother began to appraise items for the auctioneer."

It made him sick to learn of a dark side to the world Ryan didn't even know existed. "How much was I worth?"

Carrick shrugged. "I don't know for sure, but after your demonstration and from what you've said … priceless? I think the bidding would start at fifty billion and rapidly go up. There is no comparison."

"Holy shit." Ryan was dumbfounded and didn't know how to respond.

"That makes you the most expensive item in the world that's mobile. I don't know how it plays out from here, but when that money is thrown about, all stops will be pulled out."

A woman holding a toddler's hand entered the bakery, and his gut instinct began to scream. "I need to warn my mom. Now!"

Carrick handed over his cell phone, but the recording stated that his mother's phone number was no longer in service.

CHAPTER 43

When Detective Trish McCallan received the update from intelligence, she wrapped up a thirteen-hour shift and drove home. She had no choice but to wait on further developments before the case against Ryan Petey progressed. Even with her detective pay grade, she couldn't afford to live in Toronto and had to commute. Dedicated to her career, Trish never married and had no children. Dating has been a series of hits and misses over the years, and it wasn't until after her forty-eighth birthday she discovered the reason. She'd been playing for the wrong team.

Whether she was dating a woman or a man, her job came first. That's enough to stress any relationship to the breaking point. Retirement was getting closer, and while she was comfortable alone, she looked forward to a time when she could share it with someone. *However, that someone is probably going to be a golden retriever.* Until then, she lived in a one-bedroom condo near the highway in Pickering—a thirty-minute commute.

Trish threw a quick meal in the microwave and then showered. Developing a routine after work was important and helped switch off the "cop" brain and transition into civilian mode. Many officers took that time to work out, while some drank, but she liked to read. She had recently started the Harry Bosch series after catching an episode from the television adaptation. Connelly's novels were addictive, even if procedures were thrown out the window.

She was halfway through eating when an idea sparked, and Trish couldn't let go. Ten minutes later, she was dressed in jeans and an old green St. Patrick's Day T-shirt, heading west on Highway 401 back into Toronto. While off-duty, she didn't carry her Glock, but she would only ask Julie a few questions and then enjoy a few days off work.

After the officer's bodies were discovered, units entered Petey's home. Enough evidence was found to consider it an extension of the crime scene, and it was treated accordingly. Thousands of photographs were taken, and the pistol found in the kitchen was identified as police issue. However, that wasn't the murder weapon, and they couldn't find it. Ryan's bedroom had been searched, and a hard drive was previously removed from the computer. Julie escaped from her kidnappers, and her son took her place. That was the official story from the lawyer and the statement given to the police, but Trish wasn't buying it. There were no records of any flights departing the airport at that hour, and because of the surrounding rural neighborhoods, there were flight restrictions until six thirty in the morning. Like the others, she believed Ryan to be hiding until he called his mother early this morning. The story of the kidnappers and the unscheduled flight was back in play.

It was just after noon when Trish parked down the street of the Petey home. Intelligence had pulled physical surveillance and had placed cameras to monitor. Officers dressed as hydro repairmen had installed a device on the streetlamp outside, with a complete view of the front and driveway. With the importance of the case jumping several levels, she took time to study the home. The curtains were drawn, and Julie's car was in the driveway. A piece of plywood covered the front porch where the firemen had to destroy the stone slab to free her, and no others were watching the home—as far as she could tell.

Trish was never one for carrying a purse and used a man's wallet with her badge and identification. Feeling naked without her gun, she locked the car and knocked on the door.

It took a few minutes, but when Julie opened the door dressed in a knee-length blue sleeping gown, Trish was taken aback. While she hadn't met Julie previously, she had only seen pictures, and there was a sharp contrast. The woman looked like she hadn't slept in a week, with dark circles under her eyes, and was beyond taking care of herself. Her hair was a tangled mess and needed a shower. Her cheeks looked hollow, most likely from not eating properly. With her son missing and recent kidnapping, the fact that she was out of bed was a good sign. Hopefully, she had family or friends for support.

"How can I help you?"

"I'm Detective Trish McCallan from the Toronto Police Services. I want to ask you a few questions, Miss Petey." She automatically showed the badge and flipped to the ID before tucking the wallet back in her pocket.

Julie glanced up and down the street. "Where's your uniform and cruiser?"

"I'm off duty, but I'm working on your case. I just had a few questions, and then I'll leave you alone."

She hesitated. "All meetings are supposed to be with my lawyer present."

"You are not obligated to answer anything if you don't want to or are unsure if there are legal implications. I'm just trying to find your son. He may be in trouble, and I want to help."

Thanks, Bosch. That line never gets old.

It took a while to process, but Julie pushed the door open and nodded for her to come in. The kitchen had had little to no changes, and the table was to the side. Detectives and forensics had gone through every cupboard, box, and drawer. As Trish knew all too well, placing items back in their exact spot wasn't likely to happen. The living room was in better shape, and by the blankets and pillow, Julie was sleeping, resting more likely, on the couch.

"Do you have anyone that can help you?" Trish sat on an overstuffed chair, and Julie sat on the couch, wrapping a blanket over her shoulders.

"I have a sister, Jen, who lives in Vancouver, but she can't fly out here."

Trish was used to taking notes when talking and felt awkward making constant eye contact. "Do you have any friends or family overseas?"

"Overseas?" Julie rubbed a hand through her hair before shaking her head. "I don't, but my ex-husband has extended family in Italy or used to, I'm not sure. They were old."

"Has Ryan ever been in contact with them or your ex-husband?"

"Zero contact. They never reached out, and my ex is an asshole who doesn't want to know his own son." A common statement Trish had heard many times, one she didn't understand in the slightest. Julie held back a yawn.

"Does Ryan have a passport? Has he reached out to you at all?" The technique was designed to throw a person off balance, hoping they revealed more or concealed the truth. Ask a simple leading question, followed by another with a known answer to test the witness's credibility.

If Julie was flustered, it didn't show, but fatigue and stress could mask feelings. "Ryan never had a passport, and yes. He called me this morning."

Trish feigned surprise. "That's great! Is he okay? Did he mention where he was staying?"

"He said he was fine, but I know he was trying to make me feel better." Julie yawned again, and her eyes were barely open. "No idea where he was. He hung up on me."

She was going to lose her soon, so Trish made a decision. Hopefully, one she wouldn't regret or tell her captain. She needed Julie to open up and trust her. "I want to help if I can. Why don't you lay down, and I'll clean up a little? I'll be right here if you need anything."

Extending a hand to someone in need was an old ploy, and Trish felt a twinge of guilt. On duty, the move was a viable tactic to gain information, but off duty? Lines were being blurred, but if it paid off, she could get answers.

"Seriously? I could use the help."

Trish got up and extended a hand. Julie blinked several times, then reached out.

After laying the mattress flat and finding clean sheets, Julie was asleep before Trish quietly closed the door.

"I can do this." She stood with a hand on her hip, studying the mess. Before tackling the kitchen, she ensured Julie's cell phone was charging.

CHAPTER 44

After two hours of cleaning, the kitchen was done. Short of renting a steam cleaner for the tiles, it had never looked so good. The living room wasn't too bad, and it received a pass after shifting the furniture back into position. Ryan's bedroom, however, was a total disaster, and she cleared a path to the desk. Forensics couldn't find anything pertinent to the case in the mess, and most likely, they focused on weapons or drugs.

Giving up, Trish returned to the kitchen, tired. There was no sign of life from Julie, and she would probably be out for hours yet. She dug a business card from her wallet and wrote her cell number on the back with a quick note: *Give me a call if you need to talk, Trish.*

As the card was placed next to Julie's cell, the phone chirped twice and was silent. The display flashed "Not connected to the network." Curious, Trish checked her phone, and there were no problems.

When a horn sounded and a vehicle backup warning beeped, Trish dropped everything and ran to the kitchen window overlooking the front yard. A yellow appliance company truck backed up the driveway near the front door.

After twenty-six years as a police officer, she still didn't believe in coincidences.

Was the front door locked? *Shit!* As soon as she turned the deadbolt, someone knocked. The peephole showed a skinny white man, twenty-five years old, in blue coveralls, holding a clipboard. Inside the kitchen, she pulled the blinds aside as two similarly dressed men opened the back of the truck and maneuvered a box the size of a washer onto a dolly. Trish hesitated, and the man knocked again, then turned to the guys in the back of the truck and shrugged.

Had Julie ordered new appliances?

When the next knock came, Trish was on the other side of the door. "Who is it?"

"Best Deals Appliances, ma'am. Delivering your new washer and dryer."

Alarm bells were ringing. "Just leave them outside. Thank you."

The man laughed. "Wish we could. You have to inspect and sign for them. Julie Petey, correct?"

"I didn't order anything!" Trish had enough and went to get her cell phone to call for backup when the screen door opened, and the man tried the handle.

There was no response, but a shoulder slammed into the door, making the wall shake. The men in the truck had given up any pretenses of delivering. One darted up the driveway to go around back, and the other went to the front. Only then did she notice the truck had backed far enough to block the surveillance camera—if it was being monitored, no one could see.

"Where's my fucking gun!" Despite countless self-defense courses and receiving a blue belt in jui-jitsu in her thirties, Trish felt naked without her Glock. The large knife from the wooden block would have to do. She held the blade reversed along her forearm.

Blows pounded at the rear door, but the steel security bar would hold off most attacks. She picked up her phone and was about to call 911 when the front door exploded off the hinges and slammed into the closet. Trish didn't have time to think and darted around the corner, knife leading the way. Had the edge been sharp, she would have cut through to the bone, but it sliced through the material and an inch into the man's upper shoulder. She didn't notice the gun.

"Bitch!"

The hallway was narrow, and there was no room for the attacker to fire, so he punched with his left. She had fought gang bangers that telegraphed a strike less, and Trish easily ducked and grunted. The knife slammed into the man's chest with all her force, point first, and her hand slipped off the handle and along the blade, slicing her fingers.

He fell back into the wall and laughed.

The ballistic vest under the overalls saved him, and the knife fell to the floor.

A pistol aimed at her forehead from four feet away. "Get on your fucking knees."

The second man stood in the doorway, unconcerned with the fight, watching the road. Trish eyed the knife, but there wasn't a chance. The general rule for police is to maintain a five-foot distance between them and a subject, plus a foot for every inch over six feet tall. Reaction time for a gun, even already drawn, goes down inside that range. Within four feet, she had a chance.

Darting forward, she drove the palm heel of her right hand under his chin, but his head jerked, and the strike was only a graze. Yet, it was enough of a distraction for her to grab the lapel of the overalls and drive her knee into his groin. Trish tried again but hit the top of his thigh. Despite the second miss, the first did enough damage that he collapsed, whimpering and gasping for breath.

She ran into the living room, fingers dripping blood, looking for anything to use but came up short. Throwing a lamp or television remote wasn't worth it. Regardless, she ran out of time.

The second man stepped over his companion and grinned. He was six-foot-three inches, with a dark shadow of a beard and brown hair brushed to the side. Trish had seen football players smaller than him. She didn't waste her breath but stepped in close, raising her hands to guard her head.

"I like it when women fight. You wouldn't believe how much of a fucking turn-on that is." Turkish or Syrian, she couldn't tell, but definitely a pig.

Wishing she had never stopped martial arts training, Trish threw a feint at his head, then snap-kicked toward his right knee with the ball of her foot. He didn't move, and the kick bounced off with no damage. A large hand blurred and slapped her across the face when she tried the same strike on the other side.

Trish's feet left the ground, and she fell on her shoulder, seeing stars.

The first man had gained his feet and ran forward, kicking her in the ribs like punting a football into the end zone. Her ribs took the full brunt, and the air whooshed out of her lungs. Trish was lifted off the ground and flew onto the couch, ribs screaming in pain.

A hand lifted her by the hair, and she stared into the first man's face. "That fucking hurt like hell, bitch. You're going to pay for that."

While stunned and in pain, she wasn't one to give up. Her right hand grasped the side of his face, and her thumb dug deeply into his eye socket as her fingers found purchase under the jaw. Her blood smeared across his cheek, but her grip was solid.

Trish squeezed.

He let go of her hair and tried to peel her hand away, but she was strong enough to resist. As the second man grabbed her shoulders from behind, her right thumb scooped the orb out of the socket. The eyeball swung side to side like a grotesque chandelier across the man's cheek connected by the optic nerve. An arm thicker than her leg wrapped around her throat, lifting her off the ground.

Turning her head toward the inner elbow gave her enough room to breathe for at least a few seconds longer as the other man dropped to his knees. She tried kicking backward and raking the side of her shoe down his leg, but nothing worked. Fingernails dug deep gouges into the man's forearm, drawing blood, but he didn't flinch.

"You guys are pathetic." The third man walked into the living room. As everything slowly turned black around the edges of her vision, Trish tried to avoid the wet cloth the new man held against her nose and mouth. She lifted both feet to thrust forward, but he was too close. She held her breath as long as possible but inhaled when the arm around her throat loosened. The wet cloth reminded her of grass clippings after a rainfall, but the smell had a different effect. Her grip relaxed, and her body went limp.

Her last thoughts were of Julie. *Sorry, I tried.*

The man behind her laughed and didn't bother lowering her to the ground. Trish fell like a sack of potatoes and was out for the count.

CHAPTER 45

Ryan and Carrick didn't wait long for the call to give them the all-clear. After returning Ruby's car, he followed the duke's brother to a narrow townhome a minute's walk from the tavern. The living room had low beams with piles of books on the corner desk and coffee table. Instead of a television, an oil painting of a sailboat chasing a sunset hung above the fireplace.

"I'll be right back." Carrick went upstairs, and Ryan sat on the couch worrying. Last year, Julie disconnected the landline telephone since they were mainly using their cells. Ryan struggled to remember a friend's number programmed into his cell phone but came up short. Email? Twitter? He had a list of passwords in a specific file, but again, it was stored on a phone he no longer had.

Carrick came down the stairs. He had changed into a navy golf shirt, gray slacks, and deck shoes. He carried a leather bag that resembled a doctor's satchel.

"I have to see if someone can check in on my mom, but I'm unsure who to ask."

Carrick placed his bag on the floor and pulled out a flip phone. "How about I call the local police and ask for a wellness check? They'll send an officer over."

Ryan gave him the details, and when Carrick was talking with the Toronto police, he used a false name and address, citing he was a concerned uncle and Julie was going through a mental health crisis. After hanging up, he destroyed the flip phone by snapping it in half.

"It's a burner. It's time to start covering our tracks. I have a few more if needed." He sat on the couch facing Ryan. "I think it's time for us to talk. As I've said, I'm willing to help if you wish. You gave me quite the demonstration and a few more gray hairs. Fill me in on the details, and I'll help come up with a game plan. But if you wish to go alone, I'll also help and send you on your way."

Ryan took a deep breath. "Fair enough. First, I've been having these dreams. Sometimes I'm awake, and other times …"

Like his confession to a deity, Ryan didn't hold anything back and wasn't sure why. For some reason, he trusted the man, and without much besides his intuition, he had to trust it. Carrick, to his credit, didn't crack a smile or laugh. When he was done speaking, they sat in silence for a minute.

Carrick rubbed his chin. "I've been around the world several times and heard many tales, but that one takes the cake. Your friend, Crystal, is being held, so you will cooperate. You've figured that out?"

Ryan nodded.

"I'm not going to lie. There are good odds someone is also thinking of levering your mother against you."

The thought made him sick, but he agreed. "That's why I want to warn her."

"How far is Montreal from Toronto?"

He was taken aback by the question and guessed. "Five hours by car? Not too sure."

Carrick leaned forward and patted his shoulder. "I know a man there. I can't guarantee anything, but I'll see if he can check in on your mother."

"Thank you." Anything was better than nothing.

"Now, that leads me to what you want to do now and if you want help. The choice is yours, young man."

Ryan had to ensure his mother was okay, and his second thoughts were for Crystal. Not because of the physical attraction but because it was his fault she was roped into this mess. Without him, she would have been fine.

"I'd like to rescue Crystal, but I must stop whoever's hunting me." He recalled the dream and his talk with the god, adding, "I have a plan afterward, where I'll be fine. No one will be able to touch me then."

Carrick's eyebrows rose. "Last question. Do you want to go alone, or would you like some help?"

Moving granite slabs for money didn't sound like a good idea, especially if he didn't want to be found. Would he take up mining in hopes of finding a rare gem? That left committing crimes and breaking into a bank vault or robbing people. "Help, please. But I don't want anyone getting hurt."

"I'm seventy-six years old, and you wouldn't believe some of the things I've done throughout my life. I'm not proud of some of them, but I wouldn't change a thing. *You*, however, are something special, and I'd be honored to help."

Ryan held out his hand, and they shook. Carrick had a surprisingly strong grip like his brother.

"Where do we start?"

"Well." Carrick stood and opened the painting like a cupboard door. "We can play their game or make them play ours. I'm partial to the latter."

Behind the canvas was a safe, and he laid his thumb on a scanner and punched in a long code. Inside were stacks of cash at the back and jewelry boxes in the front next to several brown envelopes. Carrick removed a passport and two bundles of money, placing them into his travel pack.

"In for a penny, in for a pound," he murmured. "Try this on."

He passed Ryan a wide gold ring with two diamonds. Two black circles were on either side of the setting. The band only fit on his index finger, and he was surprised by the weight.

"That's worth 95,000 euros. Try not to lose it. I doubt you'd get that much for it, but you should know what it could be sold. At times, you may need cash or an escape fund. It's all about liquidating assets."

Ryan's eyes widened. He'd never had anything worth that much and found it unsettling. Carrick also slipped on two rings and placed his cell phone inside the safe.

When a knock sounded at the front door, Carrick wasn't surprised. "Let's go."

Ryan was shocked to see the duke's driver outside wearing a T-shirt, shorts, sandals, and a Yankees ball cap. On the curb was a white Range Rover SUV with the engine running.

"Good to see you again, Paul. It's been a long time." The two men shook hands.

"You as well, Mr. Ackley. Glad to see you are doing fine, sir."

Ryan was stunned at first, but then he smiled. He had thought everyone at the estate was killed during the attack. "Yes, thank you. Is everyone okay? I never got to thank Gemma."

He hefted the backpack over a shoulder.

"A little shaken up, but we're good. I'll be sure to pass your message along. However, I think we should be going."

"Yes, quite." Carrick locked the front door as Ryan sat in the back seat.

Once they were underway, Paul performed a series of turns on the country backroads before merging onto the highway south.

Paul glanced over his shoulder. "Sir, we'll be there within the hour."

Ryan asked, "Where are we going, Carrick? I can't fly without a passport."

"That's being taken care of, but I hope you don't get seasick."

He was about to say no, but a memory that wasn't his surfaced. A young priest named Ptah-Du-Amun glutching the gunwale of a wooden boat, violently heaving over the side, wishing he was dead, came to mind. For a brief moment, Ryan could feel the salt water spray on his face and the boat rocking beneath his feet.

His stomach rolled.

Oh shit.

CHAPTER 46

Crystal thought she would be led back to the basement cell and was surprised to be escorted outside and into a waiting car. The Mercedes still had the new car smell, but she didn't get a chance to study the driver or the surroundings. The guard had stayed with her and covered her head with a dark sack that smelled like wet burlap.

Despite being unable to see outside the vehicle, the skyline of Dubai from the eighth floor was recognizable, especially the world's tallest building, the Burj Khalifa. But that wasn't what shocked her before the elevator closed. It was the statue of Osiris between the two men.

2010, the MET gallery was robbed, and a few select pieces, including the statue, went missing. The six-foot bronze figure of the ancient Egyptian god had been on tour with the approval of the Egyptian Ministry of Tourism and Antiquities. It nearly sparked an international incident when it went missing. Crystal was in Pakistan when she heard the news of the theft and was disappointed she had never got the chance to see it. The statue was dated 2,500 B.C. and is considered priceless, one of a kind. Osiris was one of the gods of the dead, usually depicted as wrapped in a shroud and holding a staff and flail. Many statues described the god as having a green face, usually made of jade, but to all appearances, a man. There was no doubt in her mind that it was the same statue that was missing from the museum.

Crystal didn't have time to study the men and barely had time to look out the windows. Did those men steal the statue? Why did they want Ryan? The car ride wasn't long, and she was led out of the backseat into the afternoon heat. The black material of the burka quickly absorbed the heat, turning the inside into a hot, sweaty mess.

"Ah, a returning quest. It must be the service."

Crystal knew that voice and would never forget it. It was the man in the suit that kidnapped her from Ontario. She faltered, and the guard gave her a shove. She fell on a set of steps, bruising her shins and hands, withholding a cry of pain.

"Welcome aboard. If you promise to behave, we can dispense with the hood. How does that sound, Miss Kowalska?"

"I promise." She struggled but eventually gained her feet and pulled the cloth over her head.

The man stood at the entrance to the Gulfstream and gestured for her to board. He was dressed in a light green suit and a white shirt but no tie.

"Glad to hear. Please have a seat. Unfortunately, your old accommodation was removed. I'm sure it wouldn't be the same without your young man."

She took the first single seat on the right. After the lumpy mattress, it was heaven to sink into the cushioned leather.

"Go ahead and remove the face covering. Trust me. I won't be offended. But after we land, I suggest you keep it on." The pilot entered the cabin from the cockpit and retracted the stairs, sealing the jet. The man reached a far seat and pulled out a book.

Unsure of what was going on, Crystal removed the face covering.

"There are no assistants on this flight, so feel free to help yourself. There's a bar up front, and the galley has some delicious sandwiches." He then ignored her and reclined his seat to read.

As the engines fired up, her mouth watered at the thought of real food, and before the jet could taxi on the runway, Crystal made her way to the galley. However, after recalling the bathroom layout, she decided there was no way she would pass up the chance of a hot shower. Ultimately, she stuffed her face with half a roast beef sandwich as the pulsating jet pummeled her with hot water. She used the grab bar and was pressed against the shower wall as the plane left the ground, and her tears flowed unnoticed down the drain.

"I'm going to use every fucking ounce of water and every damned towel."

Crystal was content with the small victories and would take them for now. She never even looked at the phone mounted on the wall.

▲ ▲ ▲

After an hour's drive, Paul brought them to Portsmouth Marina on England's south shore. Masts from sailboats swayed, and gulls banked and dove from above, looking for fish or french fries. A young boy fished off a side pier, his rod bending with a catch or rock; Ryan couldn't tell. The breeze did nothing to remove the cloying scent of fish and saltwater. A man with piercing blue eyes and a square chin, dressed in naval whites, strode across the parking lot and escorted them through a security gate, then to a seventy-nine-foot yacht tied up to the end dock.

"I'm Captain Halvar, and welcome to the Ocean's Pearl. There is a front and upper deck, lounge, and four cabins. With the weather changing, I'd recommend staying indoors. We are also running with only one deckhand and cabin crew, so the trip may be sub-par to our traditional standards." The sunny morning was gone, and low billowing clouds raced across the sky with an eastern breeze.

"I'm sure everything will be just fine. Thank you." Carrick removed his shoes when they stepped on board, placing them in a clear plastic tub near the handrail, and Ryan followed suit.

"Welcome aboard. Enjoy your stay." The captain didn't wait and used the radio on his belt before going about his duties. "Be prepared to cast off."

The lounge had a U-shaped couch with a low coffee table facing another seating area. On the other side was a step up where the dining room and bar resided. Large windows gave a panoramic view, and the tiered ceiling had an intricate design with polished wood and recessed lighting. Carrick went to the bar, and Ryan dropped his pack inside the door.

"Where are we going?" Carrick didn't want to talk in front of the driver. He returned with a rocks glass and a few fingers of dark alcohol on ice and sat in the recliner. Ryan sat opposite the couch.

"France. It should take us eight hours to cross the channel, and we'll meet with a friend of a friend to get you a passport. After that, it's up to you."

An idea had been forming that should check all the boxes. "I have a rough plan …"

With the United Kingdom's population density comes an elevated crime rate. Since 9/11, the number of CCTV cameras has doubled every five years. The government proudly cites one camera for every eleven people in the country to control situations before they happen. In Portsmouth alone, two thousand cameras were installed along the main road and side streets. The roads and traffic were monitored, and so was the port.

When Ryan Petey climbed out of the SUV and was greeted by the captain, three cameras were recording. With the advances in AI and facial recognition software, red flags were raised, but despite the number of cameras and new advancements, they were not monitored individually. The system sent a priority message to the authorities with the screen capture and the all-points bulletin. The alert was placed in a queue behind three-hundred and fifty-seven reports.

CHAPTER 47

At midnight, southwest of Dieppe, France, in the small community of Saint-Valery-en-Caux, the Ocean's Pearl arrived at low tide. The vessel paused long enough for Ryan and Carrick to step onto the dock. Without any fanfare, the yacht turned within the tight confines of the harbor and back across the channel. During the eight-hour cruise, Ryan had time to shower and enjoy a five-star meal the chef had prepared. With traveling through various time zones and the pressure of the last few days, his sleeping schedule was a complete wreck, and he slept when he could. Though he wasn't considered a paying guest, it didn't matter to the crew. While resting, his clothing was laundered and pressed. Gemma's food had disappeared and was replaced with sealed packages of beef jerky, a crackers sleeve, and water bottles.

Ryan had thought the ship was the duke's but learned a favor was called in—good friends to have. Carrick confirmed after the arrangements with the forger and mentioned that his brother would keep a low profile elsewhere. Fingers were pointed at the attack on the estate, and the Duke wanted nothing to do with the fallout. They were on their own.

Saint-Valery-en-Caux marina relied on the honor system for those entering the country to check in with customs at the end of the docks. The hours were posted on the building, from eight o'clock in the morning to eight at night. Carrick was amused at Ryan's worrying as they casually entered the country.

Carrick led them along the walkway, and a dim light standard showed an empty parking lot. He glanced at his watch and muttered.

"Everything okay?" Ryan slipped his arms into the backpack and leaned against the pole.

"The forger knew when we arrived and should have been here by now." Carrick dug into his bag, removing another burner flip phone. He was about to dial when headlights appeared at the end of the parking lot. A white panel van's engine roared as it turned the corner, then skidded to a halt.

A man with a receding hairline, frizzing white hair, and flowing white mustache yelled out the window. "Get in. I think I'm being followed."

Ryan opened the passenger door.

"There's only one seat, kid. Get in the back. Move!"

Ryan crawled between the seats, finding a desk and computer system in the back with a bench along one side. As soon as Carrick was inside, the van darted forward, throwing him into the rear doors and knocking over a white screen.

"They've been following me since I left Paris. At least two vehicles. I didn't have time to make other arrangements or message you, so I came."

Carrick calmly buckled the seat belt. "It's appreciated. Maurice, this is Ryan. Ryan, Maurice."

"Pleased to meet you. Hold on."

The van screeched around a corner, nearly on two wheels, and Ryan flew into the bench seat. Had he not been wearing the backpack, his head would have collided with the interior wall. Ryan slid to the floor, clutching the desk leg with one hand. A thump lifted his ass into the air, and pain shot up his tailbone when he landed. "Jesus …"

"Sorry, kid. Won't be much longer."

He glanced out the window as they flew through a small picturesque town with cobbled streets and a solid wall of homes and storefronts blurring to either side. At the next intersection, Maurice barely slowed when turning left, and then he skidded to a halt. He backed into a narrow driveway between two buildings and shut off the van.

"Keep the doors closed, or the interior light will go on."

The only sounds were the engine ticking and his heart pounding as the minutes passed.

"Down!"

Carrick and Maurice ducked below the dash as a vehicle raced through the street.

"That road eventually connects to the highway south." Maurice waited a minute, then started the van. He backtracked along the streets. "Hopefully, they will follow it as we head east."

Ryan finally had a chance to examine the back of the van. The desk was against the passenger wall, filled with a computer, two printers, and four stainless-steel cases underneath. All items were secured with brackets. Tentatively, Ryan sat on the long bench as they merged onto a highway and felt a sense of relief. They were driving on the right side of the road, like at home.

"Do you know who they were?" Carrick seemed comfortable, and shaking a tail was commonplace.

Maurice chuckled. "I haven't pissed anyone off in a while, and if it were the police, they would have hung back to see what was going on. No idea, but I like to err on the side of caution."

They drove south for an hour, then Maurice turned, taking a dirt road into the countryside. There were no homes or signs, but he seemed to know where he was going. The road path led over a slight rise, and they parked in a clearing ringed by trees. He turned the headlights off but left the engine running.

"Okay, I need to get back there."

Ryan slid behind the driver's seat, and Maurice sat on the bench and turned the computer on. The monitor flipped down from the ceiling on a bracket and swung to the side. He opened the thin stainless steel case. "I only have Austrailian or American for the kid. Which one do you think is best?"

Carrick turned in the passenger seat, appraising Ryan. "Have you ever been to Australia or the States?"

"I went to Orlando once when I was ten. My mom drove. I've never been anywhere else."

Maurice didn't blink. "American it is."

He pulled out the blue passport and had Ryan sit on the end of the bench. A white screen was pulled down from the ceiling. Another case held a camera, and he connected it to the computer. "Don't smile. Just look straight into the camera."

"What about a mustache or wig?" Carrick suggested.

"When's the last time you shaved, kid?"

Embarrassed, Ryan ran a hand over his smooth cheeks, but there was a little stubble coming in on his chin. "Maybe a week ago."

Maurice shook his head. "No one will buy facial hair, but we can alter his face slightly."

He handed Ryan four sticks of gum. "Chew these and place one under your upper lip and two more in your cheeks."

Ryan shifted the chewed gum around until Maurice was satisfied, then the picture was taken. Immediately, the image appeared on the screen.

"That will work." The camera was put away, and he handed Ryan a tissue without looking. He spit the gum inside and tucked the garbage in his backpack.

"Details matter. Let's see." He enhanced the image, focusing on Ryan's brown eyes. There was a subtle hint of green, and Maurice shifted the colored amounts so there was less brown. "Now we can write your eye color as hazel. Let's work on your features."

With the software, he moved the ears lower and changed the shape. Ryan hadn't seen that graphics program before but didn't ask.

"The new picture is very close to your real face, and most custom agents will never know it's been changed. But with facial recognition, the anchor points have shifted, and hopefully, it will be overlooked. It's the details, man."

The picture was printed out and trimmed with the security features added. "This system is good, considering it's the actual unit most passport offices use for authentication."

Once the portrait was laminated to the passport, he handed Ryan a pen. "Your new name is Charlie

Lucas. Make sure you sign." His finger tapped the line. After, he added, "There is a man named Charlie Lucas living in Orlando, Florida, but he is ten years older than you and black. But don't worry about that. If they are at the stage of tearing apart the identity, then it's too late."

The last briefcase held three dozen stamps and inkpads. "You went to the Bahamas once, and let's see …" He chose a red-handled logo. "Costa Rica. Perfect. Lastly, France. You arrived yesterday." He stamped passport two on the front and the France stamp on the last page.

"Carry this in your front pocket for a few days, and it will help give it a weathered look. Don't forget to crease the spine a few times at your picture. Custom agents usually check if the book doesn't naturally open there. I have a contact that will backdate your arrival in the system. You flew into Madrid and took a train to Paris. Not all customs will give you a stamp."

Within thirty minutes, Ryan had new identification and a name.

"Thank you."

Maurice laughed. "Wait 'til the Duke gets the bill. My usual, plus mileage."

Carrick chuckled. "Excellent work, as usual. I still have two of your other passports, and they've never been questioned."

"The magnetic strips are tricky, but if you just find who the passport offices buy their equipment from, the job's easy." Maurice winked.

When a bullet pierced the side of the van, it flew between Ryan and Maurice, blowing up the monitor. A spiderweb crack destroyed the screen, and a hole punched through the other side of the van, scaring the shit out of him.

It happened so fast that Ryan didn't understand what was happening. It missed his shoulder by two feet, but the forger came within inches of death. "Holy shit!"

Before anyone could move, a man screamed, "Ryan Petey, get out of the van, nice and slow, or everyone dies."

CHAPTER 48

"Can you see anyone?" Maurice knelt on the van's floor, and Carrick peeked over the dash.

"Nothing."

"Okay, I'm going to go for the—"

Ryan didn't wait to hear about options and opened the rear doors. That bullet was well-placed and no accident. He wasn't going to chance anyone getting hurt.

"What are you doing? Get down!" Carrick whispered from the front seat. Maurice tried to grab his pant leg, but Ryan was already standing outside. He slammed the doors closed.

"I'm here. Don't hurt anyone." He called out into the night.

Two flashlights came to life and shone in his face from different angles. Ryan had no idea how many there were. It could be two. Maybe four.

"Step away from the van. Slowly."

Ryan raised a forearm to shield his eyes and spotted one man with a rifle and another standing at his side. But he couldn't see the third person. The light was too bright.

"What do you want?" Maybe he could reason with them.

"That's far enough. Turn around and lift your shirt. Any weapons?" The man who spoke had a lilt to his speech. Scottish or Irish?

They were not here to talk.

Ryan ignored the command and sang the seeking song. The notes were carried across the clearing into the ground. He discovered a large basalt deposit surrounding an underground stream. If he could shift that fault line …

Every life is precious.

"What?"

"I asked if you had any weapons. Turn around!"

Ryan wasn't talking to the men with the flashlights but to the voice in his head. It wasn't the voice of a god but the priest who died five-and-a-half thousand years ago.

There are other options than violence. Allow me.

"I don't think—" Ryan panicked when he turned and walked toward the lone flashlight. *What are you doing? That's my body! Stop!*

It is time for a lesson.

"What do you know of life, son?" The priest asked the man behind the light, using *his* mouth and lips. Ryan was trapped in a room and could only view out a window as someone else controlled his actions. Mental fists pounded against the walls in frustration.

"Get on the ground! Are you fucking insane?" The man growled.

"Cutting the thread of a person's life ahead of its appropriate time is an affront to the gods. Do you wish to reconsider?"

The other two men approached across the clearing, and the light made the shadows dance. The man before Ryan grabbed his upper arm and shouted, "I got him."

Ryan whispered. "Life can be cut short, but only with the approval of Anubis. How about I show you?"

In his mind, Ryan was screaming to no effect as his hands made a series of gestures he once viewed in a mirror. To his horror, an ankh hovered mid-air between him and the man with the flashlight. However, something was different. Not only could Ryan see the symbol, but the man could as well. The flashlight fell onto the ground as he stumbled back.

"No! Oh, shit. I'm not ready to die." The man's bladder released as his eyes bugged.

With the light out of his eyes, Ryan saw a middle-aged man with a military crewcut. He wore a black tactical vest, belt, and a slung rifle. The pistol in his hands lowered slowly to the ground, forgotten, as he stared.

"No one is truly ready, but *your* death could serve the greater good." The priest was talking in a sing-song manner, gentle and designed to calm.

Showing someone's death is a great reformer of the soul.

Please give me back my body! Ryan begged.

Soon.

Hands grabbed Ryan's shoulders from behind, but Ptah-Du-Amun didn't react.

The soldier whispered. "I have kids. I don't want to die."

Ryan was forced to his knees but didn't break eye contact. The ankh drifted closer to the soldier. The others couldn't see it.

"The choice is obvious if you wish to live." The priest spoke as if he were talking about the weather. As Ryan was forced into the dirt and his hands wrenched to his lower back, small-arms fire echoed in the night. Two targets, four rounds. A gentle mist fell on the back of Ryan's head and neck. The men to either side fell and would not be getting up again.

The soldier whimpered and stepped back as the ankh advanced, lowering his gun.

Ryan rose while reversing the hand movements. The ankh disappeared.

"It is never too late to begin your life anew. I strongly suggest you do so."

The man's pistol landed at Ryan's feet, quickly followed by the rifle, as he sobbed. "I'm sorry. The money was too good."

"Leave us."

The soldier ran into the night toward the highway.

Ryan suddenly had control over his body. "Don't *ever* do that again!"

Ptah-Du-Amun remained silent, but Ryan could feel his presence at the edge of his thoughts.

Carrick opened the passenger door and moved beside him. "Are you all right? What happened?"

The van's engine roared to life, and Maurice shouted through the open door, "I don't give a fuck what happened. Let's go."

Ryan had told many of his secrets, but this was one he wouldn't share with anyone. Ever. One moment, he was in control, and the next, he was a passenger as someone else controlled his body.

He mumbled, "I can't explain."

Carrick quickly frisked the first body but found only knives, handcuffs, and a handgun. The second man had a phone, as well as weapons. "It's locked and probably traceable."

The cell was dropped with the bodies.

Maurice honked the horn. "I'm leaving if you don't get inside. Right now!"

Once they were underway, Ryan sat on the floor, trying to block out the last few minutes as Carrick turned in his seat. "We'll be in Paris within the hour. What's next, Mr. Petey?"

Pushing aside feeling violated, Ryan had an idea, and it was time to implement the plan. "I need to buy an iPad and plane tickets."

CHAPTER 49

Ryan turned his head out of the starboard window of the airplane, trying to get a glimpse, but he could only see endless stretches of sand.

"They're thirty miles away." Carrick pointed to the southwest. "We'll be there soon after landing."

He expected to feel some attachment to the ancient land below and hoped to see the pyramids, but they were too far away. Egypt was a foreign land he had seen on television, in the movies, and on the internet, and there was no innate connection. When the *fasten seatbelt* sign dinged above, he buckled in. The plane had begun its descent, and after the long night, he was anxious.

Maurice had dropped them off at a twenty-four-hour supermarket near the airport, and Ryan's lessons for traveling while remaining under the radar began. Carrick bought prepaid Visa cards with cash and a disposable phone. "You'll be asked for the local area code when it's activated. Use zero three."

Ryan followed the instructions and was shortly registered on the Paris network.

Carrick knew the city's layout and a cab brought them to Le Meilleur des Mondes, a twenty-four-hour internet café. Using the prepaid Visa cards, he booked two tickets to Cairo and paid the upgrade fee. They were not flying first class but coach, and the price was for the V.I.P. lounge access. "A lot easier than a hotel," Carrick explained. The purchase receipt and boarding passes were sent to their respective burner phones.

The flight was due to depart just before eight o'clock in the morning, and they arrived at the airport at four. Ryan discovered that the travel hub was also a shopping mall. Book and convenience stores were next to a liquor store. What surprised him was the number of people buying clothing in the middle of the night. He had no problems finding a boutique that sold tablets. After showing the screenshots of their boarding passes and upgrade, they settled in the Emirates Lounge. Carrick realized he had left his cane in Maurice's van. Complaining about his hip, he dropped into a reclining chair. "Wake me an hour before our flight." Seconds later, he was snoring. He tried not to worry about Carrick, as the man was no spring chicken, but without him, Ryan wouldn't have made it out of the United Kingdom. Not alive anyway.

Ryan began the activation process once he plugged the tablet in to charge fully. He struggled through the first stages until the language was switched to English, not French. After that, things went smoothly. Using the phone, he created a Gmail account to register the tablet. Carrick had warned him not to log into his social media accounts, email, or applications, but the temptation was there.

Once logged into the airport's WiFi, Ryan downloaded and tested one application from the Apple Store. *Perfect! This will work.*

Ryan tried to copy Carrick's smooth demeanor as they went through security, but his fears were unfounded. They had no checked baggage, and after testing the tablet, the guard waved them through. "The real test is the customs at Cairo."

Ryan was sweating at Carrick's statement, which did nothing to help his nerves. An Egyptian prison wasn't where he wanted to spend the rest of his life. After landing and taxiing to the gate, Ryan found the airport impressive. High vaulted glass and polished steel ceilings greeted them as they followed the herd through corridors until they arrived in a massive room with thousands of people snaking through lineups. Cairo receives millions of visitors annually, and tourism accounts for nearly five billion dollars in revenue. While the lines seemed to be moving rapidly, Carrick led him to the side where a group of men and women stood against the wall, holding signs.

"VIP tours pay for the convenience of skipping the customs lineups. Sometimes, a few hundred Egyptian pounds can grease the wheels." Carrick approached a petite Japanese woman holding a white cardboard sign while Ryan stood back to wait. Cash was handed over, and the woman led them to a far line with only a few people.

"Custom declaration forms and passports." She held out a hand.

Carrick surrendered his documents, and Ryan did the same. She scanned both papers and nodded. "Stay here."

The woman skipped the line and entered the customs officer's booth, handing over the paperwork.

"Relax. Maurice is one of the best," Carrick whispered.

A bead of sweat trickled down his back, and Ryan tried not to look over his shoulder. The woman handed the officer a white envelope and collected their passports, returning within seconds.

"Thank you, ma'am. It's appreciated." Carrick slipped her another bill.

She pointed to the far gate. "No problem. Go through there. Enjoy your stay."

Ryan and Carrick were buzzed through, and without being handcuffed or thrown in jail, they were in Cairo, Egypt.

"That was the best five hundred pounds I've spent in a long time." Carrick led him down a hallway and through the luggage carousels.

"How much is that in Canadian dollars?"

Carrick chuckled. "That's in Egyptian pounds, so that would be about twenty dollars Canadian. Half that went to the customs officer, I'm sure."

Ryan found himself in a grand airport that rivaled Pearson in Toronto. Fifty-foot palm trees decorated with multi-colored and neon lights framed various stores and kiosk shops selling plastic pyramids, mummies, and sphinxes.

Carrick gestured, encompassing the airport. "It's your show, young man. What's next?"

Ryan went to the store with the knickknacks and spun the display, holding dozens of postcards. He chose a detailed map of Cairo, and his finger landed on the Great Pyramid and slid west, past a small airport and industrial area. He tapped an area one hundred miles into the desert to land on Moghara Lake. "We have to go here."

Without a word, Carrick bought the map and left to rent a vehicle. However, Ryan couldn't shake the feeling that he was being watched. He sat on a bench with his back to a wall, studying the throngs of people coming and going. The hair on his neck stood on end when an announcement came over the airport's PA system: *"Ryan Petey, please come to the information booth. Ryan Petey, to the information booth."*

CHAPTER 50

Ryan couldn't remain sitting and went to the rental booths as Carrick walked briskly toward him.

"You heard?" Ryan asked.

"Yes. We should be leaving. Now." Carrick held a sheaf of papers and a vehicle key.

The exit was nearby, only fifty feet, and Ryan led the way through a crowd of people.

"I've rented a Land Cruiser. We'll need it for the desert and—"

Ryan abruptly stopped, and Carrick ran into his back. "Bring the car around the front and take my bag. If I don't make it out, go on without me."

Carrick spun about and was confused. "What's going on? No one is watching us."

Previously, Ryan had seen an ankh appear when the kid was dying in the alley and again in downtown Toronto. For the first time, multiple symbols appeared. Ankhs hovered above the heads of a group of twenty Chinese students. Also, a family of four struggling with too many pieces of luggage. Three airline assistants on the far side of the main floor were directing people to the appropriate lineup, and an older woman was being pushed in a wheelchair—all had the black symbol above their head. Occasionally, the mark disappeared, but another would take its place. Ryan gasped when a woman carrying an infant walked past his side, and she gave him a strange look. The symbol wasn't above her head, just the newborn girl.

"Go. Now." Ryan thrust the backpack into Carrick's arms. "I'd suggest you run."

"This is the last call for Ryan Petey to come to the information booth."

Without checking to see if Carrick had left, he studied the signs and ran to the far end of the arrivals. Rude comments followed his wake as he bumped into a dozen people and slipped through a couple, moving too slowly. Against the outer wall and beside the media center was the information booth. The semi-circular desk was surrounded by Plexiglas, with two attendants working inside. Ryan ignored the symbols above their heads and rushed to the first window.

"I'm here. Ryan Petey. You called?"

The slender woman behind the counter slid a black phone through the opening in the Plexiglas. "There's been an emergency, and your father's on the line."

Stunned, he nodded, and she pressed a button and passed him the handset.

"Hello?"

"Glad I finally got through to you, Mr. Petey." The background noise and accent made it hard to understand the man.

"Who is this? What do you want?" He turned about and studied the crowds. The ankh symbols shifted to the group checking in with an airline. Two hundred people must be shuffling along the guided paths—all marked for death.

"A lot of people are going to be hurt or killed unless you decide within thirty seconds. Are you ready for the offer, Ryan?"

No!

"What's the offer?"

"You will be escorted out of the airport and go willingly. If you do that, no one gets hurt. What's your choice?"

When a young couple with a stroller lined up at the information booth, ankhs appeared above them all. Ryan closed his eyes. "I will go with you."

"Stay where you are."

Before the man hung up, Ryan growled, "If one person dies, I'll tear the world apart looking for you. Trust me. You'll kill yourself before letting me get anywhere near you."

Who said that? That wasn't me!

"I'm a man of my word. No one will die."

Ryan opened his eyes and collapsed against the counter. One by one, the symbols were disappearing across the airport. He didn't bother replying and hung up. There was no obvious sign of what was planned. A bomb? Several gunmen? Who the *hell* threatened the man on the phone? It wasn't Ryan. Fearful of his sanity, Ryan didn't have to wait long.

When the door beside the media center opened, a woman wearing a short gray skirt, high heels, and a sleeveless white blouse emerged. She paused, then walked toward him with a dazzling smile. Long red hair swayed side to side over her chest with each step, and ten minutes ago, Ryan would have been drooling over the runway model, but now he felt like throwing up.

"Are you ready, Mr. Petey?" The Australian accent threw him off balance, but he nodded.

He followed a set of chiseled calves and a tight ass through the airport to the main exit. "I'm Carrie. Pleased to meet you."

Ryan remained silent. He didn't want to have small talk with anyone who would have killed hundreds of people. Outside, the Egyptian heat hit him like a hammer. Within seconds, sweat beaded on his forehead, and he had to force his lungs to inhale the furnace blast. Squinting against the afternoon sun, she led him to a waiting black Cadillac limousine.

"Just a second."

Ryan turned in his direction as he spotted a blue Land Cruiser in line behind a small bus where a porter unloaded piles of luggage. He knocked on the window, and Carrick stepped outside.

"What's going on?"

"Sorry, but I promised to go with them. They were going to kill hundreds inside unless I agreed." Ryan swallowed the sudden lump in his throat.

"Ah, shit." Carrick ran a hand across his face and then spotted the limo. He poked Ryan in the chest. "It isn't over till the fat lady sings, kid. Remember that." He rummaged inside the vehicle and passed Ryan's backpack over.

"I will."

The limousine honked, and he turned to see the redhead standing outside, waiting with a hand on her hip. Bitch.

"Thank you for everything." Impulsively, Ryan gave him a brief hug. "Take care, Carrick."

"You too, kid. Give 'em hell, and don't put up with any shit. *You're* the man." After a final pat on the back, Ryan wiped his eyes, resigning himself to his fate. Six days after discovering the ankh in the alleyway, he wouldn't have been surprised to find one above his own head.

CHAPTER 51

"We won't be long." Carrie gestured for Ryan to get in first, and he slid to the far seat in the limousine, placing the pack beside him. She sat opposite, crossing her legs as the driver pulled away from the airport. "Just under an hour. Plenty of time for us to talk."

Keeping his eyes from wandering was nearly impossible as she shifted to reach for a bottle of water. Looking out the window helped. "Where are we going? What's the plan?"

"Would you like some water?"

"No thanks."

"I'm not good with this heat." Carrie took a sip and added, "We're going to meet some people, and you're going to help. It's that simple."

Visions of lost tombs and gold masks flickered through his thoughts. *Why would they need me to recover treasure?* "What's the job?"

Carrie stretched her legs, and an ankle bracelet jingled. "No sense in spoiling the fun. All in due time."

Ryan's eyes snapped to the side, looking out the window again. Carrie wasn't sent to pick him up so they could have a riveting chat. It was obvious where her assets lay. "Where is Dr. Kowalska?"

The question didn't throw her off in the slightest. "You will know that answer shortly."

Sorry, I brought you into this, Crystal.

Carrie removed a cell phone from a charging port near the door, and her manicured nails clicked against the screen rapidly. Ryan stared out the window as they merged onto the highway and drove south. The landscape of brown and beige was prominent, with the occasional property caring for plants and shrubs displaying their wealth. Despite the number of tourists and wealth flowing into the country, the money didn't trickle down to the average citizen. Ryan passed many homes missing a roof or gaping holes in the walls. Old vehicles were stripped of parts and left on blocks beside buildings, next to piles of garbage that disappeared around corners.

Looking after their people is the first thing any ruler should do. Ryan could feel Ptah-Du-Amun's disgust. Having a man who's been dead for thousands of years talk in his mind was the least of his concerns. Ryan could deal with it if he weren't controlling him like a puppet.

You never had poor people in your time?

The pharaoh cared for everyone, ensuring they were fed and clothed. There were problems, but this is an affront to society.

Ryan's impression changed twenty minutes later as the highway turned west. To the south were built-up homes and communities sporting green lawns and topiary bushes. Eventually, they drove across the Nile River and into another neighborhood. There was little doubt where they were going, and even Ptah-Du-Amun recognized the area.

We are close to the temple complex.

The priest's thoughts merged with the stone singer's memories, and Ryan understood the layout of the land without ever having stepped foot in the country. The temple faced the setting sun, and to the northwest was the altered sphinx in the same direction. Images overlayed of the jackal head on the lion's body and the Pharaoh Khufu's visage sculpted at a later date. The Great Pyramid would be northwest. While he had seen pictures and videos, those same images warred with a memory of a half-built pyramid with the first courses of blocks laid. In Ptah-Du-Amun's time, the pyramids were in the planning stage and had yet to begin. Ryan groaned as he struggled to make sense of the timeline and ancient memories.

Carrie had placed the phone to the side and leaned forward, knees drifting apart. "Are you okay?"

Jesus Christ. Ryan struggled to control his raging hormones at the presented view—Sharon Stone would have balked at the display. *Help!*

"Young lady, I suggest you peddle your wares on a street corner for coin or clothe yourself appropriately." The dry, humorless voice from his lips had never been more welcome.

"I never!" Carrie tugged at her skirt and sat with her legs to the side. She didn't have the decency to blush.

"I seriously doubt that much." The priest wasn't phased by her antics.

The window lowered an inch behind Ryan, and the driver spoke, "Five minutes, ma'am."

Tour busses lined the road and followed the limousine as they turned south, and Ryan saw the great pyramid through the driver's side window. Despite knowing the secrets of moving stone, he was in awe at the sheer size of the structure and the precision involved. The pyramid was the equivalent of a four-hundred-and-eighty-foot-tall skyscraper, and he had to press his face against the glass to view the summit. When the limousine followed the road as it curved to the left, the other side was just as impressive, but a gaping hole had destroyed the symmetry. The Great Pyramid had been robbed countless times over thousands of years. While some attempts were subtle, others were more direct. Ryan knew how much effort had gone into each stone and was heartbroken to see the callous disregard of the monument.

Very close.

The limo slowed as busses and tourists crowded the road, but they steadily progressed. Over Ryan's right shoulder, half the Sphinx was visible. The great carving rested in a depression, and most of the base was lost from view.

I was told the statue had to be built on the bedrock because the limestone shelf was unstable.

Once invited, Ryan had difficulty separating his thoughts from the priest's. What scared him was the silent agreement of the stone singer.

When they pulled over and parked, Ryan swallowed the lump in his throat as he prepared to step outside. Waiting was a group of men forming a column to either side of the door. Some wore a navy blue police uniform, while others wore white. All wore berets with slung rifles and pistols on their hips. At the end of the column stood an Asian man in a white suit and straw hat next to a tall man dressed in white robes and a red checkered shemagh headdress held with a black band. The slim Arab had a neatly trimmed white beard, contrasting with his more concise, overweight companion. Behind the two men, more people waited.

"Leave your bag. Let's go."

Keeping her knees together for the first time, Carrie's feet stepped outside when the door opened. Ignoring the blast of heat, Ryan followed.

"About fucking time," the Asian muttered.

"Mr. Petey, glad you could join us. Come, we have work to do." It was the same voice on the airport telephone. The Arab gestured for Ryan to join them, but he didn't move.

"Where's Crystal, and who are you?"

The Asian was about to speak when a voice cried, "Ryan!"

A woman dressed in a black burka was shoved to her knees. The guard brought the butt of his rifle into the air, and Ryan's eyes widened. The Arab screamed, "No!"

But it was too late. The ground trembled as Ryan's hands clenched with rage.

CHAPTER 52

Two things happened simultaneously. The vibrational singing of a stone singer was heard for the first time on the Giza plateau in thousands of years, and a high priest of Anubis revoked the blessing of life. With a quick hand gesture, a three-foot ankh appeared before the burly guard who had shoved Crystal. Everyone was stunned as the man screamed while falling backward when his heel caught a stone. The man's hands tried to ward off death, but it was not so easily swayed. With a strangled cry, he stopped breathing as the ankh disappeared. Two seconds had passed, and no one had a chance to move.

"Crystal. Come here, now. No one will touch you."

Ryan resumed the seeking song and explored the limestone depths beneath his feet. He had a home-court advantage, and all the guns and men couldn't do anything if he shifted the faultline. It was too bad the underground tunnel was filled with water. He had hoped to bury them alive. The ground shook again, matching his mood.

"Stop! Everything is going to be okay, and no one is going to be hurt." The Arab stepped to the side as Crystal ran to Ryan. She clung to his arm, sobbing.

The guards gasped in horror at their fallen companion, and after one look at Ryan, they stepped back.

He ignored them and allowed the fault line shift to rest. "Are you okay? What are you wearing? Did they hurt you?"

Crystal ripped the headdress off and used it to wipe away her tears. "I'm okay. They made me wear this outfit."

Ryan was baking in the heat from the full sun, and he couldn't imagine wearing a head-to-toe black robe. Carrie finally joined the two men at the end and smirked. "You got your girl back. Happy now? We have work to do."

Ryan bared his teeth and took a step forward. "I think we'll be leaving."

The Asian laughed. "Do you think it would be that fucking easy?"

The Arab snapped his fingers, and the guard nearest Ryan produced a tablet. The live camera feed showed his mother and Detective McCallan hanging from a beam with thick chains and toes barely reaching the ground.

"Mom!" His rage fled at the image, and tears flooded his eyes.

Julie lifted her head. "Ryan, is that you?"

"Where are you? I'll be there—"

The Arab snapped his fingers again, and the screen went dark.

"If you cooperate, your mother and her friend will be treated fairly. Otherwise …"

Remembering Carrick's advice, Ryan stood his ground. "I'm working *with* you, not for you. Deal?"

"Ya, fucking deal. Can we get on with it? I'm baking out here." The Chinese man waved a hand in a non-committal gesture.

Ryan spoke to Crystal. "Take those robes off. You must be boiling in there." Sweat had made the shirt cling to his back like a second skin.

"I can't. They took my clothes. I'm not wearing anything underneath."

Ryan spoke to the Arab and pointed at Carrie. "Does she work for you, or is she your boss?"

The man's eyes slowly traveled from the high heels to the top of her head. "She's my special assistant."

Ryan opened the limousine door and jerked a thumb inside. "Your assistant is wearing the wrong clothing. Get her ass in there and have them switch."

They were close to the same height, and despite the upper portions being different, it would be better than roasting in a black oven.

The Asian man laughed as Carrie was pushed toward the vehicle. The Arab ordered, "Do as he says. Move."

Ryan asked while the women switched clothing. "Since you know me so well, can you tell me your names?"

Two guards picked up the fallen man and lifted him by the arms. They made it appear that the man had fainted as a van pulled up behind the limousine.

The Arab placed a hand on his chest, giving a slight bow. "You may call me Mr. Smith, and this is Mr. Green."

"Fuck that, call me Mr. Orange. Green is bad luck."

The dead man was carried to the van, toes dragging parallel lines in the dust, and lowered inside. Several tourists were gathering on the far side of the road, and everyone had a camera.

Smith directed the guards to keep their distance as Crystal stepped out of the limo. The short skirt fit, while the blouse was too loose, it was not bad overall. She was barefoot but didn't seem to mind.

"What a difference." She smiled gratefully at Ryan.

He grinned. "It looks a hell of a lot better on you."

"Carrie, let's go," Smith called out.

"I can't, sir. The burka is too small and doesn't fit."

Before Crystal slammed the door, Ryan's eyes burned at the image of the redhead trying to cover herself with the material. Even the priest appeared amused.

"Don't care. Let's get the hell outta here." Mr. Orange began crossing the clearing, heading downhill. The eleven guards flared in a circle, ensuring the tourists were redirected. Crystal held Ryan's hand and slowly navigated her way around the sharp rocks underfoot, and once they found the pathway, she made better time.

Mr. Smith walked behind Ryan and said, "Welcome to the Valley Temple."

Fifty feet ahead, stone blocks formed the outline of a building with wide yellow security fencing blocking off the openings, except for the northern gate. The walls rose from six feet in height to fourteen and led into a wide hallway made with monolithic blocks. There was only one exit on the left leading to a long hall. A fenced-off barrier blocking an underground opening was in the middle. Plexiglas covered the pit, and everything was coated in a fine layer of sand. Ryan couldn't see below.

It connects to a series of tunnels and pathways beneath the plateau.

Ptah-Du-Amun answered the unasked question as the guards led the way, turning right at the next opening and through a gallery of pillars and small rooms. The floor was made of white alabaster stone, and Ryan ran a hand along the side of a red granite column as they progressed. After climbing a fifty-foot wooden ramp, they emerged onto a walkway path near the right foot of the Sphinx. A scattering of faded signs warned to avoid the edges, and a chain-link fence prevented anyone from going over the side. The pyramids rose in the clear blue sky against the horizon behind the great statue and causeway. Below, tourists gathered between the front feet as part of a tour, taking pictures.

Directly ahead, three guards gently directed an older man and woman back the way they came to join the group, and the remainder blocked anyone approaching from behind. Ryan was alone with Mr. Smith and Mr. Green for the first time. Crystal remained at his side.

"Okay, what is it you want?"

"To the point. I like that." Orange stepped within a foot, and Ryan enjoyed finally being taller than someone. The Asian whispered, "We don't give a fuck what you can do with stone, but I'd love to know how you killed the guard. *That* would be useful to know."

Ryan remained silent, and Smith cleared his throat before speaking. "An artifact came into our possession, confirming a long-lost myth. You will find it for us, and then you can go free."

Crystal's fingers dug into his arm, and she murmured something under her breath.

Ryan wanted to punch the smug smile off of Mr. Orange's face when he continued. "You're going to find the lost Hall of Records, asshole, or your mother will die."

Never! The high priest of Anubis was horrified, while Ryan was confused.

"What the hell is that?"

CHAPTER 53

"The Hall of Records has never been proven," Crystal said. "Rumors of lost technology, alchemy, astrology, and mathematics were supposedly sealed away as the culmination of an ancient society. Archeologists have been searching for hundreds of years and haven't found any reference or document to prove it's real. Nothing."

Mr. Smith smiled. "Correct, but don't forget mystic abilities and the history of medicine. Archeologists have never found proof, but others *have*, and it's remained a closely guarded secret. A bronze statue of Osiris was appropriated several years ago, and with LiDAR 3D scanning, we discovered the figure was hollow, and—"

"This is taking too fucking long," Orange interrupted. "We found a sealed scroll from an Osiris priest documenting the existence of a hidden temple and a map, with the Sphinx as the starting point. But when the statue was opened, the papyrus scroll caught fire. While most of it was destroyed, there was enough to prove the hall was real."

Smith pointed at Ryan. "Stone singers were mentioned, and the translation stated a path to the stars guided their steps. Lo and behold, twelve years later, you arrive and can move rocks like they were hollow. We've been searching for someone like you. The time has come for the world to find the hall."

"I may have some abilities, but I know nothing about lost technology."

Mr. Orange gave a sharp bark of laughter. "*Some* abilities? You're the most qualified to begin the hunt on the entire planet. Plus, you have Little Miss Sunshine to help. I'm sure you'll do it to save your precious mother and her girlfriend."

Ryan had no idea how the detective was involved, but there was no doubt he would do anything to save his mom. "How will I know you'll keep your end of the bargain?"

Smith pulled a cell phone out of his robes and made a call. "Release the women. Let them go." He waved the guard with the tablet over, and soon Ryan watched as his mother was lowered to the ground and three men removed the chains. Julie was carried away, and the police officer was next. "We know where they are, and I will bring them in again if you betray our trust. There is also the matter of another family member."

The guard flipped the tablet, showing pictures of Ryan's aunt walking a dog in the streets of Vancouver.

Please do not do what they wish. I won't let you!

Ryan wasn't sure how he was connected to the priest, but a god gives you a purpose and the tools to see the task done; it was up to him to figure it out. Was finding this hidden library his duty along with the other mission? The memory of the temple and walls of scrolls flickered in his thoughts. While another door didn't open in his mind, a different viewpoint became obvious.

He turned his back on the men, studying the Sphinx and the sloppy repair job to the shoulders and neck. The painted outer shell of bricks had disappeared, and instead of the smooth body of a lion, the aged corpse of a disposed pharaoh's vanity lay exposed like a rotting skeleton to the desert sun.

Turning suddenly, Ryan pointed a finger at the Arab. "Why didn't you just ask for help? Hire me to do the job? God knows I could have used the money."

The coconspirators glanced at each other, and then Smith shrugged. "Never occurred to me."

"Too fucking late, Mr. Philosophy. Are you in, or do we make another call?" Orange spat on the ground and then stared him down.

Ryan made eye contact with Mr. Smith. "I'm in, but there will be conditions."

"You fucking piece of—"

"What are they?" He grabbed Orange's shirt to forestall the eruption.

"I'm guessing you are wealthy." At a subtle nod from the Arab, Ryan continued. "You'll take care of any legal issues my mother faces. Make them go away. Next, you'll ensure Crystal doesn't lose her job or suffer repercussions from your actions."

"You want a fucking pony and a castle, too? Seriously?" Orange pleaded but was ignored.

"Anything else?"

Ryan nodded. "I'm given free rein to accomplish the task, and I never see Mr. Orange again. Your friend can fuck off. We *both* deserved to be paid for our time. Well paid." That was the first lesson he learned when starting his graphics business: no one works for free. "Also, I want my backpack." He turned to Crystal. "Do you want anything?"

Her jaw had dropped, and she stared in disbelief. "Shoes? Maybe my own clothes?"

Ryan turned to Mr. Smith. "Minor demands that will get the job done. Are we in agreement?" He stepped forward and extended his hand.

"This is ridiculous." The Chinese man's face had reddened, but Smith whispered something in his ear and gently pushed him toward the temple.

Once Orange was gone, he shook Ryan's hand. "Done, but with conditions. I will assign a group to work with you, and while they will follow your orders, they answer to me."

"Deal." Ryan didn't have to look at the sun's position or refer to the internet. He just knew. "Tomorrow is the last day before the new moon. I can't promise there is anything in the library, but I will find you the Hall of Records within twenty-four hours."

Their hands pumped once more in mid-air then separated.

Thank you, Hiram.

While Ryan had never been in such a position to strike deals or act in a position of authority, in his later years, the stone singer commanded an army of workers, gave orders, and expected to be obeyed. Failure to follow his directions could result in various actions, from a reprimand to dismissal, that would affect not only the worker but his family as well.

Sometimes, a mallet works best without a chisel as long as your mind be prompt to execute the design.

"When will you start?"

Ryan didn't hesitate. "An hour before sunrise. I need access to not only the Sphinx and grounds but also the second pyramid. I'll have a list of items ready for you. We need to rest and prepare right now, and I suggest appropriate accommodations nearby. Tomorrow will be hectic."

Mr. Smith must have worked with all types because he didn't even blink. He expected results and knew the chance of failure would result from the lack of preparation. The fact that Ryan denied any knowledge of the halls one minute to making demands the next didn't phase him.

"Second pyramid?" Crystal asked as they walked through the temple back to the limousine.

"Djoser was the first, and many errors were made as the builders used inaccurate data. We started the great pyramid seventy years later." Ryan was lost in thought, planning for the dawn, and didn't realize he had answered her question. *Fuck!*

Crystal stopped walking on the alabaster floor, and her feet shuffled in the sand. Her head tilted to the side, and she asked, "Who are you?"

Good question. The twenty-two-year-old youth was absorbing memories of others and talking with a god. Besides that, he had barely changed. "I'm still me." He held out a hand. "Tomorrow, we will find the greatest treasure and mystery of mankind. Are you in? I could certainly use your help."

She smiled, and his heart skipped at her beauty. "Do I have a choice?"

"Yes." Ryan jerked a thumb at Smith's back. "I'll have you on a plane within the hour on your way home as my final demand."

Crystal knocked his hand aside and grabbed his shirt, pulling him close. Her face was an inch away. "Not. A. Fucking. Chance."

As she leaned forward, Ryan turned his head and walked away. "Good! Glad to have you aboard."

Not only did Ryan chuckle at her subtle frustrated growl, but so did an ancient priest and stone singer. His fingers brushed against the cool granite pillars, recalling an old world that only existed in worn ruins. *It is time for a change.*

CHAPTER 54

Ryan's eyes watered as he spread the contents of the camouflage backpack over the hotel bed and shook his head at the discoveries. Carrick managed to slip his rings, a wad of cash, and the burner cell phone inside. The gesture touched his heart, and he whispered, "I hope you got out." Carrick was resourceful and had connections. No doubt he was back at the pub drinking a warm English ale.

After striking the deal, Ryan and Crystal were driven to a nearby hotel for the night. The suite had two bedrooms, a seating area, and a kitchenette. First, he wrote a list, and then Crystal added to it. He added that anyone accompanying them might wish to have similar items, then passed them to the guard outside their door. Ryan ordered room service and talked with Crystal for hours, but dawn came early, and they went to their separate bedrooms.

After a restless sleep, Ryan woke to shower and discovered everything requested on the kitchen table. "Hope someone enjoyed a late-night shopping spree."

He inserted the batteries in the headlamps and flashlights, testing each one. Despite the weight, the prybars and masonry hammer may be useful, and he tore the price tags away. Ryan wasn't sure if all the items could be obtained on short notice, but things appeared if you had enough money. The bright orange backpacks were waterproof, with a bladder on the inside pocket. A flexible straw was attached to the harness strap, and you could drink with a turn of your head. Carrying water bottles in tight spaces or while your hands were busy wasn't practical. While he may not need the climbing equipment, Ryan felt better for having it. A hundred feet of cordage, pinions, and C-clamps fit at the bottom of the pack, and he placed extra clothing and meal rations on top. Jeans and collared dress shirts would not be appropriate and were replaced with beige khaki pants and short-sleeved shirts. While resembling a jungle explorer or a crocodile hunter from Australia, the material was rugged and would dry easily. The last item wrapped in a bathroom towel was the iPad, burner phone, rings, and money—the electronics were powered down.

"Goodbye, old friend."

Ryan fondly picked up his worn running shoes and threw them in the garbage. The lightweight hiking boots were waterproof, had a rugged tread, and provided ankle support.

He started on Crystal's pack when she stepped out of her bedroom wearing a white hotel robe. "There's a coffee maker in the kitchen. Do you want a cup?"

She collapsed on the couch and mumbled, "Not a morning person."

Ryan should have asked for energy drinks but was getting used to the coffee. He'd already had two cups. It took a second mug before Crystal began to show signs of life.

"Here are your new clothes and a few things you wanted." Ryan moved the plastic bag on the table closer, and she picked it up on her way to the bedroom.

"Thank you. A quick shower, something to eat, and then I'm ready."

When the shower turned on, Ryan took her place on the couch and closed his eyes.

I need to know about the Hall of Records.

The priest hovered near the edge of his thoughts, and Ryan felt his presence but remained silent.

Do you know what a symbiotic relationship means? Ryan didn't wait for an answer. *It means I will benefit from the merger while you are in my thoughts. But you have forgotten an important fact that while you're in my mind, I'm also in yours.*

That got a response. *No!*

I'll do my best to ensure it does not become common knowledge, but in order for me to do the will of Anubis and be done with these men, I have no choice.

Ryan focused, and there was a slight resistance, then like a soap bubble, the barrier popped—he was in. He shifted through countless experiences and focused on the hall. However, a memory surfaced of a beautiful woman dancing in a long corridor, trailing flower petals to a bedroom as her robe slipped—

Enough! I will tell you what I know. Although, it isn't much. Yes, I've heard about the Hall of Records, and I had writings in my possession that were copied directly from the master tablets. But I've never been there.

The previous high priest of Anubis told Ptah-Du-Amun what he had learned from *his* master. Ryan didn't understand many references, but he discovered enough to know where to start. He was surprised to find *many* places to begin worldwide, but the main clue was less than a mile from the hotel.

"Sleeping already?" Crystal stepped out of the bedroom, hair still wet from the shower, dressed in similar clothing, but it fit better on her. She drank another coffee while rummaging through the fridge, nibbling on last night's leftovers. The clock on the microwave showed they had five minutes. Ryan went to the bathroom and had time to ensure he needed nothing else. At four o'clock, a knock sounded on the door.

In the hallway were four men dressed for combat in black military outfits, load-bearing vests, coyote-tan packs, and utility belts with holstered pistols. Like the others, the man standing closest was six feet tall and had a short crew cut. Two others were a little taller, and the last man standing down the hall must have been six foot six with the broad shoulders of a linebacker. Jesus Christ, where did Smith get these guys?

"I'm Duncan, and this is Marshal and Almond. The walking mountain is Boxcar. Don't ask." Ryan and Crystal introduced themselves.

Ryan's first impressions were good as they conducted themselves like professionals. Marshal had a short red beard, and his eyes never seemed to rest, flicking from one object to another. Almond was the darkest man Ryan had ever met, but his brief smile was brilliant, with genuine warmth in his eyes. Boxcar had the physique of a professional wrestler, with a pencil-thin mustache and a square jaw. Duncan was the oldest, with gray at the temples and in his beard. The laugh lines and wrinkles on his forehead were deep, and he appeared to be in charge.

Ryan was anxious to start but spoke up. "Before we go, make sure any electronics you wish to use again have been powered down—cellphones, tablets, and so on. I'm not sure what you've been told, but we're going to find the location of an object and then go from there. If you need to use something, let me know ahead of time. Any problems?"

The team exchanged looks, and then throat mics and other items appeared and were turned off. Duncan asked, "Our briefing was … hard to believe. Is it real?"

Ryan glanced around the hotel room, then said, "Excuse me."

At ten-foot intervals in the hallway, blocks decorated the wall in a fair imitation of the pyramid wall. Crystal stood in the doorway, grinning.

"Limestone facing, but it will do." Ryan knocked on the stone with his knuckles to prove it was real, and then he hummed the shaping song. The sconce lighting to either side of the next room flickered, as did the overhead bulb. He placed his hand against the wall and pushed. After removing his hand, a perfect impression remained in the stone, down to the wrinkles in his palm.

"Well, I'll be …" Almond pushed his larger hand over Ryan's print, but nothing happened.

Boxcar pulled a knife from a belt sheath and scraped the tip against the stone like nails on a chalkboard. "Good enough for me."

Duncan grinned. "We don't have to deal with rebel fighters or overthrow a corrupt president? This'll be a walk in the park. Let's go."

The ancients and the builders didn't wish the Hall to be found by casual seekers, but I believe we should have a chance.

Ryan shouldered his pack and followed Crystal down the stairs. His escort seemed to accept the impossible better than he did. What could go wrong?

At four o'clock in the morning, the only one awake was the night clerk behind the counter. A gray airport transfer bus awaited, and Marshal opened the door. The interior lighting was lowered once everyone was inside and had dropped their packs.

He turned to Ryan, "Where are we going, boss?"

"We're going to start at the Sphinx."

As they left the hotel, Ryan prayed to Anubis, the Christian god, and even Zeus that this adventure would be over soon and to look after his mother. Ptah-Du-Amun's last words were ominous and didn't seem promising. If distant memories of the past and an ability to manipulate stone only gave them a chance, what would it take to ensure success? Hopefully, the team of six will be up to the task. Ryan was out of options and had the promise to keep.

CHAPTER 55

One week ago, Ryan began his day in Toronto with too many energy drinks, and a shortcut through an alley changed his life. Now, he was in Egypt, taking a bus to one of the world's oldest monuments under cover of darkness, searching for a distant memory of a legend. It was just another normal Thursday in the life of a twenty-two-year-old.

"Two minutes," Marshal called out.

Duncan and the others checked their equipment, and Ryan exchanged glances with Crystal. "Are you ready?"

"Of course! For the last forty-five years, the Egyptian government has restricted access to the Sphinx. Just getting a chance to explore *that* is exciting." Her dimples made an appearance, and one of Ryan's concerns disappeared. The sparkle was returning to her eyes, and while he knew Crystal was strong, her recent experiences had affected her, and it seemed the wind had been knocked out of her sails. There wasn't much Ryan could do except be there for her, and she would open up in time. However, she was a fighter and, maybe soon, going to be the world's most renowned archeologist.

Duncan turned to Ryan and Crystal. "Due to a scheduling error, the ministry has failed to assign patrols to this area for the next few hours. Hopefully, that will give you enough time?"

"Not sure, but that should be good."

"We'll roll with the plan." Marshal turned off the bus, and Duncan lifted an M4A1 carbine rifle from the overhead luggage shelf and slung the weapon. The others followed suit, and the mood changed. The soldiers were on a mission, and it was time to focus. Ryan and Crystal slipped on their packs before stepping onto the Giza plateau an hour before sunrise.

Security lights were scattered along the dirt road and secondary parking lot immediately north of the Sphinx, where the limousine had stopped yesterday. Ryan pulled the headlamp from a cargo pocket and turned the beam on.

"Jesus!" Duncan clamped a hand over the white light. He flicked the settings until the light changed to red. "There we go. Less visible, and it won't affect your night vision."

After driving a bus with the headlights on, Ryan didn't see the big deal. "Thanks."

Crystal adjusted her headlamp before turning it on, and soon, there was a parade of red dots on the pathway heading toward the temple complex. Instead of going to the northern entrance, Ryan pointed at the yellow gate leading to the main grounds. "We need to go through there, but it's locked."

Boxcar stepped forward. "It's okay. I have the master key."

Bolt cutters appeared from his backpack, and the shackle was cut like a twig. The gate squealed open, and Ryan cringed as the sound echoed down the stone entry. Duncan closed the gate once everyone had gone through and slipped the lock through the eyelet. At first glance, it would appear secure.

There was enough ambient light from the city and stars to show the massive sculpture rising over sixty feet against the night sky. Instead of approaching between the front lion paws, Ryan led the group to the right and grinned as he ran a hand lightly over the bricks. He may have memories and can talk to men long since dead, but he was actually touching one of the world's most-known monuments—a surreal moment.

Behind the left leg, Ryan knelt at a small opening blocked by a wooden frame and steel mesh, pulling it free. The barrier was to keep out the casual tourists or slow them down enough for the guards to prevent them from entering.

"I've seen the reports on this entry. It doesn't go anywhere," Crystal whispered.

Ryan nodded and sat down with his feet dangling inside. The opening was three and a half feet by two feet, and the tunnel went straight down. "I watched the videos online, and this seems to be our best bet. Teenagers snuck in here and uploaded before the guards could get to them. There's another entryway on top of the head, and we will try if this one doesn't work."

Crystal muttered; *robber tunnels*. For several thousand years, many didn't accept that treasure wasn't buried within the Sphinx and burrowed inside. Ryan had an idea of where to go, but he was short of bringing in an excavator, so he needed an alternate route.

Ryan's feet turned to stand on the first rung of a metal ladder when Almond whispered, "Contact. Ridgeline to our north. Two men observing."

Boxcar and Marshal dropped to a knee, and the butt of their rifles planted into their shoulders.

"Get inside. Quickly. We shouldn't have any company," Duncan ordered.

Ryan climbed down the ladder, and Crystal followed. The hollowed-out cave was seven feet long and four feet wide, a drop of eight feet. Everyone fit through the opening except Boxcar. "I'm fucking stuck."

Ryan was the closest to the ladder, so he climbed. The man's barrel chest and pack were wedged against the top row of limestone bricks. A thud sounded from above, and the crack of a rifle echoed in the night a split second later.

Boxcar yelled, "They're firing at us. Get me out of here."

Another round cracked into the stone inches from the opening. Ryan sang, and Duncan winced at the intensity. There wasn't time to prevent damage to the monument, as he punched two bricks outward. Boxcar was showered in dust and sand as he fell into the pit. Duncan and Marshal eased his fall as the echo of men shouting filled the valley. Bright flashlights swept the area, illuminating the cave.

Ryan turned on the ladder. "This way."

Hidden under the overhang was a side tunnel directly opposite the entry point. Ryan crawled forward and dismantled the wooded planks blocking the shaft. As soon as there was room, he moved forward, and Crystal was on his heels. The tunnel sloped downward and was covered in a light dusting of sand. Bricks lined the walls, and the floor was worn smooth. For Ryan and Crystal, there was enough room to crawl on hands and knees, but the remainder removed their packs and shuffled forward on their stomachs. After thirty feet, Ryan stood in a bricked chamber and helped the others stand.

"Those weren't the guards from the Egyptian ministry." Marshal turned to Duncan. "Thought you said this was going to be a walk in the park?"

Boxcar's booming laugh filled the space.

Duncan ignored the question and rubbed his beard before asking Ryan, "Now what?"

The chamber was large enough for the group to stand, but no other tunnels existed. Ryan didn't need to use his abilities. He pointed to the far wall. While the bricks were limestone, a door of basalt blocks stopped them from going farther. Ryan was going to sing while removing the stone, but a grinning Boxcar tapped him on the shoulder.

"Seriously, I got this."

The six-foot-five man stepped back and then drove his heel into the bricks. The wall didn't stand a chance. A second kick enlarged the hole, and Ryan realized where the bricks had landed. "Stop! I need those. Help bring them over to this side."

Ryan carried several to the first tunnel and stacked them in the opening. As each brick was placed, he linked them together then to the limestone walls and floor. There was no lack of material, and the tunnel was quickly filled. His humming changed pitch, and the nasal vibrations made the chamber resonate. When he finished, Ryan shoved the new brick wall, which was solid—more so than the original.

"Where does that go?" Marshal peered inside the opening, looking down.

The red beam from his headlamp revealed a shaft that turned after ten feet. Duncan pulled a glow stick from his vest and bent the plastic before tossing it down. The green light hit the slope and bounced from sight, but a dim glow was visible when Ryan covered his headlamp.

"Under the Giza plateau, there are supposed to be caverns that stretched for miles, but the Egyptian government believes further exploration could collapse the Sphinx or shift the pyramids." Crystal pointed to the rough stone lining the shaft. "It's natural and not shaped."

"Almond, you're first." Duncan dropped his pack and removed a coil of knotted rope. Ryan shifted bricks to the side as the end was tossed below. Boxcar acted as an anchor, bracing himself against the wall.

Almond slid over the edge on his front, then lowered himself. The tension left the rope within seconds, followed by boots scraping against the stone.

Ryan and Duncan leaned through the opening, but he was gone. Duncan called out, "Report."

"You're going to want to send the archeologist down first." Almond's whisper carried like a shout. Ryan caught the awe in his voice. "This is amazing."

CHAPTER 56

"Hold on to the knot," Duncan said, "and you'll be lowered. There's no need to climb. Almond is right below you, so don't worry."

"I'm not that delicate." Crystal winked at the commander, and a brief surge of heat rose in Ryan's cheeks. Without trepidation, she dropped over the side, and Boxcar lowered her without effort.

"Petey, you're next." Ryan's feet soon touched the slope, and Almond helped him down the ramp, and his eyes widened. The cavern was sixty feet long and thirty feet wide with a stale, dry odor. Three great pillars in the middle supported a celestial canopy of stars chiseled into the limestone twelve feet above. Gemstones had once decorated the ceiling, forming constellations, but were now missing. There was no way of telling if the thefts were recent or occurred thousands of years ago. The red headlamps did little to show the full extent, but the eerie glow gave the illusion of stepping into a hellish landscape.

"This is amazing!" Crystal darted from wall to wall in the great room, exclaiming at each find. She tried to be everywhere at once. Colorful drawings covered every square inch of the northern border along with hieroglyphics, and the southern wall was pocked with multiple niches carved into the stone. Broken pottery lay next to bundles of sticks. A three-foot stone vase was intact and appeared pristine.

While Ryan didn't have her training, he agreed. Pigments colored a large figure pulled on a sled by several dozen men, which looked fresh. A long-beaked bird resting on a lion's back wasn't only painted on the limestone but chiseled, making it look three-dimensional. While Ryan had researched the monument briefly, he'd never seen any documents or video of the hall.

Boxcar was lowered next, then Marshal. Duncan was last, and he coiled the rope and stowed the grappling hook. "We're not the first people here." He kicked an old pop can toward a pile of garbage on the southern wall. Plastic water bottles were strewn in various locations with little disregard for the preservation of a historical monument. Remnants of a lighting system lay near the ramp with a black extension cord and dust-covered spotlights. The plastic was brittle, and the equipment was antiques. Fifty years old? Seventy?

Ryan found himself in the same situation as the previous chamber. There didn't appear to be an exit, but with the layout of the monument, there should only be one option. As Crystal exclaimed over another finding, Ryan studied the eastern wall.

A two-foot pile of human skulls rested in the bottom niche and looked untouched. The opening above held one item: an eight-inch slender clay vase corked with wood. Ryan placed his fingertips against the stone, and the low rumble of the seeking song came forth. He covered the entire eastern wall and checked the floor but only found solid limestone bedrock.

"Anything?" Duncan stood at his shoulder while the others gathered in the middle.

"Nothing. I was led to believe there's another chamber under the front paw of the Sphinx. But I'm unsure if it's real, and I don't know how to get there." Ryan was going to check the other wall when he held a hand in the air. "Do you hear that?"

"Hold up, guys. Silence." Duncan called his team.

The distant *tap tap tap* could barely be heard. Ryan didn't know where it came from, but Duncan didn't hesitate and pointed to the ramp. "Marshal."

He returned in seconds. "Someone is breaking through the other tunnel."

Duncan pointed to Boxcar and Almond, and they flanked the ramp, rifles at the ready. Then he told Ryan and Crystal, "There's only one way in here. We can hold them off, but you should get to work."

The urge to run grew, but like a hamster on a wheel, there was nowhere to go. Ryan sang again while checking the southern mural wall. Kicking a pile of plastic bottles aside, he knelt when the explosion shattered his makeshift brick wall. The ramp and enclosed hall acted as a drum, amplifying the concussive wave. Ryan dropped to the ground as a plume of dust and smoke shot into the chamber.

"Breached!" Boxcar and Almond fell back behind the first pillar, using the granite as cover.

"Petey, Doctor, behind the third pillar." Duncan joined Marshal in the middle of the room, standing with their backs to the column.

Ryan stood with Crystal, facing the eastern wall, when Almond screamed. "Flash grenade."

Despite being hidden, the flash of light blinded Ryan, and the subsequent explosion was enough to stun his senses temporarily.

A single rifle shot rang out, contributing to the ringing in his ears, and Boxcar screamed, "One for me!"

Ryan peeked around the corner, and smoke filled the end of the chamber. The headlamps resembled laser beams through the dust, and visibility was restricted.

Crystal clutched his arm. "Anything?"

"I think we should have tried another entry point. This goes nowhere." Ryan pounded his fist against the pillar as two more shots rang out.

"That's two!"

"Fuck you, that one was mine." Almond laughed.

Crystal flinched and held his fist. "Don't damage the artifacts. Besides, we can use some wisdom right now."

Ryan glanced over his shoulder at the pillar. Hieroglyphs decorated the lower half and were engraved in a band about the circumference. "Show me."

Crystal traced a finger over two birds facing left, with a stylized man kneeling behind. The pattern repeated all the way around. "This is the typical depiction of wisdom."

Ryan peeked around the corner. Duncan and Marshal lay on their stomachs, using the stone as cover. But there was another band of writing. "I need to know what that one says."

"I've already looked. It's the bowstring, symbolizing strength."

Ryan added, "The far pillar is then beauty."

Wisdom, strength, and beauty were the great pillars of our work. Hiram was proud of that statement. *Do you understand, young stone singer?*

"I do." Ryan helped Crystal to her feet and placed both hands on the stone.

"What? What's going on?"

Two more rifle shots rang out. "Bodies are piling up, Duncan," Almond shouted.

"Petey? How ya doing? Doc?"

Ryan thought aloud, "That's a fifteen-foot circumference and thirty tons."

The pillar was five feet wide and twelve feet tall, near the limits of one singer. There was no time to guess. He grasped the column with both hands and sang. The ringing in his ears from the flash bang created a false echo, and there was no time for the subtle seeking harmonics. A pure falsetto note filled the chamber, counterpoint to the occasional rifle shot.

"Grenade!"

Ryan didn't stop singing, but his hands covered his ears, and Crystal did the same. But, there was nothing in common with the first flash bang. Limestone debris showered the chamber like a shotgun blast, and the concussion wave stole the breath from his lungs.

But Ryan had learned two things. "Boxcar! I need your help back here."

"Moving!"

Almond replied, "Covering!"

The large man arrived, trailing smoke in his wake like a dragon terrorizing a village.

"What's up, Petey? You guys hurt?"

Ryan shook his head. "I will sing, and you'll move this pillar in place. It will rotate clockwise. Don't worry. I'll be helping you."

Boxcar was about to laugh but nodded when he noticed Ryan was serious. "If you say so." He slung the rifle and cracked his fingers. "Ready!"

Ryan had a problem. Over the last two thousand years, the limestone had shifted above, placing more weight on the pillar where there wasn't supposed to be any. Two stone singers would have had an easy time with the task, but he had to make do. Ryan began with the seeking song, concentrating on where the granite top had sunk into the limestone ceiling.

He nodded to Boxcar, and the man's arms wrapped around the stone.

"Now!"

The shaping song made the limestone vibrate, and dust fell from above. As Boxcar strained, a vein on his forehead pulsed with his efforts, and Ryan increased the volume. A resonance filled the chamber, vibrating the stone flooring under his feet.

"Two ropes just dropped from above!" Almond called out.

"How we doing, Petey?" Duncan asked.

Ryan ignored the chaos and wrapped his arms around the pillar, and with the sound of an oak tree splitting, the limestone ceiling cracked above his head.

Boxcar shifted his feet, and the pillar rotated an inch.

"Multiple tangos incoming!" Marshal moved forward to cover Boxcar's position.

On one level, Ryan was aware of their actions, but not only were his muscles and voice straining to their utmost in the present, but a voice was also whispering advice from the past.

"Rotate the other way, then forward sharply! One, two …"

When the assault team stepped over the bodies of their fallen men, two grenades were tossed to the chamber's far end. The explosions sent shards of pottery and bone fragments back in a hail storm of debris. Another man wearing tactical armor and a respirator mask rushed forward, a green laser sight and flashlight from his rifle leading the way as his mates covered his approach.

The first pillar was cleared, and the second. Bullets led the way while darting around the corner of the third pillar, but they ricocheted off the stone floor and into the wall—not human flesh. The remaining four men of an eight-man team searched the empty chamber for thirty minutes before giving up. After climbing the ropes, they returned to the surface. A call was made for a clean-up crew and to report that Ryan Petey had vanished.

CHAPTER 57

There was an inch clearance on all sides as he navigated the narrow confines of the tunnel. Ryan pushed forward with his toes while the sharp rock scraped along his back. The air was thick with dust, and after fifteen feet, a sneezing fit slammed his head into the stone ceiling, making his eyes water. He couldn't feel if there was blood. There wasn't enough room to bring a hand back, and they remained outstretched. Crystal would have had an easier time, but she balked at the narrow confines, and Ryan didn't blame her. Sample drilling from the surface had partially collapsed the tunnel, and there was no choice. He had to continue.

"How are you doing, Petey?" Duncan slowly fed the rope as he progressed. He had asked the same question every five minutes. Ryan wasn't sure, but squirming thirty feet had taken half an hour. However, the ceiling disappeared ahead when he tilted his head to the side.

"Thirsty and tired, but nearing the end. I'm okay."

Boxcar's booming laugh carried through the tunnel; oddly, Ryan found it comforting. If the big man wasn't worried, then he wasn't. "After that escape, the beers on me. You can do it, Petey!"

Ryan had been trying to rotate the pillar of wisdom in a circular motion, like a spinning top, but that wasn't the design. The column had to be turned to swing like a door on a hinge pin. There was no time to marvel at the narrow staircase carved into the limestone bedrock, and Boxcar practically threw his teammates down. Ryan was last, and now that he knew the design's secret, he sang while lifting, and the stone swung into position. He linked the granite pillar base to the limestone flooring to ensure no one could follow. It would take another stone singer to reveal the hidden passage.

The stairs ended in a natural rectangular cavern and continued north, but it was the narrow passageway due east where Ryan found himself. As the others recovered from the harrowing experience, he was pressed on all sides by a million tons of stone. One earthquake and he'd be squished like an ant between a hammer and an anvil.

Push, slide. Push, slide.

When his hands dangled in the open air, Ryan grinned. *I'm through!*

Covered in dirt, scratches, and sore in places he didn't think were possible, Ryan stood eighty feet underground, in the chamber under the front paw of the Sphinx. The room was nine-foot square on all sides. The walls were covered in limestone bricks the size of a bread loaf, and the ceiling was natural bedrock polished to a smooth finish. He removed the rope around his ankles and leaned into the tunnel. "I'm through!"

"Tug twice, and we'll pull you out when you're done," Duncan replied.

While Ryan had found the hidden chamber, there was no Hall of Records.

Congratulations. The high priest broke his silence. *Few have made this discovery.*

Ryan stared at the painting on the eastern wall. The shape reminded him of a handgun, and near the bottom, a dark gemstone was set into the brick. "Maybe it's a hand pointing, not a gun."

Your perceptions are skewed.

Ugh. Ryan tilted his head, and the drawing made sense. It wasn't a gun or hand pointing, but the continent of Africa. Ryan's finger found his present location on the Giza Plateau and traveled straight down, or west, in a near-perfect line through the length of the Sahara Desert to the gemstone.

"X marks the spot."

Do you believe the location should be shared with the world or held close to your chest?

Ryan closed his eyes and pictured what would happen if someone knew the map to the Hall of Records was located. Government officials would excavate a tunnel, and a full expedition would be underway within days.

"Am I supposed to be a keeper of secrets as well?" Ryan asked.

Those who use knowledge for their own use instead for the good of all are obligated to safeguard those same secrets.

Kneeling, Ryan placed his fingertips to either side of the gem, hummed the shaping song, and then pushed gently on the wall. Dust and sand trickled around the precious stone before it fell to the ground. To his surprise, the stone vibrated in response with a pure note, like a tuning fork. Leaving a hole would also point to a location, which meant more work.

More of the same material was needed when repairing a fissure or hole. Luckily, the tunnel was littered with enough rocks of varying shapes, and Ryan fit a stone the size of a chicken egg into the divot. Smoothing and shaping the plug took thirty minutes, but you couldn't tell the work wasn't original when completed. Someone would have a map but no references.

There was no point in leaving any trace behind, so Ryan pocketed the gem. Placing his hands in the loop, he gave two sharp tugs. The return journey was easier but harder on the body. He lost a layer of skin on his chin, ripped his shirt over the left shoulder blade, and a pound of sand scooped over his waistband.

"There's our tunnel rat. How are you doing, Petey?" Almond coiled the rope while Crystal brushed him off.

"I'll survive, but I will have to look at a map of where we must go next. I thought it would be the Great Pyramid, but it's much farther than that." Ryan opened his backpack, found a clean shirt, and drank water. It was then that some of the puzzle pieces came together. During Ptah-Du-Amun's time period, the Great Pyramid wasn't constructed, so any references to the hall would be older than 2,500 B.C. He was confused with Hiram's memories mixing with the priests, let alone his own.

"Maps we can get," Duncan said. "Is there an alternate way out of here?"

While the tunnel system was natural, man's hand was clear, at least to Ryan. The limestone ceiling should have dipped lower with the boulders to either side, but a six-foot opening was ahead. The path beneath his feet was smooth and only led in one direction. North.

After five minutes, the ceiling lowered, forcing Boxcar to hunch, but soon everyone dropped to their knees to progress, and Ryan paused. "Do you hear that?"

Duncan nodded. "Like a leaking tap."

"We should be well below the water table," Crystal added.

Thirty feet later, the cavern ended at a pile of limestone boulders, blocking their progress. Thin rivulets of water had worn the rock into channels and disappeared below. Ryan didn't need to hum the seeking song. There was only one boulder that could be moved. The remainder were too large and buried well below the surface.

"Need my help with this one, Petey?" Boxcar called out from the rear. He was on his knees with his rifle and pack at his side.

Duncan groaned. "We'll never hear the end of how he saved the day."

"I'm good. Thank you, though." After briefly grinning at Duncan, he sang, and his hands worked at the stone. The danger was creating a collapse from overhead, and as a precaution, he linked two larger rocks together, forming a natural arch. The boulder wasn't large, close to nine hundred pounds, and shifted easily. Once it was to the side, Ryan looked over the edge. The ten-foot water-slickened chute ended at the base of a wide stone column.

"The way out." Ryan dangled his legs over the edge and pushed off.

Ryan led the way with Marshal on his heels. After sliding around the stone, the narrow opening led into a larger cavern filled with stalactites. Water had turned the limestone into a ceiling of fangs, and the feeling of walking into a beast's mouth was hard to shake. Several mineral deposits formed into ragged columns connecting the uneven floor to the ceiling. The scrape of boots on stone created a distorted echo, and coupled with talking, it sounded like an army was traveling underground.

"These caverns connect with the pyramid?" Boxcar weaved and dodged. He was head and shoulders above everyone else.

"They should, but I'm not sure." Ryan ducked through to another tunnel on the left instead of going straight.

"You're not sure?" Marshal stopped and pointed north. "Why are we not going that way?"

"An old trick. Lick your lips and keep them moist." Ryan waited until he complied. "You can feel an air current coming from this tunnel, but there's nothing from ahead. It's a dead end."

"Keep going, Petey." Duncan laid a hand on Marshall's shoulder. "You're doing good."

Any doubt that they were on the right path disappeared when Ryan stood upright. He walked down seven steps, turned right on a platform, down another five steps, then faced the carved griffin statue. The mythical creature had the head of an eagle and the back end of a lion. The wings were captured mid-flight with a twenty-foot span, and the front talons held a skull in one, and the other rested on a spoked wheel.

"That's Nemesis, the Egyptian Goddess associated with death. She would escort the recently departed from a funeral to the afterlife and is also the goddess of fate." Crystal passed Ryan and walked down the remaining three steps. She rested a palm on the spoked circle. "No one's seen this in thousands of years."

"I don't think you should be saying that." Duncan kicked a plastic water bottle from the second landing and down the steps. "That looks old, but I don't think the pharaohs had plastic."

Marshal chuckled. "That means there's a way out. I need to see the sun and feel the wind on my face."

The tunnel soon changed from the rugged stone of a natural cavern to shaped limestone blocks, then to granite. Cyrstal mentioned they were in the subterranean chamber of the pyramid, which was not open to the public. Boxcar had to use his master key on three locked gates as they climbed long wooden ramps, four flights of stairs, and a ladder. They ascended a steep tunnel strewn with sand and limestone offcuts from the builders. When Ryan turned a corner, electric lighting illuminated their path. He stowed the headlamp as the team slung their rifles in an attempt to be subtle.

The sunlight was intense, burning his eyes, and he didn't see the guard at the end of the tunnel until the last second. The man was dressed in a navy uniform, with a rifle slung over one shoulder. When the six people emerged from a forbidden section, he turned his back on them, suddenly interested in a distant cloud.

"Fuck that feels good." Marshal tilted his chin and closed his eyes, basking in the sun.

From the elevated plateau, Ryan spotted the gray bus in the parking lot, half a mile from where they started. Full circle.

CHAPTER 58

At ten thirty in the morning, the Giza Plateau was filled with thousands of tourists. Busses shuttled people back and forth from the drop-off area, and guides led groups on a tour of the temple ruins and the Sphinx. Many preferred to wander unescorted, going to the Great Pyramid on foot. Armed government officials acted like sheepdogs, constantly keeping people from entering restricted areas. However, for a small fee, those same guards had been known to give brief tours of empty tombs. Scam artists patrolled the area like hungry coyotes, looking for prey.

The motley group walked south from the Great Pyramid across the desert to the bus. With one look at the men in tactical uniforms and weapons, tourists gave them a wide berth. Despite the armed escort, Ryan felt uneasy.

Marshal kept one hand on his holstered pistol as his eyes darted from person to person. One hand rested on his slung rifle while Duncan appeared calm and out for a morning walk.

"I don't like being in the open. Whoever attacked us earlier is still out there." Crystal stayed with him, clustered in the middle of their escort. "Are you ready to talk about what you found? What took you so long inside the chamber? Wish you could have taken pictures!"

Ryan dodged a boulder in his path and agreed. "I found a map with the location, but I couldn't leave that for others to find. I'm sure that's why we were attacked. Someone else is after the Hall of Records, maybe me as well."

"So you destroyed the map?" They were nearing the bus parking lot, and the number of tourists increased.

Ryan lowered his voice as he nodded. "Anyone could have put it back together, so I altered the stone."

Duncan asked, "Where are we going next, Petey?"

Marshal unlocked the bus, and they threw their packs on empty seats. The rifles were stowed out of sight. It took a few minutes for the air conditioning to cool the van, but it was welcome. Mid-morning, the sun was already baking, promising a hot day.

Ryan dug out his tablet and powered it up while Duncan sat beside him. Crystal leaned over the seat in front, and the others sat across the aisle. The iPad had a cellular data plan, and Ryan was rotating the map of Africa to align with the drawing on the chamber wall.

"There was a mark on the wall, due west from our position." Ryan's finger tapped near Africa's western coast. "Right here. There was nothing specific or writing, but that was the area."

Almond groaned. "That's a pretty massive country, and I've been in that area before. It's mainly desert."

"Can I see that for a second?" Crystal held out her hand, and Ryan passed the tablet across. She dropped a pin in the map before handing it back. "Is that where you saw the mark?"

Ryan rotated the screen, then nodded. "That's it."

Crystal grinned but didn't say anything.

"Spill it! The suspense is killing me." Boxcar's booming laugh filled the bus.

"As far as I know, there aren't any buildings or structures in Mauritania, but there's a natural feature called the Richat Structure. It's also been called the Eye of the Sahara."

"Do you know what it is? Are there pyramids or something?" Ryan had never heard the name previously.

She shook her head. "The richat is a natural geological formation where the earth *bubbled* with molten rock, forming concentric rings, stretching twenty-five miles across."

Only Almond appeared to understand. "The Eye is massive and will be difficult to explore. Is there any way of narrowing down the search?"

All eyes turned to Ryan, and he shook his head. "Not that I know."

Almond climbed into the driver's seat, and Duncan powered up a cell phone. "I'm going to make the travel arrangements."

Crystal explained to Boxcar how the geological dome formed and collapsed as Ryan closed his eyes. He wasn't sleeping but concentrating on memories flashing through his mind. The sending wasn't from Ptah-Du-Amun or Hiram, but a man who sacrificed his life for Anubis—Aken—and he wanted Ryan to understand something about the Eye of Horus.

Another piece of the puzzle clicked. The picture was nearly complete.

"Change of plans. I know where we have to go first." Ryan had bought the tablet for a specific reason, and it was time to put it to use. He opened the map and showed Duncan.

The commander didn't bat an eye. "Almond, we're going to need a different vehicle."

Julie Petey curled into a ball and allowed the emotions to carry her like a cork on the ocean. One minute, she was fine, and then the gut-wrenching sobs were paralyzing. Her injuries aside, she was worried about her son. *Something* was happening to him, and while she didn't know what it was, Julie knew it wasn't good—mother's instinct.

"Here. Drink some water." Trish smoothed the hair out of her eyes and helped Julie sit upright.

"Thank you." Her ribs ached, and at least one was broken. Each breath was painful, and she struggled to find a comfortable position. Her wrists were raw flesh, compliments of the chain, and constantly stinging. The original injury to her wrist still throbbed, and it was probably broken by now.

"Did you manage to sleep?" Trish asked.

Julie shook her head. "You need rest as well. You're going to pass out soon."

Trish was at her side every time she stirred or groaned in pain. "I'm good. I slept a few hours earlier while you were out."

"I think you're lying." When the water bottle was half empty, she placed it at her feet. "How's your eye?"

The men had focused on Trish, and her body paid the price. Her left eye had swollen shut, with deep cuts on her cheek and forehead. The right eye was already turning various shades of purple, but she could still see. By the way she moved, there were broken ribs as well, and not just one—her whole right side was a mass of black and yellow bruises.

"I think I could use a raw steak right about now." Trish smiled, and Julie tried not to laugh.

"Peanut butter sandwiches are not good enough for you?" Ryan had grown up on peanut butter and jam. That was still his favorite lunch. The thought of her son caused a new string of tears to roll down her cheeks.

"That's about the only thing I can eat right now. I think there may be some loose teeth." Trish sat beside her, placing an arm across her shoulders. "This will all be over soon, and Ryan will be back home, safe and sound. Call it a police woman's hunch."

The floor lurched, and the water bottle tipped off the table and rolled to the end of the room. A distant crash of thunder made the wall shake, but the light remained on. Julie didn't think her sanity would survive without the single bulb hanging from the ceiling.

She tried to chuckle, but the pain was too much and came out as a grunt. "I hope so because that fucking bucket is disgusting."

The forty-two-foot shipping container held the mattress, a six-foot plank table bolted to the wall, and the bucket at the far end—their only bathroom. Their supplies consisted of two cases of water, three loaves of bread, and peanut butter.

"I'll drop it on—"

The front of the container rose again, and the light flickered before going out.

"It's okay. I'm right here." Trish found her hand as they were enveloped in complete darkness, and the thunder drew closer. "Fuck!"

Ignoring the pain in her ribs, Julie screamed.

CHAPTER 59

While Ryan had pictured Cairo as a backwater country stuck in the past, he was proven wrong multiple times within the next twenty minutes. While Boxcar had the master key for any lock, Duncan had the cash for any purchases, including a twenty-four-hour rental for three dune buggies. The unibody design, suspension, and tires were for deep sand and were popular with tourists. The rental company upcharged for the three-seater model so that Boxcar could be comfortable but added the extra jerry can of gasoline, camping equipment, and water at no additional charge. The four men carrying pistols and tactical gear weren't enough to make the salesman hesitate after seeing the American bills.

As Duncan secured the buggies, Almond bought additional supplies, and Marshal bought lunch. While everyone had rations in their pack, a chance for fresh food wasn't to be passed up. Ryan discovered he liked the falafel of beans and chickpeas, or ta'ameye as Crystal called it, but he could barely finish the second one.

"Petey, you're with me. Doc, and Boxcar. No point in separating Marshal and Almond. I'll take the lead." Duncan loaded the packs behind the bucket seats, securing them with bungee cords.

Almond handed goggles to everyone and tan shemaghs to keep out the sand and dust.

"I'll go with the big guy, only if I can drive." Crystal threw her pack behind the seat and didn't wait for an answer. She jumped behind the wheel.

"I've always thought I deserved a chauffeur. Works for me!" Boxcar stepped over the side.

Ryan didn't bother asking and buckled the five-point harness in the passenger seat as Duncan started the engine. He kept the goggles around his neck and wrapped the scarf around his head, covering the lower half of his face.

Duncan drew his pistol and showed Ryan. "Sig Sauer P226, with a fifteen-round magazine. There is *no* safety on here except your finger. If you intend to fire, your finger goes on the trigger. Until then, your finger is extended down the barrel." Duncan demonstrated. "Assume anything you aim at will die, so always control the direction of your muzzle and keep it pointed in a safe direction. Always ensure the area *behind* your target is clear. You don't want to shoot a team member or an innocent civilian. Here's how you change magazines."

Duncan demonstrated the release and how to load a fresh magazine. He had Ryan practice several times before placing the pistol in the console between the seats and cup holders.

"I don't know what's coming, and I need my partner ready to help if required. I'll go over the SA80 rifle when we have a chance."

While Ryan didn't think he could shoot someone but then again hurled a two-pound dolerite through a man's head. Maybe the gun would be less messy. Almond finished unboxing the cell signal booster and plugged it into the twelve-volt adapter, then stowed the softball-sized white dome with the packs.

"That's it, boss. Ready."

While Ryan needed a tablet, he doubted the signal would be strong enough in the desert, and Almond had a solution. Once linked to the booster, he oriented the screen and pointed northwest. Duncan picked up the handset. "Moving out."

"Roger," Marshal replied.

"Ten-four, good buddy," Crystal drawled, and Boxcar's laugh carried across the parking lot. Soon, they were driving through the streets of Cairo.

The rental company was on the city's western edge, fifteen minutes from the pyramids. They went by several neighborhoods, a mall, and then an industrial area with warehouses mixed with factories. When the road ended, Duncan followed Ryan's finger and left civilization behind. Keeping the desert at bay was a full-time job in Egypt, with street cleaners battling the never-ending dust and sand that got everywhere. But the desert could not be tamed in such a manner.

"Relax. I have some experience playing in a sandbox." Duncan grinned. The buggy leaped forward, cresting a four-foot dune. When the wheels left the ground, he screamed, "Yahoo!"

Ryan held the tablet with one hand and the overhead bar with the other while laughing.

"Don't worry. This will get old soon. Do you have a better idea of the distance?" Duncan reset the mileage with the push of a button.

Ryan used the scale on the map; since they were off-road, the distance usually given by directions wouldn't work. "Thirty to thirty-five miles."

"We'll be there in forty-five minutes. This buggy isn't the best, but we're holding fifty miles an hour."

Farther into the desert, the more maneuvering they would have to do. The buggy may climb a hundred-foot-tall dune, but Duncan didn't take the chance. Rolling or getting stuck wasn't good for the mission. While they didn't go in a straight line, they were making good time. Ryan twisted in his seat to look behind. Almond and Marshal maintained a fifty-foot spacing. He had expected great plumes of dust to rise into the air, but buggies skimmed across the surface like a ship on the water—smooth sailing.

The sun was directly above, and Duncan wrapped the shemagh over his head. He didn't wear the goggles and pulled out a pair of sunglasses instead. As predicted, driving through the desert wasn't too exciting after twenty minutes. You could only marvel at the sheer amount of sand so many times before it became passe. Occasionally, they would navigate around rock outcroppings or drive across the ridgelines of a dune.

You are getting close.

Ryan sat upright and glanced at Duncan, but it wasn't him who spoke.

Hello?

As they crested another rise, Duncan paused, then drove toward the only feature in the immediate area—a grove of date palms. Ryan lowered the tablet. They had arrived.

The oasis had grown since Aken had been here, covering nearly a square mile, but the water was a dark brown, not clear. Only a few hardy plants grew along the edges, mainly toward the limestone outcrop. Pure white flakes rimmed the water on the eastern edge—salt. Over thousands of years, the groundwater had changed and was no longer drinkable. The only feature was to the north, where a low mountain ridge traveled west to east, two miles distant. Ryan changed the view on the tablet and guessed they were fifty miles from the Mediterranean Sea.

"Hope you're not going for a swim." Duncan turned off the engine, and the others arrived, doing the same.

Memories were calling, and he fought the desire to begin. Instead, Ryan found a water bottle behind the seat and drank. The sun was baking, and Marshal had been adamant they continued to drink, even if they weren't thirsty.

"I'm going to walk for a while. When I stop, you can bring the buggies. We'll probably need the shovels." Ryan picked up the tablet, allowing a dead man's thoughts to guide his steps.

The outcropping of rock rose along the southern shore, and he stood with his back to a large boulder. The application on the tablet was called StarChart. At home, after complaining that they couldn't view the stars from his backyard, Ryan and his friends had played with it once. When holding the tablet above your head, the night sky and names of constellations were revealed. Should you tilt the screen, the application will show a new view. The vision of the scroll with the dotted lines and holes was an archaic version of the tablet.

Ryan entered the desired date and local time. Tilting the screen to the sky, he viewed the stars where they would have been in 2,500 B.C. The bright star was the bottom left corner in a cluster, resembling a rhomboid rectangle. He held the bottom of the tablet with the top of the mountain ridge and began. Ignoring the few steps in the brackish water, Ryan focused on his target as he started the first prayer learned with the order. Each step matched the cadence, and he fell into the rhythm. Twelve minutes later, as the first prayer ended, Ryan began the second. He used the tablet to confirm he was going in the correct direction every few minutes, but Ryan wasn't traveling at night—it was the day. He used a ragged peak to act as a landmark.

When the second prayer ended, he recited the third. The next prayer was a variation of the third, but not as long. At the last word, he stopped walking. Fifty feet to his front, a great dune rose over a smooth limestone ridge. There was nothing beneath his feet but sand to mark the position. Was this it? How do I know these memories are correct?

Have faith.

Ryan faced the oasis and waved his arm in the air. He had traveled half a mile, and Duncan followed his progress with binoculars. Once the buggies left the oasis, Ryan knelt and scooped hot sand through his legs like a dog—or a jackal.

CHAPTER 60

Throughout most of Egypt, the government had installed a digging ban. Artifacts can be found almost anywhere when a civilization has occupied the land for five thousand years. Last year, a man was arrested for excavating a hole in his backyard and selling pottery, stone tablets, and a broken idol online. The government traced the seller through eBay, and he was jailed with a lengthy sentence. Despite the repercussions, many thought the risk was worth it. Rogue teams would set up at night, not only on the Giza plateau but throughout the country, and dig. Before the sun rose, they would disperse with no trace left behind. Boards covering a hole in the ground and covered with sand, which resembled most of the country, remained hidden. Crystal liked to talk while working and had more information on digging than Ryan thought possible. She was his first pick if he had to choose a partner for Trivial Pursuit.

Duncan erected a tarp between two buggies, and they alternated, resting in the shade while the remainder worked. No one questioned *how* this location was chosen or why they were searching. The team, including Crystal, accepted Ryan's expertise at face value and didn't ask questions, but that didn't stop the good-natured complaining.

"I just cleared that spot! You have to place the sand outside the hole." Boxcar worked next to Almond, and every time the shovel blades clanked together, he would shout, *en guard!*

"The sides are getting too tall for me." Almond wiped the sweat pouring down his face. "We all didn't eat magic beans as a child."

"You'd think a grunt would know how to dig a hole." Boxcar glanced furtively at Ryan, and Almond cleared his throat but didn't explain the reference. After that exchange, they worked in silence.

Once the sides of the hole were three feet over their heads, even Boxcar was having difficulty tossing the sand to the side, but the work stopped when Duncan's shovel scraped rock.

"Thank fucking, God." Marshal leaned back to sit. They were all exhausted.

Duncan cleared the sand, exposing the smooth limestone beneath, and asked Ryan, "Now what?"

"I'll let you know in a second." Ryan knelt, placing both hands on the exposed rock, and sang. The low notes carried through the stone to the depths of the earth, and he discovered not only limestone but granite nearby. A two-way radio on Almond's belt squelched, then died. Ryan pointed to the side. "Three feet that way."

After an hour of moving sand, he was nearly there.

I, too, have waited long.

Once exposed, the tunnel opening was covered by a squared slab of limestone, three feet to each side and four inches thick.

"I got this one. You don't even need to sing!" Boxcar got his fingers underneath and lifted the sixty-pound stone without effort. "We're a rock-movin' team."

The tunnel was four feet wide and five feet tall but ended after ten feet. "We're here."

Limestone walls were carved out of the bedrock, and the wall below was the same smooth red granite used in the pyramid construction. Ryan grinned. The nearest quarry was seventy miles east. Someone put a lot of effort into building this temple and keeping it hidden.

"Okay, Boxcar. Do you want to see if you have what it really takes?" Hiram, and therefore Ryan, had trained hundreds of stone singers over decades. The ability was not common, and each one found was a celebration.

"Hell ya! Excuse me, Doc." Crystal stepped to the side as Boxcar threw his shovel away and crawled inside.

"Place your hands on the stone lightly so you're barely touching it." When he followed the instructions, Ryan ignored the spectators and placed his hands on Boxcar's shoulders.

Singing between different mediums was difficult but not overly so. While starting with limestone, transitioning to granite was challenging, and a third type was even more difficult but not impossible. Focusing, Ryan channeled his abilities through another human, not stone. When placing two tuning forks with the same frequency near each other and striking one, the other will vibrate in response. The same thing can happen to people. Ryan and Hiram were listening for an echo from Boxcar's being. The strength of the echo or returning signal would reveal the potential or lack of ability.

After singing the shaping song for a few minutes, Ryan heard the response and grinned. "Congratulations! I think you could learn."

"Holy shit!" Boxcar's jaw dropped.

Ryan laughed and slapped the big man on the shoulder. "There are different levels of the stone singer trade, but you have the ability to become an apprentice."

"We're never going to hear the end of this, are we?" Marshal shook his head.

"I was apprenticed to a bricklayer once until I joined the—"

"How about we let Petey move the stone?" Duncan interrupted.

Ryan didn't understand the secrecy, but he agreed. "Let's move it together. How's that?"

Boxcar mumbled, *rock-moving team,* before Ryan placed his right palm on the granite slab and left hand over the big man's massive paw. He spoke loud enough for Boxcar to hear and not the others. "The first song any apprentice learns is the seeking song. It's used to identify the type of stone, shape, and size. You have to understand the stone before all else."

Channeling through the man was easier the second time, and Ryan discovered the granite stone was not square but an odd shape, so the ends would overlap the blocks below, allowing it to pivot.

"Can you feel anything?"

Boxcar grinned, and a sparkle made his eyes shine like a child receiving presents. "I can feel the size of the stone and its shape."

"Push in and up, like rolling a ball up a slope." Ryan changed the song and pushed.

Sand filtered through the cracks and the granite ground against the limestone. Sunlight and fresh air flowed into the temple of Anubis for the first time in thousands of years. When the slab was in line with the others in the ceiling, Ryan linked it to the walls so it wouldn't fall. A tunnel leading down to the inner chamber was visible.

"That was amazing. Thank you." Boxcar was choked up and pulled Ryan into a one-armed, rib-crushing hug.

"You have potential and an affinity for stone. Glad you enjoyed it." Ryan turned to the others. "It's safe to come down, and we'll need flashlights."

"Already ahead of you!" Crystal passed out the headlamps, and she was first down the ramp.

Some secrets should be kept. A series of memories were imparted, and Ryan stumbled, catching himself against the wall. The night of the new moon would begin in nine hours, and Ryan followed the others into the temple, wondering if there would be enough time.

CHAPTER 61

The surreal moment wasn't deja vu, but Ryan didn't know what else to call it. His fingers brushed against the walls, and sand crunched underfoot as he walked in Aken's footsteps millennia later. After his excursions, being underground was a relief, and the temperature dropped twenty degrees as he descended. Crystal's exclamation of the temple room echoed through the tunnel and chamber.

"There's no Hall of Records in here. It's too small." Marshal sounded disappointed.

When Ryan turned at the bottom of the ramp, everyone was staring at the statue of Anubis. The emerald eyes reflected the light, and Ryan bowed his head briefly in honor before they noticed his arrival.

Crystal turned to the bundles of debris on the altar and floor. "Human remains, probably sacrificed."

Ryan shook his head. "They were trapped and killed themselves to avoid prolonged agony."

She gave him a funny look, then examined the statue.

Duncan asked, "What do you need next?"

Remembering Aken's advice, Ryan hesitated. There were different levels of secrets, and he was unsure which to keep and what to reveal. He decided to err on the side of caution, and the lie twisted in his stomach. "I need everyone at the top of the ramp, near the stone we tilted. There's a pressure plate in the ground; five of you will be enough to trip it. The secrets of the temple will be revealed. At least that's what I was told."

No one had questioned where Ryan received his information, and they didn't do so now. They shuffled out of the altar chamber and up the incline.

Boxcar called out, "If you need help moving big things, let me know!"

Ryan didn't wait for them to get in position. "Excuse me, my Lord."

He pressed on the left eye socket, and the altar table clicked. Ryan's flashlight illuminated the high priest's necklace and the order's signet ring, where they rested undisturbed. There was no time to gawk. He slipped the chain over his head, hiding it with the shemagh. The ring slipped into a pocket.

"Okay, we're in position," Crystal called out, and her voice echoed down the tunnel.

"One second." Ryan slid the table back and pressed *both* eye sockets inward. The statue swung out on concealed hinges like a door. Cool sand poured outward, covering Ryan's legs to the shin. "Come on back. I have some bad news."

Seconds later, they filtered into the chamber, and Almond groaned as his flashlight flicked over the wall of sand. "Shit. Do we need to get shovels?"

Duncan sighed while Marshal swore at the discovery.

Ryan shook his head. "I don't think so." He touched the sand, and more flowed, covering him past his knees. "The tunnel has been filled in. It would take days to dig out."

Boxcar held out a hand and pulled Ryan free.

"I'd need a whole archeology team and a dozen laborers to move that much sand." Crystal glanced at the ceiling. "If the tunnel is straight and came out on the other side of the ridgeline, then—"

Duncan held a hand in the air. "What's that?"

A howling wind buffeted across the tunnel opening, and then a moan filled the temple, making the hair on Ryan's arms stand on end.

"Sand storm?" Almond asked.

Duncan drew his pistol and shook his head. "Skies were clear, and I checked the weather report. Not a chance. I think we have company."

"Fuck! My rifle's in the buggy." Boxcar's hand drifted near his holster.

"I'll check it out." Marshal didn't wait for the others and sprinted up the incline. His rifle swung into position.

"Are we done here?" Duncan asked.

"Yes." Ryan glanced over his shoulder at Aken's remains on the altar. *Sorry, I wanted to give you a proper burial.*

Duncan ordered, "Okay. Petey, Doc, stay behind me. Boxcar, watch our six. Almond, you're point. We'll go straight to the buggies and get the hell out of here. If separated, we'll meet up at the oasis. Questions?"

Almond drew his weapon and held it at the ready. Enough light filtered from the opening to navigate the tunnel without the flashlights. "Moving."

Crystal's hand found his as they followed the commander to the surface.

Almond crouched in the recently dug pit, and Duncan moved to his shoulder. Seventy-five feet on the other side of the buggies, a mottled tan helicopter touched down, buffetting a ring of sand in concentric circles.

"Fall back into the temple, and we'll—"

"I don't think so. No one is moving an inch!" Marshal yelled from behind the group.

Confused, Ryan and the others turned around. Marshal stood above them, aiming down the barrel of a rifle, keeping them in his cross-hairs.

"What the *fuck* are you doing?" Duncan yelled in disbelief.

Boxcar reached for Ryan, and Marshal fired. The bullet hit the ground inches from the big man's boots. "Don't move."

The helicopter door opened, and soldiers in tan combat uniforms sprinted toward them.

"Petey, step forward and climb out. Everyone else stays there." Marshal gestured with his chin.

"Fuck you." The betrayal triggered a torrent of rage in his chest. He began to hum when the barrel shifted, aiming at Crystal.

"If you do anything, she dies. Move now." The soldiers had arrived and spread out in a semi-circle, blocking any chance of escape.

"How much are they paying you, man? Seriously, we've worked together for ten years. I treated you like a brother." Duncan assessed the situation and came to the same conclusion as Ryan.

The soldiers carried rifles, and three stepped forward to the pit's rim.

In heavily accented English, a bald, dark-skinned man ordered, "Drop all your weapons. Do it now!"

"Petey, move." Marshal grinned. "Or everyone dies around you."

Ryan gave Crystal's hand a final squeeze. "Everything will be okay. It's me they want."

When passing Duncan and Almond, without moving his lips, he whispered, "Get ready."

They stepped aside as he trudged up the slope.

Marshal slung his rifle, and after reaching Ryan's side, he held a pistol to his head. "We'll be leaving now. Time to say goodbye."

Without warning, Ryan lunged toward the three soldiers. "Run!"

He counted on one thing. They needed him alive. Otherwise, he wouldn't have had the courage to act. Ryan crashed into the men, rifles clattering against each other as Duncan grabbed Crystal by the shoulders and threw her down the tunnel. Almond was on his heels, and Boxcar came last.

Screaming, Marshal's arm swung toward his former teammates. Three men quickly pinned Ryan to the ground, and a pure note of rage tore out his throat. The limestone shelf shook as Marshal fired, and he didn't miss. Boxcar stumbled forward, then collapsed.

While the tremor gave them crucial seconds, it also loosened the granite slab. Almond pulled Boxcar below as sand cascaded over the opening. The two-ton stone dropped with a bone-jarring thud, and two soldiers on Ryan's left lost their footing. A bullet struck the slab and ricocheted into the ground.

"No!" Ryan struggled against the men, but it was futile. He couldn't move.

"Thanks for taking care of that for me. Killing friends is always difficult." Marshal dragged Ryan to his feet, pushing him toward the helicopter. Soldiers flanked him, grasping his upper arms. Before boarding, Marshal paused. "I can't chance you screwing up the electronics."

The butt of a rifle struck him behind the ear, and his vision shrunk to a pinprick. Fears of burying his friends alive, gratefully, disappeared as he fell unconscious.

Minutes later, the helicopter hovered twenty feet while rotating about the tunnel entrance. Rotor wash shifted several tons of sand in thirty seconds, erasing footprints and covering any evidence. Only a slight depression marked the area next to the abandoned dune buggies as the helicopter flew east over the dunes.

CHAPTER 62

Almond dragged Boxcar another foot before the granite block fell, and everything turned pitch black.

"Duncan?" Crystal called out.

"Right here." When the flashlight lit up the area, he turned to Almond. "Report."

Crystal stepped aside as Boxcar groaned. "Fuck me, that hurts."

"Besides the obvious, we're lucky to be alive." Almond helped Boxcar to his feet. "The ceramic plates worked, but the .40 caliber must have packed a punch."

"You going to make it, big guy?"

"Bruises, but I'll live. What the *hell* happened with Marshal?"

Duncan led the way to the altar chamber. "He sold us out. We'll deal with him later, but I need a full inventory first. Everything."

His arm cleared the remains from the altar table, and pockets were emptied. Each man had eight magazines of 9mm ammo and 5.56 mm, along with an impressive collection of knives.

Duncan found an old pack of gum, one plastic strap from an old mission, and two glow sticks. Crystal had her flashlight and nothing else. Almond produced nearly the same items; only Boxcar had food—a melted chocolate bar.

"We don't have any water and no food to mention. Ideas?" Duncan repacked his vest while the others stowed everything away.

Crystal asked, "Boxcar, do you think you can move the stone as Ryan could? He said you had potential."

All eyes turned to the big man. "It was like being at a rock concert and listening to the lead singer. I knew the words, but there wasn't a chance I could get on stage and sing at his level. Petey mentioned I had *some* ability, but I have no idea how much."

"Damn." Duncan turned to Crystal. "Doc, what do you think?"

She hadn't stopped studying the temple but shook her head. "Two possibilities. The front door or the back."

Crystal jerked a thumb over her shoulder at the wall of sand behind the statue.

"Almond. Thoughts?"

The dark man nodded. "Whatever we do, it has to be quick. Without water, we'll either be dead or unable to move. We can't move that block, so there's little choice."

"Agreed." Duncan waded through the sand and scooped a handful. Like tilting an hourglass, more fell. "Use one flashlight at a time. I'd hate to be down here in the dark."

He removed the vest and utility belt, placing them on the altar. Duncan angled the flashlight against his pistol and got to work. Two hands scooped the sand back between his legs, and the mound quickly grew. Almond stripped down and used the same technique to shift the pile further.

"Wish I kept my shovel." Boxcar placed his gear on top and joined the work chain with Crystal. "Doc, how much air is down here? Should we be worrying?"

"Carbon dioxide is heavier than air. If you're feeling light-headed, go up the tunnel ramp. But I wouldn't worry. There should be enough in here for a week or two."

Duncan knew they wouldn't last that long without water and food. "Conserve your energy and work at a moderate pace. It isn't a sprint, but a marathon."

Boxcar chuckled as he scooped. "Do you mean at a medium pace?"

Almond laughed. "If you sing, I'm going to shoot you."

"Put your arms around me, baby…"

Duncan let them joke as long as the work was getting done. Good for morale and all that shit you're supposed to say when faced with a hopeless situation. Keep the troops busy so they don't have time to think of death looming over their heads.

"We'll take a fifteen-minute break every hour. The first one to sing all the lyrics gets an extra piece of gum." Duncan grinned as Boxcar accepted the offer, and his warbling voice echoed in the temple.

"Can't you see I need you so?"

Crystal laughed, and Almond eventually joined her. Duncan bent to the task, pushing aside thoughts of betrayal and revenge. *Come on, old man. The only easy day was yesterday.*

▲ ▲ ▲

The sensation of a twelve-inch spike being driven into his brain could no longer be ignored. It felt like his skull was cracked, and he had trouble focusing. Ryan tried to touch his head, but his hands couldn't move. Fingers felt the metal handcuffs around each wrist, and a black cloth bag over his head kept him in the dark. Slowly, he grew aware of his surroundings. The drone of the helicopter and rushing wind noise were steady.

"ETA?" Marshal asked.

Ryan swallowed the lump in his throat when the vision of Boxcar being shot replayed in his mind. *Fucking asshole!* He shifted enough to confirm his ankles were bound as well. Singing in the helicopter to fry the electronics was tempting, but he didn't know how far off the ground they were. Odds were, he'd be committing suicide. As long as he was alive, there was a chance. Until then, he would wait for the opportunity, then take it.

"Two minutes, sir."

Shortly, the helicopter touched down, and Ryan remained limp as he was carried like a sack of potatos. They didn't know he was awake, giving him an edge. *Something is better than nothing.* The sun baked him in the cloth bag, and he could only see vague shapes through the material. He was thrown in a vehicle, and the air conditioning was welcomed, but he had another problem. The necklace was missing.

A door slammed shut, and Marshal spoke. "Runway, three two."

Ryan rolled back as the vehicle drove. *I can't be killed here.* The seeking song made his chest vibrate, and he matched the tone to the engine noise. For a minute, nothing happened, then a *ding* sounded.

"What was that?" Marshal asked.

"Engine light. Probably due for an oil change." The man sounded American and older.

Ryan increased the volume, and the results made him grin. The vehicle lurched, and another warning signal sounded. The driver sounded puzzled. "I don't know what's wrong."

"I do."

The muzzle of a pistol pressed against Ryan's temple. "Shut the fuck up."

"Go ahead and shoot me, asshole." He continued to sing. The shaping song had the desired effect, and the vehicle shuddered and died. Something held the note a split second longer, and Ryan realized the gemstone from the map was still in his pocket. Like the bluestones of Stonehenge, the precious gem acted as an amplifier. But the ring was missing. *Fuck!*

"It's not a far walk, sir." The driver tried turning the key over, and a series of clicks made Ryan chuckle.

"Fucker!" The pistol slapped him in the head, but the bag absorbed most of the blow. The pain was worth it. Marshal opened the door, and Ryan knew what was coming next. He was yanked outside, landing hard on the ground. Unfortunately, he was on an airport tarmac, and the multiple compounds in asphalt wouldn't react to his singing. He could have sunk Marshal to his knees if he was on stone.

"Get up."

"I can't, idiot. Remove the handcuffs and untie my legs." Ryan laughed.

"Jesus *fucking* Christ." Marshal lifted him by the belt, and with a quick dip, Ryan was thrown over his shoulders.

As soon as he started walking, Ryan spoke, "I have to pee."

"I swear to God. I *will* shoot you in the leg."

Marshal was struggling after five minutes, and then suddenly, he threw Ryan down like a sack of potatoes. "Here he is, sir."

Ryan waited to be knocked out, but a syringe was injected into his thigh instead. "You're going to pay for this, asshole …"

Ryan was unconscious for the second time within an hour, but this time, he had company on his journey into darkness.

CHAPTER 63

2565 B.C. Giza Plateau

The white linen sheet was lowered by four men at each corner, draping over the small body on the stone table. Marwa's shaking hand tilted the copper bowl, and goose blood flowed over the hot coals in the brazier. The thick fluid bubbled as the cloying metallic odor rose to assault the senses. She tried not to vomit and clutched the jade ankh necklace.

I have done this a hundred times; don't be sick.

Last week, her seven-year-old daughter complained of sharp abdominal pains and stopped eating. The healers tried everything, but an hour ago, Tahini passed away in her sleep with Marwa at her side. As a priest of Anubis, she knew the importance of death, and

Tahini no longer suffered. That knowledge did little to appease the living or mend her heart. The young priestess had never had to bury a family member before, and grief shredded her soul.

The four men left the torches in the sconces and filed out of the temple, leaving the priestess alone to finish the ritual. But she couldn't do it.

"My baby." Grief-stricken sobs wracked her body. "Bring her back, my Lord!"

Marwa collapsed on the stone floor, and the bowl of goose blood splattered over her white robes. A fresh round of tears poured down her face when a hand squeezed her shoulder.

"I got the message and came as fast as I could." Ptah-Du-Amun was breathless. Marwa knew her husband had run across the plateau for days to be here at this moment. Her hand found him and drew strength from his presence.

"Our baby girl is gone." Marwa struggled to her feet and collapsed in his arms. Strong arms held her up and caressed her long, dark hair.

"It's okay. I'm here." He tried to soothe her, but it had the opposite effect.

Two hands shoved him hard, and she screamed. "It's *not* okay. Tahini is dead!"

Marwa didn't realize she was punching her husband in the chest until he held her wrists.

"Her transition from this world to the next will be assured. Let's finish the prayers, and may our Lord's guiding hand carry her soul through the afterlife."

Any form of rational thinking was gone. When Marwa latched onto an idea, she couldn't shake it. "It's only been an hour. There still may be a chance for Tahini."

The look of horror on Ptah-Du-Amun's face didn't sway her thoughts. "No! It is forbidden. Fate's wheel has spun, and mortals cannot reverse its turn."

While she was young for a priestess, not yet having seen her third decade of life, her husband taught her not only the three prayers but also the fourth. He would be a high priest within the year, and Ptah-Du-Amun had passed along the restricted knowledge.

"Leave me alone. Now." Marwa placed her hands on Tahini's shoulders. There was no time to wait or follow the ceremony—she began the fourth prayer. The gods will *not* decide her daughter's fate. A mother knows best.

"No! Please don't. You have no idea of the dangers." Her husband pleaded, but it was too late.

Seconds after the words rang out in the stone temple, Marwa's mind was elsewhere. She was soaring through a cloudless gray sky surrounded by pinpricks of fire twisting and dancing to a nameless beat. In a pattern she didn't understand, some lights disappeared while others came into existence. At first glance, she was surrounded by hundreds, then thousands of sparks as Marwa continued her journey, but soon she traveled alone.

Until she came to the great barrier, seconds or hours could have passed, but there was no way to tell in a realm without time. The black wall was infinite in all directions, and the enormity of the task nearly crippled her resolve. But thoughts of a newborn suckling at her teat, Tahini's first steps, and her gentle voice singing while at play pushed Marwa into action.

In a realm where sound translates to energy, prayers have power.

Her pleas struck the great barrier like a hammer, making the surface ripple. But repeated efforts had no results, and Marwa grew desperate. Blind with love, loss, and grief, she hurled herself at the wall. A light flare wrapped around her before Marwa crossed the great divide. As one disappeared through the mortal barrier, a spark entered the realm of humanity from the beyond.

▲ ▲ ▲

"It's okay, honey. I have you." Ptah-Du-Amun wrapped Tahini in the white sheet, holding her to his chest. His daughter didn't need to see the sacrifice her mother had made. Let her memories of Marwa never be altered.

He stood beside his wife for fifteen agonizing minutes, not daring to interrupt. Tales of the mind never returning were but one of the warnings he had learned from the high priest. The first was never to make demands of the gods. Ever. The consequences were dire, or the price too high.

Ptah-Du-Amun stepped over his wife with a gentle hand, rubbing Tahini's back. He would prepare a warm bath and make her favorite soup.

She snuggled into the crook of his neck and murmured, "I love you."

With a final look at the crumpled form on the stones, he whispered, "I love you, too."

CHAPTER 64

Waking up in an airplane was an experience Ryan wished would change. His hands were handcuffed in his lap, but the ties around his ankles were gone. Instead of a jet, he was leaning against the window of a commercial plane. Wiping the drool from his chin, he looked over his shoulder to learn he was the only passenger. Any thoughts of singing vanished as the plane flew above the clouds. Long stretches of sand were below, and in the distance, an aqua-marine ribbon stretched across the horizon. Luckily, he sat in the emergency row over the port wing. In case there were any troubles, he'd make a quick exit.

While shaking off the effects of the drugs, he whispered, "I'm sorry about what happened with your wife, Ptah-Du-Amun."

Knowledge can be painful, but you can benefit from others' experiences.

Not only had Ryan lived those last moments as Marwa, but he had also learned the fourth prayer's correct intonation. As a singer, he knew that sound and vibration could have repercussions on the physical world. But with the right notes, the spiritual as well. The version used with the star chart, while technically correct, lacked the nuances.

"Your daughter?"

She lived a full life and gave me many grandchildren.

Ryan was having trouble wrapping his mind around the time shift across millennia. Even Ptah-Du-Amun's great-grandchildren have been gone for thousands of years. He got the courage to ask something that's been bothering him for the last week. "How can we talk if you've been dead for a long time?"

The priest's wry humor shone through. *You know the answers already. You'll figure it out.*

"Great. Totally helpful."

When the *fasten seatbelts* sign chimed, Ryan thought it was a joke, but a flight attendant appeared from the cockpit. She was a slim brunette in a dark blue dress suit. Turkish Airlines was embroidered on the upper chest. "Seat in the upright position, and fasten your seatbelt."

"Excuse me. Where is everyone else? Where are we going?" Ryan followed her instructions.

"All seats were purchased, and the flight will land at Chinguitti, Mauritania. We'll be arriving in eight minutes. I hope you enjoyed your flight. The local time is 18:00 hours."

She reached over and snugged his belt tighter before returning to the cockpit.

The aircraft banked, and the landing gear deployed as they descended. Ryan had smoother landings, but they didn't crash, so he didn't complain. Before taxiing, the cockpit door opened, and Marshal stepped out. He was dressed in the same tactical gear, but his rifle was missing.

"Showtime. You ready, Petey?"

"Do I have a choice?" Ryan unbuckled and stood in the aisle. He didn't want to be manhandled by the scumbag.

"You'll find out soon enough." Marshal stepped between the seats and gestured for Ryan to go first.

The flight attendant opened the door, and a wave of heat flowed into the craft. Two ground crewmen wheeled a staircase to the side.

Marshal spoke. "Hold on a second, kid. I want you to know this is nothing personal, and I did this just for the money. However, I've heard about the people that are *really* running the show, and you don't want to fuck with them."

Ryan remained silent but raised his eyebrows.

"No. Seriously. They have more power than governments and more money than countries. Do what you will with this information, but if you follow their rules, there's a chance you can walk out of this alive. You've saved my bacon, and I appreciate it. Listen to me or not, but I'm telling you the truth."

Marshal gestured for Ryan to descend first. The Chinguitti airport was a fraction of Toronto's, consisting of one-story buildings, a hangar, and a maintenance shack. Refueling trucks were parked at an angle near the main road. The country beyond the airport grounds was stark and resembled a Martian landscape: the harsh, rugged terrain combined volcanic rock, dark red sand, and basalt.

"We'll be leaving within the hour. Our escort is waiting in the terminal." Marshal maintained a ten-foot distance; one hand never left his holstered pistol while crossing the tarmac.

Can volcanic rock be manipulated like granite, Hiram?

Ryan studied the hellish countryside, and there would be little doubt he would soon be in the thick of it.

The structure is different and responds like a mineral or crystal. A song was altered to achieve success.

Ryan was lost in the lesson when he entered the terminal, nearly bumping into a dark-skinned man wearing a blue suit.

"Ah, Ryan Petey. A pleasure to finally meet you."

Duncan had sand in places where he didn't think it was possible, but their efforts produced results. The temple room floor was three feet deep and leveled with the table's surface. Boxcar was a powerhouse, flinging material out of the room to the base of the ramp in a steady stream for the last hour.

"How are you doing, Doc?" Duncan leaned against the wall to catch his breath.

The altar table acted as an anchor, supporting the slide's base, allowing the team to tunnel through the top portion next to the ceiling instead of moving the broad expanse. With her back to the roof, there was no danger of being buried alive, and she tunneled like a mole. Loose material was scooped and flung underneath her body. Then she would slide down, pushing the piles with her feet. Duncan left his arms in the sleeve of his shirt, stretching the material to act as a paddle.

"Thirty-five feet and going strong. I could really use a beer, though." Crystal began to plow another wave of sand toward Duncan.

They agreed to work as hard as possible before dehydration was an issue. There was no rescue coming, so they pushed. The only people that knew where they were wanted them dead, except Petey.

Duncan flung the sand back to Almond, who pushed it to Boxcar. The system worked, but the only unknown variable was the tunnel length versus the available space. Crystal was optimistic but admitted she didn't know the depth of the ridgeline. They would at least go down fighting if the escape route were longer than the temple.

"Did someone say something about beer? I could drink a case right now." Almond wasn't the only one who was thirsty. When you know you can't drink, you want it more.

"I'll buy the first round. After that—"

Crystal screamed, and the sound was cut off as the tunnel collapsed. Duncan had a brief glimpse of her light before it was extinguished like a candle in a hurricane.

"All hands on deck. Dig!" Duncan didn't waste any time and flew at the wall of sand like a man possessed.

CHAPTER 65

Ryan asked, "Do I know you?"

The man was an inch taller and portly. A short white beard, round glasses, and brown fedora should have placed him on a movie set. "Iain Barkhouse. I'm here to verify the validity of any artifacts recovered for my employer."

The nasal tone and British accent set Ryan on edge, and while he wasn't prone to violence, the thought of punching Barkhouse gave him great pleasure. "Bathroom?"

Barkhouse tilted his head and looked at him over his glasses. "Pardon?"

"I need to use the facilities. Excuse me." Ryan stepped around two armed guards in blue uniforms and slung rifles to the bathrooms. The terminal had a counter along one side and two rows of six plastic chairs in the middle. A man worked behind the counter on a computer, and a woman stood ready to check luggage; both wore gray suits with white chevrons on their shoulders.

Ryan took his time, and when he returned, Marshal was sprawled on a chair talking with Barkhouse. He was about to sit at the far end when two white trucks pulled up to the double doors on the tarmac.

Marshal jumped to his feet. "Okay, Petey. Where to now?"

The guards and Barkhouse faced him, waiting. Ryan shrugged. "No idea."

Marshal let out a nervous chuckle. "Game's over, man."

"The Richat Structure is twenty-five miles across and, to put it mildly, fucking huge." Barkhouse pushed his glasses up his nose with an index finger. "If you can't narrow it down precisely, I'll be making a call." His hand slipped into his jacket and paused.

Ryan sat in the black plastic chair, leaning back. "Go ahead and call. Let them know Marshal's to blame."

The two guards scowled, then took a step forward.

"Woah! Calm down." Marshal's hand drifted toward his right hip. "I have no idea what you're talking about."

"He stole a few things from me, and I need them. Without it, we can just sit here all night. If you can order a pizza, that'd be great." Ryan's heart rate spiked, and the headache throbbed in response. They needed him *more* than he needed them. *I'm the golden ticket—your move, asshole.*

Barkhouse held out his hand, and Marshal dug in his vest pocket, pulling out the necklace and ring. He handed them over. "Just a few souvenirs. I didn't know they were important."

Ryan was relieved when the items were in his hand, and Ptah-Du-Amun echoed the sentiment. Not only was the necklace the high priest's symbol of power, but it was also a map. The diamond was the key. When Crystal explained that the Richat Structure was also known as the Eye of the Sahara, Aken's memory of the necklace surfaced. The precious stone resembled an eye. The tip of the falcon's beak wasn't centered on the gemstone but pointed to the upper-left corner. It was a long shot, but there were no other leads to narrow it down. However, the similarities were too close to be ignored.

"No matter what happens, these items are mine. That's not negotiable. Are we good?" Ryan stared the Englishman in the eye. Maybe it was his tone or confidence, but Barkhouse nodded. "We'll travel to the northeast corner of the structure. If there's a map, I can pinpoint the location better."

The first taller guard spoke in broken English. "There will be one in the truck, sir."

Ryan didn't wait for an escort but marched outside. He climbed into the first vehicle's back seat. Barkhouse sat in front, and a guard joined him in the rear. Marshal and the others went in the second truck.

The guard spoke to the driver in a language Ryan wasn't familiar with, and shortly, a folded map of the area was passed back. He didn't need to refer to the necklace. Aken's memory was near perfect.

"Right here." Ryan's finger tapped the outer ridge of the structure. The handcuffs clinked. He held them out to the guard, but the man shook his head.

The information was relayed to the driver, and Barkhouse studied the map before pulling out his phone. No doubt he was updating his boss.

"We'll be there in an hour or so," the guard informed Barkhouse. "The road only goes so far. After that, we'll have to walk."

Ryan stared out the window, holding back a smile. They were letting a stone singer loose in a world filled with rock. *Payback's going to be a bitch.*

▲ ▲ ▲

Duncan was shoved aside as Boxcar took over. His massive hands were nearly the size of shovels, and each scoop was more than he could have done. He worked with Almond to clear the area, but it was a losing battle. The sand covered their knees, and a particularly long avalanche swamped the altar table, covering their vests and weapons, but Boxcar didn't stop.

Like sand pouring from one half of an hourglass to the other, momentum took over. A steady stream flowed into the temple, and Duncan ordered, "Boxcar, stop! Get back in here. We need to clear more space."

The three men had been together for ten years and worked well as a team. Tons of sand were moved within minutes as the flow increased.

"There's a light ahead!" Duncan called out. "I can see Doc as well. I'm going in."

The agile man flew up the river of sand while Almond and Boxcar continued to work. A hand was flat against the curved ceiling, only visible above the elbow, marking her location. He didn't need the headlamp anymore. Through cracks in a pile of rocks, sunlight flooded the corridor.

"Hold on, Doc. I got ya!" he scrambled closer and grasped her forearm, pulling her free.

For a second, he was confused, but when Crystal's head popped out of her shirt. She was panting and flushed but alive. "Thank you!"

"Quick thinking, Doc."

By placing the fabric over her nose and mouth, she could breathe. When seconds counted, you did what you could to survive. *Smart move.*

"No more digging. Can you make your way to the rocks?" Duncan shouted down the tunnel, "Almond, you're first, Boxcar second. Leave the gear. Carefully make your way up."

"Fuck ya!"

When Crystal tilted a rock over, a beam of sunlight had never looked so good, and he wanted to weep with joy. *Appreciate the good moments. You'll need them when things go bad.*

Another good moment he looked forward to was sending a bullet through Marshal's head. It will be the best ninety-three cents he ever spent.

Crystal wiggled through, and once outside, she widened the opening. That's one tough woman. She would have made a great soldier.

Duncan climbed out next, then helped the others. Ten minutes later, he discovered the buggies and gear were left behind. That was their second mistake. The first was not killing him outright.

He powered up the satellite phone in his pack and made the call. Marshal had a ninety-minute headstart.

"Watch your six, asshole. I'm coming for you."

CHAPTER 66

Ryan knew the word bleak, but now he had a visual to go with the definition—the landscape of the Richat Structure. Thirty minutes of traveling across the countryside revealed scrub bushes struggling to survive, a train of wild camels kept their distance, and a howling wind that shook the truck like a toy.

He toyed with disabling the vehicle, but the guard kept an eye on him, not the landscape. Ryan's head still ached from the last time he was knocked out, and he didn't want to go through that again. Various scenarios played out in his mind, and making the ground shake or throwing rocks was hard to compete with a rifle pointing at your head.

Iain Barkhouse held up his phone, showing him the screen. "That area of the structure is barren. The ridgeline is steep, and there's no way the trucks will make it."

While the Richat Structure resembled an impact crater twenty-five miles wide, Ryan was assured the occurrence was natural. The depression had a sharp ridgeline for most of the circumference, and it would take months to explore on foot fully. Ryan wasn't sure a helicopter would be faster. Too many details would be missed.

"As I said, I'm unsure of the exact location, but I'll figure it out when I get closer. However, this could take a few days or a week. No street signs are pointing to the Hall." Ryan had peeked in the truck bed. No one had brought any food, water, or shelter. They may have resources and money but they couldn't plan a birthday party without failing.

Barkhouse returned to his phone. Maybe the situation was becoming apparent. Iain spoke to the driver and turned left at the branch. "There's an old trail that will work."

Ryan glimpsed the screen and wondered if they had hijacked an orbiting satellite. The topography was beyond Google Earth. The truck slowed as the terrain grew more rugged, but the tires and suspension were up to the task. Ryan and the others held onto the grab bars as they were bounced around. With the elevation, the view outside the window changed. The concentric rings making up the structure stretched for miles, but a flash of white caught his eye. "What's that over there?"

From a distance, the bright white walls of the cliff resembled snow or an ice sheet.

"The Sahara was once a tropical forest, but before that, the ocean waters flooded the low ground. Sodium deposits ring the structure."

While everyone was focused on the trail, Ryan studied the necklace. The detailed carving was a marvel; he doubted modern technology could do such work. Tilting the diamond allowed the fine lines of each feather to pop. On the other side, a series of scratches resembled a slanting number sign. The gem was definitely a diamond, and any markings would be intentional, including the scratching. The remaining six stones and the ankh were free of design. Ryan placed his hand behind the stone, and the scratches lined up, not with the beak, but with the falcon's eyes.

"Can I see your phone? I need to look at the contour map."

Barkhouse grumbled but unlocked his phone before passing it over.

Changing the angle, Ryan studied the mountain ridge north of the eye. Two peaks resembled the tips of a soaring hawk's wings, and the worn mound in between could have been the head. Time had eroded the stone, but he knew where to look.

Ryan found the location on the paper map and pointed. "Here."

"This better not be a wild goose chase." Barkhouse took his phone back and showed the driver the new heading.

The truck bounced down a slope before turning in direction. Ten minutes later, Ryan had guessed correctly. While eroded, the curve between the two peaks could have been from a bird of prey. When the ground became too rugged, the driver stopped. Unfortunately, they were a hundred yards away, only a few minutes walk.

Ryan held his wrists out to the guard again. "Where the hell am I going to run to out here?"

At a nod from Barkhouse, the man removed the cuffs.

The desert wind swirled a plume of dust in his face, and Ryan wished he had sunglasses. Without waiting on the second truck, he walked north to the ridgeline and revised his opinion of the abundance of desert life. Smooth tracks of sand were marred with small footprints, and dozens of red ants tore a winged insect apart. Under a pile of rocks, Ryan spotted a tan mouse as it darted to safety. Ahead, birds the size of sparrows flitted from scrub plants to stones, searching for food.

Truck doors slammed, and the guards yelled to each other as he trudged uphill. Ryan had gained fifty yards when Marshal sprinted to his side.

"What's the plan, Petey?"

"I was hoping for ruins or a sign, but there's nothing here." Ryan was torn. Half wanted to find the Hall of Records, and the other side wanted to take everyone for a twelve-mile hike, running in circles.

Marshal pointed to the top of the ridgeline. "You have to change the perspective to obtain a full visual. Shout which direction to go, and I'll mark the spot."

He may be a murdering asshole, but the advice was sound.

After five minutes, Ryan climbed to the highest elevation in the immediate area, the ridge's left wing-tip. Satellite imagery was good, but the human eye could pick out details that a screen couldn't. Four guards, Barkhouse, and the two drivers remained with the truck, and he did his best to ignore them. How far could those rifles fire?

"Son of a bitch."

Marshal was correct. Shallow depressions at the base of the ridgeline formed a rectangle the same size as the truck. "Over there!" Ryan yelled and directed Marshal to stand at the location.

Before descending, Ryan fought the temptation to run. The countryside stretched miles north and was as flat as the prairies. There was no place to hide. The sun would be down in a few hours, and huddling in a pile of rocks with snakes and scorpions wasn't appealing. Resigned to his fate, he went to join Marshal.

The guards stayed with the truck, and Barkhouse joined him. "You've found it?"

"I think so."

Ryan knelt at the corner of the depression and dug using his hands. After ten inches of sand, he found a stone shelf. While more porous than granite or limestone, sandstone was an excellent material for building an underlying structure but wasn't waterproof. Ryan wasn't sure how long ago the ocean flooded the Sahara and left the salt deposits, but anything stored underground could have been destroyed. However, everything would be good if the hall was built after the waters receded. There was only one way to find out.

Fingertips pressed against the sandstone as the seeking song made his chest resonate with the deep notes. The vibrations carried deep into the ground and painted a picture in his mind of the strata. Not sorry about your cellphone, asshole. Ryan increased the volume for good measure, but it wasn't required. He was kneeling on the door to the Hall. There was nothing else it could be. The sandstone slab was six feet wide, eighteen feet long, and two feet thick. The walls supporting the door were shaped basalt blocks that withstood the test of time.

"I need a shovel." Ryan brushed the sand off his knees.

Barkhouse spoke to Marshal. "See what you can find in the trucks."

After a few minutes, he returned with the guards and drivers. They carried an assortment of make-shift implements: tire jacks, a green cooler lid, a clipboard, and a Yeti thermal mug.

Barkhouse took the mug. "That's mine. Get digging where you're told."

Ryan outlined the depression with the heel of his boot as Marshal and Barkhouse watched the others dig. He found a stone shard the size of a dinner plate and went to work.

The sun was a hands-width above the horizon when the sand and rock were cleared, exposing the stone underneath. "I'm going to need some help. Get your fingers under the edge, and we'll lift this to the right side." Ryan tapped the ground next to a sprig of acacia with his foot. The plant was four inches tall and the only sign of anything green in the immediate area. It had to be a good omen.

The guards laughed, and the driver shook his head. "'Ders no chance."

Marshal had seen his work previously and crouched to his left, hands grasping below the lip. Ryan didn't wait for the others and sang. The sandstone slab weighed sixteen tons, but over countless centuries of weathering, the ground had shifted, pinning the stone in place. The guards backed away when the pure notes of the shaping song made the earth vibrate.

Barkhouse shouted. "Get in there and help, or you're not getting paid."

With two men straining, the slab rose several inches, grinding against the basalt before it was stuck. But two additional men on either side made the difference.

As a plume of stale air billowed out, the door to the Hall of Records opened for the first time in five thousand years. Maybe longer. One end of the rock sheet was lowered and they pivoted the other side to reveal wide steps carved into the sandstone shelf and volcanic rock which led down inside a dark pit.

"Get the lights," Barkhouse ordered to the driver.

Ryan couldn't wait. He descended into darkness.

What were they going to do? Shoot him?

CHAPTER 67

The first twenty steps had basalt bricks lining the walls, then transitioned to igneous rock. The magma had melted the dense stone, forming a tunnel, and the flow levels created concentric ridges and grooves near the ground. The opening resembled a subway tunnel, flat along the bottom, and tapering walls of smooth, gray stone tilted inward, forming an arch overhead. Warnings of foul gasses killing stone singers in deep tunnels surfaced from Hiram, and Ryan stopped at fifty feet to get a feel for the cavern.

Footsteps scraped from above as Barkhouse led the guards inside. Bright white light flooded the tunnel from the handheld LED tubular lights, turning night to day. After another thirty steps, Ryan paused on a platform until the others joined him. One of the world's wonders lay before his feet, and the moment didn't fill him with apprehension or fear but reverence.

When the guards arrived with Barkhouse, the lights were lowered onto the tripod stands.

"Holy shit." Marshal stood at his side. Stairs led from the platform, hugging the wall in an arc, to the floor below. The chamber was sixty feet round, with a thirty-foot ceiling. Statues of the gods ringed the room, carved into niches every fifteen feet. Many were depicted with animal faces, and Ryan found the jackal at the base of the stairs, Anubis. Ra stood at the far side with a falcon head, holding a great staff. The ibis-beaked Thoth wore robes, holding a scroll between two hands. The warrior goddess, Sekhmet, had the head of a lioness, but instead of being ready for battle, she held a crooked branch with rounded leaves and flowers—the healer aspect.

The Eye of Horus carved into the polished granite floor was nearly the same size as the chamber and ringed with hieroglyphics. Ptah-Du-Amun studied the Hall through Ryan's eyes, and he tried to understand the engravings, but the symbols were foreign. *The writing is older than recorded history.*

The chamber had not been immune to the ravages of time. The northern wall was sheeted in a thick layer of salt, and the ground was littered with rubble. While the arched ceiling had withstood earthquakes, floods, and the harsh climate of the Sahara, pieces had fallen onto the Eye.

"Yes, it's very nice. Go find the records."
Barkhouse flicked his sausage-like fingers. "Set up the lights on the far side. I don't want him doing anything I can't see. Once you're done, wait at the top of the steps. Marshal, you stay here. We're nearly finished."

The guards and drivers placed the lights on the chamber floor and one on the landing before leaving. They talked excitedly in hushed whispers while stomping up the stairs. Ryan descended fifteen feet to the main floor.

"Watch him," Barkhouse ordered Marshal.

The carving of Anubis was seven feet tall, and Ryan bowed his head when passing.

Guide my steps, my Lord.

Ryan paused before each niche to pay his respects. Was the sun god real? He would have laughed at the thought eight days ago, but knowledge had changed his perspective. The statue of Thoth was the only visual reference to learning, and it was worth investigating first. Ryan ran his fingertips over the granite and marveled at the technique. The scroll was no thicker than two playing cards and, with brilliant lighting, nearly translucent. But the scroll was smooth— no writing or marks.

Ryan studied the granite floor. It was made with twelve-foot blocks, shaped and fitted so close together that the seam disappeared. Smooth as a countertop and placed with precision.

"Well?" Barkhouse's nasal tone carried in the chamber, setting his teeth on edge.

"This is the Hall of Records, but it's empty. I'd mentioned I could lead you here, but there were no guarantees." Ryan stood in the center of the chamber and gestured. "I think at one time this chamber was full, but it looks like someone has—"

"I don't care about any of your previous deals. I don't work for them." Barkhouse chuckled. "You thought I was with *those* people? I know better than to court death in such a manner."

"I've chosen my side as well," Marshal shouted. "You have to have some idea where the artifacts could be hiding?" Marshal stood at the platform's edge, watching Ryan like a hawk.

"I thought I told you to stay outside …" Barkhouse turned when footsteps pounded down the steps.

Then all hell broke loose.

The sharp retort of a rifle was amplified in the chamber tenfold. Before Marshal could draw his pistol, the impact flung him through the air, falling fifteen feet off the platform to land in front of Ryan. The hooded figure dressed in black smashed the rifle butt into the side of Barkhouse's head, and the plump Englishman crumpled like an empty crisp bag. Marshal struggled to breathe with a hole in his chest as blood pooled on the Eye. He wouldn't be getting up again. When another figure in black darted down the steps and flew into his arms, he couldn't speak.

"Ryan! Oh my, God." Crystal squeezed him in half, and the pistol in her right hand dug into his back.

Almond ran down the tunnel. "We've got company coming in hot. We have to leave. *Now!*"

"Come on, Petey." Duncan threw back his hood. "Time to go."

CHAPTER 68

"How did you get here?" Everything was happening too fast, and Ryan had trouble processing.

"I'll see what I can do to slow them down." Almond darted up the stairs.

"Petey! Let's go." Boxcar yelled from the surface.

"I can't leave here." There was only one place to hide anything in the chamber; if he could figure it out without singing, others would also. "Leave and take Crystal with you!"

"Then I'm staying, too." Crystal threw her backpack aside and tucked the pistol in the small of her back. "You aren't getting rid of me that easily!"

The time for making decisions was gone. Boxcar and Almond thundered down the steps, taking positions to either side of the tunnel, back to the wall. "Incoming."

Duncan ran down a few steps, then jumped. He stood in front of Ryan and Crystal, rifle at the ready. "The stairs will act as a funnel, and we should be able to hold out. Hopefully, you have another escape plan, Petey."

The shuffle of steps grew louder, and when the long white robes appeared, Duncan's head lifted from the rifle's sight. "Boss?"

The Arab, Mr. Smith, gasped. "This place is marvelous." Wide-eyed, he stared at the statues and the carving on the floor. He didn't notice the body at his feet or Marshal bleeding out below. "At last."

"It's the least I can do."

Ryan's heart froze when he heard the man's voice. The Arab was followed by another, along with a rigid tapping on alternate stairs marking his arrival.

Carrick Ackley, dressed in a black suit and tie, came down the last step.

Ryan's jaw dropped. "Sir?"

"Beautiful, isn't it?" Carrick stood behind Mr. Smith, left hand on his shoulder. When the cane fell, the Arab gasped and struggled. "I find this a fitting place for your burial chamber."

The Englishman pushed the Arab to the ground. The knife in his hand dripped blood onto the white robes as the dying man's moans filled the ancient chamber.

"What are you doing?" Ryan's mind was reeling. How could Carrick do this? What's going on?

"It's obvious, young man." Carrick wiped the blade on the robes before sheathing it on his belt. "Taher double-crossed me, hoping to steal the treasure. I left enough slack on his leash to finish the job, but he had to learn his lesson."

"Drop the knife!" Boxcar stepped forward, aiming for the side of Ackley's head.

"Oh, I don't think so." Four others were coming down the stairs. The bald black man and an older man escorted two people with black cloth bags over their heads. The two men were the Duke's security guards from the estate. *No!*

"Mr. Petey, are you ready for the incentive?"

At a nod from Carrick, the tall man removed the bags.

"Mom!"

"It's okay, honey. Just listen to Mr. Ackley, and everything will be okay." His mother and Detective McCallan were beaten and bruised but alive.

"You said you were going to help them!" Tears flooded Ryan's eyes, and he had trouble seeing.

"I said I would send a man from Montreal to check in on them. He also kindly shipped them over to avoid any problems like this." The second, smaller man held two handguns to the back of the women's heads.

"It seems, Major, you're officially unemployed." Carrick looked down on Duncan.

"That's true." Duncan's voice and rifle never wavered.

"How could you do this, Carrick?" Ryan knew the answer, but he had to hear it.

The Englishman's laugh made the hair on his neck stand on end. "The money, of course. Alone, you were worth untold billions, but the actual artifacts from the Hall of Records? Trillions? I'm about to find out rather soon."

"So, this was all about the money?" Ryan stepped in front of Duncan, making him lower the rifle. His mother was up there, and he had to protect her no matter the cost.

"I'm the auctioneer to the world's elite. Of course, it's about the money. Now, let's get on with things. Where are the records?"

Ryan shrugged and did an exaggerated scan around the room. "Someone beat us to it."

Carrick snapped his fingers, and the man behind Julie kicked her knees out. She screamed as she was pinned to the floor with the pistol in the back of her head. Almond and Boxcar stepped forward.

"If you don't throw down your weapons, the women die. I also have others outside, ready to come in, but I thought we could handle this in a civilized manner." Carrick could have been talking about the weather for all the emotion in his words.

Ryan's heart leaped in his mouth when his mother cried out, but the response frightened not only him but the others in the room. The bedrock rumbled, and a piece of the ceiling fell at Ra's feet. "If you harm my mother, we will all die together."

The seeking song traveled through the granite slabs to the igneous layers beneath the Hall of Records. Even deeper, long-buried lava tubes connected to the fault line, and the effort to shift that much stone would exhaust him, but would be worth it.

Carrick wasn't nervous. "Here's the deal. You give me the records, and you all go free. That's it. Easy peasy, lemon squeezy."

Ryan trusted the man as far as he could throw him. "How do I know you're telling the truth?"

"Don't trust him, Ryan!" Crystal whispered at his side.

Carrick gestured to the two men, and the handcuffs were removed from Julie after she was helped to her feet. McCallan scowled and rubbed her wrists.

"You ladies are free."

"Everyone goes free, or there's no deal." While Duncan and the others worked for Mr. Smith, he didn't want them to suffer the same fate. Mixed feelings aside, they were good men.

"If all weapons, including my men's, are lowered and placed on the ground, you find the Record and hand it over. We all go on our merry way."

Ryan turned to Duncan. "Do you trust him?"

"He's all about the money and the deals. Follow through, and I believe he'll stand by his word."

Boxcar and Almond lowered their rifles at the same time as the others. Duncan placed his weapon down as well.

"Okay, Ryan. Now it's your turn." Carrick used the cane to point in his direction.

My Lord, what do I do? Guide me!

CHAPTER 69

Ryan closed his eyes and waited for an answer, but Anubis wasn't speaking, nor was the priest or stone singer. The silent answer came to him from an unlikely source. His mother. Her pleas and condition tore his heart in two and left him no leeway.

"Deal."

Ryan took a step back and caught a subtle head shake from Marshal. A bloody hand clasped to his chest controlled the bleeding, but by the amount pooling, he didn't have long. Strangely, Marshal didn't have an ankh about his body. Maybe he wasn't dying?

Ryan knelt in the middle of the chamber, placing both hands on either side of the pupil. The deeply carved Eye was lined with the same material as the two-foot eye—black agate. But the orb wasn't as deep as the granite, only eight inches. There was a void under the cap, along with another stone plug. Singing didn't give him enough information, but he knew where to start.

"Boxcar, I need help."

The big man frowned at Carrick before coming down the stairs. "What do you need, Petey?"

Ryan tapped the black agate with a finger. "I'm going to lift this up a few inches, and I need you to hold it in place. I'll need a flashlight to see inside. Something isn't right."

Boxcar plucked a tactical light from Marshal's belt and turned it on. "Ready."

The shaping song filled the chamber with the melody, and he wasted no time. Ryan dug his fingers into the solid granite to either side of the agate eye. The fitting was absolute perfection to the one-thousands of an inch, and the stone slid like wet glass when lifted. Ryan held the disc an inch off the floor.

"Okay, Boxcar, don't let it drop."

Ryan grabbed the flashlight and examined the underside.

"Shit."

Silvered metallic wires were wrapped through the stone, holding a stone vase underneath. Ryan shifted the flashlight to the other side, and the thin-walled vase held a liquid. The wires extended to the second disk below.

"It's a rather simple trap. If you break the top or pull too hard, the vase breaks. I've dealt with a lot worse.

Trust me. Hold the top. I got this." They switched positions, and then Boxcar removed a Leatherman multi-tool, and his large fingers wrapped around the stone vase. The four wires were clipped, and Ryan placed the disk to the side to find the stone below, which was riddled with holes.

"I'm guessing it's acid."

"Let's see what it was guarding." Ryan placed his fingers in the openings and pulled the second stone free.

Boxcar shone the flashlight inside, and the reflections made the ceiling dance like moonlight off a still pond. Ryan removed the cylinder and held it against his chest. The material was light-weight, like aluminum, but shone like polished stainless steel.

Every surface was scribed with ancient writings, pictures, and diagrams. He had thought it was a cylinder, but the metal was rolled, like a scroll, but two feet tall. Ryan guessed the length would be thirty feet or more once opened.

"Last knowledge of the ancients." Ryan held the record in one hand and the acid in the other. "I'll bring it to you, and you leave. Right?"

Carrick couldn't take his eyes off the prize but shook his head. "No offense, but if you keep your distance, things will work out better. The girl can hand it to me."

"Can we study it first?" Crystal pleaded.

Carrick tapped Barkhouse with a polished black shoe. "That was his job. Just bring it here. I have a flight to catch."

Crystal turned the writings in her hand and slowly walked up the stairs, no doubt memorizing as much as possible. She was three steps from the top when the ankh appeared over her head.

Ryan's heart lurched. "No!"

Crystal stepped over Mr. Smith, with a puzzled look on her face, turned to face him. "What's wrong?"

"Nothing's wrong. I'll take that." Carrick plucked the cylinder from her hands.

Before anyone could react, Trish McCallan drew the pistol from Crystal's waistband, bringing it up in a practiced motion to shoot Carrick. But the tall black man was faster and within reach. His hand clamped over hers, and his left elbow connected with the police woman's temple.

As Trish fell, the Sig Sauer P226 bucked when the trigger was pulled.

CHAPTER 70

Ryan was already moving before Crystal hit the floor with Duncan close behind. The ankh was pulsing in the final stages.

"Sir, move!" The shorter guard spun Carrick toward the stairs and practically carried his charge away, with the taller man acting as a shield. Carrick's cane clattered to the ground as they escaped.

Trish was struggling to sit when Ryan stepped over the Arab. Julie threw herself in his arms, "Ryan!"

"I'm okay, Mom. Help Detective McCallan. Everything's okay now."

Ryan knelt beside Crystal as the ankh flickered once, then faded.

"No!"

His trembling fingers brushed Crystal's hair out of her eyes. The bullet hit her in the upper chest, and she died instantly.

"Oh, Doc." Boxcar was at his side, and a big hand gently patted Ryan's shoulder. "I'm so sorry."

Tears fell in a steady stream from Ryan's face.

Outside, a helicopter flew over the chamber opening, and the thumping rotor wash quickly disappeared.

"Duncan. Can you get my mom out of here? I want to be alone for a few minutes, then close the Hall."

"No problem, Petey. Doc was a tough woman." Duncan and Almond collected the rifles and helped the others up the stairs.

"Do you need me?" Boxcar's eyes were full of tears as well.

"I got this one. I'll be there soon."

Ryan held Crystal's hand as Boxcar joined the others.

When they were alone, Ryan whispered, "I'm so sorry."

Barkhouse still hadn't moved and could be dead. Mr. Smith lay five feet away in a twisted heap, but somehow, Marshal's faint, gurgled breathing carried up the stairs.

Help me! Ryan pleaded with Anubis.

Two arms slipped under Crystal's body, and he struggled to his feet, cradling her like a child. Ryan's boots slid in the pool of blood, but he made it to the chamber floor. Gently, he laid Crystal at the jackal's feet.

"Please help. She doesn't deserve to die." Ryan bowed his head in reverence, but there was no response. Placing one palm on her forehead and another on her chest, Ryan took a deep breath before beginning the fourth prayer.

No! Stop before it's too late, Ptah-Du-Amun begged. *There's no way to cheat death.*

Hiram's words echoed in his mind. With the right frequency, anything was possible.

While he wasn't sure of the meaning of the words, they still had power—ancient whispers of the gods given to mortals. When Ryan's eyes opened, he was near the ceiling, watching Marshal fighting to live and himself kneeling over Crystal's body.

Ryan continued to rise through the rock, emerging into the night sky. He was lost in the chant as the pleas of the high priest faded. The life force of his mother and the others flitted about on the ridgeline like sparks from a bonfire. As twilight shifted to black, he was surrounded by darting motes of light swirling like an ocean current around and through him in a never-ending dance.

Marwa's memory merged with the present when Ryan halted at the infinite black wall of death. In a realm where sound translates to energy, prayers have power. The fourth prayer was never designed to bring someone back from the other side but to escort a person to the afterlife. But further actions required a sacrifice.

Ryan rose to his feet.

Frothing red bubbles trickled from Marshal's mouth, but his eyes were still aware.

"Robert Peter Morris, your death is assured, but your afterlife is not. Would you sacrifice yourself for a chance at rebirth? Fate's wheel spins, and you must decide." Ryan had no control over what was happening, but he was without fear.

Marshal's eyes widened at hearing his true name, and a lone tear escaped. With his last breath, Robert whispered, "Yes."

Ryan's hand cupped the rising spark as the mercenary passed, and he was back at the infinite wall. A gentle breath blew the lifeforce from his palms, and with a flash of light, it crossed the great divide. A beam of energy shot out of the barrier, circled Ryan once, and disappeared.

Crystal's gasp of breath brought him back to the chamber. The rise and fall of her chest filled him with joy and wonder. *Thank you, my Lord.*

Ryan clasped her hand to his chest and waited. Crystal's eyelids fluttered as she woke.

"Hey." Her dimples made his heartache.

"Where is everyone? I was dead." Her cheeks were flushed, and the twinkle was back in her eyes.

Ryan grinned. "You were just mostly dead."

Crystal sat upright and lowered her shirt. The hole in her chest was gone, and a white scar was the only sign of an injury. "Is it over?"

Dying and returning to life wasn't a common occurrence, but after helping her stand, Crystal was steady on her feet.

"Yes and no." Ryan frowned. "Did you feel that?"

He waited a few seconds, and when the chamber shook, Crystal's eyes widened. "Was that you?"

Ryan shook his head and knelt. He didn't sing long before bolting upright. "We don't have much time!"

"What's wrong?"

Another stronger tremor shook the Hall, and pieces of the ceiling fell. The salt deposited on the wall cracked.

"I may have started something that's beyond my control. At least, I think it was me, but it could have been someone else." He glanced at the statue before continuing. "The fault line shifted, and the lava tubes are filling with molten rock." Ryan wanted to preserve the ancient hall but couldn't hold back a force of nature.

The next tremor toppled the statue of Ra, and the salt sheet broke free, shattering into a million pieces on the granite floor.

"Holy shit!"

Ryan pulled Crystal to the stairs, but she yanked his hand away. "Look!"

He was stunned and wanted to stay, but they ran out of time. "Is that my backpack?"

Crystal handed it to him. "I thought you might need your clothing or something."

He dug inside and found the tablet still wrapped in the towel. He powered it on.

"Perfect! You're amazing!" Ryan grinned ear to ear. "Take as many pictures and videos as you can. We don't have much time."

A lamp toppled with the next quake, and a fine line of dust filtered from the ceiling. Crystal wasn't wasting a second. The built-in video camera was recording. She focused on the newly exposed wall, the floor, and the statues in the recesses.

"We have to go!" Another quake cracked the granite slab at the base of the stairs, and the shifting floor buckled his knees. Crystal continued to record as he scooped the backpack and helped her up the stairs.

She paused on the landing for a final picture, and then, hand in hand, they ran to the surface.

Duncan stood at the opening, white as a sheet as they emerged. "Holy shit, Doc."

"It was only a flesh wound." Ryan laughed. "We should clear the area. It's going to get *very* hot here rather soon."

Duncan led them to the waiting helicopter, and shortly, they circled the glowing red pit that was once the ancient Hall of Records.

CHAPTER 71

Three weeks later, Toronto, Canada.

Ryan grabbed the mug and poured himself a coffee, adding half a spoon of sugar. The days of waking up to an energy drink were over, but he didn't miss it, especially after Crystal explained what they did to your liver.

"I'm heading out, honey. I'll be back in time for lunch." Julie came into the kitchen and gave him a hug and kiss. The therapy sessions have already produced results, including finally allowing his mother to sleep through the night. His dreams, however, had been a wild ride since leaving the Eye of the Sahara, but he had an excuse his mother didn't—the ability to speak with the dead. Her injuries were fading, but the scars on her mind would take longer to heal. The plaster cast on her wrist would come off in five weeks.

"Do you want me to go with you?" He's always offered, but his mother declined.

"I'm good. Love you."

"Love you too, Mom."

After three hectic weeks, he was finally relaxing without looking over his shoulder at every turn. During the three-hour helicopter flight to Rabat, Morocco, Ryan had learned what happened to his mother and Trish McCallan. Carrick Ackley will answer not only for his crimes but for the abuse. His first mistake was allowing Ryan to go free; if he made one, there would be others.

Duncan couldn't take them home, but the consulate in Rabat spoke with the Canadian government and worked on their behalf. The Moroccan health care system applied stitches or bandages where needed. While Mr. Smith, Taher, had not followed through with any monetary payment for Ryan, his legal resources were top-notch and saved them millions. Teams of lawyers dealt with not only the police but also their transition into the country. Thirty-six hours later, they landed at Toronto Pearson Airport. After the lawyers worked with customs and immigration, everyone was taken home by interns at the firm.

Ryan finished a second cup of coffee and toast when the doorbell rang. While the Toronto police had officially stopped the investigation, officers stopped by over the last couple of weeks to ensure no other problems or issues arose. Ryan knew they were fishing for information, but he politely referred them to the lawyer and told them to have a nice day.

When he opened the front door, he was confused by the large man in a blue golf shirt and khaki shorts who was not a police officer. "Hi, Petey."

"Boxcar!"

Ryan slapped his hand and went in for a bro hug, but Boxcar wasn't having any of it. Ryan's feet left the ground, and his ribs creaked with the massive bear hug. "Hope you're doing good, man."

"Come on in. Can I get you a coffee?"

"I won't say no to that." Boxcar kicked off his shoes, and moments later, Ryan joined him in the living room with a mug for each.

"It might be a stupid question, but how did you find me?" Ryan sat on the couch, and Boxcar sunk into the recliner.

"I used to be an officer in the intelligence battalion and know my way around computers, not just a rifle." Boxcar looked sheepish. "I did some snooping. Hope you don't mind me stopping in unannounced."

"Of course not, but I can guess why you're here." Ryan placed the mug to the side and leaned forward. "Stone singing, maybe?"

Boxcar chuckled. "When you sang, I could *feel* the stone. Not just with my fingers, but in here." He tapped his forehead.

"Apprenticeships are a serious matter, and years of commitment are required. But, if you're willing to put in the effort, I can—"

"Boxcar!" Crystal flew across the living room, and the big man barely had time to stand before she leaped into his arms. Ryan enjoyed the view but made a mental note to buy longer T-shirts.

"Doc! I'm glad you're still alive."

"Me too." Once her feet touched the ground, she ran a hand through her tangled hair. "Hold on a second. Coffee first, then we can talk."

Shortly, she returned with a mug and sat beside Ryan on the couch.

"How are Duncan and Almond?" Ryan asked.

"After ten years of working together, we're going our separate ways. On good terms, though. I've decided to give up mercenary work." Boxcar tugged at the golf shirt. "I'm going to be a civilian for a while."

Ryan's eyebrows raised. "So, you're unemployed?"

"Yes, and by the way, my name is Luke Phillips. I'm from Saint Louis, Missouri."

"Nice to meet you, Luke." Ryan raised his coffee in a salute.

Crystal asked, "Can I still call you Boxcar?"

Luke laughed. "That's been my name since I played football in college. Yes. Not a problem."

"Good! Since you're unemployed …" Crystal grinned at Ryan, and he nodded. "I'll get the pictures and map." She disappeared downstairs.

"And put on some pants!" Ryan called out before turning to his friend. "First, about the offer of teaching you what I can about stone singing. I will gladly do so, but I have a confession."

Crystal returned, still dressed in his T-shirt, but had time to slip into shorts. She held lengths of rolled paper and a stack of pictures. She spread them out on the coffee table.

Ryan continued. "When I mentioned Carrick Ackley took the Records from the Hall, I wasn't being truthful."

Crystal used the mugs to hold the corners of the world map. Her dimples appeared as she showed Boxcar the pictures. "I took these before the Hall was destroyed."

He studied the images, turning them at various angles. "It's a map, but I'm unfamiliar with it."

Ryan placed it flat on the table. "If this large land mass in the middle is Antarctica, then this…"

Boxcar caught on quickly. "Got it. This is South America, and this would be Australia."

"Right." Crystal showed the other pictures they had developed. "These are the seven continents, each marked with the triangle."

Boxcar turned to the world map, where Crystal had copied the symbols. "So, this triangle in Africa was the Hall of Records?"

"Yes." Ryan didn't have to wait long before Boxcar caught on.

"There are six other Halls!" Excited, he flipped through the remaining pictures and notes.

"The ancients didn't place all their knowledge in one place, but scattered them throughout the world." Ryan tapped a location. "This is Cholula, Mexico."

"If I have the translation correct, hidden there is the Halls of Medicine." Crystal smiled.

"Knowledge was divided into seven aspects or categories: medicine, astronomy, music, geometry, logic, spirit, and arithmetic."

"Which one did Carrick get?"

Ryan laughed. "He got the collective knowledge of stargazers and astrologers. Carrick can now predict when a solar eclipse will occur, how many days until the winter solstice, and other information useful for the average farmer six millennia ago."

"Oh my, that's hilarious." Boxcar's laugh made the walls shake. "What's your plan?"

"Ultimately, I will start a new order dedicated to Anubis, a learning center. Knowledge *should* be shared, not stored away for thousands of years." Ryan rolled the maps and stacked the photos. The god's vision was clear, and he would do his best to see it through after what happened.

Boxcar pointed to the sheet on top. "What's that?"

Ryan smiled at his first sketch of the ankh. "The ancient sign that started everything. A sign from the gods."

Crystal added, "The ankh is supposed to be the symbol of life, but after fixing translations and talking with Ryan, I've discovered the real interpretation. The ankh is the key to reincarnation."

Ryan knew Boxcar didn't understand, but Crystal's hand found his, and her look made his cheeks flush.

"Well, Luke from Saint Louis. Crystal and I are going to each continent to recover the ancient records." Ryan stood, then held out a hand. "Are you with us? If you're up for it, there will be time for training."

Boxcar didn't hesitate and shook his hand. "I'm in! But this isn't going to be cheap. How are you going to finance the operation?"

"Carrick Ackley has graciously made a donation." Ryan removed the gold ring from his index finger and dropped it on the table. There was no point in mentioning that a stone singer could easily find rare minerals and gems. He'd save that news for later. "Ready to change the world?"

Ryan wasn't just talking to Boxcar and Crystal but also to the dozens of voices in his head. Scholars, builders, fishermen, and laborers, the common people of an ancient time who had dedicated their lives to Anubis, had also offered assistance. Their resounding *yes* gave him shivers.

Crystal grinned. "Of course, but first, more coffee!"

Smiling, the newest high priest of Anubis went to make another pot. With one foot in the past and another in the present, Ryan looked forward to a promising future. All the signs were there.

ABOUT THE AUTHOR

David grew up in a small town east of Toronto, Canada. He has had many interests throughout the years, including the military, martial arts, playing guitar, and reading, and in his own mind, he is quite an excellent angler. David is married, has one daughter, and misses his chocolate lab daily.

Feel free to write to David at:
author.david.darling@gmail.com

AFTERWORD

Did you ever have a moment of clarity and could envision an entire situation or project from beginning to end? That's what happened with The Egyptian Enigma. I was writing another novel, and I couldn't shake the idea. When that happens, I usually write a quick page of notes, maybe a first chapter, to place me on track later, then file the story in my ideas folder. However, the story and concept were screaming in my ear with this novel, dying to be typed. So, I placed Noah Hunter on hold to finish this book, and I'm glad I did! I enjoyed the research and learning more about the Egyptians—time writing is never wasted.

Stone Singers—Where did that come from? I watched a documentary on the scoop marks at a quarry near the pyramids. The resemblance to someone using an ice cream scoop on solid rock is very strong. My immediate reaction and thoughts were simple. "*The ancient Egyptians used sonics to carve and manipulate monolithic stones.*" Is it likely? Not really, but from that rogue idea, a novel was born. Point of note: after I finished the story, I saw some remarkable things done with sonics, from levitation to surgeries. Maybe singing to stones isn't so outrageous.

The research: namely, what is real and what isn't. Stonehenge: Yes, forty-three bluestones are used in the construction and have resonate abilities. The Avebury henge north of Stonehenge is real, but are they connected? Anything I've found about the two henges supporting each other is speculation and has not been proven. I saw a map reporting proposed ley lines converging at each location, which was enough for me to run with the idea. To be clear, no science has proven that ley lines exist, and scientists have treated the report with kid gloves.

The Sphinx: Let's start with the monument's age. Officially, the monument was built in approximately 2,650 B.C., and the proposed original head was that of a lion. When the Great Pyramid was built, the lion's head was re-carved into the present form we see today. However, there *was* speculation that the original was that of Anubis. Again, there is no solid proof. Are there entrances into the Sphinx? Yes! There are a few, and the one I mentioned in the story (behind the rear left foot) is real. I've seen the video where two men climbed down, showing the bottom and ladder. The side tunnel *does* exist, and in the video, it was boarded across with planks. Ground penetrating radar has shown tunnels and a possible cave system below the monument and plateau, including a small chamber under the front paw. The Hall of Records? No idea! The antiquities minister isn't forthcoming with any findings nor allows exploration without his consent or involvement. The Sphinx has other entrances, like the hatch I mentioned on top of the head. They were reported to be "Robber Tunnels" and lead nowhere. But that same minister spent three weeks exploring inside the monument … suspicious, and I'd love to know if there is a conspiracy cover-up! There are videos out there claiming the Sphinx is 12,000 years old, placing it on par with Gobekli Tepe, but again, every idea has been shot down. The watermarks on the limestone around the monument are natural when the water *does* flow through the area. The limestone shelf can be cross-sectioned at any location, and the water rivulets are also there. It does make for a good story, though!

The Richat Structure is a natural phenomenon in western Africa, made millions of years ago by a caldera volcano. The concentric rings were from collapsing domes of earth that have eroded into the shape of an orb—hence the name, Eye of the Sahara. LiDAR scanning happened during the spring of 2022, but again, the results have yet to be released, and that information is being held tight. Why? No idea. But don't forget that civilizations have flourished and collapsed on the African continent for nearly ten thousand years. You can dig nearly anywhere and find relics of a forgotten past. There are also rumors that the Richat Structure is the lost location of Atlantis. It is a great premise, but it isn't possible.

The Hall of Records is a myth passed down for thousands of years, nearly as old as Anubis. Coincidence? As I finished this novel, the north face corridor was discovered on the Great Pyramid! An unexplored tunnel above the main entrance that hasn't been seen in thousands of years is making the rounds on the news. There are still things to be learned, and maybe fiction will one day be fact.

I have been an avid reader of James Rollins, Boyd Morrison, Steve Berry, Wilbur Smith, and Brad Meltzer's novels, where they stretch reality and blend it with facts and history. Not only do I recommend their books, but I hope that one day, *The Egyptian Enigma* can be placed on the shelf next to such adventure works, and those authors will enjoy the novel they inspired.

If you enjoyed the story, please leave a review wherever you purchased. Reviews are a currency greater than gold to writers, and they help the algorithms make their novels viewable to others. Something as simple as "4 Stars – I liked it" helps. I hope you were entertained regardless of what is true and what isn't within the story. That's the point of a novel: to momentarily take you away to the land of imagination.

I would also like to thank Clay Stafford and the entire support team at the writing conference, Killer Nashville. *The Egyptian Enigma* was nominated for a Top Pick for the Claymore Award for Best Action Adventure Novel. I will not know how I did until the end of August, but to make it this far, two years running, is an honor. I have met so many wonderful people and formed friendships at Killer Nashville, and I encourage others to attend. I will be back! Speaking of friends I met in Nashville, thank you to Cindy Dees and Bruce Coffin for their help and assistance. Shifting my mindset is difficult (ask my wife!), but I took your words and lessons to heart; this story is the result.

Thanks to C.E. Albanese and his wife for their assistance with the following short story, *Memories Never Fade*. I hope you enjoy it.

On a side note, who do you picture playing the characters should this novel go to film? Let me know!

January 2024
David Darling

Memories Never Fade

With the morning sun at his back, Paul Horne smoothed out his uniform and straightened the brass-colored sergeant chevrons pinned to his collar before wrapping his knuckles against the screen door. His hands moved with military precision, a testament to the habits ingrained during his enlistment and years of service. However, there was no need to knock; this place was his second home, but good manners prevailed.

A moment later, he heard the shuffling of feet and pulled open the screen door.

His grandmother left the kitchen, wiping her hands on a white apron. Her eyes watered, and a smile washed over her face when she turned the corner. The faded blue dress with yellow sunflowers was familiar, and her slippers brushed against the oak floor with each step. The small woman hugged him on the threshold. Her arms could barely reach halfway around. The embrace and the scent of her kitchen, a blend of warm spices and freshly baked goods, was a soothing balm.

"About time you stopped by," she said. "I missed you."

She barely reached Paul's chest, and her perfume reminded him of the flowers in his mother's backyard. All the stress he had carried for months was pushed aside with one simple hug, and the tightness in his chest vanished as his shoulders finally relaxed. His grandmother was a refuge, a sanctuary against the chaos he'd faced overseas.

"I missed you, too, Grandma." Tears rolled down his cheeks as the sudden dam of emotions threatened to overwhelm him.

She stepped back and reached up to wipe his face. Then, arms that had rocked him to sleep as a child pulled him down. Instead of the usual peck on his forehead, she kissed the new scar under his eye before releasing her hold.

"Are you okay?"

The inquiry into the marks he carried, both visible and hidden, was not surprising. His grandmother rarely missed anything. "I'm okay. Now."

"You always were a horrible liar. Have you been home?"

Paul shook his head. "I was going to surprise Mom and Dad, but I wanted to see you first."

She gave a short chuckle. "Well, you *are* my favorite grandson."

"I'm your only grandson." Paul laughed at her favorite joke.

"That's why you're my favorite." She cleared her throat. "I have something for you. Come on in."

The urge to continue was strong. "I must get going. I'll come back this afternoon if that's okay?"

"No problem, dear. Hold on." She entered the house and quickly returned with a red and green tin box. His grandmother had used that same container all his life after baking. It bore the marks of countless desserts, each a symbol of her love.

"Here you go. I just made your favorite cookies. Bring them with you and make sure you share them, young man." Her stern words were followed with a sly wink.

"Yes, ma'am." He smirked when a memory surfaced. As a boy, he had eaten half the tin of date squares while riding home on his bike. Paul's mother had been furious, and two decades later, that story was often retold.

His grandmother laughed. She understood and always had. "You better get home. Go. Do your surprises."

Paul stepped forward and gave his grandmother another embrace. "Love you, Gram. I'll be back later."

"Don't worry about me. Everything's fine here. I love you, too, Pauly. Tell your mom and dad I love them, as well. Promise?"

"Will do." He bent and gave her a quick kiss on the cheek.

"You better go before I start crying. After you talk with your parents, come back here, and we'll talk. We have a lot to catch up on. Welcome home."

At the black Chevy truck, Paul waved goodbye. In response, she flicked the front porch light on and off, as always. He climbed behind the wheel, honked, and blew her a kiss before leaving—the same gesture he had done for nearly three decades. The cookie tin sat beside him on the center console, and he drummed his fingers on top to the music. His heart had lightened despite the tears.

He turned right at Bloomer's Flower Shop, avoiding the main streets downtown, and took the side roads. His mother should be out in the gardens before the day grew warm while his dad puttered around the garage. The streets were a journey through his past, a reminder of the winding pathways he'd taken in his youth on his bike, then later in his first car. He loved that blue Ford Mustang almost as much as the truck. Each turn carried the echoes of laughter and adventures long gone—a lifetime ago.

Paul's fingers brushed a small, polished silver pendant hidden against his chest. The piece of shrapnel had nearly taken his life. IEDs had killed half his section while patrolling a highway in the Helmand province, and the thin scar under his left eye was a constant reminder of how close Paul came to joining his friends in Valhalla.

Paul parked two homes away and turned off the truck. He walked up the sidewalk with the cookie tin in one hand and an army duffel bag in the other. He had guessed correctly. His mother was weeding the front garden, lost in the aroma of rich earth and growing things. It was her sanctuary of tranquility, a stark contrast to the chaos he'd known overseas, that his mother took solace in daily.

"Excuse me, but I seem to be lost."

His mom looked over her shoulder, and Paul noted her puffy, bloodshot eyes. She burst into tears while crossing the lawn in three steps and threw herself into his arms, crying.

"Oh, my God! My baby boy is home. *How*? When?"

Paul dropped the duffel bag and held on to the container with one hand while picking up his mom with the other. He spun her in a circle before letting her down.

"I'm back a little early."

"Paul!"

His dad came around the corner. The dark circles under his eyes and hollowed cheekbones were too prominent for Paul to ignore. His father froze for a second in shock before his jaw closed, and his feet finally moved. Seconds later, they embraced, crying simultaneously. *This* was the moment that helped get him through the times he felt like curling into a ball, screaming at the world. It was a reunion of hearts, a healing balm for wounds too deep to see. The love of his family. It filled his soul and made the life of a soldier possible.

"When did you get in?" His mom wiped her eyes on the back of her hand. She couldn't stop smiling.

"Late last night. I wanted to surprise you."

His dad chuckled. "You certainly did. Your commanding officer called yesterday and—"

"It was obviously a mistake." His parents always interrupted each other, and today was no exception. Without warning, Paul's mother gasped and stepped back, hand clutching her chest. Her eyes remained fixed on the container. "Where did you get that?" she whispered.

After holding up the red and green tin, Paul smiled. "Sorry, this wasn't my first stop. I went to Grandma's house."

"Oh, my God…" His mother collapsed into a crumpled heap on the lawn, shaking.

Shocked, Paul stepped forward to catch her, but it was too late. He rested a hand on her shoulder as he knelt. "What's wrong? Mom?"

His dad turned white as a sheet. He also couldn't take his eyes off the cookie tin. "We didn't want to tell you this far into your tour, son, but your grandmother passed away two weeks ago. There was a house fire, and she couldn't leave in time."

His father's confession was like a lightning bolt from a cloudless sky. Unexpected. Paul chuckled to hold back the shadows that had followed him for the last four months. "Nice try. I was there just six minutes ago. She's fine."

His mother met his eyes and shook her head. "We are *not* joking, Paul. Your Grandmother died from smoke inhalation fifteen days ago."

He could still smell his grandmother's perfume on his uniform. He stared at the tin, and Paul didn't know what to say as he removed the lid. Neatly stacked under the waxed paper were dozens of fresh chocolate chip cookies; they smelled delicious. He showed them to his parents.

"They're still warm. Grandma had just baked and handed them to me. She wants me to come back and visit."

Paul's mother picked up a cookie and took a bite. The chocolate stretched in a thin line before snapping like a delicate thread, and she muttered. "They taste just like hers."

He spoke about what happened and described Gram's light blue dress and apron. He helped his mom to her feet, and Paul realized she was in shock. Seeing his mother in that condition twisted his stomach into knots, and he felt helpless. His mother rubbed the scar on his cheek. The faint residue of pink lipstick was transferred to her thumb.

"What's going on?" Her voice barely reached his ears.

The situation was making Paul's head spin, and he stumbled. The lid fell at his feet, forgotten.

His father gasped. "Come with me, son."

Paul passed the container to his mom's shaking hands. "Everything will be okay, Mom. I love you."

"I—I …" She couldn't finish the sentence. His mother clutched the tin tight against her chest, and her sobs followed him down the street.

At the truck, he had trouble with the passenger door; it had always stuck. Paul's father had to open it from the inside.

"Is Mom, okay? What's happening?"

His dad held up one finger. "Just hold on."

With one look in his father's eyes, Paul waited. He had seen that expression all his life and knew when to push it or not. They turned left onto Maple Street shortly, and his father parked outside the house.

Paul's jaw dropped when he finished processing what his eyes were trying to tell him.

The tightness rushed back into his chest, and his left eye twitched as Paul stared out the passenger window. A sense of foreboding washed over him, and a feeling made the hairs on the back of his neck stand on end.

"No!"

It was a surreal tableau, a scene from a horrible nightmare. Paul checked to make sure he was awake. Once a bastion of memories and refuge, his grandmother's house lay in ruins from the fire's fury. The walls had collapsed into the basement from the blaze. The once pristine lawn was scorched from the intense heat, and the lush garden was ash. Eight-foot blue-wired fencing surrounded the property to keep everyone out, and the burnt smell lingered in the air like a shroud of sorrow.

Paul's forehead rested against the passenger window as his heart pounded double time. A wave of emotions threatened to overwhelm and bury him; outrage, sorrow, anger, and despair warred for dominance. The demons inside howled like the cries of his fallen brothers, drowning out the present and reality.

The lurking darkness nearly swept him away, but he returned when a firm hand squeezed Paul's shoulder like a lifeline.

"This isn't possible," Paul whispered. "I was just here…"

When the floral scent stirred from his uniform, his jaw unclenched, and a gentle smile made the corners of Paul's mouth twitch. The faint perfume was a whisper from the past, a reminder of his grandmother's presence. It was a comforting fragrance, a witness to their bond, and it eased the tightness in his chest.

Paul's trembling, calloused hand pressed against the passenger window in farewell.

"There's something else I have to tell you, son." His father's hand dropped from Paul's shoulder to rest on the passenger seat.

The moment stretched for an eternity, and it took a heroic effort to look away, but he eventually met his father's eyes. "Yes?"

"We got a call yesterday from your commanding officer. We know about the roadside bomb," his father's voice filled the truck cab with sympathy.

"Yeah." Paul's hand went to the pendant on his chest and nodded. "That was a close one."

"No, son. It was *not* close." Tears rolled down his father's cheeks, making Paul's chest ache. "It was fatal."

It took a second to notice how his father's hand rested on the truck seat below him.

"I don't understand …"

"That makes two of us, but I'm grateful for this moment. Your mother and I will always love you." A shaking finger pointed out the passenger window. "I think someone is waiting for you."

In the blink of an eye, things were different.

The gardens were now full of early spring flowers, and the grass was short and recently trimmed. Sparrows chirped while darting in and out of the white hibiscus. Nothing had changed since Paul had played here as a little boy. Remnants of his rope swing still hung from the high branches of the towering elm, but the board was long gone. Sitting on the front porch, his grandmother waved to them both. A small table between the wicker chairs held two glasses of iced tea and a plate piled high with cookies.

"Don't worry about your mother, Paul. I'll take care of her." Paul found himself standing outside the truck, but the door never opened. His father rolled down the window. "Give Hazel our love."

Understanding, Paul reached under his uniform and removed the identification tags with the shrapnel piece. He passed them through the window. "I don't need these anymore, do I?"

His father remained silent and shook his head while clutching the tags in a white-knuckled grip.

Paul turned toward the porch light and took a step when the sweet scent of lilacs filled his being. With each pace, his body faded until nothing was left but a clear voice filled with sorrow and acceptance. "Say goodbye to Mom. I love you too, Dad."